ANGEL MEADOW

by

Bill Rogers

First Published December 2014
by Caton Books

First Edition

Whilst this book is based on factual research, and actual police operations are referred to as background context, all of the characters in this book are fictitious, and any resemblance, if any, to actual persons, living or dead, is purely coincidental. Any references to businesses, organisations, places or localities are intended only to give the fiction a sense of authenticity. All of the events and behaviours described as taking place in those settings are fictional.

A CIP record for this book is available from the British Library

Published by Caton Books

Paperback ISBN: 978-1909856-14-1

Cover Design by Dragonfruit
Design and Layout: Commercial Campaigns
Proofreader: Sarah Cheeseman

Chapter 1

The wind sliced through her fine silk blouse. She shivered. He placed his arm protectively around her shoulders. She snuggled closer. They turned away from the muted sounds of alcohol-fuelled camaraderie, and headed south down Rochdale road towards the city centre.

He glanced at his watch. It was three twenty-nine a.m. Just over an hour until sunrise. No matter, tomorrow was Saturday. She had a weekend off, so no need to set the alarm. They would stir at the same time, sober enough to indulge in the kind of quality sex that right now was out of the question for both of them. Then a leisurely shower, a coffee and brunch in the Marble Arch Inn.

She stumbled. He held her tight, and waited until she had recovered. They stood still for a moment, listening to the sounds of the city. Taxis ferrying the last of the clubbers home. A distant police siren wailing its way southward down Oxford Road. The occasional white van heading into the city centre with new stock for the Sunday shopping bonanza.

As they reached the corner of Angel Street an ambulance, blue lights strobing the night sky, swung out of Addington Street and hurried up Rochdale Road towards the North Manchester General Hospital.

They turned right. Only a couple of hundred yards

and they'd be home. The upper storey of the Angel Inn, stark white above the dark green walls below, appeared to hover in mid air. Just beyond it a single light glowed in one of the windows of the nearest apartment block. To their left, armadillo like, loomed One Angel Square, the landmark headquarters of the Co-operative Group.

'Nearly there,' he said as they reached the corner of Style Street.

She lifted her head from his shoulder.

'What was that?'

'What?'

'That!'

This time he heard it too. A woman's voice. Low on the wind, pleading.

'No! Please, no!'

She straightened up, suddenly sober and alert.

'Harry, do something,' she said.

'Like what?'

'Call the police.'

'And tell them what?'

'What d'you think? That there's a woman being attacked.' She sounded angry.

'We don't know that,' he said.

She placed her hands on his chest, pushed herself free and made to run towards the sound. He grabbed an arm, causing her to stumble. He caught her as she began to fall.

'Let me go,' she cried.

'Don't be stupid,' he said. 'You don't know what you're getting us into.'

As she struggled to free herself she began to scream, and then to yell.

'Police! Help! Police!'

'What did you do that for?' he said.

'To frighten him off.'

'You don't know it's a him.'

'Don't be stupid.'

She reached into her bag for her mobile phone.

There was the sound of someone spitting, twice, close by. They froze, straining to hear. Just the sound of sporadic traffic, and the wind moaning among the trees in Angel Meadow.

'There,' he said, gently releasing his grip. 'You've frightened him off.'

'Him?'

He laughed nervously.

'Okay, you win. A man, just discovered he'd been wasting his time.'

In the soft glow of the street lamp he saw her grimace.

'Men! You're all the same,' she said. 'One track minds.'

'Present company excepted.'

Her snort suggested otherwise.

He took her hand, placed his other arm around her shoulder, gave her a hug, and felt her relax.

'Come on, have-a-go hero,' he said. 'That's enough excitement for one night.'

Lights had come on in two other apartments, their occupants disturbed by her screams. He saw a blind half raised. A face, backlit, peered into the night.

'I hope they haven't rung the police and put me in the frame,' he said. 'That's all we need.'

Chapter 2

Kate woke to the sound of birdsong. On top of the duvet lay an arm encircling her chest. He was snoring softly. She gripped the edge of the duvet with both hands and bounced it up and down until his arm slid off, enabling her to to turn and face him.

He looked so peaceful with his hand tucked into the pillow, cradling his face. A sound sleeper, he was rarely troubled by the murky depths he plumbed by day. It had been over a year, long before they finally tied the knot, since the once recurrent nightmare of his parents' deaths had surfaced.

Tied the knot. What kind of metaphor was that? It didn't feel like a constraint, being married. They both had their independence, and separate jobs of equal worth. She still met with her friends and colleagues outside of work, and he had started going to the gym again. And to that crazy Nags Head reading group, the Alternatives.

Her hand slid back under the duvet, and settled on her burgeoning stomach. She smiled. Burgeoned to be strictly accurate. She didn't care what all of her singleton friends seemed so eager to assert, that children tied you down, that life would never be the same. Of course it wouldn't. It would be better. More challenging, but definitely more fulfilling.

A sudden kick, followed by a jab that could only

have been an elbow, made her laugh. It was as though their baby had read her thoughts, and was urging her not to become complacent. I'm here. I'm coming. You'd better be ready!

Tom must have felt it too. He stirred. Opened a bleary eye. Then the other one. Focused.

'What did you do that for?'

'Good morning to you, too,' Kate replied. 'And it wasn't me, it was Junior. Apparently, it's your turn to get breakfast.'

He rubbed his eyes with the knuckles of his index fingers.

'Junior Caton is already hyperactive,' he complained. 'What's he going to be like by the time he's walking?'

'She is perfectly normal,' Kate retorted. 'In the third trimester we were told to expect movements from baby at least thirty times an hour.'

'Movements, not a Saracens versus the Barbarians Rugby Cup Final.' He turned onto his left side, and snuggled back into the pillows. 'Anyway, I thought we'd agreed not to find out the sex until it was born.'

'We did, and I haven't,' she said. 'I've just got this feeling.'

'And mothers always know,' he mumbled.

'This mother knows it's your turn for breakfast,' she said, delivering an elbow of her own.

They sat up in bed with the pillows stacked behind them. Tom had opened the blinds, revealing the view across Milliner's Wharf, along the Medlock Valley, over Crime Lake, beyond Oldham, to the swell of the Pennine Hills between Diggle and Littleborough. This view, and the stunning sunrises across the fringe where wild moorlands collided with urban industrial sprawl, was one of the reasons they had bought this apartment. That they could also see the Greater Manchester Police Headquarters buildings at Central Park, was not. It was a constant reminder that Kate could have done without.

The tray lay across his lap. They had drunk their coffee and fruit juices. A few accusative crumbs the only remaining evidence of croissants and toast. Tom swung his feet to the floor, lifted the tray clear of the duvet and carried it to the dressing table.

'Have you decided yet?' she asked.

'Decided?'

'About your paternity leave. One week or two?'

He slid back into bed beside her.

'I told you,' he said. I'm happy to take the full two weeks if you want me to.'

'Happy, but not delirious?'

'That's not fair. I'm looking forward to this baby as much as you.'

She grimaced, and placed her hands on either side of her belly as though trying to lift it.

'No, I don't think so. When you've carried a baby for eight months, going on nine, then you can say you're looking forward to it as much as me.'

'You know what I meant. I'll do whatever it takes.'

She relented.

'I know you will. But I want you to apply for one week. You'll be a nightmare if you're not at work. The girls will take it in turns to come round to help out and keep me company. I'd prefer that. Anyway, a week's plenty of time to train you up.'

That sounded ominous.

'Train me up?'

'Nappy changes, night feeds, breakfast in bed every day.' She grinned. 'At least you've made a start on that one.'

He decided to quit while he was ahead. He would

genuinely have been happy to stay at home for the full fortnight, but she was right. He'd probably be climbing the walls by the end of it. Not that he wasn't going to be a Modern Dad. After all, he was going to be there at the birth, wasn't he?

Kate had her iPad open and clicked on a document.

'Choosing your post-maternity outfits?' he asked.

'Already done that,' she said without looking up. 'Just checking the first draft of my dissertation.'

'On a Saturday?'

'Unlike you, I don't distinguish between work and pleasure,' she said. 'I enjoy them both.'

'Serial and multiple acts of murder: an exploration of offending by women, singly and with partners,' he quoted. 'Not everyone's idea of pleasure.'

She looked up.

'You remembered?'

'Not something you'd forget in a hurry. Unlike the last one. What was it? Model serial drivers?'

'To what extent do existing models of offender behaviour provide a basis for the construction of models for the drivers of serial murderers in Britain, based on the characteristics of those murderers?'

'Hardly slips off the tongue,' he observed. 'Anyway, I've been meaning to ask, I thought that was for your PhD. How come you're doing another one?'

She sighed and set the iPad down.

'You weren't paying attention, were you? Although to be fair you were in China on that trafficking case when they had the graduation ceremony. I started out on an MPhil/PhD. Normally the one leads straight into the other, but because I was given the teaching role they let me split them.'

He remembered now.

'Don't you have to finish your PhD dissertation within four years regardless?'

'Normally, but they made an exception. I've got till the end of January.'

'It's a good job you've got maternity leave then,' he said, without thinking.

She rounded on him.

'I see, so you think it's going to be a doddle? Fitting it in around eight breastfeeds a day, nappy changing on demand, bonding with Junior, cooking, washing, cleaning, ordering home deliveries, not to mention keeping house for a desperately overworked Detective Chief Inspector?'

He was tempted to say it had been her choice, but common sense, and the survival instinct, prevailed.

'I've told you, I'll do whatever you need me to do around the house.'

'When you're here. Nightfall to sunrise, and those weekends when the murders and rapists decide to take a break themselves. Which is rarely.'

That wasn't strictly true. The last couple of months had been quiet. All of the murders and manslaughters had been Category C, with the perpetrator known from the outset, and cleared up by the appropriate teams. He'd shifted that much paperwork he was secretly hoping something would come up. He wasn't going to tell her that.

She saw the hurt in his eyes, and softened. She placed a hand over his, and squeezed gently.

'That was unfair of me, Tom. You're a good man, and a husband of whom most of my friends are envious. And you're going to be a brilliant father. Don't pay any attention to my outbursts.' She tightened her grip. 'But don't you dare put it down to hormones. I alone am allowed to do that.'

She let go and pushed back the duvet.

'I'll need a special favour from you though.'

He sensed her hesitation.

'Go on.'

'In a few months, October time, when the baby's settled, and moving onto formula feeding.'

'Go on.'

'I'll need you to look after her…'

Her again. He hoped she wasn't going to be disappointed.

'…while I nip down to Ashford.'

'Ashford in Surrey?'

She nodded.

He read her expression. Assertive defensive.

'HMP Goldstone?' he said.

'Yes.'

Her Majesty's Prison, Goldstone. The UK's sole young adult and women only prison. The largest of its type in Europe. A purpose-built, top-security facility. There was only one reason she would be going there.

'You're going to interview their serial and multiple murderers?'

'Yes. I have to. A PhD is about original research. That means working from sources. I don't have any option but to do some face-to-face interviews.'

'If the perpetrators agree to talk with you.'

'They will. Egotism and self-justification. It's part of the profile.'

It wasn't as though it would be the first time. She had interviewed scores of violent men and women. Psychopaths, sociopaths, and everything in between. It was what made her such a good profiler and investigative psychologist.

'I'll come with you,' he said.

She bristled.

'I don't need my hand holding, Tom. And I won't need patronising just because I'll have recently given birth.'

'I meant travel with you, Kate, and stay in the hotel. So we could all be together. There's no way I'd be taking our baby into that place.'

He didn't really want her going in there either. These were the most dangerous women in the country. One had recently planned to escape by killing a warder, and severing the finger of another to use it to beat the biometric fingerprint recognition system. If she hadn't been grassed up by a couple of the other prisoners she might well have pulled it off. And the fact that the place was privately run didn't exactly fill him with confidence.

The sound of the phone cut short her reply. It was the landline. She picked it up. Listened. Shook her head. Lobbed it onto the bed.

'It's for you.'

She walked into the wet room, and closed the door behind her.

'Sorry, boss,'

Caton was surprised to hear Acting DI Stuart's voice on a Saturday morning. There was no need to ask her why she had rung. It was an apology to which he had become accustomed. One that still caused his heart to skip a beat, the blood in his veins to stir. As a detective he was more sensitive than most to the infinite variations of pitch and tone in the human voice. Sensitive enough to distinguish from those two words between a brutal assault, rape, and a violent death.

'Where?' he said.

'Angel Meadow.'

It was all he needed to know. Everyone in the team was aware that he liked to come at it cold. Without preconceptions.

'How come it's you that's telling me, Jo?' he said.

'I called in to get something I'd left behind yesterday. I was there when the call came in.'

He noted the hesitation. They weren't supposed to take work home with them. It wasn't just about work–life balance; paperwork lost or stolen could mean the end of a promising career. Most of them did it though, especially if they were in court the following morning. Including him.

'Where was the duty officer?' he asked.

A longer hesitation.

'In the canteen.'

'Who was it, remind me?'

'DC Hulme.'

Poor Jimmy Hulme. He'd be kicking himself for missing that call.

'Make sure he does the rest of the ringing round, Jo,' he told her. 'Except for DI Holmes. You call and tell him I'll pick him up in fifteen minutes. Then you get on down there and hold the fort till SOCO turn up.'

'Right, boss.'

He put the phone back on the charger, and opened the door of the wet room. Kate was in her bathrobe, rinsing her electric toothbrush under the tap.

'You'll need to shower,' she said. 'Your razor is fully charged, I just tested it. I'll go and make you a bacon sandwich, and a flask of coffee. There's no telling how long it'll take for a mobile kitchen to arrive on a Saturday.'

'I'm sorry, Kate…' he began.

'Don't!' she said, pointing her toothbrush at him. 'It's just how it is.'

She brushed past him. In the doorway, she turned to face him.

'And you were right, Tom. It has been quiet lately. So don't apologise. Just go and do what you have to do. I'll be fine.'

Chapter 3

'You didn't have to pick me up.'

Gordon Holmes levered back his seat, and stretched as best he could.

Caton glanced across at him.

'Have you looked at yourself?' he said.

His DI flipped down the sunshade, peered at his reflection, in the mirror and grimaced.

'I see what you mean.'

He flipped the sunshade back.

'Even so,' he said.

Caton watched as a cyclist and a white van went through the lights on red. Where was a squad car when you needed one?

Holmes leaned forward, and gave them a couple of whoops of the siren. The van driver touched his brakes briefly, glanced in the mirror and kept going. The cyclist looked over his shoulder, lost concentration, wobbled perilously close to the pavement, then recovered and turned left between the barriers on Liverpool Road, supposedly closed for sewer repairs. The lights changed, and Caton set off along Deansgate.

'You told me you were going to watch Spain v The Netherlands with the lads last night,' he said. 'Followed by Chile and Australia.'

'So?'

'What time was that?'

'Eight o'clock start. The second one finished at one p.m. Bit of a let-down, both of them.'

Caton stopped for the lights at Kendals.

'So, five hours of serious drinking time. Plus one for the road. You reckon you'd pass a breathalyser?'

'Probably not.'

'Probably not? Two pints an hour, that's eleven pints. Twenty-two units minimum. Your liver's working flat-out to process one unit an hour, plus an hour. You'll still be over the limit at teatime.'

Holmes shrugged.

'I keep telling you, it's not worth it,' Caton said.

As though to prove the point a marked car appeared at the entry to St Ann's Street. The officer looked across at them with that familiar cool appraisal that made even Caton feel somehow guilty. A flicker of recognition crossed his face. He gave a slight nod as the lights changed, and Caton pulled away.

'What about you, boss?' said Holmes. 'Don't tell me you didn't crack open a bottle of red.'

'A half bottle.'

'Pull the other one. I bet you drank the full bottle, what with Kate not drinking.'

'I saved the other half for tonight.'

Holmes laughed.

'Sometimes you slay me,' he said.

'Better me than the drink,' Caton replied.

A female police officer and a Police and Community Support Officer stood at the entry to Angel Street. Seventy metres further on they could see the tapes marking the outer cordon. Caton was directed to the temporary car park normally reserved for workers on the Noma building sites, just a few metres away. They took their murder bags from the boot, and set off.

This area was completely different from how Caton remembered it when he worked out of Collyhurst. Then it had consisted of derelict land, abandoned terraces, decrepit Victorian warehouses. The once notorious Beer House was now the gastro Angel Inn, with a plump pink cherub for its pub sign. The former Co-op car parks serving the iconic insurance and headquarters buildings were now a vast building site. Due for completion in 2027 this would be small town in its own right. The Co-op's equivalent of Port Sunlight, or Saltaire. Providing they got over the current crisis. He hoped so. Manchester owed a lot to the Co-op. So did the whole of the North of England. He vaguely remembered his mother collecting the 'divi' stamps. She had been fiercely loyal to the concept of customers having a sense of ownership, and sharing in the profits. It would be shame to see that go just because of one bad appointment, and a rash attempt to diversify. £800 million had already been invested in this development. It was unthinkable that that might also be at risk.

'What d'you reckon, boss?' said Holmes. 'Sliced egg or Ocean-going liner?'

'What?' he said.

'This place. One Angel Square. What d'you reckon?'

Caton had seen photos of it from above, taken by India 99, the Force helicopter. In those it looked like a ship's funnel. From down here he thought it had the appearance of something out of a futuristic video game. Either that or a giant shiny beetle. At over a million pounds to build it was the greenest, most sustainable building in Europe. Out here, away from the city centre, away from the redbrick and stone-clad buildings that were the historical heart of the city for which he felt such affection, it didn't matter so much what it looked like.

'Liner,' he said.

They had reached the outer cordon. The tape was tied between a downspout on the side of the apartments on the corner of Simpson Street, and the wooden fencing that bordered the building site. A woman PC was busy checking the IDs of a pair of Scenes of Crime officers, and entering their names in the crime scene log. Residents were leaning over the side of their balconies, gawping. One couple were seated at a table, having their breakfast while taking in the scene below. Caton found their voyeurism chilling.

Checked and recorded, they walked on in silence towards the cluster of trees ahead of them. No casual observations, no playful banter. The skyline filled with towering cranes, empty, still and skeletal, their operators just now rising from their beds on what promised to be the start of a glorious weekend. Flaming June. For some.

They turned right onto Styal Street and headed past the first of two more apartments blocks. These balconies were also crowded. Caton cursed inwardly. Those on the upper storeys must have a bird's-eye view of the crime scene. Facebook, Twitter, YouTube and all the rest would already be sharing images around the globe. Every parent, partner and friend with a loved one not yet returned from a night on the town fearing the worst. They stopped at the entry to the parks, guarded by three uniformed officers.

Caton took a deep breath, and closed his eyes. He tried to visualise what he remembered of this immediate area from his time at Fort Collyhurst. Behind him, where the apartments now stood, had been derelict terraced houses. On the three remaining sides stood warehouses and factories spanning over one hundred and sixty years of manufacturing. In the centre, St Michael's Flags and Angel Meadow. Seven acres of run-down parkland, frequented by homeless persons, alcoholics and drug addicts by day and night. Few children ventured there then, except to kick a football across the weed-filled flagstones before disappearing into the side streets as dusk fell.

'Boss?'

DI Holmes was anxious to get on with it. This eagerness for the hunt was Gordon's greatest asset, and his Achilles heel. It meant that he drove his investigations forward with a determination and pace that left little or no time for reflection. For alternative points of view. To think outside the box that was the Murder Investigation Manual. Except that even in the manual they spoke of 'creating slow time', of 'putting your foot on the ball'. Fat chance of that with Gordon, head down, racing for the corner flag.

He opened his eyes. Twin wrought-iron frames marked the entrances. The one to the left St Michael's Flags, the other to the right Angel Meadow. Beyond them he could see that both parks had been re-landscaped. There were solar-powered lights beside the pink tarmac paths, flower beds and wildflowers in patches beneath the sycamore and silver birch. Benches were dotted around.

A police notice on the nearest lamp post warned motorists to remove all satnav equipment and clean off suction-pad marks. Some things never changed.

Gordon had already entered Angel Meadow. The two Scenes of Crime Officers were now thirty metres ahead of them on the path that bisected the park. Caton flashed his ID at the officer by the entrance, and set off in pursuit.

Chapter 4

The path descended. Seventy metres from the entrance it bisected another that formed the western perimeter of both parks. An officer in tactical aid gear sent him to the right. Almost immediately he encountered parallel lines of red and white scene-of-crime tape marking the inner cordon. A decontamination tent was being erected. Beyond it more tape hung between metal staves either side of a trail of Benson's ubiquitous green plastic duckboards marking the crime scene pathway. They led from the path into the clump of trees immediately ahead of him.

Holmes was shrugging on his Tyvek suit. Caton placed his murder bag on the ground, took out his own all-in-one and began to put it on.

'It was only a matter of time,' said Holmes.

'What was?' Caton replied.

'Another one. Down here.'

Caton zipped up his hood, and began to put on his over-shoes.

'I'm not with you.'

Holmes pulled a face. The one he thought denoted frustration but that most people interpreted as boredom.

'The Angel of the Meadows!' he said.

Caton closed his bag, grasped it firmly, and straightened up.

'They didn't find her here,' he said. 'It was back there.' He nodded south-west towards One Angel Square, just visible above the trees behind them. 'When they were digging the foundations.'

Holmes shrugged.

'Near enough,' he said. 'They could be linked. You know what you always say coincidences.'

Caton stepped up onto the first of the duckboards.

'And what do I say about jumping to conclusions?'

'Could be a copycat,' said his DI as though he hadn't heard.

Caton didn't dignify it with a reply. His only concern was what lay ahead.

The duckboards continued for fifteen yards between the trees, and terminated beside the redbrick perimeter wall, where they formed a semicircle to create a viewing platform. There were four others already there. Jack Benson, the lead crime scene officer from Caton's team, the two other scenes of crime officers, one of whom was setting up a camera on a tripod, and Joanne Stuart, recently promoted to Acting DI.

'The Force Medical Examiner is on her way, sir,' she said. 'She should be right behind you.'

'Dr Tompkins?' said Caton.

'Yes, sir. She said she'd try to get hold of Professor Flatman too, since he'll be doing the post mortem.'

'He won't thank her for dragging him in on a Saturday morning,' Holmes observed.

'For once, you'd best try not to upset him then,' said Benson.

'While we're waiting for the FME, run me through what we have here,' said Caton, even though it seemed self-evident.

Her back was against the redbrick wall. She was sitting facing them. She wore a navy jacket over a white blouse. Her legs were splayed out in front of her. Her skirt had gathered up behind her as she slid down the wall, exposing the pink of her knickers at the sides. At the front, the hem was barely a pelmet. Auburn hair, showing black at the roots, framed an oval face. Her eyes were open. Her expression showed fear and surprise. There was a hole in the centre of her forehead. Her jacket was open, and there was second hole in the centre of her chest, just to the left of her breastbone. It would have been easy to miss but for the red against the white of her blouse.

'When we arrived,' Benson began, 'DI Stuart and I, we found a very agitated elderly woman sitting by the side of the path hugging a border terrier. A PC from Collyhurst was sat with her. Apparently, the dog had run off into the trees, then started barking. When it didn't come back she went in after it. Found this.'

He pointed to the body.

'She had the wits to get out of there, and ring 999 on the mobile her son gave her so he could keep tabs on her.'

'Where is she now?' said Caton.

'In an area van on Gould Street. The dog wouldn't stop yapping, and the owner looked ready to croak it.'

'Okay, then what?'

'We made an initial reccy, checking for physical evidence as we went forward towards this point. Signs of footprints on the grass, broken twigs, scraps of clothing caught up on the trees. Anything the perpetrator or the victim could have brought to the scene, or left behind.'

'And?'

'The ground has been dry for the past two days, so no real footprints. No obvious signs of disturbances or trace evidence, but...'

He paused and looked to Joanne Stuart, who held up a large evidence bag and a smaller one.

'A handbag,' she said, raising the larger one. 'We found it under a tree on a direct line from the path to here.'

'Hers?' said Holmes.

'It's a reasonable assumption.'

'Have you looked inside?'

'No, sir. I thought I'd wait for you.'

'Thank you,' he said. 'And it's boss, alright?'

'Yes, boss.'

'And?'

She raised the smaller one.

'A shoe. Navy blue, high heeled. It was five yards back there, close to the handbag. Heel's broken. It's definitely hers.'

She pointed to the matching shoe half on, half off the victim's right foot.

'Anything else?'

'No, boss,' said Jack Benson. 'Nothing that looks as though it might be relevant. There's plenty of rubbish though.'

He pointed to the detritus gathered along the foot of the wall. Empty lager cans, crumbled bags, used condoms, assorted bits of clothing. Even a faded bra and several pairs of knickers.

'I'll make sure that forensics check it all, obviously.'

'Obviously,' said Gordon Holmes.

It wouldn't be the first time a perpetrator used existing rubbish to conceal something he didn't want found on him.

Caton bent down to get a clearer view of the wound to her forehead. The hole was a fraction smaller than a one-pence piece. It was almost a perfect circle. The centre was thick with congealed blood and other matter. Probably a mixture of brain and splintered bone. Because her head had not fallen back, only a trickle of blood had formed a trail down her forehead, and along the left side of her nose. The edges of the hole were lightly pitted, and dusted with what looked like soot. Her eyes stared back at him, seeking answers he was unable to provide.

He felt an almost overwhelming surge of sadness, and had to put a hand down on the duckboard to steady himself. It was the first time he had felt like this in his nineteen years with the Force. He had no idea why. He tore his eyes from hers and straightened up.

'Have you found any cartridges?' he said.

'Not yet,' Benson replied. 'We had a good look before I had the duckboards laid. But if they're here, we'll find them.'

'Obviously,' said Holmes.

'What's obvious?' said a deep cultured voice.

They stepped aside to allow Sir James Flatman through. Despite his stoutness, the ill-fitting Tyvek all-in-one, and the fact that he was a good head shorter than any of them, he still managed to appear distinguished. It was the combination of silver hair, aristocratic nose and intelligent eyes. Eyes that twinkled as they lighted on DI Stuart. Playfully lecherous eyes, if such was possible. Bizarrely so, since everyone knew, him included, that he was wasting his time.

'Thank you for coming, Sir James,' said Caton, ignoring the question because he knew any answer would be met with a sarcastic riposte.

'Might as well,' the Home Office pathologist replied. 'Only missed a round of golf. And since I'll be doing the PM I thought I may as well see it in situ.'

It, not her, Caton observed. A way of coping with the job rather than callousness. In his experience all pathologists had a grim sense of humour, and an impressive range of distraction techniques.

'Is there room for a little one up there?'

Carol Tompkins, the Force Medical Examiner, waiting patiently at the back.

'Oh yes, Dr Tompkins,' said Flatman as though she was an afterthought. 'We arrived together. Don't really need her now, but since she'd made the effort thought she might as well tag along. Always helpful to have an assistant.'

He sounded like a Sir Lancelot Spratt impressionist. The irascible surgeon from the 'Doctor in the House' series to which Caton's father had introduced him.

Joanne Stuart took a deep breath. Caton sensed her biting her tongue. Benson asked the two SOCOs to move to the back to make room for the FME. She joined Flatman, apparently untroubled by his arrogant sexism.

'Okay,' said the professor, kneeling with some difficulty to the right of the body. 'Let's see what we've got.'

He leaned forward to examine the wound in the centre of the forehead. Unbidden, Carol Tompkins inserted a tympanic thermometer in the victim's left ear. Flatman looked up sharply.

'I'll take a rectal reading when the tent arrives,' she said calmly pre-empting his comment.

Flatman grunted, and turned to look up at Benson.

'Has this been photographed yet?'

'Not yet,' the Crime Scene Manager replied. 'We were just about to.'

The pathologist sighed, and stood up.

'Well, get on with it then,' he said. 'Then I can have a proper look.'

'The current body temperature is 26.5 degrees Celsius,' said Carol Tompkins. 'The ambient temperature is already 21 degrees Celsius. It's going to be a scorcher today.'

'So,' said Flatman, 'assuming the normal 1.5 degrees drop in body temperature per hour from the moment she deceased, that equates to seven hours, subject to the ambient temperature at the time of death, and in the hours following.'

'It was 17 degrees at three a.m., 18 degrees at six a.m., and 20 degrees an hour ago, at nine a.m.,' said Joanne Stuart, holding up her iPhone, and surprising them all.

'In which case,' he said, 'it's likely that her temperature fell a little faster over that period. So, subject to the rectal temperature, and confirmation of those figures, DS Stuart kindly–'

'DI Stuart,' said Gordon Holmes.

Flatman inclined his head in a mock bow.

'Well,' he said, 'not before time. Now, where was I? Oh yes, subject to confirmation, examination of stomach contents, insect activity, initially it would suggest a time of death between five and seven hours ago.'

He paused to direct the SOCO taking the photos.

'I want a close-up of that wound. And the eyes.'

When the cameraman had finished, Flatman knelt down again. He placed the thumb and index finger of his right hand over the wound, and eased it open as best he could.

'Ruler!' he said.

Anticipating the request, Benson handed him a plastic ruler with black markings. The pathologist placed it across the centre of the wound.

'Nine point eight millimetres,' he said. 'Circular, no stellate lacerations.'

He lifted the ruler and reapplied it across the centre of the wound, and the pitted skin surrounding it around it.

'Stipple tattooing has a radius of four centimetres,' he said, sitting back on his haunches. 'Absence of powder marks.'

'So, a 9mm bullet fired from intermediate range,' Gordon Holmes pronounced.

'Very good, DI Holmes,' said the pathologist, for once without a trace of sarcasm. 'And how would you describe intermediate range?'

'One foot to three feet,' Holmes replied without hesitation.

'Mmm,' said Flatman.

Bending forward again, he examined the eyelids, the jaw and the neck. He raised the left arm, and then lowered it.

'Rigor mortis is twenty-five per cent advanced, which supports our initial estimates of the time of death.'

He stood, placed a hand on either side of the head, and eased it forward until he could see the back of the skull.

'You're lucky, Chief Inspector,' he said. 'The bullet is still in there. Just. She must have been standing against the wall.'

Caton had a vision of her leaving the path, fleeing through the trees, stumbling, hobbling forward, turning, backing away until the wall brought her to a stop. Standing there frozen with fear. Knowing that she was about to be executed. Knowing that there was no escape.

Flatman pulled the body gently towards him.

'Can you lift her jacket and blouse back please Dr Tompkins?' he said.

They had both ridden up to expose the lower back. The FME raised them as far as she could.

'Her back has lesions where she scraped against the wall,' said Flatman. 'Presumably as she slid down it. No exit wound. Lividity in the lumbar spine where she has not been in contact with the wall tells us that she has not been moved. This was where she died.'

He nodded to the FME. Together they laid her back in the position in which she had come to rest. He knelt again and unbuttoned her blouse. He had some difficulty easing the left side away from her chest because the blood had congealed. Dr Tompkins handed him a scalpel, which he took without comment, and used to cut the fabric free.

The bullet had passed through the centre panel of her bra, sucking some of the fabric inwards. He used his gloved fingers to locate her ribs.

'The bullet entered between the third and fourth ribs,' he said. 'Approximately two centimetres from the sternum. Dead centre of the heart, give or take.'

He sat back, then used his hands to push himself up from the duckboard. Caton hooked a hand under his armpit to help him up.

'That's as much as I can tell you for now,' Flatman said. 'Probably enough for you to be getting on with. Dr Tompkins will I'm sure be happy to carry out the remainder of the examination in situ?'

At least he had the grace to check that she was willing to do so.

'Of course,' she said.

'Thank you, Carol,' said Flatman. 'Perhaps you'd like to join me when I do the PM?'

'If I'm free,' she replied.

He turned to Caton.

'Have to be Monday morning, I'm afraid. It'll take you the rest of the day to finish here I expect.'

He pushed back the sleeve of his Tyvek and consulted his watch.

'If I hurry, I'll be able to join them for the last nine holes.'

Chapter 5

Caton, Stuart and Holmes, found a bench and sat down to take stock. Behind them Carol Tompkins was hard at work beneath a white tent. Jack Benson was directing an inch-by-inch search of the area within the inner cordon.

'Let's run through it again,' said Caton. 'See if there's anything we've missed. We're thinking one offender, one victim. This is the primary murder scene. There is no sign that the victim was bound, no evidence of a struggle, no other injuries.'

'The fact that she'd dropped her handbag, lost her shoe, suggests she was trying to get away though,' Joanne Stuart observed.

'No defence injuries,' Gordon Holmes pointed out. 'So it's unlikely the perpetrator will have sustained any injuries himself. Scratches, bruises, that sort of thing.'

'No doubt about the cause of death,' said Caton. 'Two 9mm bullets, either of which would have been fatal.'

'That narrows it down,' said Holmes. 'Semi-automatic pistol, rifle, Uzi sub-machine gun.'

Caton shook his head.

'Not a rifle, not from that range. Nor a sub-machine gun. These were single shots, close up, with pinpoint accuracy.'

'Like an execution,' said Joanne Stuart.

'Exactly.'

'Neither of the cartridges has been found,' said Holmes. 'That suggests the perpetrator is forensically aware.'

'And cool, calm and collected,' said Caton. 'Almost professional.'

'Ex-forces?' suggested Holmes. 'A hired gun? A gang enforcer?'

'A police firearms officer?' said Stuart.

They both looked at her.

She shrugged. 'What? You're always saying discount nothing.'

Caton nodded.

'Fair enough,' he said. 'How do we think the perpetrator exited the scene?'

'Just walked back along any one of the paths and disappeared into the side streets,' said Holmes.

Caton was not convinced.

'I spotted a camera covering both entrances,' he said. 'Someone this professional is unlikely to enter or leave that way.'

'There's no camera on the Old Mount Street/Gould Street entrance,' said Stuart. 'I had it checked.'

'What about the apartments?'

'They've got cameras, but they're all trained on the entrances to the buildings. Don't even cover the streets.'

'Could've climbed over the wall,' said Holmes.

'It's ten feet high down this end of the park,' Joanne Stuart pointed out.

'Except for the railings,' said Caton.

'What railings?' said Gordon Holmes.

'While you were talking to Benson, I slipped into the bushes,' he said. 'I followed the wall for ten metres or so either side of the place where the body lay. Just a few metres to the west there's a gap in the wall filled by twelve spiked iron railings with a bar across the top. Presumably it had once formed the north entrance to the parks. The railings were about five feet high. Easy enough to scale.'

'What's on the other side, boss?' said Joanne Stuart.

'Aspin Lane,' he told her. 'The railings are immediately opposite the back of the Charter Street Mission.'

'The Ragged Children's School,' said Holmes. 'That's how I remember it.'

It was how Caton remembered it back when he was in the MGS Historical Society, and the Charter Street Ragged School and Working Girls' Home was a museum. Testament to the time when it was Manchester's first Victorian Industrial School, providing clothes, clogs, food and education to the children, and breakfast to destitute adults.

'Not any more,' he said. 'Now it's the King of Kings Independent Christian School.'

'A boarding school?' said Holmes hopefully. 'Maybe they heard something?'

'A day school,' said Caton. 'There's nothing else on Aspin Lane. Just a couple of car parks. It heads down under the railway onto Danzig Street. From there you've got three or four possible exit routes, including paths across the open ground covered in shrubs that goes up to Collyhurst and Smedley. Loads of places to leave a car. Beggar all CCTV. It's the way I'd go.'

'If the perpetrator did go that way, there's a good chance there'll be trace evidence,' Stuart pointed out.

'Benson's got it covered,' Caton told her. 'What's next?'

He returned to his forensic strategy mental checklist. His deputy beat him to it.

'Nothing to suggest it was sexually motivated,'

said Holmes. 'Not unless he put her knickers and bra back on.'

'It's been known,' said Joanne Stuart. 'But I agree, not this time.'

'The PM will tell us for sure,' said Caton. 'What about the offender being forensically aware? It looks as though the casings were retrieved. Not that it's going to help him all that much. Not with the bullets still in the victim.'

'If they were picked up,' said Stuart, 'it ties in with our theory that this was a professional killing.'

'You're right, Jo,' said Caton.

He ran the back of a gloved hand across his forehead to wipe away the sweat. Then he turned back and looked towards the trees.

Shadowy figures moved slowly inside the tent, partly masked by the leaf-laden branches.

'Was anything taken from the scene?' he asked. 'Any trophy items? Anything valuable suggesting this was for gain? A robbery gone wrong?'

'We won't know for sure until we find out if she was wearing jewellery or a watch last night,' said Joanne Stuart. But the perpetrator did leave this behind.'

'Perpetrator, Caton noted. Not once had she assumed a male attacker. Only he and Gordon had done that.

She held up the evidence bag containing the handbag.

'Let's have a look then,' said Caton. 'It's our best chance of establishing the victim's identity.'

The three of them stood up. Stuart opened the as yet unsealed evidence bag, carefully removed the handbag, and lay the evidence bag on the bench seat and smoothed it flat. Then she opened the handbag and, one by one, lay the contents on the evidence bag.

There were four keys on a key ring; a pair of sunglasses in a case; two small packs of tissues; two pairs of navy-blue cotton knickers; an opened pack of paracetamol; two 14-unit packs of Durex Real Feel condoms, one still sealed; two sticks of lipstick; a compact case containing powder and mirror; a nail file; a rape alarm; a mobile phone; a bottle of hand sanitizer; a tube of K-Y Jelly; and three dark chocolate Kit-Kat bars. DI Stuart found a zip compartment. Inside was a small transparent freezer bag containing banknotes.

'It's like a Tardis,' said Holmes.

'This is nothing,' she said. 'The average woman's handbag holds forty items.'

'No ID, and no diary or address book,' observed Caton.

'At least we know what she did for a living,' said Holmes.

He picked up the open pack of condoms.

'Four left. Someone's been busy.'

Stuart counted the money.

'One hundred and seventy pounds exactly,' she declared.

Holmes rubbed his chin with the back of his hand.

'Doesn't sound a lot for a night's work.'

'You need to keep up, Gordon,' she said. 'This isn't Belle de Jour we're talking about. The going rate on the street for ten minutes is only £10 to £15. It's only £50 for half an hour in a brothel. Even less in a walk-up room.'

'The bag looks like it's worth a bit though,' he said, fingering the gold Scottie dog tag.

'It's a Radley,' she told him. 'Genuine, too. Between £130 and £160 in the shops. Half that in TK Maxx if you're lucky.'

Holmes pointed to the knickers.

'Hardly what you expect of someone on the game,' he said.

'A lot of the girls wear cotton,' she told them. 'Synthetic ones can increase the chance of infection apparently. I don't understand why she was wearing high heels, though. Makes it harder to get away if you feel threatened.'

'Vanity?' said Caton. 'Especially if the street's your shop window.'

He picked up the keys and examined them.

'Two front door keys – one Yale and one to fit a two-lever lock. No back door key. An apartment perhaps?'

'What are the other two, boss?' asked Holmes.

He held them up for the others to see.

'Suitcases?' he said.

'Or anything you can put a little padlock on,' said Holmes.

Caton replaced the keys.

'I don't understand why she didn't use the rape alarm,' he said.

Gordon Holmes picked up the rape alarm and pulled the key ring. The pin flew out. Nothing happened.

'The battery's probably buggered.

'Then why keep it?' said Caton.

'I'd have thought she'd have a weapon of some kind,' said Holmes. 'A pepper spray maybe.'

'Aside from the fact that it's illegal,' said his Stuart, 'the girls are advised not to carry any weapons that could be used against them.'

'No drugs either,' said Caton. 'Unless you count paracetamol. Or anything to suggest that she might have been a user.'

'If she wasn't, that would be unusual,' said Joanne Stuart. 'It's been estimated that up to 95 per cent of prostitutes are problem drug users.'

'Who can blame them?' said Holmes. 'It would take more than drugs to get me on the game.'

'Don't worry, Gordon.' She grinned. 'Nobody would want you.'

Caton picked up the mobile phone, and turned it on. It wasn't password protected. He tried the contacts folder, but it was empty. He flicked through the last numbers dialled. None of them meant anything to him. According to the dates and times she hadn't made or received a call in over four days. He clicked on the account. O_2 Pay As You Go.

'At least we can get them to track where she's been when it's been turned on,' he said. 'That might give us something. An address, for example.'

He put it back down.

'You can bag them up again, Jo,' he said. 'Then seal and label it. We'll get forensics to make them a priority.'

A youthful uniformed officer came down the path towards them.

'Chief Inspector Caton?' he said.

'Detective Chief Inspector Caton to you, lad,' said Holmes.

The young man looked embarrassed.

'I'm sorry, sir, ' he said. 'I mean... Detective Chief–'

'It's alright,' said Caton. 'My colleague is just winding you up. It's a habit he has.'

'Yes, sir,' said the constable. 'I was told to tell you that the Mobile Incident Room has arrived.'

'Right,' said Caton. 'Tell them we're on our way.'

Chapter 6

The Mobile Incident van was parked off-road in the entrance to the United Utilities facility on Gould Street. Close to the northern entrance to the park. Away from prying eyes on the balconies of the apartments. Close enough for potential witnesses to drop in. The Divisional Commander, whose officers had helped to secure the scene, handed over to the Tactical Aid Team, and left. Detective Chief Superintendent Gates, Caton's immediate boss, had just arrived. He quickly brought her up to speed.

'Motive?' she said, scanning the Fast Track menu on the whiteboard attached to the side of the van.

'Too early to tell, ma'am,' he said. 'If the handbag does belong to the victim, and we have yet to establish that, and she was on the game, then there are possible motives connected with that.'

'A disgruntled punter wanting his money back? Or robbery?' she said.

He shook his head.

'Unlikely. There's nothing to indicate that sex had taken place. And in either case, why kill her? He could have just picked up the handbag and left.'

'Her pimp then?'

'That is a possibility,' he said. 'Although I've rarely heard of a pimp killing one of his own assets. Even if he thought she was cheating him by lying about the number of customers she'd had. A beating to teach her a lesson, or a slash with a Stanley knife where it won't put off the punters. Not a cold, calculated murder. We don't even know if she had a pimp.'

'Drugs then,' she persisted.

'There's no evidence that she was using or dealing,' Caton told her. 'But if she'd fallen foul of a drugs gang, if they thought she had informed on them, or might, that could be reason enough.'

'That's where most of our shootings have come from over the past four decades,' she observed.

She sat down and ran her fingers through her hair.

'By the way, I've had the Press Office issue a preliminary press release confirming that an incident has occurred and a body has been found. Further information will be given out at a formal press conference later this afternoon. That should keep them off your back for a while. Buy you some time.'

'Thank you, ma'am' he said. 'I appreciate that. I'd appreciate it even more if you could handle that press conference.'

'Don't push your luck, Tom,' she replied. She smiled thinly. 'I'll see what I can do.'

'Acting DI Stuart is liaising with Scenes of Crime and Forensics to fast-track whatever evidence is gathered,' he told her. 'DI Holmes has organised the door-to-door to identify potential witnesses among the residents. He's got PCSOs and traffic wardens recording and reporting index numbers of all vehicles currently or previously seen in this vicinity. He's sent officers to seize CCTV images from all of the adjoining buildings. I have two of my team working with Division to track down all of the prostitutes known to work this area.'

'And their pimps?' she said.

'And their pimps.'

'And your priority is?'

'Identifying the victim.'

'And your best hope is?'

'The other prostitutes, her mobile phone and CCTV images, assuming she lives locally.'

'Failing that?'

'A public appeal.'

'Using a post mortem photo?'

'It's all we have at this stage.'

She frowned.

'Hardly ideal.'

If only you knew, thought Caton. He'd seen that look in the dead woman's eyes, trapped by the onset of rigor mortis. He had a feeling that once the muscles had relaxed again it would still be there, frozen in time. Haunting him until her killer was caught.

'Excuse me, ma'am.' Gordon Holmes stood in the doorway. 'Only I've got two witnesses outside who reckon they may have heard the murder.'

'Heard it?' said Caton.

'Heard the victim, at any rate,' said Holmes.

'I'll leave you to it, Tom,' said Helen Gates. 'Give me a call when you get back to the Incident Room.'

Gordon Holmes stepped aside as she left the van, then ushered a young man and a young woman up the steps. They were both in their mid-thirties. He was dark haired, medium height and slim. She was taller, blonde haired and of athletic build. They both wore tracksuit bottoms, loose-fitting T-shirts and sandals. They looked tired, and pale. As though they'd just got up.

'This is Mr Harry Watts and Miss Alenka Ajek,' said Gordon Holmes. 'Mr Watts is an administrator at North Manchester General Hospital; Miss Ajek works there as a doctor.'

'As a Senior Registrar actually,' said the young man.

'And this is my boss, Detective Chief Inspector Caton,' Holmes continued. 'Just tell him what you told me.'

'Please,' said Caton, 'sit down.'

It wasn't difficult for them to choose a seat, there were only two. Caton perched on the table, with his Deputy alongside him.

'Is it true a woman's been murdered?' said the woman.

Caton could see that she was close to tears.

'I'm sorry,' Caton told her. 'At this stage all I am able to say is that there has been an incident. We are examining a body, but the circumstances surrounding the death are as yet unexplained.'

'This body,' she said, 'it is in the park?'

'Yes.'

It was hardly a secret. Most of the residents would already know exactly where it was found. And in what condition.

She turned to the young man.

'What did I tell you!' she said. 'We should have done something. You should have let me!'

He placed his hand on her arm.

'Alenka,' he began, 'it would only have–'

She pulled her arm away as though his hand had burnt it, hugged her body and bowed her head.

'Let's start again,' said Caton. 'What is it that you think you heard?'

'Did hear!' said the woman, raising her head. Her eyes were defiant through the tears. 'We did hear it.'

Caton raised his hands in submission.

'Okay,' he said. 'Just tell me what it was you heard.'

'A woman's voice,' said the man.

'Pleading,' said the woman.

'Pleading? How did you know that she was pleading?'

'Because of what she said.'

'And how she said it.' The man again.

'What did she say?'

'No! Please, no!' said Alenka Ajek. 'Just like that. Pleading. Like she was pleading for her life.'

Caton looked at the young man for confirmation. Watts nodded in agreement.

'What time was this?'

'Half past three this morning,' he replied. 'I know because I'd only just looked at my watch.'

'And where were you exactly?'

They told him about leaving the party. Walking down towards their apartment block. Hearing the woman pleading. Alenka wanting to go and help. Him pulling her back. The was recrimination started again. Caton interrupted.

'Mr Watts is right,' he said. 'Assuming what you heard was connected to this incident, I can tell you that you wouldn't have been able to make a difference. In fact, it's likely that one or both of you would have become victims yourselves.'

The couple looked at each other. That went some way to assuage the guilt that they were feeling.

'You could have rung the police though,' said Gordon Holmes. 'At least then we might have caught whoever did it.'

Their faces fell.

Nice one, Gordon, Caton reflected. There you go again with your size tens.

'What were we going to tell them?' said Watts. 'We didn't even know for sure where it was coming from. It could have been something of nothing…' His voice tailed off.

'Only it wasn't,' said his partner.

'Besides, we thought the people in the apartments would have rung you,' said Watts unconvincingly.

'They were nearer.'

'What people?' said Holmes. 'You never mentioned other people.'

'Lights came on in some of the windows,' said the woman, 'when I screamed. We could see them at the curtains. Lifting the blinds.'

'You screamed?' said Holmes.

She blushed.

'To frighten him away.'

'How did you know it was a man?'

'That's what I said,' Watts interposed.

She shrugged.

'I just assumed.'

'It was a reasonable assumption,' said Caton. 'Was there any kind of response to your scream?'

She shrugged.

'The lights came on.'

'Someone spat,' said Watts. 'Twice.'

'Spat?'

The detectives looked at each other.

'How exactly?' said Caton. 'Can you repeat the sounds you heard. And the interval between them?'

'A silencer,' said Holmes. 'He used a silencer.'

Caton nodded. The sounds he'd made were identical, with three seconds between them. Given the distance the couple had been from the crime scene, it was exactly what silenced shots would have sounded like. The first to the heart; the next one the head shot after she'd slid down the wall. When pushed, they'd both agreed that each time there was a hint of an echo. Just what you'd expect from a suppressor. Not a spit though. He looked at the map on the table. Not from one hundred and sixty-five yards away.

'It must have been them,' said Holmes. 'Too much of a coincidence, and the timing's spot on.'

Caton agreed. Five to seven hours the pathologist

had said. Three thirty would make it just over six and a half hours up to the time that Flatman had arrived at that calculation.

'If only they'd used their bloody mobiles to dial 999,' said Holmes bitterly. 'I bet they're quick enough to post selfies on social media.'

'At least it narrows down our passive data search parameters, especially the CCTV,' said Caton. 'And it corroborates one theory we had about the perpetrator.'

'Which is?' said Holmes.

'That we're looking for a professional. Someone used to handling guns. And that it was almost certainly pre-planned. Who do we know that walks around with a suppressor in their pocket as well as a 9mm handgun?'

Chapter 7

At half past eleven Caton judged it time to head back to Central Park. The first bags of physical evidence from the scene were on their way to forensics. DI Stuart was now overseeing the on-site Loggist, and the Exhibit Officer, as well as helping to triage the residents of the apartments queuing up to tell their stories of disturbance in the early hours. Gordon was liaising with the Tactical Aid Search Team and the Neighbourhood Police Team. His main priority was identifying the victim, closely followed by making sure that all of the footage from the scores of CCTV cameras was being seized. Not an easy task with so many of the business premises closed for the weekend.

'I'm off,' said Caton. 'As soon as DS Carter gets here, brief him to take over, then you come and join me in the Major Incident Room.'

He was just about to get into his car when someone shouted his name. A PCSO and a detective from the Divisional Neighbourhood Team were sprinting up Angel Street towards him. He shut the door and sat on the bonnet to wait for them.

'We know who she is sir, the victim,' said the breathless detective constable. 'Tell him, Val.'

'Slow down, and take your time,' said Caton. 'You can start by telling me your names.'

The woman was clearly the fitter of the two, her

breathing undisturbed by the sprint.

'PCSO Hymer,' she said. 'This is PC John Rowlands. We're from the Collyhurst Neighbourhood Team.'

'And you think you've identified the victim?'

'We have identified her, sir,' she said.

'How so?'

'From the photo and the description sent to our hand-helds,' said PC Rowlands.

He held up the device. From the screen the victim's face stared back at Caton. Her eyes still challenging him to find her killer.

'We know her as Irish Meg,' said the PCSO. 'She's a working girl.'

'Only been here a short while,' said the PC.

'Never given us cause to nick her,' said his colleague. 'But I've had a word with her a couple of times. We both have. Just to check she was okay.'

'Okay?' said Caton.

'You know,' she said. 'Safe.'

The full import of what she'd said hit her. She grimaced.

'She worked Corporation Street,' said PC Rowlands. 'She started off on Elizabeth Street in Cheetham, but she was hassled off there.'

'Hassled by whom?'

He shrugged.

'She didn't say, did she, Val? We assumed the pimps, or the other working girls.'

'Do you know where she lived?'

They both shook their heads.

'It's a pity we didn't have reason to nick her,' observed the PCSO. 'Then she'd have had to give us an address.'

'It's generally pretty quiet round here,' said the PC. 'Nothing like this.'

He looked at the image on the screen again, shook his head, switched off the device and placed it back in his breast pocket.

Caton remembered it when this patch had been a hive of nefarious activity.

'What do you call pretty quiet?' he said. 'Say within the last month?'

'Two anti-social behaviours, one on Angel Street, one on Almond Street,' said Rowlands.

'And a robbery on Sand Street,' added his colleague. 'A bag snatch. The guy had a knife. Suspect as yet unidentified. Probably a druggie.'

'And that's it?'

They both nodded.

That was the thing with the way crime statistics were reported now. They had them at their fingertips. Come to that, he could have looked them up himself on the www.police.uk crime mapping site, just like any member of the public could.

'The odds are one of the other girls will know where she lived,' said the PCSO.

'How quickly can you find out?' said Caton.

'We could start with Menthol Mandy up Rochdale Road?' said PC Rowlands. 'She'll still be in bed. She favours her beauty sleep on a Saturday morning.'

'Menthol Mandy?' said Caton.

'You don't want to know, sir,' said Hymer. 'Trust me.'

Caton was back in the Incident Room at Central Park when the news came through. Hymer and Rowlands had an address. He let DCS Gates know, and then called Gordon Holmes.

'Has Carter arrived?'

'Yes, boss.'

'Then hand over to him and head over to Ancoats.

Quick as you can, Gordon, and get Benson to lend you a SOCO, just in case. We have an address for the victim. You'll find me parked up on Sherratt Street.'

Caton waited impatiently with Detective Constable Hulme outside the five-storey redbrick Victorian facade of Victoria Square. An impressive four-sided block of flats with English Heritage status. Not like the rubbish they threw up in the sixties and seventies.

'I've never been inside there, boss,' said Hulme. 'I did see it on TV once though. Some crime drama.'

'It's quite something,' Caton told him. 'The first municipal housing in the city. Over two hundred single and two-room flats. Home to just short of a thousand people in its heyday.'

He pointed to the one of the turrets that stood at each corner.

'There were communal laundries and drying rooms in those; still are. Only now there's a see-through glass and steel lift as well. There's a community centre, and a garden in the middle with lawns and benches. A Housing Association at its best. It's a warden-controlled facility for the elderly and retired. Not much crime here, not in real life.'

'In London they'd pay hundreds of thousands for a flat in a place like this,' Hulme observed. 'Only they call them apartments and penthouses.' He grinned. 'Who said, a rose by any other name would smell as sweet?'

'That which we call a rose by any other name would smell as sweet,' quoted Caton. 'It was Juliet.'

He saw the look of bemusement on the DC's face, and experienced a frisson of pleasure and having finally got one over on their resident pub quiz champion.

'Of Romeo and Juliet?' he said.

'Oh, right,' said Hulme 'He knew a thing or two, did William Shakespeare.'

'He's not the only one,' said Caton, pointing to a street at right angles to them with rows of neat double-fronted terrace houses on either side. Window boxes full of plants hung from low black railings that marked the boundaries of each house.

'What's that street called?'

'Anita Street,' said Hulme, reading the name on the large new sign attached to a pole.

Caton pointed to the much smaller original sign attached to the wall of the house on the corner.

'Anything strike you about that sign?' he said.

'No,' said Hulme.

'Have a closer look.'

Jimmy Hulme crossed the road and approached the sign.

'Someone's had a go at it,' he said. 'Chopped a bit off by the looks of it. That's all.'

'That's because it was originally called Sanitary Street,' Caton told him. 'On account of the fact that every house had a water closet, and there were proper drains and sewers, and fresh water supply. Only about fifty years ago someone, presumably a resident, decided it was embarrassing. So they bastardised it so that it read ANITA STREET. The name stuck.'

'Can't say I blame them,' said Hulme. 'These houses would fetch close to a half a million quid in Chelsea. If I lived here I'd have done the same.'

'Tut tut, Detective Constable,' said Caton. 'Criminal damage.'

The DC's reply was interrupted by the sound of Gordon Holmes' titanium Mondeo screeching round the corner and skidding to halt beside them. A white-faced, white-suited SOCO emerged from the passenger side and walked towards the boot, one hand on the roof to steady herself. Holmes hauled himself from his seat and closed the door behind him.

'You do know that expenses for the use of your own vehicle aren't going to cover six-monthly replacement of tyres and brakes?' said Caton.

'You did say "quick as you can," boss,' Holmes reminded him as he headed towards the boot to assist the SOCO.

She was lifting out a heavy black plastic case. Holmes reached in and retrieved a black backpack for her.

'There you are,' he said cheerfully.

She scowled at him.

'If you've damaged any of this you can pay for it.'

'Don't worry, he will,' Caton assured her.

Holmes looked up at the Victoria Square flats.

'Don't tell me she lives in there?' he said. 'I thought that was zimmers only.'

'Is there any 'ism that you haven't managed to subvert?' said Caton, arming his car and then leading them across the road and down towards the corner with Ancoats Street.

'I'm doing my best,' his Deputy joked. 'What I need is an incentive.'

'How about a transfer to traffic?' said Caton. 'I'd give you a week before you were on your final warning.'

DC Hulme started to laugh, until he saw the look on his DCI's face.

Caton took them round the corner, past Kutters unisex hair salon, a string of Chinese businesses, including a hair and beauty salon, and two indeterminate trading businesses. Indeterminate unless you could read Chinese characters. He checked off the numbers and stopped outside a shop with a steel shutter down, no sign over the top and a single wooden door with a steel surround.

'This is it,' he said.

'Where our victim lives?' said DC Hulme.

'Lived,' said Holmes.

'According to Menthol Mandy,' muttered Caton.

'Who?'

'You don't want to know.'

Caton stabbed the second of the four buttons on the steel plate to the right of the door. When there was no reply he kept his finger on the buzzer.

'Whose flat are you buzzing, boss?' said Gordon Holmes.

'Not the victim's,' said DC Hulme.

The three of them turned to see if he was being serious. He was. The other two detectives should have known better. Hulme's pedantry was already a legend, and he'd been with the team less than a year.

'Another working girl,' said Caton, removing his finger momentarily, then applying it again. 'She lives in the one below our victim's. Our source says she found her the flat.'

'Are you sure she's in, boss?' said Hulme.

The speaker squawked. A stream of abuse left them in no doubt where they should shove their heads before they left.

'Nice,' said Holmes. 'Can't wait to meet her.'

Caton depressed the button again and spoke into the speaker.

'This is the police, Chantelle,' he said. 'Please don't make us break this door down. It'll only annoy your neighbours, not to mention the landlord.'

This time the curse was muted. There was a louder buzz. The speaker squawked.

'The door's open,' she said. 'I'm on the third floor.'

Chapter 8

'Less than half a mile from where she died,' observed Gordon Holmes as they trooped up the stairs. He was carrying the SOCO's kit bag, leaving her free to hump the metal case. 'If she was working Corporation Street, Angel Meadow would have been on her way home.'

The door to the flat on the third floor was wide open.

'In here,' shouted the occupant.

Caton led the way down the narrow corridor that doubled as a hallway, and as a means of separating the bathroom and toilet from the lounge. The walls were painted oatmeal, and the laminate oak floor was clean and unscuffed. Someone had been burning scented candles; the place smelt like Lush at the Trafford Centre. It was not at all what he had expected.

In the lounge was a cream sofa, and two small matching armchairs. A stainless-steel coffee table stood on a white rug. There was an artificial gas fire set into the wall. She was standing beside a large screen television, with her back to the window that looked out onto Oldham Road. Her shoulder-length bottle-blonde hair was mussed and unkempt. Devoid of make-up, her oval face looked tired and creased, with dark shadows beneath sharp eyes the colour of blue-green glass. With the exception of those eyes, she was plain, but her face had a good bone structure.

Caton could see how a little make-up might transform that face, especially when viewed beneath street lamps.

Holmes came alongside him.

'Well, well, well,' he said. 'If it isn't Chantelle Shifnall.'

She scowled at him.

'Gordon Bennett! It's Detective Constable Holmes. You haven't changed. Except around the middle.'

'Detective Inspector,' he told her.

She pulled her pink bathrobe tighter around her waist, tied the belt in a bow, and folded her arms defensively.

'Nice to see someone's gone up in the world,' she said.

Holmes turned to Caton.

'Chantelle and I go back a long way. When I was working out of Bolton, and she was working Shifnall Street. Hence the nickname.'

'Not my choice,' she said. 'It's the one you bastards used when you nicked me.'

'Not your real name though, Chantelle, is it?' said Holmes. 'What was it? Lesley…?'

'Lesley Leanne Friend.' Said with a hint of irritation.

Holmes smirked. 'That's it!' he said.

'What?' she bristled. 'You thought that was funny? Being called the lessie's friend. Why d'you think I call myself Chantelle?'

'Enough, Gordon!' said Caton.

It was her turn to smirk.

'Gay Gordon,' she said. 'I'll be sure to remember that.'

DC Hulme made a poor attempt at smothering a chuckle.

'Miss Brown,' said Caton. 'Or would you prefer Friend?'

'Chantelle,' she said. 'Chantelle will do. Now, why don't you just tell me why there are four coppers in my flat and then let me get back to sleep?'

'Please,' said Caton, 'I think you should sit down.'

'Why? It can't be my dad's dead, because he drank himself into the grave years ago. And if it's my mother, I'm not interested.'

'It isn't,' said Gordon Holmes. 'It's your friend, Irish Meg.'

Her face paled visibly beneath the artificial tan. She placed one hand on the windowsill beside her. For a moment Caton thought her knees might give way. He put a hand out to catch her. She waved it away and sank into the nearest armchair.

'Irish,' she said. 'Poor Irish. I warned her.'

Caton signalled Holmes to take the other armchair, then sat down on the sofa facing her. He looked up at the SOCO and directed her to sit beside him.

'You warned her, Chantelle?' he said. 'Why did you warn her? And what did you warn her about?'

She pulled a tissue from the pocket of her robe, blew her nose and put the tissue back.

'About working alone,' she said. 'About getting into a punter's car without having someone note down the registration. About walking back here on her own in the dark. Obvious stuff.'

'Obvious to girls who have been at it for a while,' said Holmes. 'She was new, wasn't she?'

'New to Manchester,' she replied. 'I don't think she was new to our line of work, though. I know she worked Elizabeth Street in Cheetham Hill for a couple of weeks before she came down here.'

'Why did she move?' asked Caton.

'She was being hassled by some of the other girls. And a guy wanted to pimp her. Said she needed protection. Then offered her drugs. When that didn't work he threatened her.'

'Threatened her. How?'

'Told her it was him she need protection from.'

She raised her hand to her face and gestured with it.

'A slash here with a double-bladed Stanley knife. A slash there. Career over. You know how it is.'

They did. Parallel scars that only plastic surgery could hide.

'Did she tell you the name of this man?' said Caton.

She smiled grimly.

'She didn't tell me, I didn't ask. No point. She was more worried about it happening here.'

'Did it?' said Holmes. 'Might it have done?'

She shook her head.

'We've got a bit of a worker's cooperative going down here. We watch each other's backs. The first hint of a pimp moving in and we let the Neighbourhood Team know. They warn them off.'

Caton nodded. It was part of the strategy that followed on from the Policing and Crime Act 2009. The emphasis had shifted to the kerb-crawling clients soliciting for sex, and the pimps who fed off and intimidated the prostitutes. If the girls were caught engaging in sex acts in overtly public places they could be fined or given an ASBO. Otherwise they tended to be left alone.

'You haven't asked me what happened to Meg,' he said.

She fingered the tissue in her pocket, but didn't remove it.

'I don't want to know. Not unless she's coming back.'

'I'm sorry, Chantelle,' he said, 'but her body was found in Angel Meadow. Among the trees beside the wall that borders Aspin Lane.'

She didn't need to know any more than that. The less they revealed, the better. The greater the chance that she might surprise them with what she knew.

She seemed nonplussed.

'What is it?' he asked.

'We never walk across the parks alone at night,' she said. 'None of us do. Meg wouldn't either. It's asking for trouble.'

It was exactly what Caton had thought from the outset. On the other hand, she had to take her clients somewhere. They all did.

'Do you know where she went with her punters?'

'Somewhere close by, in their cars,' she replied. 'Down by the railway. Under the arches on Fitzgeorge Street. Wherever your lot don't have a surveillance van parked up.'

Fitzgeorge Street. Where the body of Roger Standing CBE had been found in his car. It reminded Caton of the amorous couple caught on CCTV that night.

'But not in the parks?' he said.

'Not on our own,' she said. 'And certainly not after the lights have gone out.'

'When are they switched off?' he asked.

She told him. She was right. There was no way the victim would have gone down there of her own free will.

'I knew there was something wrong,' said Chantelle Brown, as much to herself as to them.

Nobody spoke. They all new to wait for her to explain. She looked up at their expectant faces.

'Last night,' she said, 'about seven o'clock. She'd been out. I don't know where. When she came back she knocked on my door. She was really upset. Crying. I made her come in and brewed us both a cup of tea. She said someone had been in her room. The door was open and her stuff had been moved around.'

'Moved around?' said Caton. 'Was anything taken?'

'I asked her that. She just shrugged. Then she said her money stash and her mobile phone were still there. She doesn't have…' She checked herself. 'Didn't have much of any value that I ever saw.'

'Did she lock her door when she went out?' said Holmes.

She looked at him scornfully.

'What do you think?' A single woman, living on her own. In rental property. Round here. Of course she did. Mind you, the only times I've been up there when she's been going in or out she just pulled it to.' She shook head. I never just rely on the Yale.'

She looked at them as though daring them not to believe her.

'I don't. No way. I use both locks. Every time.'

'Did she have any idea who it might have been?' Caton asked.

She shook her head.

'She said she had no idea. I think that's partly what bothered her. If it wasn't a thief or someone she knew, who was it? That'd bother me. I asked her if she thought it might be a punter who'd followed her. Or that guy who wanted to pimp her.'

'What did she say?'

'She didn't. I don't think she was listening. Then all of a sudden she started crying again. Only this time it was more like weeping. She was unconsolable.'

'Inconsolable,' said DC Hulme.

'What?' she said.

'It doesn't matter,' Caton told her. 'Please go on.'

'Anyway, Meg was heartbroken. I could see there was nothing I could do. She left and went back up to her flat. I left her to it. She was still there when I went out about nine o'clock. It was the last time I saw her that night.'

No one spoke. They jut sat there filling in those final hours in their mind's eye.

Caton broke the silence.

'When did she start to work on your patch?'

'About a month ago. I spotted her the first night she arrived. I always like to check out the opposition. It was me that told her about the flat. How it was vacant. It worked for me too, because it's good when there's more than one of you living in the same building.'

'Did Meg ever talk about being stalked or harassed down here?' asked Caton.

She shook her head again

'No. Though we've all had punters who get fixated. But so long as they're prepared to pay for it they can see us any time they like.'

'But what if you come across one you don't trust?' asked Holmes.

She pulled a face.

'I don't trust any of them. But it's the ones that want to mix it up with a bit of violence, or a lot of violence, that you've really got to watch out for. Or sometimes there's a quiet one who's just really scary. Creepy. Like you know, he's capable of really bad things, and maybe it's only a matter of time.'

'What do you do about them?'

'Say no. Then steer clear.'

'What if they persist?'

'You still say no, but you make sure all the other girls have his description, and that of his car, even the licence number. Sometimes we'll take a photo when he isn't looking. Show it around. We let your lot know too.'

'Has there been anyone like that recently?' asked Caton.

'No. Not for a couple of months. There was one. Thin, sweaty, dead eyes. But he was before Meg came on the scene.'

'Have you got his photo?' said Holmes.

'I'd have to look. But I think so.'

'We'll need to borrow your phone,' Caton told her.

'No way!' she protested. 'I need that for my business.'

'It'll only take a minute,' he assured her. 'Just so my colleague here can copy the photos.'

He indicated the SOCO sitting next to him.

'Alright,' she said. 'But just the photos. I don't want you copying my contacts.'

She got up and went into another room, returning a minute later with a mobile phone. She handed it to the SOCO, who placed it on the coffee table and opened her case, to reveal, among other things, a small laptop.

'So,' said Caton as the SOCO got to work, 'she never said she was worried about a punter?'

Chantelle sat down again.

'No. Mind, there was odd something the other night. We were in a bar. O'Malley's. Having a quick DC.'

'DC?'

She smiled that thin smile again. 'Dutch Courage. It helps if you have a drink before you start your day. Not too much, mind. Don't want to put off the punters. They like to kid themselves you really want to do it with them, not that you're too pissed to care.'

'You were in O'Malley's?'

'I was facing the door, force of habit; she was looking into the room. I was talking to her about something of nothing when I realised she wasn't listening to me. She was listening to the couple on the table behind me. I joked about it. Said she might just as well get her mobile out and start texting her mates for all that I was entertaining her.'

'What did she say?'

'She laughed it off.'

'And this struck you as significant because?'

'Because no sooner had I started babbling on than she'd tuned in to those two again. I looked round a couple of times to see what was so interesting, but all I could see was the back of this guy's head. When I turned back she'd gone white, pushed back her chair and was standing up, wanting to go. "Are you alright?" I said. "I need some air," she said, and headed for the door. Didn't even finish her drink.'

'What did you do?'

'I threw mine down, then went outside. She had her back against the wall and her head between her knees. I thought she was trying to be sick, but she wasn't. She was just catching her breath. Then she straightened up. "I'm alright," she said. "Just a bit dizzy there for a moment."'

'What did you think was happening?'

'Looked like a panic attack to me.'

'What happened then?'

'We set off back to our pitches.'

'Did she say anything about the couple she'd been listening to?'

'No.'

'But you think this panic attack was something to do with them?'

'To be honest, I've no idea. But it did seem a bit of a coincidence.'

'And you didn't get a good look at them?'

She shook her head.

'Not really. I mean, I did turn and glance at them as I reached the door. But like I said, all I could see was the back of one of them, and the top of the head of the other. They were laughing about something.'

'Did you hear any of the conversation she was listening in on?'

'I was too busy listening to myself. Mind...' Her forehead wrinkled as she tried to remember. 'I do remember one of them had an Irish accent, a bit like her own but stronger. The other one sounded local. There was something, though. The local one kept putting on this Irish accent, or was it Scottish? Anyway, every time he did it that's what set them off laughing.'

Caton was running out of questions. She was beginning to look exhausted too. Emotionally drained, and even more tired.

'A final question for now, Chantelle,' he said. 'Did Meg ever let slip her surname?'

She shook her head.

'No, never.'

Her expression was apologetic, as though it was her fault she had never winkled it out of her.

'Don't worry,' he said, 'I'm sure the landlord will know. She must have had to provide some kind of identity.'

She laughed.

'What's so funny?' he said.

'You're joking, right?' she replied. 'All he's interested in is the deposit, and regular payments. He's lucky to rent that place and he knows it.'

'What happens if a tenant defaults?'

'If we miss one payment, we're out. He changes the locks and takes our belongings down the pawn brokers in lieu of the rent.'

'He can't do that,' said DC Hulme. 'He'd be in contravention of the Landlord Tenancy Agreement. He has to serve a Section 21 notice first.'

'Is he for real, Mr Holmes?' she said.

'I often wonder,' Gordon replied.

Caton stood up, and the others rose with him.

'Thanks for your cooperation, Chantelle,' he said. 'One of my officers, probably DC Hulme here, will come back when you've had a rest and take a formal statement from you, but right now we'd better take a look at your friend's flat.'

The SOCO reached across and handed back Chantelle's phone. Caton took a card from his pocket.

'If you think of anything else, my contact details are on here.'

They were filing out of the room when DC Hulme stopped in the doorway.

'Just one thing if I may, Miss Brown?' he said, surprising them all. 'Why did you all call her Irish?'

On the face of it, it was a daft question. Caton couldn't wait to hear the answer. Sometimes the simplest question was the most enlightening.

'Because of her accent,' said Chantelle. 'It wasn't that obvious, but it was there. I mean, she didn't talk about Ireland or where she came from. We all just assumed. Because of her accent.'

She smiled to herself.

'Funny, she never complained about us calling her that. In fact, I think she was secretly pleased by it.'

'North or South, would you say?' said Hulme. 'Northern Ireland, or the Republic? Her accent?'

They waited as she thought about it.

'I'm not an expert, she said, 'and like I say, it wasn't that strong. But if I had to choose, I'd say Northern Ireland.'

Chapter 9

'It's not a lot to go on,' said Holmes as they trudged up to the next landing. 'That stuff about those two blokes. Worth a trip to O'Malley's though, to see if the bar staff remember them. Maybe they're regulars. Might even be able to put faces or names to them.'

The door to her room was locked.

'Her intruder must have had a key if she did pull it to when she went out,' said DC Hulme.

'A child could open this,' said Gordon Holmes dismissively. 'All you need's a pick-gun.'

The SOCO put her case down and examined the Yale-type lock.

'You're half right, Detective Inspector,' she said, straightening up.

'Which half?' he said.

'The bit about a child being able to do it.' She placed an index finger against the face of the lock. 'So long as the child had access to a bump lock.'

At first Caton wasn't sure what he was looking at. Then she slid her finger back a little and he could see a slight indentation in the brass plate immediately above the keyhole.

Caton knew the theory. The specially designed bump key was inserted part way in, then bumped in hard and fast. It had the effect of pushing the pins up above the shear line. Providing a light rotational force was applied to the key before the pins fell back again, the cylinder would turn and the door could be opened. Apparently, it had become the professional burglar's method of choice.

'I thought bumping didn't leave any traces,' he said.

'Depends how much force is applied, and how new the lock is,' she told him. 'In this case the lock's been replaced recently, and this indentation isn't the result of regular wear. He'd need to know what lock it was though, otherwise he'd have to carry a bunch of different bump keys around with him.'

She reached into her case and removed an evidence bag containing the keys they had found in the victim's handbag. She inserted the brass key into the lock.

'Here we go,' she said.

The key turned, and she pushed the door open.

'I'll go first,' she said, 'if that's okay?'

Caton nodded in agreement.

As they waited for her to give them the all-clear, Caton breathed in deeply through his nose. There was a fresh, clean smell. Sweet, but not cloying. Like a good wine from Alsace.

'Gloves on, but try not to move anything,' said the SOCO from the door to the lounge. 'Not until I've taken some photographs. If you have to pick anything up put it back where it came from.'

'Seems a bit OTT,' muttered DC Hulme. 'It's not as if she died here.'

Gordon Homes rounded on him.

'In the case of any suspicious death the victim's home is treated like a crime scene until we know otherwise. Especially when we have reason to believe it's been broken into. You should know that by now.'

Caton started by having a quick look around.

The apartment was nowhere near as smart as Chantelle Brown's. There was a dirty tartan carpet on the floor of the hall and in all of the rooms other than the kitchen, where cheap red artificial tiles had been laid. The house was sparsely furnished. A divan bed with a duvet in the single bedroom, a scuffed white leather two-person sofa and a matching pouffe in the lounge. The eighteen-inch Samsung television had seen better days. Instead of a coffee table there was a stack of small teak tables, on top of which stood a lamp with an orange shade. There was no fireplace. An electric heater stood against one wall. On the window ledge was a small glass vase which held a wilting spray of freesias.

He went into the bedroom. The divan was pressed up against the wall. Beside it was a small locker with a drawer beneath which was an open compartment. In the corner of the room was a single pine wardrobe. He opened the wardrobe. Four dresses, three skirts, an anorak and a three-quarter-length coat hung from the top rail. On the lower rail he counted two pairs of jeans and three pairs of slacks. A small shoe rack held six pairs of shoes and a pair of three-quarter-length boots. A large hatbox on top of the wardrobe held matching pairs of bras and knickers. A second held three handbags and a pile of tights. All in all it represented a fraction of Kate's collection back home on the Wharf.

He turned his attention to the bed. The duvet had been pulled up over the pillow. A much-worn teddy bear sat by the headboard as though on guard. He lifted the bear, turned back the duvet and examined the sheets. The bed had been slept in recently. The sheets were crumpled, but clean. He lifted the pillow. Beneath it was a pair of white cotton pyjamas. It seemed she'd had a thing about cotton. He replaced the pillow, drew the duvet back up and replaced the teddy bear.

In the side table drawer were tissues, a handkerchief and a cardboard box. He lifted the lid. The box contained two diaphragms and a part-used tube of spermicide. Beside it was a prescription box of 21-day contraceptive pills made out to a Maureen Flinn. He took out his notebook and wrote down the name, and the name of the prescribing pharmacist. He opened the box and slid out the tab of pills. There were fifteen pills left. He slid them back and replaced the box.

He crouched down to explore the open shelf beneath the drawer. There was a thick black book that looked like a Bible. He picked it up. The title was picked out in faded gold leaf. The St Andrew Daily Missal. He opened it. On the flyleaf was an inscription in blue ink.

To our beloved Maureen on the occasion of her First Holy Communion. June 14th, 1981. All Our Love, Mummy and Daddy XX

Different coloured ribbons marked different sections of the book. Caton tried each in turn, but could see nothing of any immediate significance. He made a note of the inscription, and then put the Missal back where it came from, next to a small round plastic box. The lid of the box was transparent. He could see that it contained a black rosary with a silver crucifix. He stood up and looked around.

On the widow sill were two photo frames. One had a photo of a girl of about twelve years of age in her school uniform. He thought he could see a likeness in the smiling face to the dead woman in Angel Meadow. It was something about those eyes. The other photo was of a middle-aged couple – a man and a woman – raising champagne flutes to the camera. They looked very happy. An anniversary perhaps, or a cruise. He turned the frames over to see if there was anything written on the back. There was not. He put them back on the sill, and used his mobile phone to take a photo of them both.

Caton sat on the bed for a moment and tried to put himself in the place of the woman who had lived here. He imagined her putting her clothes away, slipping on her pyjamas, turning back the duvet. He reached down between his legs and lifted the duvet. There was a drawer. He had missed it before because it only ran along the bottom half of the bed. He pulled it open. It contained a multipack of condoms, a pair of slip-on sandals and a biscuit tin. He lifted the tin out and placed it on the bed. He lifted the lid. Someone whistled. It was Gordon Holmes, standing in the doorway.

'There must be hundreds in there,' he said.

Caton lifted out the three bundles of notes. They were each of a different denomination, and wrapped in red elastic bands like the ones the postman regularly left on the pavement outside his apartment. The bundle of twenty-pound notes was by far the thickest. Holmes watched as Caton counted.

'Six hundred and fifty-five pounds,' he said as he placed an elastic band around the final bundle and put them back in the tin.

'So why didn't the burglar take it?' said Holmes, echoing Caton's thoughts.

'There's no evidence there was a burglary,' said Caton, 'apart from Charlotte Brown's third-party account and that dent on the faceplate of the lock.'

He replaced the tin, closed the drawer and stood up. It was only then that he noticed another photo frame lying face down on top of the bedside table. It was a wooden frame the same colour as the table. He picked it up and turned it over. The frame was empty. Just a faded piece of backing cardboard.

'Maybe the thief had a photo fetish,' joked Holmes.

Caton followed him, deep in thought, to the kitchen. A clean dinner plate, a knife and fork, and a paring knife lay in the drainer on the side of the sink. The fridge contained a half-empty pint milk bottle, five apples, three eggs in a container, some canned food and several boxes of takeaway meals for one. A box of breakfast cereal stood in the middle of the small kitchen table, accompanied by a bowl, a spoon and a mug.

'Meagre fare, but organised,' Holmes observed.

They went into the combined bathroom and toilet next. There was barely room for the two of them, let alone DC Hulme, who had finally ceased shadowing the SOCO. It was just as Caton expected. Clean, neat and sparse.

'Come on,' he said, 'let's get back to Central Park and leave her to it.'

'Shame we didn't turn up anything,' Holmes remarked as they trooped down the stairs.

'I wouldn't say that,' Caton replied.

Chapter 10

DI Stuart was still at the scene, while the rest of the team were back in the Major Incident Room. Ged had cleared as many of the whiteboards as possible, and designated one half of the room exclusively for Operation Stardust.

'Don't blame me,' she said. 'The computer chose it.'

'A computer with a sense of humour,' said DC Hulme.

They stared blankly at him.

'Don't tell me you don't know?' he said.

'Enlighten us, Jimmy,' chorused Holmes and Carter. It had become a standing joke.

Unabashed, he cleared his throat.

'Operation Stardust 1 was a military operation of the Delaz Fleet against the Earth Federation in UC 0083.'

His audience rolled their eyes.

'Come on,' he said. 'The Gundam Wiki series? The Japanese TV animations?'

'Can anyone tell me what Japanese animations have to do with a woman lying dead in Angel Meadows?' asked Caton, emerging from his cubicle.

'Yes, boss,' said DC Hulme, to another chorus of groans.

'Don't bother,' said Caton, turning his attention to the list of actions Gordon Holmes had just finished writing on the board.

'Potential Suspects,' he read. 'Pimps.'

'As far as we know she didn't have one,' said Holmes. 'Nor is there anything to suggest that she was being hassled into letting herself be pimped on her new patch.'

'What about the one up in Cheetham that was rumoured to have been threatening her?'

'Cheetham Neighbourhood Team are chasing that one down for us. They have a couple of names. Promised to have him found by end of play today.' He shrugged. 'You know how it is; these blokes are like vampires, they only come out in the dark.'

'Punters?' said Caton.

'We don't know of any regulars she may have had,' said Benson. 'After all, she'd only just started working the Corporation Street triangle. But I've got a list of everyone arrested or stopped on suspicion of soliciting in that neighbourhood in the last six months. They're all going to get a visit.'

DC Hulme whistled.

'That's going to be a lot of relationships in trouble,' he said.

'Serves them right,' said Holmes. 'If you're going to play away, you've got to expect your friends to come calling.'

'Drugs Supplier,' said Caton, reading on.

Holmes rubbed his chin.

'No evidence that she was a user, but we'll have to see what toxicology turns up. Like you said before, boss, we can't discount the possibility that she'd stumbled onto something big and they saw her as a threat. DCI Lounds says we're barking up the wrong tree, but he's promised to look into it.'

Caton moved on to the next set.

'Witness Interviews. Where are we up to?'

'They're being collated, cross-referenced and put straight onto the system via the mobile Incident Room,' Benson told him.

Caton nodded. Joanne Stuart was already proving to be a capable pair of hands, rising to the challenge of promotion just as he'd promised DCS Gates she would.

'Any statements deemed to be significant,' he said, 'I want those witnesses to be re-interviewed by one of this team.'

CCTV was the next on the list.

'Tactical Aid have been brilliant,' said his Deputy. 'We reckon they've got everything they could, given it's a Saturday. We'll still chase the rest come Monday though. I've got two officers working on it full-time.'

He moved across to the wall map at the centre of which was the crime scene. He indicated the route with his left forefinger.

'So far we've got her walking down Oldham Road close to the time her friend says she heard her leaving her flat. Then we've got her in Swan Street, Miller Street and finally, onto Corporation Street. There's footage of her up and down Corporation Street. We've even got her getting into a number of cars. Three so far. Before you ask, we've got the makes and models, and the licence plates. They're being checked. Nothing so far.'

'Fingerprints?'

'DS Stuart–' Holmes began.

'Acting DI,' Caton reminded him.

'Sorry, boss.' He looked genuinely embarrassed. 'I didn't–'

'It's alright, Gordon,' said Caton. 'Just get on with it.'

'Acting DI Stuart came up with a great idea,' he said. 'She's sent over to Longsight for that mobile fingerprint scanner they're trialling. You know, like the ones the Met uses? She's going to persuade SOCO to use it on the victim in situ.'

Before Caton could comment, one of the DCs called over.

'Boss, you're going to want to see this.'

They crowded round his desk, and focused on the monitor. It was a live feed of the Press Conference DCS Gates had promised. Caton didn't know whether to be miffed that he hadn't been invited to attend, even if he had been called on to speak, or relieved that for now he was out of the glare of publicity. He smiled when he saw who was to be the spokesperson. Martin Hadfield, Assistant Chief Constable of Crime. Either he'd pulled rank, or she was playing politics. Letting him put his noose in the neck, as he seemed to make a habit of doing these days. Hadfield leaned into the mike.

'Shortly before 9 a.m. this morning, police were called to Angel Meadow Park close to the Northern Quarter and the City Centre, following reports that a body had been found. I can confirm that the body was of a woman, believed to be in her thirties. Enquiries are ongoing to identify the individual, and a post mortem has been scheduled. I can also confirm that the death is being treated as suspicious, and a murder inquiry has been launched.'

Hands shot up. Voices called out.

'Is it true she was shot?' shouted one.

'Can you can confirm that the victim was a prostitute?' called another.

'Do you suspect a sexual motive?' one demanded.

'Is there any connection with the Angel of The Meadows?' asked another. 'Are you looking for a serial killer?'

The ACC looked distinctly uncomfortable. The woman from the Press Office leaned across, placed a hand over the microphone and whispered in his ear. As she sat back, he leaned into the mike again.

'I urge anyone with information about this incident, including the possible identity of the victim, to call us direct by dialling 101, or by visiting your nearest police station. If you wish to pass on information anonymously, you can call Crimestoppers on 0800 555 111 or fill out our secure and anonymous online form. I must stress that people should not use the GMP Facebook or Twitter pages to report this or any other crime-related information.'

Before anyone could respond, he was on his feet and out of there.

'You did well to miss out on that one, boss,' said Holmes.

Caton was more concerned about the fact that information he would have preferred to stay out of the public domain a little longer was already out there. The woman who had found the body, probably. Nothing he could do about that.

'Right,' he said. 'Everything seems to be in hand. It's going to be a long day and a long night. I'm going to nip home, have a wash and brush up, and get changed, then I'm back here for the duration. The rest of you can do the same if you need to, but check with DI Holmes first. I don't want a mass exodus. And give your nearest and dearest my apologies, and tell them not to expect to see you this side of tomorrow afternoon.'

Chapter 11

'Hi, Kate!' he called as he closed the door behind him.

He found her working at the desk in the lounge. She stood and came to meet him. They kissed.

'This is a nice surprise,' she said. 'I didn't expect you back this side of midnight.'

He grimaced.

'It's a flying visit, I'm afraid. I need a shower and shave, and I wanted to see you, if only briefly. Then I've got to go back. You know how important the first twenty-four hours are.'

'I'll make you something while you're getting changed,' she said. 'Mixed bean soup, with poached eggs or beans on toast to follow. You choose.'

'Poached eggs,' he told her. 'And a mug of tea. I can only take so much coffee.'

He was still drying his hair when the landline rang. Kate came into the bedroom and lobbed the handset onto the bed beside him.

'It's Harry,' she said. 'Don't be long, I've just put your eggs on.'

'Hi, Tom,' said his son, his voice brimming with youthful exuberance. 'Guess what?'

'Wigan are hoping to bounce back?' said Caton, bracing himself for the response.

'What do you mean, hoping?! Defo they're going

to do it. Then you'd better watch out.'

Caton was tempted to wind him up a bit more by suggesting they hadn't a hope in hell, but then remembered that he too had once been young and believed that anything was possible.

'I hope they do,' he said. 'City could do with a bit of competition.'

'Anyway,' said Harry, 'Mum's got a new boyfriend. And he's a footballer.'

'A footballer?'

Caton had visions of a fit, overpaid, self-obsessed, poorly educated young man having a swift fling with the mother of his son, before moving on. Worse still, not moving on. He ran his hand through his hair, knotted his tie and walked through into the lounge.

'She can tell you all about him herself,' said Harry. 'Got to go, Dad. Things to do.'

And he was gone.

'Tom?' It was Helen. 'He's told you then?'

'A footballer, Helen?' he replied, making no attempt to hide his incredulity.

'Don't be so bloody stereotypical,' she said. 'I'd expected better of you.'

'Have you forgotten Okowu-Bello and the Frozen Contract case? That may just have jaundiced my view of footballers a little.'

'Firstly, that was hardly typical,' she replied. 'Secondly, he's a former footballer, now a coach. And thirdly, before you ask, he's more or less my age.'

'More, or less?'

'He's only two years younger.'

'I thought you said the nuns told you you should always marry a man older than you?'

'They did. Because women mature so much faster than men. As you're clearly intent on proving. Anyway, who said anything about getting married?'

Caton decided it was time to change the subject.

'How does Harry get on with him?'

'Fine, and vice versa. You've no need to feel threatened.'

He decided to let that ride too. She was right of course. It was what really bothered him. She could date whoever she liked. Marry whoever she pleased. He had no rights over her. It was all about Harry. He sat down at the kitchen table.

'Can I ask you a question, Helen?' he said. 'Nothing to do with this.'

'Try me.'

'You were raised a Catholic?'

'Yes.'

'At what age do Catholics make their First Holy Communion?'

'Why?' she said. 'You're not thinking of becoming a convert, are you?'

'No. Humour me,'

'Seven or eight. Nearer seven, I think. Nowadays they do them all at once though.'

'All at once?'

'First Confession, First Communion, Confirmation.' She laughed. 'From Sinner to Soldier Christ in one day.'

Caton placed the phone back in its cradle.

Kate put his plate on the table and sat down opposite him, nestling a mug of tea in her hands.

'Don't tell me you're discussing your cases with Helen now?'

'No. I didn't tell her what it was about, I just needed to clear something up.'

'And did you?

'I think so.'

'Are you going to tell me,' she said, 'or is that strictly for former girlfriends?'

She was smiling, but he knew she was smarting inside.

'These eggs are perfect,' he said. 'Soft and runny.'

'Don't change the subject,' she responded.

'We found a prayer book in her room. The St Andrew's Missal. There was an inscription inside.'

'What's the significance of that?'

'The inscription was dated June 14th, 1981. If Helen is correct, that means the victim would have been seven or eight at the time. Which means that now she would be forty-three to forty-four years of age.'

'If it is her missal.'

'Bit of a stretch if it isn't. Same name. Meg's short for Margaret, surely?'

'Megan, Megara, Meredith and Morgan,' she added unhelpfully. 'Megan's on my list for our daughter.'

'If it is a daughter,' he replied.

She reached across the table and clattered him on the head with her tablemat.

She waited until he'd finished eating and was sitting back sipping his mug of tea.

'Angel Meadow,' she said. 'Wasn't there another body found there a few years ago?'

'Yes. Her body, or to be more accurate her skeleton, was found when they were excavating the land where the Co-op's new headquarters has been built.'

'That's it,' she said. 'They think she was killed about forty years ago. There was a lot of talk about it being a sex killing. Why was that?'

'She was naked below the waist. Her dress, bra, jumper and tights were near the body. One shoe was missing. There was a lot of speculation about it having been taken as a trophy.'

'It could just as easily have come off when she was being moved.'

'Exactly. She'd been wrapped in a carpet and moved from wherever it was she had been killed. Easy to see how a shoe could have come off.'

'How did she die?'

'She had a fractured jaw, fractures to her neck and a broken collarbone. The best guess was that she'd been beaten to death.'

Kate shuddered.

'Did they manage to identify her?'

He took a sip and set the mug down.

'We think so.'

'Only think so?'

'A professor of Anthropology at Dundee used a mould of the woman's skull to create a forensic facial reconstruction in clay. Carbon14 dating of her teeth and bones narrowed down her age, and the time she was believed to have been killed. That together with descriptions of the clothing and intensive missing persons enquiries led the team to Tanzania, where a family had contacted them.'

'So why can't they be certain?'

'Because when it came down to it they couldn't get a sample of DNA from the family. I never found out why exactly. It may have been the authorities out there, or the family themselves.'

'So we'll never know?'

'It doesn't look like it.' He drained his mug dry. 'On the upside, while they were doing all that delving into missing persons they were able to eliminate twenty-one people who weren't missing after all, reunite six others with their families and locate over forty more.'

'Doesn't sound like there's any connection with your victim.'

'Shot twice at close range, with clinical accuracy. Clothes undisturbed.' He shook his head. 'It won't stop the press speculating though.'

Kate stood up and began to clear the table.

'Do you want my professional opinion?' she said, knowing full well that he would. 'It's not the kind of MO you'd expect. It sounds more like an execution than a crime of passion, jealousy, anger or rejection. Certainly not sexual deviance. And I've never heard of a serial killer whose choice of weapon was a gun. Other than to disable a victim first.'

Caton didn't want to dwell on what that might mean.

'There's no evidence that robbery was a motive either,' he said. 'Although we can't discount the possibility that she knew the perpetrator, or was carrying something they wanted.'

She returned and sat back down at the table.

'The fact that no attempt was made to hide or dispose of the body would fit with a punishment killing,' she said. 'You know, sending a message at the same time.'

'Risky though,' he observed. 'Because sending a message implies that others would know he, or she, was the killer.'

'Or had commissioned the killing,' she said.

It felt odd to be discussing a brutal murder across the table with a heavily pregnant woman. Caton wondered if it was true that an unborn child could hear what people were saying outside of the womb. If so, he hoped their child was not going to be some kind of genius, blessed with total recall.

He pushed back his chair and stood up.

'I'll have to go, Kate.'

'Hang on,' she said, heading for the kitchen.

She returned with a small plastic container, which she thrust into his hand.

'Cheese and tomato. Should keep you going for a while. Has to be better than a pastie, or a deep-crust pizza.'

Caton raised his eyebrows.

'You must have mistaken me for Gordon,' he said.

He leaned forward to kiss her and attempted a panda hug. Where their bodies met he felt a sudden ripple of energy surging between them.

Kate's face beamed with delight.

'I think she's learning to jog,' she said.

He was walking to the car when his BlackBerry pinged. He had a text message. He stopped and opened it up. It was from Joanne Stuart.

Check your tablet. We have an ID!

As soon as he was in the car he opened his tablet and went straight to the secure email exchange. There was a message from DI Stuart, with an attachment.

We got a hit on her fingerprints! Maureen Flinn. Age thirty-eight. Single. Enhanced records search threw up seven arrests for soliciting going back twenty odd years. Most recent in Birmingham 2009; Newcastle 2011; Hull 2013.

He clicked on the attachment. Like all mugshots it did her no favours, but it was definitely her. The shoulder-length hair was black, not auburn, but it framed the same oval face, fine cheekbones and sad, intelligent, questioning eyes.

He exited the program, closed down the tablet and started the car. He looked in the rear-view mirror, indicated and pulled away from the kerb.

'We will get him, Maureen,' he murmured. 'I promise.'

Chapter 12

Swiping his card as he entered the Headquarters building triggered an alert. He was directed to the reception desk, where there was a message waiting.

'Assistant Chief Constable Hadfield asks that you go immediately to Interview Room three,' he was told. 'And speak with a Cindi Hoenan.'

Speak with Cindi Hoenan? Not question Cindi Hoenan? And why Hadfield? Why not Helen Gates, his immediate boss? There was only one way to find out.

She stood as he entered the room. Sharp eyes behind a pair of black-framed retro spectacles. Black hair in a loosely layered pixie cut. Subtle make-up. She wore a red cardigan over a white blouse. Both hands on the table. No wedding ring. A loose-fitting black pencil skirt below the knees, and ox-blood patent leather shoes with a low heel. Intelligent. Office work or people services, he thought. An administrator perhaps, in local government. Or something like a health visitor.

She thrust out a hand for him to shake. He took it, reluctantly. Her grip was firm, cool and confident.

'Cindi Hoenan,' she said. 'With an i.'

'Detective Inspector Caton,' he replied. 'Please sit down.'

He sat opposite her.

'So, Miss Hoenan,' he began. 'What can I do for you?'

'Ms Hoenan,' she replied. 'And I think you'll find it's what I can do for you?'

'In respect of?'

She seemed surprised that he had not been told.

'In respect of the murder of the person we both know of as Irish Meg.'

Caton took his notebook and a biro from his pocket.

Both know of.

'You have my full attention, Ms Hoenan.'

'Among other things,' she said, 'I am Chair of the Manchester Sex Workers Cooperative.'

The slight uplift of one eyebrow told him that she had registered his poorly concealed surprise.

'Last Tuesday we held a meeting to discuss the response of the National Collective of Prostitutes, to whom we are allied, to the outrageous proposals presented to a Parliamentary Committee by an organisation advising the government.'

Caton had no idea what any of this had to do with him, but he was beginning to understand why Martin Hadfield had ducked out of this one.

'I'm sorry, but I don't understand what this has to do with–'

She raised an imperious hand.

'The victim, Irish Meg, the investigation into whose murder I gather you are leading, attended the meeting. She came with one of our regulars, Chantelle. I gather you've already met Chantelle?'

Caton put his biro down and folded his arms. It wasn't a conscious response. It was an automatic reaction to the way in which she seemed determined to exercise control. He could see her as a dominatrix.

'What relevance do you think the victim's

attendance at your meeting might have to her death?' he said.

She shrugged.

'I don't know,' she replied. 'It's your job to find out things like that.'

'Are you suggesting that she was killed because she had attended your meeting?'

'I'm not saying that. But she was killed because she was a sex worker. What are you doing about that?'

Now he understood. This was not about providing information, it was about political leverage with a small p.

'We have no evidence that her death had anything to do with her profession,' he told her.

She smiled.

'So you agree that sex work is a profession?'

'Not in the sense that it requires specialised vocational training. Only in the sense that a profession is also a career.'

She crossed her legs, as though settling in for a long debate.

'You can take it from me, Detective Chief Inspector, that it does requires specialised vocational training. On-the-job training maybe, but training nevertheless. Have you any idea how much health and safety knowledge is required, not to mention counselling skills? Some clients simply want you to listen while they talk. We sex workers save more marriages than your average marriage counsellor. That's why this idea the government is proposing about decriminalising sex work and criminalising those who pay for sex is bollocks. It doesn't work in Sweden, and it won't work here. It'll just mean more girls like Meg getting killed.'

Caton had had enough. He closed his pocket book, replaced his biro and stood up.

'Ms Hoenan,' he said, 'my job, as you so succinctly

pointed out, is to investigate the unlawful killing of a young woman, not to debate the law surrounding prostitution. Thank you for your interest, but unless you have any information that may assist my investigation I'm afraid I'll have to ask you to leave.'

He didn't care that he sounded like a PR mouthpiece, only that she got the message and couldn't hold anything he said against him.

She appraised him coolly for a moment, then unfolded her legs, smoothed her skirt, pushed back her chair and stood.

'Hounding men seeking the services of sex workers is driving vulnerable women into taking greater risks,' she said. 'Meeting and servicing clients in isolated places. Adding to their own vulnerability, our vulnerability. Mr Hadfield understood that. Do you, Chief Inspector Caton?'

He walked past her and grasped the door handle.

'I understand what you are saying,' he told her. 'Fortunately my current responsibilities do not include enforcement of the Policing and Crime Act 2009 in relation to soliciting and loitering for the purposes of prostitution. All I can promise you is that my investigation will not involve hounding anyone unless we have good reason to believe that they may have been involved in this young woman's death.'

He opened the door and stood back.

She stared at him intently for a moment.

'Just so long as you do get him,' she said.

Then she walked towards him. Her eyes never left his. Shoulders back, hips tilted forward slightly, one foot in front of the other, she radiated elegance and controlled sexuality. She could have been a model, he reflected. She paused in the doorway and smiled thinly.

'At least,' she said, reading his thoughts, 'you didn't ask what a girl like me is doing in a job like this.'

'Don't ask,' he said in reply to Joanne Stuart's quizzical gaze. 'Just tell me about our victim.'

The image he had seen on his tablet, copied and enlarged, was now centre stage on the board in front of them.

'Maureen Flinn. Forty-four years of age. Place of birth not known. Employment history not known – apart from those seven arrests for soliciting. We do have a series of addresses, each associated with those arrests. Mainly rented flats and several hostels.'

'Hang on,' said Caton. 'How come we don't have more than this? She must have had an NHS number, national insurance and tax references, credit history.'

'These weren't major offences,' she said. 'You know how it is. In most cases she was simply cautioned. A couple of fines. One ASBO. Looks like each time she was arrested, she simply moved on.'

'As long as they had a name, date of birth and a place of fixed abode, in those days nobody was going to want a complete history,' reflected Gordon Holmes. 'Even if they decided they did, she was probably long gone by the time they got round to it.'

'We should start with her name and date of birth, and then work forwards,' said Caton.

'Assuming the name is spelt right, and she didn't lie about her age,' said DC Hulme.

'Based on those assumptions,' said Joanne Stuart, 'Duggie Benson came up with forty-seven names in the UK register of births and the electoral register. He's trawling through them.'

'What if she was born in Eire?' said DS Carter. 'Or Canada, or the USA?'

'Or Australia,' said Hulme.

'We'll have to release her photo,' said Caton. 'Newspapers, TV, Facebook, our Twitter page.'

'Fortunately we may not need to,' she said. 'We

may already have a lead.'

'Why didn't you say so?' he said.

'Because I wasn't given a chance?'

She had a point. And it wasn't like her to grandstand. Gordon perhaps, but not her.

'Go on.'

'Duggie found a Maureen Flinn, the right age, on a social services database. Twenty-seven years ago she was allocated a place on a supported housing scheme in Oldham.'

'Twenty-seven years ago our victim would have been seventeen years old,' Caton reflected. 'The age at which young people in care have to move out of local authority care homes into a flat, a mate's house, or–'

'Supported housing!'

'Thank you, DC Hulme,' said Gordon Holmes. 'I Wouldn't have got there in a month of Sundays.'

'Duggie is trying to cut his way through all the data protection gatekeepers,' she told them, 'to see if we can't get a copy of her records.'

'That shouldn't be a problem,' Caton observed. 'It's not as though the victim can give her consent.'

'So long as our victim and their former client are one and the same,' she said. 'Duggie's sent them a copy of her photo. He's waiting for someone to confirm, or otherwise.'

'Tell them to hurry up,' he said.

Twenty-seven minutes later he was looking at a summary on a single side of A4. The bare bones. The original file, he had been informed, would be made available to him at Royton Town Hall.

Maureen Flinn had first come to the notice of Oldham Social Services at the age of thirteen and a half. She had been referred, on behalf of the parents, by one of the council's education welfare officers. The child had been temporarily excluded from one high school on three different occasions for disruption and non-attendance. Caton had never been able to get his head around the use of suspension as a sanction for truancy. I t sounded more like a reward than a punishment. What chance was there of rebuilding relationships with the school after an even longer period of absence?

Finally, the school had lost patience and she was permanently excluded. She lasted three months in her new school and was back on the temporary exclusion merry-go-round. No details were given. There was a period of seven months when she was being educated at home. Then, aged fifteen years and two months, after running away from home twice, and trashing a classroom at her next school, she was officially taken into care and placed in a residential home. The next entry, one year and ten months later, recorded her leaving care. A housing association address was given as her destination. After that, nothing.

Caton placed the sheet of paper on his desk and sat back.

'What happened, Maureen?' he said to the cubicle partition. Not at the end obviously, he already knew how it had ended. Nor in the middle; he could have written that story with a high degree of accuracy. A young girl, straight from care. Low self-esteem, poor prospects, no support mechanism. There was a twenty per cent chance that she would end up living on the streets, and a more than fifty per cent chance that she would end up living off them. It was the time before that interested him. The years that should have overflowed with unconditional love and excitement, and joy in learning. Innocent eyes, bright with expectation. When had that all gone wrong? And why? It wasn't his concern, he knew that. Not unless it had a direct bearing on the investigation. But he couldn't help wondering. Otherwise, what was she? Just a name and a body, dissected, sewn together and lying in a fridge. That wasn't who he was seeking justice for. It was for the life that had been, and still could have been had it not been snatched away.

On his desk was the note that Duggie Benson had attached to the sheet of paper. It contained two names, Anne and Michael Flinn, and an address. He picked it up, put it in his pocket and stood up.

He had to push his way past the throng of reporters and cameramen outside as he left the building. Cindi Hoenan was giving forth. Her voice followed him down the path to the car park.

'This government's policies have raised unemployment, lowered wages, cut benefits, pushed women into debt and made more women homeless. That is why so many have turned to prostitution to make ends meet. These proposals to criminalise clients paying for consenting sex are simply going to put more women at risk. At the same time they are going to deflect the police away from investigating the trafficking of girls, rape and the murder of sex workers such as our sister here in Manchester, in order to persecute those engaged in buying and selling consensual sex.'

She wasn't interested in Maureen Flinn. Nor would the millions be who saw and heard Cindi Hoenan on the news that evening. This juxtaposition of her death with her occupation would reassure the readers of the red tops. He could see them shrugging, turning the page, checking the Euro Lottery results. Those with far right leanings would have seen it as the inevitable consequence of a life of sin. God's judgement. Not a thought for how an innocent little girl in a First Communion dress could end up three decades later slumped against that wall in Angel Meadow.

Chapter 13

A neat detached bungalow on the outskirts of Oldham, perched on a slight rise, on the road to Scouthead. The rear patio windows looked out over rolling hills, dotted with sheep, towards the Pennine escarpment beyond Uppermill. His idea of a retirement idyll.

Caton had called in first at Oldham Social Services and collected a copy of the full report. It was safely locked away in the boot. From what he had speed-read, the Flinns had nothing to reproach themselves for. Their daughter had been well and truly out of control. Had they not sought the help of Social Services, she would have been taken away from them by the courts. And now they had this to contend with. Some idyll.

Anne and Michael Flinn sat side by side on the sofa. Their hands entwined, their knuckles white, like their faces. Perched on the edge of their seats, they looked ready to flee at a moment's notice. He could tell that the news he had brought had been both long awaited, and a brutal shock. They were devastated when he told them. Half an hour had passed. Only now, their cups of tea lying cold and untouched on the coffee table, did he feel able to ask his questions.

'When did you last hear from your daughter?'

Michael Flinn glanced at his wife. Head bowed, her nod was barely perceptible.

'May the 17th, 1997,' he said. 'It was a Friday. Maureen had just moved into a housing association flat the council had organised. They notified us that she was moving. Not that we were aware that they had to. We decided to go round and see if there was anything she needed. If there was anything we could do to help her settle in.'

He shook his head, more in sadness than in grief it seemed. Indeed, there was a sense of wistfulness that ran throughout his account.

'She wouldn't let us in. In fact, she would have slammed the door in our faces if I hadn't had my foot across the threshold. She was angry that we were there. In hindsight, I don't think it was that she didn't want to see us. I think it was that she didn't want us to see her. Not like that.'

'Like that?' said Caton.

'She was wearing a thin T-shirt with some obscure slogan on the front. You could tell that she had no bra on underneath. Her skirt was pelmet-short. Bare legs and high heels. Her hair short and badly cut. And she was thin. Pitifully thin. She stood there trying to project such fierce independence, and yet we could tell that she was frightened.'

'Frightened?'

'Of what she was doing. Planning to live alone in that pathetic flat, with hardly any possessions. Without family or friends. No lifeline. No job.'

'You asked her to come back home?' Caton guessed.

'Of course we did,' said his wife. 'We pleaded.' Her voice tailed off. 'Of course we did.'

Her husband eased one hand free, and placed his arm around her shoulders.

'But her pride wouldn't let her,' he said. 'That and the guilt she wore like a hair shirt.'

'Guilt? In what sense did she feel guilty?'

He shrugged.

'For having let us down. For having let herself down. And something else we never understood. Something before she came to us.'

'Before she came to you?'

The look on both their faces was one of surprise. They looked at each other. He saw the realisation dawn. Their faces softened.

'She was adopted, Chief Inspector,' said Michael Flinn. 'We adopted her when she was nearly five. We assumed you knew. That Social Services would have told you.'

'I've only seen a summary of the care report,' he told them. 'Adoption wasn't mentioned.'

They shared another knowing look.

'Do you believe in nature or nurture, Chief Inspector?' said Michael Flinn.

'I haven't really given it that much thought. Although with a child on the way I suppose I should have done.'

Indeed I should, he reflected. With Harry being brought up by Helen, and me an occasional father in his life, I ought to at least have thought about it.

'Most people don't,' Flinn replied. 'Unless they happen to be adoptive or foster parents. In such cases the answer has a fundamental effect on how you choose to parent. And how you respond when things don't turn out as you expect.'

'It was the first question we were asked when we applied to adopt,' said his wife quietly.

'And how did you reply?'

He read their body language and instantly began to apologise.

'I'm sorry, I shouldn't have–'

'It's alright, Chief Inspector,' said Michael Flinn.

'It's a question we have revisited time and time again.'

'Nurture,' said his wife. 'We chose nurture.'

Anne was a nurse,' her husband explained, 'and I was a teacher. Of course we chose nurture.'

'And now?' said Caton, sensing that there was sub text begging to be heard.

Their answers came together, and yet were a world apart. Neither looked at the other.

'Nurture,' said the husband.

'Nature,' said the wife.

Nobody spoke as the implications of that divide circled the room and then settled like of dust on layers that had been there for decades.

'It's a paradox that my wife chooses nature,' said Michael Flinn at last, 'because believing that ought to lift the burden of guilt that she feels. If there really was little that could have been done to modify Maureen's behaviour, to compensate for her innate personality, then there would be no one to blame. Least of all ourselves.'

He hugged his wife a little closer. She let him, as though powerless to resist.

'Equally,' he continued, 'since I chose nurture, I ought to have a sense of guilt, and I do not. Sadness, regret, but not guilt.'

He leaned forward, picked up his cup of tea, discovered that it was cold and set it down again.

'I suppose,' he said, 'the reality is, that it's always a mixture of both, and there is no point in trying to make sense of it, because you never will.'

Caton felt sure that he was right. Especially given that their daughter had already had a previous life, had been nurtured, for better or worse, through what many consider to be the most formative years in a child's development. Even before she came to them, her future was being formed in ways over which they had no control.

'So that was the last time you saw Maureen?' he said, deliberately changing the subject.

'She made it clear that she did not want to see us. She lived on the other side of town. Frequented places that we did not. We thought that if we did as she asked she might, in time, come round.'

'But she didn't?'

'No. Instead, as soon as she was eighteen she left Oldham. No forwarding address. To all intents and purposes she disappeared from our lives forever. Until now.'

'Did you make any attempts to find her?'

'We tried. Internet searches. Putting her name into Facebook. Anne even enrolled in Friends Reunited as a mythical former pupil of her high schools in the hope that she might come across a reference to her there. She wasn't officially a missing person, you see. She had chosen to move on.'

'And you didn't really want to find her,' said his wife in the same quiet voice. 'Not really. You were too scared of what you might discover.'

Her husband didn't bother to deny it.

'It helped me to sleep at night. Most nights, that is,' he said.

'What about friends at school, in the neighbourhood, when she was in care?' said Caton. 'Might she have kept in touch with any of those?'

They looked at each other and then shook their heads.

'She didn't really have friends,' said Michael Flinn. 'She was a bit of a loner. A satellite rather than a star was how a primary teacher described her.'

'She was quite withdrawn when she first came to us,' said his wife. 'We assumed that she was shy, but it was more than that.'

'By the time she was in high school we had become quite concerned,' said her husband. 'That's when she was first referred to an educational psychologist.'

A loner. That was how her fellow sex worker Chantelle had described her.

'Was she ever bullied at school?'

Again, they shook their heads in tandem.

'Not that we knew. I think the other kids were wary of her,' he said.

'Wary? Why wary?'

'It was something several of her teachers mentioned over time. She was intelligent, fiercely independent and radiated a kind of toughness. She wanted to be alone, and no one dared invade her personal space.'

Caton thought that was surprising in view of her choice of occupation. But then he'd known a lot of prostitutes, and some of them had all of those qualities. Even though they invited men inside their personal space in a literal sense, it was always on their own terms.

'Did Maureen ever try to find her birth mother?'

He had expected it to provoke a reaction. Unease, disappointment, anger even, but he could tell from their expressions that it had been a far more careless question. Unworthy of a detective.

'Maureen's mother was already dead when she came to us,' Michael Flinn replied stiffly. 'Her father too.'

'I'm sorry,' Caton told him. 'I shouldn't have presumed.'

Flinn waved his apology aside.

'You weren't to know,' he said. 'With all these programmes they have on television nowadays, children reunited with their mothers, it was a reasonable assumption.'

'Never a mention nor a thought for the adoptive parents,' said his wife bitterly.

'Mr Caton doesn't want to hear about that,' said her husband, clearly used to the tirade of complaints that would otherwise have followed.

'We had been trying for five years before we discovered that we had been wasting our time. It was my fault,' he explained. 'Firing blanks. We were both distraught. It was worse for Anne; for her it was like a bereavement. One that has never really gone away.'

He squeezed her hand and fell silent. Caton waited patiently for him to continue.

'When we were accepted for adoption it was like a new world had opened up. There was a shortage of newborn infants at that time, but we were happy to wait. Then we were told that there was a little girl who they thought was a perfect match. But there were complications. She was four and a half years old, and it would mean going over to Ireland for the final stage of the process. When they told us that she had lost her parents in tragic circumstances we felt this overpowering urge to help her. We didn't hesitate for a moment. Three days later, we were on the ferry.'

'She was beautiful,' said his wife. 'A mop of black curly hair. Wide eyes. Rosebud lips. She looked so sad and lost sitting there on a chair too big for her, hugging a teddy bear for all she was worth.'

'It was love at first sight for both of us,' said her husband. 'For Anne and me, that is. For Maureen it took a little longer. Three weeks later, we on our way back to Oldham. As a family.'

Caton knew very little about the process, but three weeks sounded like a very short time.

'What did you learn about the circumstances of her parents' deaths?' he asked.

Flinn shook his head.

'Very little. Just that they had been a very close and happy family, but that there'd been a tragedy. They said it would be better all round if we knew as little as possible.'

'And we were advised not to discuss it with Maureen,' added his wife. 'Because it would simply resurrect intensely painful and potentially damaging memories that she had clearly managed to suppress.'

'You see,' said her husband, 'That's how it was in those days. No such thing as bereavement counselling. Now we understand understand how problematic it must have been, keeping all of that locked away in her head. How much better it would have been if she'd been helped to come to terms with it. To find closure.'

Caton had first-hand experience of child bereavement. He wasn't so sure it was as easy as they seemed to think. He had not been allowed to attend his parents' funeral. Nor had he ever cried. Then or since. At least not for them. He had often found himself discreetly wiping tears from his eyes at other people's funerals. Even those of people he had never known in life, except as victims of misfortune, misadventure or homicide. He only had to hear the strains of 'Abide with Me' or 'How Great Thou Art' for the tears to well up. He had often wondered if that was some kind of transference, an indirect mourning of his own loss. Kate would know. But he had never summoned the courage to ask her. He felt sure she already suspected. "You have issues," she had told him once, when they were watching some film or other with a mildly tragic ending and she caught him pretending to blow his nose in a surreptitious attempt to mask his emotions. She had been more direct the first time she had experienced one of his nightmares.

"You should see someone," she'd said. "It isn't going to go away, and you never know how it might manifest itself in other ways." But it had gone away. Within days of her agreeing to marry him he had felt as though a weight had been lifted from his chest. No more flashbacks to the accident that had killed his parents. Now he slept soundly every night no matter what horrors the day had presented.

'Can you let me have details of the adoption agency you dealt with?' he said.

They both looked at each other, and then back at him.

'Is that really necessary?' asked the husband.

'To be honest,' he said, 'I'm not sure. I won't be until I've spoken with them. But this is a murder inquiry and I can't afford to ignore any lines of enquiry, however unlikely they may seem.'

Michael Flinn stood up.

'Very well,' he said. 'I'll go and get you the details.'

Caton heard him moving around upstairs and the sound of a printer. Five uncomfortable minutes later, he was back with a brown A4 envelope.

'I think you'll find it's all here,' he said. 'I made you a copy of the originals, if that's alright?'

Caton stood and took the envelope.

'I'm afraid I'll have to ask you to come into Manchester as soon as you are able,' he said, 'to formally identify Maureen. I'll send a car to collect you and bring you back.'

'Please don't apologise, Mr Caton,' said Michael Flinn. 'It's so long since we've seen our daughter. We need to see her one more time. To say goodbye.'

'And to tell her that we're sorry,' whispered his wife.

'I keep telling you, Anne,' he said, 'there is nothing to apologise for. We did our best. I don't think there's anything we could have done differently that would have made a difference.'

Caton didn't doubt it for a moment. It was clear that these two had loved their daughter unconditionally, suffered deeply as she spiralled out of control, and agonised over their decision to allow the council to take over. For the next twenty-seven years they had hoped and prayed that one day they would answer the door and find her standing there. Instead of her, it had been him. Instead of reconciliation and redemption, he had brought them grief. Of course they had done their best. But Anne Flinn would never be able to accept that fact. She would continue to blame herself until the day she died. Moreover, despite her husband's assertions to the contrary, Caton had the feeling that deep down he would always wonder what more he could have done.

Michael Flinn showed him out.

'You know, Chief Inspector,' he said as they stood on the doorstep, 'in a way you have brought us closure. I never really believed in that word, that concept, but I realise now that we no longer have to worry about where she is, what she's thinking, what's happening to her. To go to bed every night praying that she is safe. To wake in the early hours of the morning imagining the worst. Well, now the worst has happened. Now she is free and so, in a way, are we.'

He looked over his shoulder to check that his wife was not within hearing distance.

'Anne will eventually come to realise that. Then we can remember the little girl who brought so much love and happiness into our lives, and thank God for the privilege of having had that time with her.'

Caton closed the gate behind him and walked to his car. He hoped that Michael Flinn was right. It was the least the two of them deserved.

Chapter 14

Gordon Holmes' response was characteristically succinct.

'Wild child. Into care. Out of care. Off the radar!' he said. 'No surprises there then.'

'Tell that to Anne and Michael Flinn,' said Caton.

'You know what I mean, boss. It's like the plot for a Jimmy McGovern film about all that's wrong with the care system. What was that Prison Reform Trust report called?'

'A Stepping Stone into Custody.' said Caton.

Holmes nodded vigorously.

'Exactly. One per cent of children are officially "looked after". But they represent between twenty-five and fifty per cent of the prison population, depending on who you believe. Only question is, do they end up getting looked after because they're destined for a life of crime, or is the care system responsible?'

Caton sighed. 'Nature or nurture?'

'A bit of each?' said Joanne Stuart. 'They go into the system vulnerable and a bit damaged, and come out the other end totally wrecked.'

'Like first-time offenders getting a custodial sentence,' observed DC Hulme.

This was a theme that Caton had heard debated more times than he cared to remember. Talking about it changed nothing, other than to vent their frustration that so much of their work, and the associated misery for others that it brought, could have been avoided by proper investment in prevention. That was for the policymakers. Their job was to bring offenders to account, and to keep the public safe.

'Look,' he said, 'I have no idea whether the years our victim spent in Ireland before she was adopted by the Flinns have any bearing on this investigation. It seems unlikely, but we can't rule it out. On the other hand, it's pointless any of us rushing off across the Irish Channel without good reason. Not when there are so many avenues to explore here first.'

'That's a shame,' said Holmes. 'I could do with a trip away.'

There was a chorus of assent.

'Settle down,' Caton told them. 'Avenue one, the autopsy. What does that tell us?'

'The full report is on your desk, boss,' said Holmes. 'The short version is as follows.'

He consulted his notes.

'The victim suffered cerebral brain damage from a gunshot wound to the head. The bullet passed straight down the midline, causing catastrophic damage to both hemispheres of the brain and the brain stem. There would have been immediate loss of function. Almost simultaneously a gunshot wound to the heart passed through two ventricles and the pericardium, causing cardiogenic shock. Basically the heart was unable to pump fast enough. At the same time there was massive loss of blood into the pericardium and beyond into the chest cavity. Had she not already suffered the brain injury, hypovolemic shock resulting from extensive exsanguination would have killed her.'

It was exactly what Caton had expected to hear.

'Any other injuries?'

'No, boss. Nor was there any sign of disease or illness, other than some vaginal scarring from historical lesions consistent with her occupation as a sex worker, and some early indications of mild osteoporosis.'

'Tox results?'

'Negative for alcohol and for illegal drugs. There were, however, traces of an SSRI.'

'Selective serotonin reuptake inhibitors,' translated Hulme. 'For depression.'

Holmes pointedly ignored the interruption. 'Normally used in the treatment of depression,' he said.

Hardly surprising, Caton reflected, given her history and occupation.

'I don't suppose you know what kind of side effects they have?'

Holmes waved his notes triumphantly.

'Headaches, nausea, dizziness. They can make you jittery apparently. Then there's insomnia sometimes, low sex drive, and inability to have an orgasm.'

He grinned. 'Although I'd have thought those last two were a distinct advantage to a sex worker.'

'Gordon!' said Joanne Stuart, shooting him a dirty look.

'It's a shame you didn't come with me to meet her parents,' said Caton. 'I'm sure that would have been a comfort to them.'

'I'm sorry, boss,' he said. To his credit he managed to look it.

'We didn't find any of those pills in her handbag or her flat,' Caton observed. 'Nor was there any record of a prescription.'

'I thought that was odd, boss,' said his Deputy. 'Then it occurred to me that whoever broke into her flat could have taken it, to stop us tracing her identity from the prescription.'

'He must have known we'd find out eventually,' said Joanne Stuart. 'Though I suppose he'd think it would buy him time.'

'Time for what?' said Holmes.

'To cover his tracks. Sort out an alibi. Dispose of the gun. Disappear. Who knows?'

'There's another reason,' said Caton. 'Motive. If we know who the victim is, that helps us to work out why she was killed. Who knew her, and might also have had a motive to kill her. But if the perpetrator did take the drugs, then why did he leave that box of contraceptive pills, complete with her name and the pharmacist's details on it?'

They had no answer to that.

'What else was missing from her flat?' he asked.

'A photograph,' said DC Hulme. 'At least it's a reasonable assumption there was one, given the empty photo frame.'

'Exactly,' said Caton. 'But the perpetrator must have known that we would get an identification as soon as the embalmers waved their magic wands and enabled us to publish a photo of her to the media. That's why he didn't bother to hide the box of contraceptive pills. So it wasn't her face he was trying to hide, but someone else's.'

'Himself or herself,' said DC Hulme. 'The perpetrator, that is.'

'Or somewhere else,' said Stuart. 'A place that people would recognise. A place that might connect him to the victim.'

'We won't know till we find that photograph,' said Gordon Holmes, rubbing his chin. 'The only trouble is, we aren't going to find it until we find the perpetrator. Catch 22.'

Caton was trying to order his thoughts.

'Is there anything from the CCTV?' he asked.

'Not a lot, boss,' said Joanne Stuart. 'Certainly no suspects seen entering or leaving the scene during an hour period prior to the first attender on scene.'

Caton looked at the map of the area around Angel Meadow and St Michael's Flags.

'But there must have been people going in and out of there?'

'There were,' she replied. 'A dozen in all, including the couple who claimed to have heard our victim call out. Two were sex workers. One was a homeless person. The remaining seven were all residents returning home after a night on the town. They've all been interviewed and eliminated.'

'What about men soliciting sex? We must have captured some car registrations.'

She shook her head.

'Wrong time of night, boss. They're all tucked up in bed with their unsuspecting wives and partners that time of the morning.'

'Or too pissed to get it up,' someone muttered from behind their monitor screen.

Caton made a mental note to deal with him later. That was the trouble with this open-plan space; it invited earwigging and thoughtless interventions. He looked at the Murder Investigation Manual Checklist beside the board. It looked as though they were stuck on the TIE phase. Trace, Interview, Eliminate. There were just three more categories they hadn't covered.

'What about the rest of the people with access to the scene? Ones who would have already been in the area and had no need to leave it? The residents of those apartments, for example?'

'All in hand, boss,' Joanne Stuart told him. 'Every one of them is being interviewed, even if repeat visits have to be made to catch them in.'

'People associated with the victim?'

'We think we've traced all of her fellow sex workers,' she said. 'They've been keen to help. Stands to reason; they don't want to be next. As for Maureen Flinn's clients, that's proving problematical. She kept herself to herself, and she hadn't been on the patch that long, so…' She shrugged.

'Keep at it,' he said.

That only left MO suspects. Persons with previous convictions for the same or similar offences. It had been established early on that there were none. Murder of a female sex worker by gunshot wounds to the head and heart. Professionally executed. All the hallmarks of a professional contract. Head, and heart. That was one of the things they taught firearms officers. One of the things he had been taught. Unless there is time or a need to choose your target, aim for the chest first. A larger mass, easier to hit, instantly disabling. Then the head shot. The kill wound.

'Boss!'

His Senior Analyst hurried towards them. He looked unusually excited.

'We have a match on the bullets.'

He thrust a sheet of paper into Caton's hand.

Caton stared at the three sets of images, obviously taken through a macroscope. The contrasting black and white striations and nicks looked like a barcode, and might as well have been for all the sense they made to him, except that even he could tell from these magnified images that they matched.

'The one from the head shot was distorted and partially fragmented,' Benson explained. 'But this is the one that penetrated her heart. It was in good nick. Fortunately, they reckon the gun hadn't been used much, if at all, since the original record was made.'

Below the images was a copy of that record provided by the National Ballistics Intelligence

Service. But it was the original source that caught Caton's interest; it was from the database of the Police Service of Northern Ireland. He read on past the detailed and incomprehensible forensic analysis to the summary.

The bullet submitted by Greater Manchester Police – case number GMP 789/42 – shown in images A1, B1 and C1 – is a 9×19mm Parabellum .4SW calibre full metal jacket, ball bullet. The cartridge is 8 gram, 123.5 grains capacity. Date of manufacture 1972.

This bullet has been found to match three bullets and associated cartridges originally entered onto the Royal Ulster Constabulary database, now the Police Service of Northern Ireland database. Case Number RUC 58976/17/11/78.

Both bullet and cartridge are consistent – as are the striations identified above – with the Browning Hi-Power Mark 1, locked-breech, semi-automatic, single-action, recoil-operated pistol.

The 9x19mm parabellum bullet. Caton had fired them himself during his tactical firearms unit training with GMP, although from the third-generation Glock 17C pistol rather than the Browning historically favoured by the British Army and NATO Forces.

'Northern Ireland,' he said, handing the paper on to his Deputy for the rest of them to read. 'During what was euphemistically know as the Troubles.'

'I got on to the PSNI,' said Jack Benson. 'Quoted their reference, and they sent me this.'

He offered another sheet of A4.

'Read it out,' said Caton.

'The three bullets and their associated cartridges were recovered from the scene of an attack on Castlederg Police Station in County Tyrone in 1978. The perpetrators – believed to be members of Provisional IRA – were pursued by an armoured car carrying troops from the Rockcliff Ulster Defence Regiment base. Fire was returned. A roadside bomb was activated causing the armoured car to leave the road and overturn. The perpetrators escaped over the border into Donegal. These bullets and cartridges were among those recovered from the scene. The perpetrators were never identified. The gun was not found, nor was there any evidence that it was used in subsequent attacks or killings.'

'Bloody hell!' Gordon Holmes exclaimed. 'Looks like that trip is back on, boss.'

Caton had no trouble persuading Helen Gates that he should travel across the Irish Sea. After all, they had no other leads. There was, however, one sticking point.

'I'd like to take DI Holmes with me,' he said.

'No way, Tom,' she replied. 'A case of this magnitude? If you're not here, you have to leave your Deputy in charge.'

'Then it'll have to be DI Stuart.'

She frowned. He could tell that she was computing the cost. Two single rooms instead of a double. Martin Hadfield would have something to say about that.

'She'd bring an added dimension,' he said, pressing his case before she had a chance to commit herself. 'Especially with the nuns.'

'In my experience,' she said, 'nuns are far more easily charmed by a sycophantic male. A pretty female with hair, make-up and a dress sense like Stuart's, simply reminds them of what might have been.'

'With the male officers of the RUC and the PSNI then,' he reasoned. 'You know how it is, ma'am.'

She feigned mild surprise.

'I don't know whether to feel outraged or complimented.'

'I'm sorry, ma'am, I don't follow.'

She raised her eyebrows.

'Oh, I think you do. We both know what you were about to add and thought better of.'

'What would that be, ma'am?'

'I bet you've charmed a few in your time,' she said.

'I wouldn't have been so presumptuous, ma'am,' he said. 'However, if I had been, surely it would been a compliment rather than an outrage?'

'I doubt you'd want Acting DI Stuart to know why she was going with you,' she said, changing tack. 'She isn't exactly known for her anti-feminist views.'

It was getting out of hand. He had never meant it to go down this route. He was sure that she knew that. She was just teasing him. He didn't take the bait.

'Very well,' she said at last. 'How long do you think you'll need?'

'I won't know till we've done some digging,' he said. 'A day to get there and back. Three days minimum over there. A week tops.'

'Five days maximum,' she said. 'I shall be appointing a Reviewing Officer six days from now. If I don't, I'll have ACC Hadfield and the Chief Constable breathing down my neck.'

He stood up.

'Thank you, ma'am.'

He turned in the doorway.

'I'll give Chief Superintendent McCarthy of the An Garda Síochána your best wishes, shall I, ma'am?'

He had the satisfaction of seeing her blush. So much for all that simulated indignation.

'Get out,' she said. 'Before I send for Security.'

The other three women in his life gave very different reactions. DI Stuart was delighted to be at the heart of the investigation, particularly since it involved both travel and, as she'd put it, 'proper detective work'. He sensed that she would have preferred Gordon to go with him and for her to lead the investigation while they were away. If that was so, she'd given no indication of it. That was typical of her. It was what made her one of the most valued members of his team.

Kate had seen it as an opportunity to work on her dissertation, and to finalise everything for her impending confinement. Although that hadn't been the phrase she had used. It sounded too much like imprisonment, she had said. He didn't think labour sounded any better. In fact, he seemed to recall reading somewhere that in the eighteenth century, guests who came to celebrate a new birth were offered 'groaning' bread, 'groaning' cake and even 'groaning' beer! He resolved not to share that with her. Not until after the birth.

Helen Malone was far less amenable.

'Ireland?!' she said. 'Harry was supposed to be coming to you this weekend.'

'It would have been problematic even if I hadn't been going,' he told her. 'This is a major murder investigation.'

'Well, you could have let me know sooner. And you can forget about seeing him at all for the next three weeks. We were leaving next Friday for Majorca, but I'll see if we can get an earlier flight.'

'We?' he said.

'Me, Harry and Jake. Do you have a problem with that?'

Actually, he did. Leaving out the fact that he still hadn't met this Jake, it meant that she was taking Harry out of school. Not something he approved of, or would ever contemplate doing with any child for whom he had custody. Only he didn't have custody, just voluntary visiting rights. And his trip to Ireland had hardly placed him on the moral high ground.

'I hope you have a nice time, Helen,' he said. 'Give Harry my best.'

'I will.'

She sounded mollified, which on balance was a good result. He replaced the phone and went to find his passport.

Chapter 15

'Just seven miles, according to the satnav,' she said.

Caton nodded, his eyes glued to the twisting road passing through unfamiliar territory, conscious that at any moment a tractor could appear around a bend and force him to reverse until he found a gap in the hedges into which to squeeze the car.

'It's very pretty,' she said. 'Monaghan.'

There was a clear blue sky with a dusting of clouds. The temperature was 22 degrees Celsius according to the on-board computer. A patchwork of lush green pastures, punctuated by woods and bright yellow fields of rape, filled the rolling hills as far as the eye could see. Every so often they passed a substantial farm with freshly painted walls and neat fenced paddocks reflecting proud owners making a good living from this land.

'It is,' he said. 'The Borderlands is what it's been since partition in 1921. Along with the counties of Cavan and Donegal. All part of what's still known as Ulster, and yet legislatively part of the Republic of Ireland.'

'A bit like the Scottish Marches,' she observed. 'With Dumfries and Galloway, and the Scottish Borders on one side, and Cumbria, Northumberland and County Durham on the other.'

He laughed.

'Once upon a time perhaps, when the Border Reivers raided back and forth, but not any more.'

'Who knows?' she said. 'If the Scots vote for independence, there could be all manner of smuggling and pillaging back and forth across the border.'

'Nothing like they experienced here during the Troubles,' he said grimly. 'But from what I read on the Internet, while we were coming over, the farmers in the north of the county still have plenty of problems to contend with.'

She closed the map on her lap and turned to give him her full attention.

'Like what?'

'Like over a third of them losing substantial numbers of sheep and cattle to rustlers, as well as tractors, 4x4s and other high-value equipment.'

'I bet that's pushed up their insurance,' she said. 'Not just for them, either.'

'It's not just them that should be worried. They suspect that a lot of these cattle will have entered the food chain through dodgy abattoirs. Some of the animals had only recently been given doses of penicillin and other drugs. Without the normal withdrawal period to allow the drugs to leave their system, these could be entering the human food chain, with unquantifiable consequences.'

She grimaced.

'I think I'll go vegetarian while I'm over here.'

'Who said the meat's only being sold here?'

He rounded the corner and braked smoothly to a halt. Twenty metres ahead, a farm worker stood in the middle of the road holding a red flag. Behind him a herd of hefty, irregular-patterned black and white cows sauntered from one side of the road to an open gate into a field on the other side.

'Holsteins?' she wondered.

'They could be Friesian,' he replied.

She grinned and pointed at the temperature indicator on his screen.

'On a day like today?'

He smiled and shook his head.

'Don't give up your day job.'

They watched the last of the cows enter the field and the farm worker raise a hand in thanks as he closed the gate behind them.

'Probably Holstein–Friesians,' he said as he switched on the ignition.

'Not like you to hedge your bets, boss,' she said, settling back for the final few miles. 'Which reminds me, I didn't thank you for asking me to come with you.'

'I didn't have any choice in the matter,' he replied, straight-faced.

For a moment she thought he was serious, then she caught the twitch at the corner of his mouth.

'Very funny,' she said. 'No, seriously, I'm really looking forward to this.'

'I did have an ulterior motive,' he confessed. 'In choosing you.'

She sat up.

'Now you've piqued my curiosity.'

He glanced at her, and then quickly back at the road.

'I have a feeling this is going to be tricky, Jo,' he began. 'There's a lot of angst about historical abuse in children's homes. And here we come, sticking our noses right in the middle of it. I don't expect them to be laying down the red carpet. I needed someone capable of showing a bit of tact and sensitivity.'

'Thank you, boss.'

She sounded genuinely pleased. And really touched.

'Don't thank me,' he said. 'There wasn't a lot of competition.'

She laughed. How could she not, imagining Gordon Holmes and Jimmy Hulme trying to woo over defensive and suspicious nuns and social workers?

'I know what you mean though,' she said, when she'd finally recovered. 'You weren't the only one doing your homework on the plane.'

'Really?'

'Yes, really. I had the same concerns as you, so I looked it up.'

'And?'

'It was horrific. There was one article posted only yesterday about the bodies of eight hundred babies that have been found in a septic tank at a home for unwed mothers run by an order of nuns.'

'Not aborted, surely?'

'There was no suggestion of that, nor was there any evidence that they'd died of mistreatment. The records showed two babies dying every week. Only there were never any graves for the mothers to visit. Now they know why. There were plenty of non-church institutions implicated too,' she said. 'State and voluntary. I suppose it was an entire culture's attitude towards children.'

Caton nodded.

'Seen and not heard,' he said. 'Except in these cases they weren't seen either, except by their abusers.'

'I didn't find anything specific about Monaghan,' she told him. 'But there's loads of stuff about abuse in the Republic, and there's a major Northern Ireland Institutional Abuse Inquiry.'

'It was inevitable,' he said. 'First the priests, and then the residential homes. And those films, The Magdalene Sisters and Philomena, brought it into everybody's consciousness.'

'It wasn't just here,' she said. 'All those poor boys in America, Canada, Australia. There are at least seven major investigations going on right now across the UK. Not to mention the ones into how the Home Office managed to lose a hundred and fourteen files about allegations of abuse by an alleged ring of paedophile MPs.'

'Well, here is where we are,' he said, pulling in beside a pair of iron gates between two high walls.

'Looks idyllic,' she said.

Beyond the gates, a metalled driveway led past manicured lawns to a three-storey honey-coloured stone building with gothic windows and a circular tower topped with a cross.

'Appearances can be deceptive,' he said.

She nodded at the bright new security cameras on the wall and the state-of-art answer phone panel.

'Children safeguarding,' she said. 'Closing the stable door?'

He lowered the window and reached out to press the call button.

'Better late than never.'

Chapter 16

'Mrs Wade will see you now,' said the receptionist.

They were in a modern glass and steel extension to the building that had little in common with the narrow convent corridors which had led them here, footsteps echoing behind them.

'Mrs Wade?' said Caton. 'We were led to believe this was a convent.'

From behind came a throaty laugh. They turned to find a short, plump, cheerful-looking woman standing in the open doorway of an office.

'As you can see, Detective Chief Inspector,' she said, 'I am definitely not a nun. Although given the trend towards mainstream clothing, perhaps it is not that evident. Though you'll find no nuns here with whom to compare me.'

She stepped to one side.

'Come in and make yourselves at home.'

The office was sparsely furnished. A wooden work desk that could have come from the IKEA catalogue, four polished steel and leather chairs, and a coffee table. She waited for them to sit, and pulled up a chair to join them. She offered her hand to Joanne Stuart first.

'Ellen Wade,' she said. 'Senior Administrator.'

'So this is no longer a convent?' said Caton when

the introductions were over.

'It hasn't been for over a decade. Vocations have dried up I'm afraid, and it was only a small Order in the first place.'

'But it is still a children's home?' asked Joanne Stuart.

'Not as such. Not like in the old days, when it was the Convent of St Bride and St Cera. There is still a nursery and infants section, and a small Special Needs school, both of which are residential, but the numbers are small.'

'So what is it that you do here?' said Caton.

'We are part of the Child Protection & Welfare Services arm of the North-East Children and Family Services provision for Cavan, Monagahan, Meath and Louth.'

She smiled.

'It's quite a mouthful, I know. Essentially, aside from the special school, we provide residential care for infants and young children who have experienced serious emotional or physical abuse or neglect, and are deemed to be at risk. We also provide outreach support to families with significant child welfare issues, and training in children safeguarding. A small but important part of our work is in delivering an adoption and fostering service. Hence the small numbers of children in residence here.'

'It's a very large building,' he observed.

'Ah, but the bulk of it is offices. Our outreach work involves teams of clinical psychologists, social workers, social care leaders and family support workers. Many of them have offices here. You could say this is the hub from which all of the work radiates.'

She pushed her chair back a little, stretched out her legs and folded her hands in her lap. She looked at each of them in turn. Her expression was thoughtful rather than suspicious.

'I'm not really clear why you are here. I understand that your phone call said it was to do with a girl who was adopted from here back in the 1980s. That wasn't a lot to go on. And the convent was never one of those that became embroiled in the abuse scandals that have marred both Church and State.'

The two detectives looked at each other. That was one possibility ruled out.

'We're not here about child abuse,' Caton told her. 'At least, not as far as we are aware. This is a murder investigation.'

'Murder?'

'That's right,' he said. 'The person we now know as Maureen Flinn, adopted from here in 1980 by Anne and Michael Flinn, was found murdered in Manchester.'

She crossed herself.

'That's terrible. How was she killed?'

There was no point in hiding it; now she had the name she could simply look it up on the Internet.

'She was shot.'

'Shot?!'

Whatever she had been expecting, it was not that.

'But I don't understand what it could possibly have to do with the convent,' she said.

'Nor do we,' he told her. 'But we have to find out everything we can about her life.'

She placed her hands on the arms of her chair and levered herself up. She winced as she did so, favouring her left hip.

'I understand, but I'm afraid that as far as I can tell she was never actually here.'

Caton frowned.

'Mr and Mrs Flinn were adamant that they collected their daughter from here,' he said. 'And the adoption papers are on the convent's headed notepaper.'

He began to open the envelope he had brought with him.

She crossed to her desk.

'I don't need to see it. Your office faxed a copy over.'

She picked up a blue bound file from her desk and handed it to him.

'Here are the lists of the birth name and subsequent adoption name of every child adopted or fostered in that year, not only from this home, but from every other home in the North-East region. We hold the central registry, you see.'

Caton scanned the lists. Five pages of them.

'Could the record have been misplaced?' said Joanne Stuart. 'In a different year perhaps?'

Wade came and sat back down.

'I wondered about that. It can happen when records are computerised. So I had my staff check the three years on either side. Then I had the physical files for the convent checked. I'm sorry, but there is no record of a Maureen Flinn. Nor is there a record of any child adopted or fostered from here on the date shown in your papers.'

'What does that mean?' asked Caton. 'That it was an illegal adoption?'

She pursed her lips.

'Not necessarily.'

'I don't follow.'

'There is a difference between illegal and unrecorded,' she said. 'Or simply "missing".'

'Like the other one hundred and fourteen files,' said DI Stuart as an aside.

'I beg your pardon?' said Mrs Wade.

'My colleague is referring to another matter,' he reassured her.

'There is another issue that bothered me,' she said. 'The birth name of the child in the papers you sent me is missing. That is not merely unusual, it is a serious breach of legal protocols.'

'I wondered about that myself,' he said. 'Could it be that she was abandoned and nobody knew her mother's name?'

She shook her head.

'Even if that had been the case, the Church into whose care she seems to have been given would have provided her with a Christian name and a surname.'

'Whatever the reason,' he said, 'it may explain why the file was never recorded, or subsequently went missing.'

'I can't help you there. But there may be someone who can.'

'Who would that be?'

'The copy of the adoption order among the papers you sent me had names and the signatures of the judge who made the order, the sponsors and a witness.'

Caton opened the envelope and took out the original he had brought with him. Joanne Stuart leaned across so that she could also read it.

'Judge Henry Hoey,' he read. 'Sponsor, Father Michael O'Leary. Witness, Sister Agatha... I can't make out the surname. And it isn't printed.'

'Toomey,' she told him. 'Sister Agatha Toomey. The Judge and the priest are no longer with us I'm afraid, but Sister Agatha is still alive. She's living in a small retirement home for nuns gifted to the Diocese of Clogher by a banker in the 1980s.'

She handed him a business card.

'Here is the address. It's about thirty miles away. You'll find the phone number and the postcode on there too. But don't rely on your satnav. Not unless you want to end up in the Atlantic Ocean.'

He thanked her for her help, and she accompanied them to their car.

'One last thing, Detective Chief Inspector,' she said. 'I wouldn't hold out too much hope. There's no telling what, if anything, she'll remember. It was her ninety-first birthday last month.'

Chapter 17

It was late afternoon before they arrived at the home. It was smaller than either of them had expected. A detached Edwardian double-fronted house, it promised five or six bedrooms at the most.

He parked the car on the semi-circular gravel drive, and Joanne Stuart rang the bell. She had to press it several times more before someone finally arrived.

Through the glass-panelled front they could see a woman punching numbers into a code box by a second interior door. The door swung open and then closed behind her as she approached them. She wore a navy-blue short-sleeved top over a matching pair of trousers. Of medium height, she was sturdy, with muscular arms. She opened the door, but left them standing outside.

'How can I help you?' she said, her eyes and her tone equally wary.

Caton had already decided not to show his warrant card. Outside his jurisdiction, despite the fact that he had the same powers of arrest as back home, it could easily be construed as seeking to mislead in a way that could harm future relations that they might come to rely on with the local Garda. They had been informed, of course, that he and DI Stuart were on their patch. It was standard protocol. But they wouldn't take kindly to them misrepresenting their status.

'Good afternoon,' he said, with what he hoped was a charming smile. 'My name is Tom Caton, and this is Joanne Stuart. We are here to see Sister Agatha Toomey.'

'You're not relations?' she said.

'No,' he replied. 'We are hoping we can have a little chat with her about her time at the convent of St Bride and St Cera.'

Her eyes narrowed as she crossed her arms and clenched her fists, causing her muscles to stand out even more.

'You're journalists!' she exclaimed, managing to make the word sound like an obscenity.

'No, nothing like that,' said Joanne Stuart, hoping to rescue the situation.

But the woman wasn't having any of it.

'Hoping to rake up some muck to sell your rag,' she said. 'Well, you'll find none here, so be off with you!'

The inner door opened and a man half her size came to join her.

'What's the matter, Grainne?' he said.

'There's a couple of Journos here,' she replied. 'Wanting to quiz poor auld Sister Agatha. I'm telling them they're wasting their time.'

'We are not journalists,' said Caton, holding up his warrant card. 'We are police officers from England engaged in a murder investigation.'

The woman gave him a withering look.

'Police! So why the hell didn't you say so in the first place?'

'It's alright, Grainne,' said the man, 'you can leave this with me. You'd better go on inside and see to the ladies before all hell breaks loose.'

He waited until she had entered the code and passed through the interior door, before turning back to them.

'It's teatime, you see,' he said. 'If we don't watch them, one half won't be eating a thing and the other half will be tucking into someone else's cream cake. Which wouldn't be so bad if they weren't diabetic.'

He laughed nervously.

'Police you say? From London?'

'From Manchester,' said Caton. 'My name is Tom Caton. I am a detective chief inspector. My colleague here, Joanne Stuart, is a detective inspector. I didn't mention that to start with because we have no legal status here, and no automatic powers of arrest. Strictly speaking, we are outside our jurisdiction.'

'I can see that,' said the man. 'My name is Aiden Kelly. I'm the Manager of Carmel House. You'd best come in.'

He closed the front door behind them and asked them to use the disinfectant hand wash dispenser before releasing the inner door.

'It's as much for your benefit as the residents,' he confided. 'You wouldn't thank me for letting you leave with a bladder or bowel infection.'

'Too much information,' whispered Joanne Stuart.

'Don't mind Grainne,' he said when they were safely inside. 'She was only doing her job. We've had all sorts trying to wheedle their way in here.'

He showed them into a side room that was clearly his office.

'Take a seat, why don't you,' he said. 'I'd offer you a drink, but the staff are all busy right now with it being teatime. But you'll be alright in about twenty minutes if you can hang on that long.'

He sat down behind a large wooden desk. His chair must have been raised because he was on a level with Caton despite standing a full foot shorter. His head was tiny, even in proportion to his body. It gave him the appearance of a child who had aged long before his time. His eyes, however, were sharp as they darted from one to the other of them.

'A murder investigation, you said. Now you have me intrigued, Mr Caton. What's it about exactly?'

'What I'm about to tell you is in strict confidence, Mr Kelly,' said Caton. 'If it gets out at this stage it could obstruct our investigation.'

Obstruct was over the top, he knew, but he had the feeling this man enjoyed a bit of gossip. The manager raised his eyebrows a fraction, but his no response suggested that he understood.

'We have reason to believe,' Caton continued, 'that the victim was adopted, as a four year old, from the convent of St Bride and St Cera. Sister Agatha Toomey's name appears on the adoption order.'

'Good Lord,' said Kelly. 'That must have been a good while ago? Sister Agatha has been here with us for the past fifteen years, and before that she was in the missions in South America.'

Caton wanted to give away as little information as possible, although once again he realised that Kelly only had to do a search on the net and then put two and two together to arrive at four. It wasn't as though there had been that many murders in Manchester in the recent past, in spite of what the media and all those fictional TV series led you to believe.

'It was a long time ago,' he confirmed.

'So what could it possibly have to do with Sister Agatha?' the manager asked.

'I have no idea,' said Caton. 'And I doubt very much that it does. But we have to find out all we can about the victim, and it may be that Sister Agatha can tell us something about that child that will be an important piece in the jigsaw.'

Aiden Kelly sucked his breath in through his lips and shook his head in a manner that did not bode well. For a moment Caton thought he was going to refuse to give them access to his charge, which he had every right to do.

'Well,' he said to Caton's surprise, 'you can have a go, of course you can. But I wouldn't hold out too much hope. She has what the doctor politely calls cognitive impairment. We call it dementia. Whatever you care to call it, it comes down to the same thing; her memory's shot.'

Caton's heart sank. It was a long way to have come for a dead end. Joanne Stuart leaned forward.

'Is it just her short-term memory, or all of her memory?' she asked.

Kelly looked at her with faint amusement.

'Her short-term memory, for sure. As for the rest of it, who knows? We don't get to talk to her about her past that often, we're far too busy coping with the here and now.'

He looked at his watch.

'They should be finished any time soon. I'll get you both a drink while we get her back to her room, then you can find out for yourselves.'

'No wonder her memory's dodgy,' said Joanne Stuart when the door had closed behind him. 'If they can't find the time to chat with her about her life, what chance has she got of remembering any of it? I've got an aunt in a care home and they asked my nieces to make up a memory book for her, full of photos from way back right up to when she went in there. The staff get it out two or three times a week. It's surprising how much she does remember even though she's got Alzheimer's.'

'It's a pity we don't have a photo of Maureen Flinn when she was a child,' he said. 'At least that would have been something to jog her memory with.'

'There is one thing we could do that is appropriate,' said Joanne Stuart.

'Go on?' he said.

'Pray!'

For some reason Caton had expected the room to be small and dark, like a Carmelite cell, but with a disturbing odour of urine and disinfectant. In fact, it was twice the size of his and Kate's bedroom, with a huge window that looked out onto the gardens. There was a single bed with a bright flowery duvet, two bedside tables each with a lamp fixed into the wall, a dressing table and mirror, and a small desk, with a chair in front and a padded kneeler beside it. There were two wardrobes, a chest of drawers and a door, which he assumed led to some kind of en suite bath or shower room. On the walls were a number of religious prints, including The Sacred Heart, the Virgin Mary being Assumed into Heaven, and a female saint wearing a white wimple and a black cape over a brown habit. The room smelt of freshly fallen pine needles underfoot on a damp autumn evening.

Sister Agatha Toomey sat in a comfortable armchair by the window, staring out at rose beds nearing the end of their first flush. She was wearing a thick brown fleece over a white blouse, loose-fitting blue cotton trousers and a pair of black shoes. Her lips were moving silently. Her hands were in her lap, and her fingers were constantly on the move. It was as though she was saying her rosary on an imaginary set of beads. She seemed unaware of their presence in the room.

'I'm happy for you to stay,' said Caton.

'No, I'll leave you to it,' said the manager once he had drawn up the two occasional chairs and set them facing her. 'I'm sure you'd prefer it that way, and my being here wouldn't make any difference one way or the other.'

He paused in the doorway.

'At any rate, I don't have to worry about whether or not the two of you have been police checked, now do I?'

He laughed at his little joke and closed the door.

'I'm not so sure about his being here not making any difference,' said Joanne Stuart. 'He'd do my head in, never mind hers.'

Caton looked at Sister Agatha and shook his head despairingly.

'I'm beginning to wonder what we're doing here,' he said. 'None of it's going to be admissible, and we don't even have Maureen Flinn's original name.'

'Is that you, Maureen?' said the nun in a voice so firm that it took them both by surprise. She stared straight at Joanne Stuart. 'Is it you, Sister Maureen, come to call me for vespers?'

'No, Sister,' said Joanne Stuart as gently as she could, 'it isn't Sister Maureen. My name is Joanne.'

The nun smiled. Her face seemed to lose twenty years in an instant. She reached out her hand.

'Is it you that's come to take me to vespers, Joanne?' she said.

Joanne Stuart moved her chair a little closer and took her hand in hers.

'No, Sister,' she said, 'it isn't time for vespers yet. We have come to talk with you.'

For the first time Sister Agatha became aware of Caton's presence. Her stare was unblinking, and gave nothing away; to Caton, who was used to reading people's faces, it was disconcerting.

'Do I know you?' she said at last. 'You're not a priest, are you?'

'No, Sister,' he said, 'I'm not a priest.'

They had both agreed not to tell her that they were police officers, nor anything about the investigation. They felt sure that it would only perturb her. Aside from the ethics of frightening an old woman it would only make it harder to find out what they needed to know. Nevertheless, he felt guilty about being less than honest. Bizarrely, the fact that she was a nun seemed to make that even worse.

'Ms Stuart and I have just come to have a chat with you,' he said. 'About the old days.'

She turned her eyes onto Joanne Stuart. For an old woman, her eyes were clear and penetrating.

'Is that Stuart with a "u" or Stewart with a "w"?' she said.

Caton had been asked enough times if his own name was spelt with or without an 'e' to know what was going on in her mind. It was the perennial filter common throughout this island, and most of all in the North and the Borderlands; are you Catholic or Protestant? He'd always thought it simpler to ask, and far more likely to be accurate.

'With a "u",' she replied.

Caton watched the smile creep over the nun's face, and smiled inwardly himself. If only she knew. Not only had DI Stuart been baptised in the Church of England, but she was also a lesbian in a long-term civil partnership.

'The old days,' said the nun wistfully. 'I think about them a lot,' she said. 'The trouble is, they're not as clear to me as they used to be.'

She turned to stare out of the window, as though hoping to find something there.

'Did I know you back then?' she said. 'In the old days?'

'I don't think you did,' said Joanne Stuart.

She gestured to Caton to hand her the envelope he had brought with him. She opened it, sifted through the contents and pulled out a photograph.

'But I think, Sister Agatha,' she said, 'you may have

known this little girl, and her mother and father.'

Sister Toomey stared intently at the group in the photograph. The hands with which she held it were mottled with liver spots and the dark-blue veins knotted like tiny ropes strained at skin that was paper thin. They waited for some sign of recognition, but it was impossible to tell what she was thinking. She began to trace the outline of the little girl with the index finger of her right hand. Then she smiled, and began to stroke the little girl's face.

'I was seven,' she said. 'Mammy and Pappy were so proud. I was the first, you see.'

They waited for her to continue, but she just sat there stroking the photograph.

'You were the first what, Sister Agatha?' said Joanne Stuart, misunderstanding. 'The first to become a nun?'

She looked up and frowned, then returned her gaze to the photograph and began to smile once more.

'To make my First Holy Communion,' she said.

She turned and spoke directly to Caton.

'There were seven of us,' she said, her voice full of nostalgia. 'I was the first. Father Mulhearne was the priest, God Bless him. And the Bishop was there.'

Her face clouded over for a moment.

'Or was that the Confirmation? Maybe it was, maybe it wasn't. But the Bishop was there with his mitre, and his crozier and his ring,' She smiled at the memory. 'And his crux pectoralis,' she said, 'hanging on his chest. I couldn't take my eyes off it. And the Communion Breakfast.' Her eyes lit up. 'We had cakes, and jelly, and ice cream, and Gerald knocked his juice over...'

She began to cough, and when it seemed she might not be able to stop, Caton got up to go and fetch help, but then it stopped as suddenly as it had begun and he sat down again. She wiped a dribble of saliva from the side of her mouth with the back of her hand.

'Are you alright, Sister?' said Joanne Stuart. 'Would you like a drink of water?'

She seemed not to understand, so Joanne Stuart repeated herself. This time she nodded.

Caton looked around the room. There was an enamel jug and a plastic beaker on a tray on top of the chest of drawers. He went to investigate. The jug was two thirds full of water. He poured some into the beaker and handed it to his colleague.

Sister Agatha continued to clutch the photograph with both hands, so Joanne Stuart held the beaker close to her mouth. She dipped her head and drank in tiny sips. When the nun sat back in her chair, Joanne Stuart placed the beaker on the window sill beside her.

'The little girl in the photo,' she said, 'it isn't you, Sister. That's a little girl whose adoption you arranged when you were at the Convent of St Bride and St Cera. Those are her adoptive parents.'

She waited for the nun to look again at the photograph. But she didn't. Instead, she stared out of the window again.

'Suffer little children to come unto me,' she said fondly. After a moment she turned back and looked directly at Joanne Stuart. 'There were so many of them,' she said. 'So many wains. Their mothers too poor, or ignorant, or feckless.'

She shook her head and looked out of the window again. She could easily be talking to the roses.

'We did what we could, you see. Found them mummies and daddies. Good Catholic homes. So many of them.' Her voice trailed off.

She looked down at the photograph still clutched in her hands. When she spoke again, her voice was almost a whisper.

'Like poor little Caitlin,' she said.

'That's Maureen,' said Joanne Stuart, correcting her. 'Maureen Flinn.'

Caton reached across and placed a warning hand on Stuart's arm.

The nun turned her head and looked at them. This time her voice was firm and reproachful.

'Caitlin,' she said. 'This is Caitlin Malone. God help her. Her and her sister.'

'Her sister?' said Caton. 'Do you remember the name of Caitlin's sister, Agatha?'

The nun looked down at the photograph again.

'Finnoula,' she said. 'Caitlin and Finnoula Malone.'

Then she stared out of the window again. After what seemed an age she shook her head. When she turned towards them there were tears in her eyes.

'Suffer little children,' she murmured, stroking the face in the photo. 'Suffer little children.'

Chapter 18

'What on earth did you say to her?' asked Aiden Kelly. 'I knew I shouldn't have left her alone with you.'

She was still in her chair, but her eyes were closed and she was gently snoring. Whatever it was the manager had given her, it had worked.

'It's not what you think,' said Caton. 'All we did was show her a photograph of a child and its parents. It seemed to bring back a memory that upset her. That's why I sent for you.'

'We weren't to know that it would trouble her,' said Joanne Stuart. 'It came as a surprise when she actually recognised them.'

Kelly frowned and opened the door.

'Well, I hope you got what you came for,' he said. 'Because you'll not be quizzing her again. Not without a warrant from the Garda and the permission of her doctor. And I can tell you now, you're not likely to get that.'

He accompanied them to the front door.

'Goodbye to you,' he said.

'Thank you for giving us the opportunity to speak with Sister Agatha,' said Caton. He paused. 'Please, Mr Kelly, if I could just ask you one more question?'

The manager puffed.

'Get on with it then.'

'Sister Toomey said she was the eldest of five.

Would you happen to know what's become of the others?'

Kelly sighed.

'I would, since it's all in her records. One sister died of TB, another of scarlet fever and a third of typhoid fever. Her brother became a priest. He died of a heart attack twenty years ago. She's no one left. You're the first visitors she's had in over a year, apart from the lay Eucharistic Minister who brings her communion once a week, and look at the mess you've made of it.'

He didn't wait to see them drive away.

Caton stopped outside the gates, switched off the engine and turned to his colleague.

'Do you think we could have got any more out of her?' he said.

'I doubt it,' she replied. 'She wasn't just upset, she was all over the place after that. You didn't have any option but to call the manager. We'd have been failing in our duty of care.'

Caton grimaced.

'I got the distinct impression that Mr Kelly thought we already had.'

'You don't think he'll make a formal complaint, do you, boss?'

'I doubt it. Even if he does, what's he going to say? That an elderly woman, not used to receiving visitors, became upset when she was shown the photo of a family?'

'That a couple of Brit' policemen interrogated a poor, auld, sick, defensive nun, and reduced her to tears?' She laughed. 'I think not. For a start, you invited him to stay and he declined. How's that going to look?'

Caton nodded.

'Good point,' he said. 'But I still hope he doesn't say anything to the Garda; we may need them to help us track these girls down.'

'That was a turn up, wasn't it, boss?' she said. 'Her mentioning a sister.'

'If it was a sister,' said Caton. 'Could have been a cousin or some other relative.'

He lapsed into silence, reflecting on the fact that it now seemed that his former girlfriend Helen Malone, Harry's mother, shared the same surname as the victim.

'I don't want to dampen your spirits,' she said, 'but we don't even know if she was talking about the girl in the photograph. About our Maureen Malone.'

'The thought had occurred to me,' he said. 'We'll just have to find out. Have you got your iPad with you?'

She retrieved her handbag from under her seat, took out her GMP issue tablet, flicked it open and switched it on.

'What d'you want me to do, boss?'

He scratched his head.

'For a start,' he said, 'you can find out who holds the register of Births and Deaths for the Republic of Ireland,' he said.

'I'll need a Wi-Fi connection,' she told him.

She waited for her tablet to search for a network. Slowly a list began to appear. She grinned.

'Well, what do you know?' she said, with a mischievous expression on her face. 'Scholastica House has a Wi-Fi connection that doesn't require a password. Aiden Kelly will never know how helpful he's been.'

'Don't forget it's not secure,' he said.

She was already busy entering the search algorithms.

'I know,' she said. 'I'm not going to be opening any GMP files or using my passwords.'

In about twenty seconds her face lit up.

'The General Register Office, Government Offices, Convent Road, Roscommon,' she announced. 'There's an email address, a fax and a phone number.'

Caton switched on the satnav and waited for it to load.

'Is there a postcode?' he said.

She gave it to him. He entered it and selected the Find Route option.

'It's only sixty-two miles from here,' he announced. 'Journey time two hours and twenty-seven minutes.'

'That's a long time for sixty-two miles,' she observed.

'There are no motorways, and lot of minor roads,' he said. He looked at his watch. 'They'll be closed before we get there. Give me the phone number, Jo.'

He was put through to the woman who dealt with enquiries from the Garda; she was only too happy to help.

'No, you don't have to go through the Garda,' she told him. 'But I will need something in writing. If you could get your people to fax an official request through to the number I'll give you, I'll be happy to fax the information back by return. Will that do you?'

'That would be wonderful,' he said.

A quick phone call to Duggie Benson set it up. They didn't have to wait very long. Caton's phone rang. He put it on the loudspeaker.

'Boss, it's Duggie. They've sent over what you asked for. I've just emailed it to both your accounts. It's just a question of how long it takes to arrive.'

'Thanks, Duggie, that's brilliant,' Caton told him.

'I know, boss,' came the cheerful reply.

'Don't push your luck,' said Caton.

'There's just one thing,' said Joanne Stuart. 'We'll be opening it up on an unsecure network.'

Caton thought about it.

'I doubt that Kelly spends his time hacking people's computers,' he said, 'let alone his residents. And there's no one else within a mile of here.'

'It's your call,' she said. 'I hope it doesn't come back to bite us.'

'Bite me,' he said.

She didn't look impressed.

'It's my iPad,' she said, opening up her email account.

The message was already there. There was one attachment.

'Bugger!' she said.

'What is it, Jo?'

She turned the tablet so that he could read it for himself. The message was short and succinct.

We have no Birth record of either a Caitlin or a Finnoula Malone for the period identified in your request. There are, within ten years either side of that period, individual Birth records related to both names. I have attached a list for your information. If there is anything more we can do for you please do not hesitate to contact me personally.

A name, phone number and email address appeared below the message.

'Open the attachment,' he said.

There were twenty names in all, scattered throughout the Republic. Twelve Finnoula Malones, and eight Caitlin Malones. None in County Monaghan.

'Ten years is a massive window,' he said. 'There is no way our Caitlin is one of these.'

She logged out of the account and went to the home page.

'Perhaps she was talking about two other girls,' she said. 'She must have had hundreds pass through her hands.'

Caton shook his head.

'I don't think so,' he said. 'That reaction was too strong. There is one other explanation.'

'Go on,' she said.

'Monaghan, Cavan and Donegal,' he said. 'What do they have in common?'

Her eyebrows furrowed.

'They're all part of the historical region of Ulster?'

'And?'

It took a second or two for her to work it out.

'And they're all Borderlands!' she exclaimed. 'They all border the North.'

Hurriedly she logged back into the Wi-Fi connection. It took her even less time than before to come up with a second address.

'The General Register Office for Northern Ireland,' she said triumphantly. 'Oxford House, 49–55 Chichester Street, Belfast. BT1 4HL.'

Caton looked at his watch.

'It's too late now,' he said, starting the engine. 'But at least we won't have far to go in the morning.'

They booked in to the Titanic Quarter Premier Inn in the centre of Belfast, which was as good as it was going to get through GMP's central booking service. As far as Caton was concerned it was better than adequate, and ideally situated, two minutes from the Waterfront and, as it turned out, only 300 yards from the Registrar Office they were to visit in the morning. Caton had just finished unpacking when the internal phone rang. It was Joanne Stuart.

'I've just had a word with the concierge,' she said, 'and when I told him we were looking for an early dinner he recommended the Arc Brassiere at the Waterfront Hall. It's only a spit away, and well within budget. What do you think, boss?'

'Sound's great,' he said. 'Do you want to tell him to go ahead and book us in?'

'Okay. There's just one thing. They only serve until just before the curtain goes up in the main theatre, so we'll have to get our skates on.'

'No problem,' he replied. 'I'll come as I am, if that's alright with you? Just a quick once over with the electric razor.'

She laughed.

'I'd start worrying if you told me were going to dress up to come out with me.'

'I hope you remember you said that,' he told her. 'I consider it a licence to dress down. Just so long as you're happy to be seen with a shlump?'

'In the foyer in five minutes, boss,' she said. 'Or I'll go without you.'

Caton smiled. She sounded just like Kate.

'That was great, wasn't it?'

She wiped a crumb from the corner of her mouth with her serviette.

'It was,' he agreed. 'Good value too.'

He had gone for the Gracehill black pudding, potato bread and grilled tomato, with chive aioli, and an eight-ounce chargrilled sirloin, braised shallot, button mushrooms and red wine gravy. She had the crab, avocado and wild rice timbale, crème fraîche and crisp breads, and the confit leg of duck, pickled red cabbage, fondant potato and parsnip purée. They had finished by sharing a selection of local cheeses, oatcakes and chutney. The steak and the duck were pink, just as they'd expected, and the house Chilean merlot was fine. The bill came in just under £50, which, once they'd deducted the cost of the wine which he'd pay for himself, would be acceptable as subsistence, and keep the accountants happy. Public scrutiny was so tight under the new Police and Crime Commissioner that the details of all Chief Officers' expenses were up on the Web for everyone to see. It followed that the expense claims from other ranks came under meticulous scrutiny.

Joanne Stuart had talked throughout the meal and not expected a great deal of response, which had suited Caton. Having been single for so long after his divorce, Caton had become used to dining alone. Since his relationship with Kate that had changed. But he secretly admired the insistence of Camilleri's Ispettore Montalbano on silence in which to savour one's food.

They left the Waterfront Hall and started to walk around the impressive circular building.

'I didn't know you spoke Yiddish,' she said.

'Sorry?'

'Shlump? A dowdy person. Looked it up on my iPad.'

'That's not what your tablet is supposed to be used for.'

'How will they know it's not connected to our investigation? Something one of the witnesses told us?'

'An Orthodox Jewish Irish witness?'

'How about Alan Shatter? He was the Irish Minister of Justice and Equality, and Minister for Defence, up until he resigned two months ago. I looked that up too.'

Caton laughed.

'I bet he isn't a shlump.'

She stopped and looked out over the water at the reflections of the coloured lights from the building dancing on the surface of the water. Then she turned and looked up at the impressive Waterfront Hall.

'It's some building,' she said. 'Like a cross between the Manchester Library Theatre and the Manchester

Conference Hall,' said Joanne Stuart.

'Without the history,' Caton replied. 'I'm not knocking it mind, but nothing can beat classical stone-built Victorian.'

'This will be part of history,' she said. 'Just like the Lowry, and the Imperial Museum North. And they all look amazing lit up at night.'

'Come back in a hundred years,' he said, 'and see if they still look the same.'

They started walking again, around the building and then back towards their hotel.

'I sometimes feel strange to be enjoying myself like this when there's so much sadness in the world,' she said.

'Strange or guilty?' Caton asked.

'Well, guilty I suppose. Even more so since I joined the Major Incident Team, where the day job brings you face to face with the worst side of human nature. With murder, manslaughter and rape. How about you, boss? Do you ever feel like that?'

'Sometimes,' he admitted. 'After a particularly bad one. But more often I feel angry, and a bit depressed. But no more guilty than when I'm sitting on the sofa with a takeaway and a glass of red in my hand watching Sport Relief footage from a famine-hit region of Africa. And you know how long that lasts.'

She nodded thoughtfully.

'I know what you mean. We wouldn't be able to function at all if we couldn't compartmentalise. I think it's a bit like putting stuff in quarantine. It's still there, but you don't have to think about it.'

'That's why so many of our single colleagues seek refuge in the pub after a particularly nasty incident,' he said. 'Only it's more anaesthetic than quarantine.'

'Not just the single ones,' she said.

'True.' He was thinking of his Deputy. Wondering

if Gordon's drinking was beginning to escalate. 'I'm lucky I've got Kate to go home to, and you're lucky you've got Abbie. Speaking of which, I'd better give her a ring before she rings me.'

'And I'd better give Abbie a call,' she said. 'Shall we tell them what we had for dinner, and that we had a romantic stroll on the waterfront?' She grinned. 'Or did we just have a club sandwich in the hotel with a half of Guinness?'

He took out his phone, and switched it on.

'What do you think?' he said.

Chapter 19

They had an early breakfast and set off. The Register Office turned out to be just over 300 yards from the hotel.

Oxford House appeared to be wrapped in large, shiny stainless-steel tubes. Given that the building to its right had been demolished, Caton had an uneasy feeling that the role of the tubes was to keep it standing. It didn't help that the office to which they were directed was on the ninth floor.

'No problem,' they were told. 'Would you like me to do the search for you? It'll save you time.'

Four minutes later, he was back with the results.

'Here you go,' he said, placing a printout on the table in front of them. 'Finnoula Malone, born at 6 p.m. on the 8th of January 1973, St John of God Hospital, Newry. Caitlin Malone, born at 4 a.m. on the 18th of January 1975, also at St John of God Hospital, Newry.'

He smirked.

'April must have been a busy month in the Malone family.'

He saw the look on their faces and quickly continued.

'Parents Michael John and Rosaleen Brianna. Is that what you were looking for?'

Caton read through the rest of the details. The

mother's occupation was given as housewife, the father's as farmer. He pointed to the address.

'Where is this exactly?'

'As you can see,' said the man, 'it's in Crossmaglen, which is about forty-five miles south-west of here. I can't say exactly where, but I think it's down near the border. I can bring you a map if you like.'

'That won't be necessary,' Caton said. 'But do you think you could print out a census return for this address around the time these children were born?'

'That'd be 1971, or 1981,' said the man. 'Which would it be?'

'Both of them,' said Caton. 'And while you're at it, could we have the most recent one too, please?'

While they waited, Joanne Stuart dug out her iPad and searched for the address in Google maps.

'Here it is,' she said. 'Drumboy Road. He was right. It doesn't matter whether you head east, west or south, it's less than half a mile to the border.'

Caton leaned back in his chair.

'So,' he said, 'we have two young girls living in the North, who suddenly end up in the care of nuns over the border in Monagahan, at least one of whom is adopted to a couple from Oldham.'

Before they could begin to speculate on how that might have happened, the clerical assistant was back. He had the printouts in his hand and a confused expression on his face.

'I've done as you asked,' he said, handing Caton the printouts. 'But as you can see, it's really odd. They're all there in the 1971 census, but after that nothing. Right up to 2011.'

It was true. In 1971 Michael and Rosaleen Malone were recorded as living on the farm with three children: two sons, Michael aged eleven and Padraig aged ten, and a daughter Aileen, aged thirteen. In both the 1981 and the 2011 census the farm was shown as unoccupied.

'Maybe they fell on hard times and had to move away,' said the clerk. 'It's not that unusual. Especially with farmers.'

Caton handed him back the printout of the 1971 census.

'One last thing,' he said. 'Could you bring us the death certificates for this family?'

'That's going to take a little longer,' he told them. 'Can I get you a drink while you're waiting?'

This time when he returned he looked both serious and confused. He handed the printouts over without comment and stood there waiting for their reaction.

Caton had to read each of them twice just to be sure.

Michael, Rosaleen, their sons Michael and Padraig, and their daughter Aileen shared the same place and time of death. Nine p.m., on the 2nd of October 1979, at the farm where the family lived. They also shared the same cause of death. Multiple gunshot wounds. They had not simply died, they had been killed.

'God, that's terrible!' Joanne Stuart exclaimed.

'You're right,' said the clerk. 'But it's not unheard of. They were bad times you know.'

Caton looked up at him. Barely into his twenties he had experienced none of this. It was all a part of history to him, albeit recent history.

'Caitlin and Finnoula Malone,' said Caton. 'Could you check if there are death certificates for them too, please?'

'I already did,' he replied. 'When you said this family, I assumed you meant that to include the two other daughters. There's nothing for either of them, thank God.'

'I'm afraid that's not entirely the case,' Caton muttered. 'For one of them at least.'

He instantly regretted saying anything at all, and didn't bother to elaborate. The likelihood of this young man being able to keep something as explosive as this to himself was about as likely as him not posting a selfie of himself with Lady Gaga on YouTube. The less he knew, the better.

'If you wanted to find a record of the details behind a tragedy like this, where would you start in Belfast?' he asked.

'Something like this? That's easy,' the clerk replied. 'The Irish News and Belfast Morning News. It's only a spit away.'

'I'm curious, boss,' said Joanne Stuart as they turned into Donegal Street, just half a mile from the Registry building. 'Why didn't you start with the Police Service of Northern Ireland? They're bound to have the most comprehensive report.'

'Because,' he said, 'before I go looking at any official accounts I want to know what we're dealing with. The official adoption papers didn't even record our victim Maureen Flinn's birth name.'

Ten metres ahead, on the opposite side of the road, a large sign on the blue painted ground floor facade of a modest redbrick building proclaimed IRISH NEWS Ltd. But Joanne Stuart had other things on her mind.

'Well, look at this!' she exclaimed.

She had stopped outside a narrow-fronted grey building with steel grills across the anonymous front door. Anonymous but for the fifteen-foot-high poster above it. A red fist rose from an imperial laurel wreath, with a red star beneath it, the name KREMLIN – SINCE 1999 in large Cyrillic characters, and a legend above: THE ULTIMATE GAY CLUBBING EXPERIENCE.

'Abbie pointed this out on TripAdvisor,' she gushed. 'But I never expected to come across it.'

'If you're thinking what I'm thinking,' he said, 'you can forget it.'

'Oh, come on, boss,' she said. 'It's probably like AXM or Lamaars, and you've been in both of those.'

He looked at the statue of Lenin standing beside the poster, his right arm raised in a neo-fascist manner, pointing the way to a classless, stateless, humanist future.

'Somehow I doubt it,' he said. 'Anyway, I forgot to bring my glitzy glamour outfit.'

'Don't be such a stick in the mud,' she said. 'There's a restaurant, a disco, karaoke. You'd love it.'

'I'm not sure it'll sit well on my expense claim form,' he said.

'My treat,' she told him.

'Sorry, Jo,' he replied. 'How's it going to look when someone posts you and me on Facebook? Police officers engaged in a murder investigation on the razzle in Belfast nightclub! Like those Met' officers in that football star's private box.'

'That's not the same at all,' she said. 'They were accepting his hospitality when they were supposed to be interviewing him as a suspect.'

But he was already halfway across the road, heading for the newspaper offices.

'We don't have a librarian any more,' they were told. 'She left us last year. You could try the central library, I'm sure they have copies in one form or another.'

'But you do still have archives?' said Caton.

'We do indeed,' she replied. 'It's just the bodies we don't have any more.'

He dredged up that special smile again and took out his warrant card.

'Would it help if I told you we were police officers, and this was part of a murder investigation?'

She barely glanced at his ID. Her eyes widened.

'A murder investigation?' she said. 'Are you with the Historical Enquiries Team?'

'No,' he admitted. 'This concerns a current investigation.'

She eyed him shrewdly, her journalistic curiosity aroused.

'With historical roots?' she said.

'Perhaps,' he replied.

'If I can mange to find someone to hunt through the archives, would you be prepared to give us a heads-up on this?' she asked.

Caton frowned.

'You wouldn't be looking to blackmail a police officer?'

'Certainly not,' she said, with a mischievous smile. 'For a start, with blackmail you need a dirty little secret, and you've not done anything wrong that I'm aware of and secondly, for a police officer you're a bit out of your jurisdiction, are you not?'

So much for her not having clocked his ID.

'Furthermore,' she continued, 'you've already given me the year and the names. What's to stop us following up on this ourselves?'

Game, set and match. At the very least, he decided, they could muddy the waters. Worse still, with the resources available to them, plus knowing the patch and living there, they might even outpace the investigation itself, with potentially serious consequences.

'Okay,' he said. 'I promise if we make a connection I'll let you know at the same time that we release any press statements in Manchester. You'll already be a step ahead of the rest of the media. It's the best I can do without prejudicing the investigation, and I'm not prepared to do that.'

The smile that had been sitting on her face broadened.

'Fair enough,' she said. 'I'll see what I can do. It make take some time, so while you're waiting you might want to have a look at CAIN.'

'Cain?'

'In capital letters,' she said. 'Never know what you might find.'

'Go on then, Jo,' said Caton as he watched the woman from the news desk depart.

'Why didn't you bring your iPad out with you, boss?' said Joanne Stuart. 'I'm going to have to keep charging mine.'

He moved out of reach.

'Because I knew you were coming with me, and I thought it would give you something to do.'

She took the tablet from her bag.

'You'll regret that,' she said.

It seemed to take ages to launch.

'I told you,' she said. 'Look at the battery. It's only got five per cent life left.'

While they waited she took out the charger lead and looked around for a power point. All of the sockets seemed to be for computer leads, but eventually she was directed to the hospitality area where she hijacked the socket for the electric kettle.

CAIN stood for Conflict Archive on the Internet. A website launched in 2009, it contained a digital archive of source materials and other information relating to the conflict in Northern Ireland, including the background, key issues and main events. Of most relevance were the databases covering the victims and survivors, and in particular the chronological listing of deaths.

'1979, Jo,' he said, even though she was already clicking on it.

A series of entries appeared. There were one hundred and twenty-three in all. Over half were accompanied by a photograph of the victim.

'This is just one year,' she said. 'I had no idea.'

She scrolled down to October, passing on the way names that leapt out at Caton. Airey Neave, MP, Conservative Party Spokesman for Northern Ireland, killed by a car bomb in the Houses of Commons car park; Lord Mountbatten, the Queen's uncle, killed by a remote-controlled bomb on his boat as he left Mullaghmore Harbour in County Sligo. Although only six years old at the time, Caton remembered his parents' shock and disbelief, and with the news of Mountbatten's death, swiftly turning to sadness in the case of his mother, and anger in his father.

'Here we are,' she said. 'October 2nd.'

And there they were. Each name was accompanied by a photograph. It was obvious that Maureen Flinn, or Caitlin as they now knew her to be, had been the image of her mother Brianna. The likeness was evident too in her brother Padraig in particular. The faces were haunting in their own right, but the fact that Caton and Joanne had seen the defiled body of their daughter, and sister, was heart-wrenching. Neither of them spoke as they read the bare details that accompanied each photo. Details that said so much, and yet so little.

Status: Civilian (Civ), Killed by: Non-specific Republican group. (REG)

Shot at home, together with other members of the family during suspected internal dispute.

'Those poor kids,' said Joanne Stuart as they stepped out onto the street.

'At least it gives us possible motives,' said Caton.

'If whoever did it still thought that dispute wasn't finished until the entire family were dead, but thirty-five years? That's a hell of a vendetta.'

'I was thinking more along the lines of covering it up,' he said. 'What if those little girls were witnesses?'

'Either way,' she said, 'please tell me we're not embarking on an investigation involving former members of a Republican terrorist organisation?'

'Whatever it takes, wherever it takes us,' he said. 'Besides, it said suspected internal dispute. In other words they still don't know for certain who did it.'

'What now?' she said.

She thought Caton looked more troubled than he had since they'd left Manchester.

'I'd say,' he replied, 'that the priority is to find Finnoula Malone, or whatever she is now known as. The preservation of life is the first rule when arriving at a crime scene, only right now it's about preventing the crime from happening.'

'If we're not already too late,' she murmured.

'Sorry?' he said. 'I didn't catch that.'

'I said I didn't know you were a Lifehouse fan, boss,' she lied, patting the pocket in which she kept her iPad. 'Whatever it Takes. It's track four on their Who We Are album.'

'Keep looking,' he told her. 'You might want to try the US Navy.'

Chapter 20

For the first time since they had arrived on the Irish mainland it looked like they may have come up against a brick wall.

'Have you any idea what we're up against here?' said the inspector officer they had been allocated for their enquiry.

It was clearly a routine he'd repeated on scores of occasions, and had off pat. He didn't wait for them to reply.

'We were given one hundred and seventy-five staff to examine all the deaths attributed to the Troubles between January 1969 and the Good Friday Agreement in 1998. That's 3,268 and 2,516 incidents, or cases if you prefer. Do you know how many of those cases we've been able to start?'

'No,' replied Caton, even though he clearly wasn't expected to.

'One thousand and forty-four,' he said. 'One thousand and forty-four!'

That sounded like quite a lot to Caton, even without the shouting.

'And do you know how many we've managed to complete?'

This time they merely shook their heads.

'Five hundred and eight-five!' he thundered. 'Five hundred and eighty-five. That's only got us as far as

1973. And you want to know about a case that happened in October 1979?'

He sat back in his chair and crossed his arms.

'I suggest you come back in five years time, sir,' he said. 'If we're still here.'

They didn't give up. Caton knew that the team was divided into two smaller teams: an Investigation team staffed by the Police Service of Northern Ireland, and a Review team staffed by officers from mainland UK forces deemed to be independent in the sense of never having been involved in, or directly touched by, the conflict. There just happened to be several officers from GMP seconded to the Review team, one of whom, Jack Layer, he knew really well. They arranged to meet in a café about a mile and a half away.

'This is a bit cloak and dagger, Jim,' said Caton after the introductions had been concluded and they were sitting with their coffees in front of them.

'You couldn't have come at a worse time, Tom,' he replied. 'The HMIC report brought everything to a halt. We've got a new boss. The whole process is being reviewed. And there's an embargo on releasing any future reviews to members of the victim's families, let alone the public or the press.'

Caton blew on his coffee and took a sip.

'What did Her Majesty's Inspectorate of Constabulary have to say that was so damning?' he asked, tearing a piece off his Danish pastry.

'Wasn't it something about way you'd been dealing with statements from the army and the police?' said Joanne Stuart.

Both Caton and Jack Layer pretended not to be surprised.

'Dead right, Detective Inspector,' said Layer. 'Except that it wasn't me.'

She laughed. 'Jo will do fine since we're not working together.'

'Well, Jo,' he said, 'it was mainly down to a few rogue officers in the Investigation team, which is composed mainly of retired officers, many of whom served in the old Royal Ulster Constabulary. It's a mute point as to whether or not they'd misinterpreted their remit, or had flagrantly resolved to accept everything that representatives of the state told them, as against members of the public, and proscribed organisations like the IRA, UDF, PIRA and so on. Either way, it meant that historical statements by police and services personnel, and current reiteration of those statements, were not being rigorously tested.'

'In other words,' said Caton, 'they could have lied at the time of the incident, and continued to lie, and HET officers weren't ever going to challenge that?'

Jack Layer nodded.

'Exactly. Which meant that former terrorists could be arrested and charged, but there was little likelihood that police and service personnel who'd deliberately committed murder or had overstepped the mark would ever be brought to book.'

'Which makes a mockery of the whole process,' Joanne Stuart observed.

'Right again,' said Layer. 'And threatens to undermine the Good Friday Agreement.'

'So where are you up to right now?' said Caton. 'And where does that leave us?'

He shook his head.

'Not a lot's happening. Nor is it likely to until they've decided on the future of the Historical Enquiries Team. None of the victims' families are going to trust our findings as things stand. As for your investigation, I'll see if I can get you a look at the file. We won't be doing anything with it anytime soon.'

He looked at his watch and pushed his chair back.

'I'd better be going. They'll be wanting to know where I've been. Everyone's paranoid right now.'

He stood up.

'Just one thing, Tom. It would help no end if you could put in a written request. Nothing fancy, so long as it looks official.'

'It is official, Jack,' said Caton. 'This is a murder investigation.'

They gave him a fifteen-minute head start, then made their way back to the PSNI headquarters building. It took less than five minutes to complete the form, but when the civilian clerk took it without so much as a glance at the contents and dropped it into what was clearly an OUT tray, Caton made his presence felt.

'If you take a look at my request,' he said, 'you'll find that I have marked it urgent. My colleague and I are only over here for a few days and we are conducting a murder investigation.'

'We're conducting three thousand plus murder investigations,' muttered one of the other clerks who had been earwigging.

'The big difference,' said Caton, staring straight at him, 'is that ours took place less than a week ago.'

He turned his attention back to clerk sat in front of him.

'At the very least, failing to expedite this request would amount to lack of cooperation between two UK police forces, and worst it could be deemed obstruction. So, are you going to get out from behind that desk and find someone who can give us immediate access to this file, or do I have to get my Chief Constable to ring your Chief Constable?'

The man climbed reluctantly to his feet and sloped

off, clutching the request form as though it was a hot potato.

'I should have asked him his name,' said Caton. 'That's always good for a bit of leverage.'

'Gerard T Meaney,' said DI Stuart.

'What?' said Caton.

'His name is Gerard T Meaney. It's on his name tag.'

'I didn't really need to know it, did I?' he said smiling. 'Not now anyway.'

Five minutes later, a sheepish Gerard T Meaney returned and asked them to accompany him, through two doors accessed by swipe cards and down a corridor to an interview room. He stood aside to let them enter.

'Someone will be with you shortly,' he said, before hightailing it down the corridor.

'That's a bit cryptic,' said Joanne Stuart. 'Someone.'

Caton chose a seat on the opposite side of the table, facing the door.

'It's an improvement on no one,' he said.

Joanne Stuart sat beside him. She had just placed her bag on the table when the door opened. A woman walked in, followed by a man holding a lever-arch box file. He closed the door behind him. Caton and Stuart stood up.

'Detective Sergeant Margaret Riordan,' said the woman, holding out her hand.

She looked to be in her mid-fifties. Medium height, with a pale freckled complexion and curly red hair, sharp green eyes and a welcoming expression.

Her colleague placed the file on the table and held out his hand.

'James Burke,' he said. 'Detective Chief Inspector, retired.'

He was a head taller than his colleague. Oval faced,

his hair had receded to the point where all that was left was a wispy shadow in the centre and short grey stubble on the sides. His eyes were also grey, with a jagged yellow ring around each pupil. Caton was thinking how distracting they must have been for any suspect Burke had interviewed.

The four of them sat down.

'As you'll have gathered from our accents, we are both from this side of the water,' said the man. 'I served with the RUC, and then the Police Service Northern Ireland until nine months ago. Margaret is seconded from the PSNI.'

'Though I'm due to retire in just over a year,' she said with a smile. 'Bring it on.'

James Burke steepled his fingers.

'We are part of the team involved in reviewing the policies, procedures and standards used by the Historical Enquiries Team to date, and to implement the recommendations of the Inspectorate regarding future investigations by the HET.'

'But not their investigations?' said Caton, wondering why these two had been the ones to bring him the report.

'Well, that too,' Burke replied. 'We can hardly review their procedures without looking at how investigations and reviews have been carried out to date. But our role is not to re-investigate; it's simply to determine if appropriate procedures have been followed.'

'Our understanding,' said Caton, 'is that the case we have requested sight of has not yet been the subject of an HET investigation.'

'That's correct,' Burke replied. 'So you're probably wondering why Margaret and I have involved ourselves? Well, I'll tell you. When it was mentioned that you wanted to see it with regard to a recent murder, it aroused a great deal of interest among the Command Team.'

'It surely did,' said DS Riordan. 'And not just them.'

'So,' her colleague continued, 'they decided to take a little peek before it was brought to you.'

'And that's why we're here,' Riordan said.

Caton and Stuart looked at each other. So far this was as clear as the M60 in rush hour.

'See for yourselves,' said the former Detective Chief Inspector, opening the box file and pushing it across the table.

The papers filled the box, but it was clear from the cover sheet that this was a summary, containing extracts of key files and overall findings. The bulk of the witness statements had not been included.

'Where is the rest of the file?' Caton asked.

'Here in this building. In the PSNI Records section. I know what you're thinking, but there's nothing suspicious in that. It was normal for the HET to receive a summary file for every one of the cases they were due to investigate, so they could cross-reference them. They would only request the full file when they were ready to begin the investigation of that particular case.'

It made sense to Caton. There would not have been the space to store everything, and what would have been the point?

'Read on,' said Burke, 'and all will become clear.'

'Or not,' his colleague added.

They were only five pages in when the penny dropped. Caton and Stuart stared at the sheet of faintly yellowed paper. Across the table Burke and Riordan smiled knowingly at each other.

'You've found it then?' said Burke.

'These names,' said Caton, pointing to the thick black stripes randomly spread across a dozen or so of the lines on the page, 'they've been redacted?'

'Bravo,' said the Irishman. 'And not just there, but throughout the documents.'

'Is this common practice?' asked Joanne Stuart. 'Or is it just this case?'

Burke folded his arms and sat back in his chair.

'It is unusual, but not unique. Usually a case has been made that service personnel would be at particular risk if their names were to be revealed, even within the service.'

He could see the confusion in the faces of those opposite him.

'You have to remember,' he said, 'that these cases relate to a period when to all intents and purposes there was a war going on.'

'And the first casualty of war is truth,' said Caton.

'That might be so,' Burke replied. 'But not in this case. 'There are legitimate reasons to protect undercover police officers, or intelligence officers, or soldiers who exercised their duty appropriately but in doing so were certain to become the target of terrorists. Even on the mainland, courts have allowed soldiers to give evidence anonymously and from behind a screen.'

'Sections 74 to 85 of the Coroners and Justice Act 2009,' said Joanne Stuart.

Burke and Riordan looked at her with a mixture of surprise and respect.

'DI Stuart just passed the Inspectors' Board,' he told them. 'She'll have forgotten it all in a couple of months.' He tapped the sheet he was holding with the back of his hand. 'Without these names there is no way you can investigate or review this case.'

'Except that when the Historical Enquiries Team do come to reopen that case,' said Burke, 'we'll have access to those names in the full and original record. But not until then. And I'm afraid you may find it as difficult as we would to get them before then.'

'But not impossible?' said Caton.

'Not impossible. Just bloody difficult, and very time-consuming.'

'In the meantime,' said Caton, 'is it okay for the two of us to work our way through this, and make some notes?'

Burke placed his palms on the table and pushed his chair back. His colleague followed suit.

'Not a problem,' he said. 'So long as you leave it exactly as you found it. It'll be a long day. I'll send someone to bring you some drinks and find out what you want for lunch.'

'Do yourselves a favour and stick with sandwiches,' said Margaret Riordan, with a knowing wink.

'And don't forget,' said her colleague, pointing at the camera high up in the corner beside the door, 'Big Brother is watching.'

Chapter 21

'That was some double act they were doing,' said Joanne Stuart.

'I wonder if it was just for our benefit,' Caton replied, pointing at the camera. He lowered his voice to a whisper. 'Let's assume not. Just to be on the safe side.'

He took off his jacket and hung it over the back of his chair. She did the same with hers. He turned up his sleeves to the elbow. She undid the top button of her blouse, and kicked off her shoes.

'Right,' he said. 'Let's get on with it.'

Caton placed the summary sheet on top of the pile and closed the lid. It was four thirty in the afternoon. The tabletop was littered with empty plastic cups, water bottles and several paper plates.

'Let's get out of here,' he said.

It was about as much as either of them had said to each other in the past five hours. There had been plenty of Ooohs, and Aahhs, a handful of Oh my Gods, and the occasional mild swear word. Nothing that might have meant anything to anyone watching or listening in. They were putting their jackets back on when there was a knock at the door. James Burke entered.

'I just thought I'd pop in and see where you were up to.' His smile spoke volumes.

'We're done,' said Caton, pushing the box across the table. 'Thanks for your help.'

'You're welcome,' said Burke. 'Did you find what you wanted?'

Caton couldn't tell if he was fishing for information or simply being polite.

'Let's just say that it was interesting,' he said. 'But what we really need now are those names.'

The Irishman nodded.

'I thought you might say that.'

He placed a card on the table and pushed it towards Caton with his forefinger.

'This is who you need to speak to. She's not available right now. But if you come back bright and early in the morning, I'm assured she'll be willing to see you.'

Caton picked up the card and turned it over.

'Assistant Chief Constable Anne Reed,' he said. 'I'm impressed.'

Burke held the door open and stepped aside.

'Eight thirty a.m.,' he said. 'And don't be late. Apparently she's got a busy day.'

'Right,' said Caton as soon as the gates closed behind them. 'I don't know about you, Jo, but I need to clear my head. I propose that we go back to the hotel, freshen up, and then meet in the bar.'

'That's a relief,' she replied. 'I'm exhausted, mentally and emotionally. I could do with a shower, and a stiff drink.'

An hour later they were in a quiet corner of the bar lounge, nursing a Hendricks and tonic, and a pint of Guinness. Caton wiped the condensation from his glass with the napkin and lifted the glass to admire the rich creamy head above the deep dark body.

'You know what they call that, don't you, boss?' said Joanne Stuart.

'A pint of Guinness?'

She shook her head.

'The blonde in the black dress.'

He raised the glass to his mouth and drank deeply.

'This pint, by any other name,' he said, wiping his upper lip with the napkin, 'would taste as sweet.'

'Funny that,' she said. 'I've always found it smooth and creamy, but definitely dry.'

'Artistic licence.'

'Mmm.' She took a sip of her gin and tonic. 'I've always been in favour of artistic licence myself. The next time you forget to leave your phone on, and Kate rings me to find out where you are, I'll tell her I last saw you in the bar with a blonde in a black dress.'

He ripped open the packet of cheese and onion crisps and offered them.

'No you won't. Not unless you're intent on keeping that Acting Detective Inspector label.'

'Have you seen the name of these?' she said, taking a handful of the golden crisps. 'TAYTO. That's the Irish for you. Having a great laugh at their own expense.'

Caton helped himself, washed them down with another mouthful and carefully placed the glass on a beer mat that read: Beer is proof that God loves us and wants us to be happy.

'We can't put this off forever,' he said. 'How about if you tell me how you see it, and then we do a bit of brainstorming?'

'Fair enough,' she said. 'While we've both got a clear head.'

She went to take her iPad from her bag but he stopped her.

'Just the initial story. From memory. We can look at the details later. You do the crime scene, I'll do the findings.'

She smiled sweetly.

'I'll do my best, boss, but you know what my memory's like.' She tapped the side of her head with her knuckles. 'A sieve, apparently.'

He grimaced.

'I'm sorry, Jo. I shouldn't have told them you'd only just passed the Board. I was just trying to break the ice.'

She wasn't letting him off the hook that easily.

'At my expense.'

'I won't do it again.'

'You'd better not.' She smiled again. 'Boss.'

Stuart had toughened up considerably since the Cutacre investigation, Caton realised. She was more than ready to take on a team of her own. It would almost certainly mean her leaving his squad. He would miss her a lot, he realised, but it would be criminal to hold her back.

'You have my word,' he said. 'Now, can we get on?'

She laced her fingers together and steepled her thumbs. Caton had noticed before that it was how she prepared when remembering and retelling. They were all different, he reflected. Gordon rubbed his chin. Kate placed her hands in her lap. He liked to lean back in his chair with his hands clasped behind his head. The infinite variety of human beings.

'Tuesday, October the 2nd, 1979,' she began. 'Five seventeen in the morning. The Royal Ulster Constabulary receive a call at the Crossmaglen Barracks. The caller claims that there has been some shooting heard in the vicinity of Drumboy Road, one and a half miles away from Crossmaglen, and close to the border with the Republic. When asked for more information the caller gives the name of a farm, and adds, "They're innocents, God help them," and rings off. This being bandit territory, they suspect it may be another attempt to lure them into a terrorist trap. They ring the much larger joint RUC and Army Barracks at Bessbrook Mill, twelve miles to the north. Bessbrook tell them that there is a patrol in the area that they're diverting to Drumboy Road. In the meantime, two constables set off from Crossmaglen in a Land Rover. It goes without saying that they are told to proceed with caution.'

She sipped her gin and tonic.

'How am I doing so far?'

'Faultless. Keep going.'

She steepled her fingers.

'The constables arrive at the farm. Lights are on upstairs and downstairs, but there is no sign of life. The front door is open. Inside the parlour there is a faint acrid smell in the air that they both recognise as the residue of gunfire, and another stronger, more metallic smell. They move past overturned chairs to the adjacent open-plan kitchen. The body of a man lies on the floor between the two rooms. There is a rifle beside his outstretched arm. A woman's body lies across another, smaller body on a bench by the kitchen table, as though protecting it. They move around the table and find the far bench upturned, and the bodies of a young boy and a slightly older girl sprawled on the floor. All of them are dead. All of them have been shot. Multiple times.'

She took another sip and carried on.

'They search the rest of the house and find it empty. They report in, and are about to search the barns and other outbuildings when the Army patrol arrives. The patrol makes sure the main building is clear, and then searches the rest of the buildings. They discover a cache of weapons under a tarpaulin poorly concealed beneath a stack of hay. An hour later, an RUC major crime scene team of detectives arrive, together with forensics and a pathologist.'

She picked up her glass.

'Your turn, boss.'

Caton leaned back. He smiled as he realised that he was clasping his hands behind his head.

'The perpetrators were never found. Nor was any forensic evidence discovered – fingerprints, fibres, DNA – that could be linked to known suspects. The father was allegedly a suspected Provisional Irish Republican Army sympathiser, associated with a brigade responsible, among other things, for a recent deadly reprisal against an Ulster Defence Force paramilitary unit, and the death of two officers in the Ulster Defence patrol that confronted them as they fled the scene.'

He paused for a drink. She grinned, and pointed to his nose and upper lip. His napkin was already soaked, so he swiped the back of his hand across his mouth and used the palm of his other hand to massage the creamy residue into his skin.

'Guinness are missing a trick,' she observed. 'Moisturiser for Men.'

'Stop it,' he said. 'I'll forget where I'm up to.'

'The bullets?'

'Okay. The bullets retrieved from the father, and the other bodies, were from an M16 rifle that had been used in a raid on a border police station at the time of Operation Motorman in July…'

'1972.'

'1972. The gun by the father's outstretched hand, which incidentally had his fingerprints on it, was an AK-47. It had been fired, but no bullet was found. There was gunfire residue on the father's hands and clothing. The cartridge case was under the kitchen table. Both weapons were consistent with others found in the cache.' He paused. 'Remind me, Jo.'

She tapped her iPad, tapped a file, and scrolled through the pages.

'There were two RPG-7 rocket launchers, one Bren gun, a dozen grenades, four M-16 rifles, five AK-47s, a Browning 9mm pistol, two shotguns and twenty boxes of ammunition. Oh, and a small amount of explosives, and some timers and detonators. It emerged that the Browning had been taken from the body of a member of the Defence forces in an ambush; most of the others were traced to two shipments in the 1970s, one from the US and the other from the Lebanon via Cyprus and Antwerp. Both thought to have originated with the Al Fatah branch of PLO.'

She looked up.

'That's a hell of a haul.'

'By no means the biggest they came across,' he said. 'But sizeable. Anyway, the conclusion that the Royal Ulster Constabulary came to was that it was the work of the UDF, the IRA or the PIRA. Let's take each of those in turn.'

'The UDF,' Jo said. 'The most obvious. Sworn enemies of all the Republican organisations. They'd also been subject to several humiliating ambushes and assassinations. On the other hand, they would have been operating deep into PIRA territory, dangerously close to the border.'

'And,' he added, 'drawing even more attention to themselves, and away from the traditional Republican targets – the Defence Forces, and the UK Government.'

'What about the IRA?' she said. 'They had even less interest in drawing attention to themselves. And wouldn't they have been more likely to want to steal a PIRA arms cache, rather than just murdering the quartermaster and his family? As I understand it they were against killing innocent civilians.'

'Fair point,' he acknowledged. 'As for the Provisional IRA, they'd have even less reason to kill their own alleged sympathiser. Even assuming it was a punishment killing, say because they thought he was informing on them, there's no way they'd leave all those weapons behind.'

'You said he was allegedly a PIRA sympathiser. I thought the report was more definite than that.'

'It was. But it didn't provide any evidence to back up that assertion. It seems to me that it was just a bit too convenient a label.'

'Come on, boss,' she said. 'What about that cache of weapons?'

'I know,' he said. 'It looks bad, but who's to say someone else didn't hide them there without his permission? Or maybe he wasn't given any choice in the matter? Look after these for us, or else!'

'Is that likely?'

'No less likely than giving them to a known sympathiser to look after. Who better to get to hide them than someone no one would suspect?'

He picked up his glass and swirled it, staring thoughtfully into the liquorice-coloured whirlpool.

'What are you thinking, boss?' she asked.

'There is another possibility.'

Intrigued, she sat up, leaned closer across the table and lowered her voice.

'Go on.'

'That Army patrol,' he said. 'Conveniently close to the crime scene, yet they don't arrive until after those two constables. When they do get there, they trample all over the crime scene before the detectives and forensics officers arrive. And it's them that discover the arms cache.'

'You're not suggesting…'

'It wouldn't be the first time,' he replied. 'And who

would have a better motive than them?'

'But his wife and children too?'

'I know.'

He emptied his glass.

'Do you want another one?'

'I'm fine,' she said. 'I'll have a glass of wine with my dinner. Speaking of which, I don't know about you but I'm starving.'

'Me too,' he said. 'Let's go.'

As they stood up he flipped the beer mat over.

I'm sick of all the Irish stereotypes. As soon as I've finished this pint I'm going to start a fight.

He smiled grimly, and muttered to himself. 'I know exactly how you feel.'

The barman overheard, and watched as they left the lounge. He shook his head and reached for another glass to shine. That was the English for you. Couldn't even handle a pint of Guinness.

Chapter 22

The barman would have been more impressed had he observed Caton demolishing the classic Ulster Fry at the famous Brights Restaurant a couple of blocks south of their hotel. Joanne Stuart scoured the Early Bird Breakfast menu and settled for the famous Yankee Bagel: maple cured bacon with Yankee-style eggs on a toasted bagel.

'Assistant Chief Constable,' she said, pushing her empty plate away, 'that sounds ominous.'

Caton wiped the final vestiges of the eggs from his plate with the remains of the fried bread.

'It usually means either a warning, or a reminder not to tread on anyone's toes and to make sure we keep them in the loop.'

She reached for her cup. 'Are we going to?'.

He swallowed the piece of fried bread and washed it down with a slug of coffee.

'Which?' he said. 'Tread on anyone's toes, or keep them in the loop?'

'Either.'

He grinned. 'Yes, and no. That's how it usually goes. It's virtually impossible to avoid treading on toes, and never wise to keep the locals entirely in the loop.'

'Especially,' she added, 'when it's obvious they don't plan to reciprocate.'

'Exactly.'

She pointed to his empty plate.

'I suppose you know you've got a reputation at work for being a bit of a health freak? All that hot water to drink, sensible food, and visits to the gym. Is that what you really have for breakfast every morning?'

He laughed.

'I wish. Kate would have a fit if I expected that every day, even if I cooked it myself.' He smiled ruefully. 'Which I'd have to. The nearest I get is two bacon croissants on a Sunday morning, with a cafetière full of coffee and a copy of the Observer.'

'Don't worry, boss,' she said, 'your secret's safe with me. By the way, I Googled ACC Anne Reed last night.'

'I'm impressed,' he told her. 'I'd have done the same, but I dropped off the second my head hit the pillow.'

She placed her iPad on the table and brought up the notes she'd made.

'Assistant Chief Constable Anne Reed. OBE and Queen's Police Medal for Distinguished Service. Single. BA in Sociology, and MA in Criminology from the University of Leicester. Twenty-six years' police service, all of it in Northern Ireland, with the exception of three secondments: one to Strathclyde Criminal Investigation Branch; one to the FBI Academy's National Executive Institute programme for senior law enforcement officers; and one to the Security Service.'

Caton's eyebrows arched. 'MI5? Which office? Here, London, Glasgow, Manchester?'

She shook her head.

'It didn't say. She's worked in just about every department in the RUC and the PSNI, including being a Divisional Commander, and also Head of the Organised Crime and Major Investigations teams. And how about this? Given the direction our own investigation seems to be heading, I thought you'd be interested to learn that she did a spell recently heading up what they call legacy issues.'

'Meaning?'

'Basically, the Retrospective Murder Review Unit, and the Historical Enquiries Team.'

'No wonder she wants a word with us,' he said. 'Recently, does that mean she no longer has that role?'

'That's right, she doesn't. At the moment, among other things, she's Head of Criminal Intelligence, and Liaison with Counter Terrorism Command.'

Caton checked his watch.

'In that case,' he said, waving to catch the eye of the waiter, 'best not keep her waiting.'

They arrived with twenty minutes to spare, which was just as well, because it took over half that time to fill in their details and get through security. They were ushered to the ACC's office at precisely eight thirty a.m.

'Punctual,' whispered Joanne Stuart. 'Prepare for the headmistress routine.'

'Headteacher,' Caton responded with a grin. 'You should know better, DI Stuart.'

She was about to stick her tongue out in response when their guide opened the door.

'Close escape,' Caton whispered.

'Really? What was, DCI Caton?'

Assistant Chief Constable Anne Reed sat behind a beech desk. Off to the right, on an easy chair beside a coffee table and a small bookcase, sat a man in his late forties wearing civilian clothes. Short and exceptionally slim, with a pale complexion and tousled cropped hair the colour of copper, the ACC was wearing a white shirt, her jacket draped over a chrome valet stand in a corner of the room. The black tie and the epaulets with their white insignia of two crossed tipstaffs within a laurel wreath, added to the bleak formality of her appearance, broken only by the amused expression on her face.

'Sit down, please,' she said, pointing to the two chairs on the other side of the desk.

As he sat down, Caton he realised that the way in which the chairs had been set up meant that it would be impossible, without turning their heads, to see the face of the other man in the room.

'As you have no doubt gathered,' she said, 'I am Anne Reed. The gentleman behind you is Mr Wetherall. I invited him to sit in. He and I have a meeting to attend in precisely…' She glanced at the clock on the wall behind them. '…seventeen minutes. So, let's get on, shall we?'

Caton debated whether to ask her who exactly this Mr Wetherall was. On balance, he decided, it was probably best to leave it. If she didn't want to tell him it was likely that all he'd get would be a cover story of some kind. It didn't mean, however, that he wouldn't try to find out. She looked from one to the other of them, eyebrows raised, indicating that she expected one of them to say something. He was not going to make it that easy for her.

'Well?' she said, with a hint of frostiness in her voice.

'We were led to understand, ma'am, that you wished to see us,' said Caton. He immediately realised that he must sound like a difficult sixth former sent to the headteacher to explain himself.

The ACC's eyes flicked over Caton's right shoulder, sharing her frustration with the mysterious Wetherall.

'Let's not mess around, Detective Chief Inspector,' she said. 'I don't have time for it. As I understand it, you have had sight of the summary of an historical RUC/CPS/Northern Ireland Office report in which certain names have been redacted for security reasons. You are now requesting sight of the full report, including the names and identity of those protected witnesses. Am I right?'

'Yes, ma'am,' he replied.

The ACC folded her arms, and sat back in her chair.

'Given that the said report relates to a thirty-five-year-old case that occurred entirely within what is now the jurisdiction of the Police Service of Northern Ireland and the Northern Ireland Public Prosecution Service, I'm sure you'll understand that we are entitled to know the basis for your interest in this case, and would need a very convincing argument as to why we should reveal those names to you.'

Before he had a chance to reply, she extended her right arm in front of her, hand raised, as though stopping the traffic.

'Particularly since,' she continued, 'the case in question is currently being reviewed by the PSNI Historical Enquiries Team.'

Caton waited to see if she had finished. A fraction too long, judging by the way her forehead furrowed and her eyebrows came together in a disturbing straight line.

'With respect, ma'am,' he said, knowing full well the signal that phrase would send, but unable to think of any other way to preface his next remark, 'I have been assured that although it is among those due to be reviewed by the HET team, this case is not currently being investigated or reviewed.'

He had no idea if it was the with respect or the fact that he had contradicted her, but her expression made it clear that she was seriously pissed off with him.

'Just answer the question,' she said through gritted teeth.

'Certainly, ma'am,' he said, hoping that he sounded both transparent and reasonable. 'The case with which DI Stuart and I are engaged concerns the murder of a British subject in Manchester. In the course of our investigation it has emerged that, as an infant, the victim was formerly resident in Northern Ireland, and was adopted by an English couple via the Republic of Ireland. I did explain that when I initially liaised with PSNI Belfast. Subsequently, whilst here, we have established a direct link between the victim and the events in 1979 which are the subject of the report of which we are requesting sight.'

'A direct link?'

'Yes, ma'am.'

Her eyes narrowed.

'You'll have to give me more than that, Detective Chief Inspector.'

Caton had decided to give away as little as possible, because he knew that if he did there was a very real possibility that the HET would be told to bring the case forward and start reinvestigating it straight away, with all that that would mean for his own investigation, but also because he had no idea if there were reasons why someone might want to tamper with the facts or run interference. In the end he decided he had little choice but to do as she asked, and give her something substantial.

'Our victim, ma'am,' he said, 'was killed by two gunshot wounds, to the head and to the heart.' He paused for dramatic effect. 'We have just established that she was a member of the same family that was the subject of the redacted report. Her family were also killed by gunshot wounds. We believe that she may have been a witness to those killings.'

The silence in the room had the intensity of an electric charge as Reed and Wetherall made connections and computed implications. The sound of the chair behind Caton scraping the floor sliced through their thoughts like a knife across a glass bottle.

ACC Reed looked up at the sound. It was clear from the expression on her face that she was taking her cue from Wetherall. She shifted her gaze back to Caton.

'It would have expedited matters,' she said, 'if you had told us this before.'

'We only found out yesterday, ma'am.'

He wasn't sure if she believed him, and he didn't care one way or the other.

'Mr Wetherall would like to ask you a question,' she said.

'Before he does,' Caton replied, 'could I enquire as to his standing in this matter? It is after all a confidential police matter.'

She slammed her hands down on the table.

'For God's sake!' she said. 'Mr Wetherall is my guest and I can vouch–'

'It's alright, Anne,' the man interjected smoothly. 'If I was DCI Caton I would want to know.'

He stood up and walked to the window to the right of the ACC, where he perched his bottom on the sill. For the first time, his height became apparent. He was short. So short as to be almost vertically challenged. Standing like this his head was only on a level with the ACC's. What he lost in stature he made up for in presence. His face was perfectly symmetrical. His hair artfully tousled to boyish effect. A Saville Row suit contained a trim yet muscular body. Bright, intelligent eyes appraised the two English detectives.

His voice was smooth and confident, hinting of a private education.

'My name,' he said, 'is Graham Wetherall. I represent the Northern Ireland Office. I'm sure you're aware of the role of the NIO, but since many people are not, I'll just remind you. The remit is to ensure the smooth working of the devolution settlement in Northern Ireland, to represent Northern Irish interests within the UK government, and reciprocally, to represent the UK government in Northern Ireland.'

He paused to see if they were following him although, as with all government speak, it purported to tell them everything whilst telling them nothing at all.

'Good,' he said, taking their silence as affirmation. 'So, my question for you, DCI Caton, is don't you think that it would be best to let ACC Reed know what precisely it is that you need to know, and let her team, with its substantial resources, dig it out of the report and send it on to you? That way you can pop back home and concentrate your efforts on tracking down the perpetrator in your own jurisdiction.'

His smile indicated that he thought it more of a rhetorical question than one that required any thought at all.

Caton didn't see it that way. Beside him, Joanne Stuart sliding her iPad from her bag.

'Actually, Mr Wetherall,' he said, 'I don't. Because until we have read the entire report I will not be in a position to tell ACC Reed precisely what it is I need to know.' He smiled. 'I'm sure you are aware of the concept of not knowing what it is you don't know?'

'So you tell us what you do know,' said ACC Reed, 'and we will let you know what it is that you don't know.'

'Please tell me if I've got this wrong, ma'am,' said

Joanne Stuart, taking all three of them by surprise, 'but as I understand it, according to CPS guidance in relation to cross-border investigations and prosecutions, the following factors should be considered.'

She read directly from her iPad.

'Whether the prosecution can be divided into separate cases in two or more jurisdictions; the location and interests of the victim or victims; the location and interests of witnesses; the location and interests of the accused; and potential delays.'

She put the iPad down.

'The victim was located in Manchester. That gives DCI Caton and I primacy over the pursuit of the perpetrator or perpetrators. Having others, however well intentioned, filter information in relation to the investigation is likely to create difficulties in putting together a case that will satisfy the CPS. There is no case to pursue in Northern Ireland in relation to the killing of our victim. Attempting to divide it into two would be highly problematic, and cause unnecessary delays in identifying and tracking down the perpetrator. So, surely it makes sense that the HET here in Belfast begin their investigation and review of the historical case at a time convenient to them, and in the meantime allow us full access to the information to enable us to do our job?'

She smiled innocently.

'Or have I got it completely wrong?'

Caton wasn't sure which of the three of them was most shocked. He certainly hadn't seen it coming, and neither had ACC Reed. The man from the Northern Ireland Office was the first to recover.

'Well put,' he said. 'And most succinctly, if I may say so.'

ACC Reed looked ready to protest, but he leaned forward and placed an arm on her shoulder.

'It's alright, Anne,' he said. 'I am sure that DCI Caton and DI Stuart can be trusted to exercise due discretion in their handling of this information. And who knows? It may be that their own investigation throws up information helpful to the Historical Enquiries Team when they come to review the case themselves.'

Anne Reed looked far from convinced, but it was obvious to Caton who was really in control here. She glanced at her watch. She was already late, assuming there really was a meeting to attend.

'Very well,' she said. 'But just remember to stick to your own remit. It is not your role to reinvestigate the historical case. And if you do discover anything relevant to your own investigation, then I expect you to let me know.' She paused. 'Personally. Do you understand?'

Chapter 23

'What the hell was that all about?' said Joanne Stuart as they waited in a seminar room for the case notes and the report to be brought to them.

'God knows,' said Caton. 'Although I do have my suspicions. You were brilliant in there by the way.'

She came as close to blushing as she was ever going to.

'Thanks, boss. But to be honest I was bricking myself. I still wouldn't rule out a complaint to DCI Gates, or worse still the Chief Constable.'

'I don't think that's going to happen. True, we were both sailing pretty close to the wind, but, as you so bravely pointed out, we had common sense and CPS guidelines on our side.'

'What are these suspicions then?' she asked. 'And what was that Wetherall man doing in there?'

He looked around to make sure that no one was listening in. Apart from the two behind the desks who were busy in conversation themselves, and the security guy by the doors, there was who might overhear.

'If I'm right, he's at the heart of the matter. That official speak he gave us about the remit of the Northern Ireland Office comes down to two things. Making sure nothing upsets the hard won and very fragile political stability over here, and safeguarding

UK national security.'

'I don't see how our getting to read the unredacted report is going to threaten either of those two things,' she said.

'Bear with me,' he said. 'The Northern Ireland Office is hand in glove with the Security Service.'

'MI5?'

'Exactly. Since 2007 they've held the brief for security in Northern Ireland, and have a base over here at the barracks in Loughside. And who did you say Anne Reed had a secondment with?'

Her eyes lit up.

'The Security Service. So you think they're the ones who are most concerned?'

Caton nodded.

'Do you remember how Wetherall introduced himself? He said, "I represent the Northern Ireland Office." He didn't say he was actually with them. And when he talked about their remit, he said the remit, not our remit. What does that suggest to you, Jo?'

'That's he's not with them at all. That he's with the Security Service.'

'But he didn't want to divulge that,' said Caton. 'Or at least he didn't want to spell it out.'

She was still trying to make sense of it.

'But what has this got to do with MI5?'

The door opened and a woman entered, wheeling a carton on a two-wheel trolley.

'Hopefully,' said Caton, 'we are about to find out.'

It took the whole day for them to plough through the case notes and the report. Now they were on their way back to the hotel having agreed that it would be best to share their thoughts in the privacy of one of the bedrooms. They were at reception waiting for their keys. As one of the receptionists handed over the keys, her colleague came across to join them.

'I had a really strange experience earlier,' she said. 'A woman came in asking for your room numbers. She said she had a letter for each of you, and it was extremely confidential. If possible she'd like to slip them under your doors.'

'What did you say?' asked Caton.

'I told her there was no way that we could divulge a guest's room number, but I'd be happy to keep them safe for you and make sure you got them when you returned.'

'Well done,' said her colleague.

'Yes, thank you,' said Caton. 'So do you have them?'

She shook her head.

'That's the funny thing. She gave them to me and then a minute later asked if she could have them back. She said she'd forgotten to include an attachment. So I gave them back to her and off she went.'

'How long ago was this?' said Caton.

'About two hours ago.'

'And she hasn't been back?'

'No. That's what I thought was odd. That's why I thought I'd better tell you.'

'Thanks again,' he said. 'You did right. Has anyone told you you'd make a great detective?'

She blushed.

'No.'

'Well, they have now,' Joanne Stuart told her. 'And take it from me, he knows what he's talking about.'

They waited until they were in the lift.

'Oldest trick in the book,' Joanne Stuart observed. 'Hoping the receptionist would tell her and, failing that, waiting to see which numbered boxes she'd put the letters in.'

'Only she didn't, and the boxes are out of sight,'

said Caton. 'Which is why she asked for them back.'

'What do you reckon, boss? MI5 planning to bug our rooms?'

He shrugged.

'Or firing another warning shot across our bows.' He grinned. 'Maybe they were hoping to install video cameras in the hope of catching us in flagrante.'

She laughed.

'They'll have a hell of a long wait. If only they knew, eh boss?'

The doors slid open.

'If they're as smart as they're supposed to be they already do,' he said.

They spent ten minutes exploring every inch of his room, including dismantling the phone, peering inside the lamps and under the bed, and checking the walls and ceiling for evidence of covert wireless surveillance cameras. When they'd finished, Caton made them both a coffee and switched on the TV, with the sound on low.

'This is exciting,' she said, dunking a shortbread biscuit into her coffee.

'Sometimes it doesn't hurt to be paranoid,' he replied, doing the same.

'Although I don't see how anything we've read so far could be a danger to national security,' she said.

He nodded.

'On the face of it, I agree. Seven and a half hours of ploughing through those depressing autopsy reports, witness statements, and pages and pages of conjecture, and what have we got that we didn't know already?'

'Those names,' she said. 'Whatever it is they're afraid of, it must have something to do with those names.'

'Did you notice anything about the witness statements?' he asked.

'You spotted it too?' she said. 'There was something fishy about all of them. The neighbours heard nothing, saw nothing, know nothing. So who rang the police in the first place? The constables who arrived first at the scene, their statements were virtually identical. And the ones provided by the Army patrol fitted together like a carefully crafted jigsaw.'

'That's a great analogy,' he said. 'And spot on. What's more, the RUC CID investigators must have realised all that too, but there's no evidence they tried to dig any deeper. It looks as though they just accepted it all at face value. No wonder they never managed to identify the perpetrators. And the strangest thing of all…'

She finished it for him.

'There was no mention of our victim, or her sister. It was like they'd never existed.'

'Exactly. The neighbours must have known about them. The local constable, too. So how come no mention?'

'And what about the wider family?' she pondered. 'They must have wondered what had happened to them. And assuming they already knew, how come they didn't offer to take in Finnoula and Caitlin rather than allowing them to be split up and adopted?'

They drank their coffee while they thought about it.

'Another thing,' said Joanne Stuart. 'Why did they blow up that cache of arms after they'd recorded the details? Why didn't they take them back to the Bessbrook barracks?'

'It was standard practice at the time,' he told her. 'The main concern was to put them out of the reach of the terrorists. There was always the possibility that they were booby-trapped I suppose, plus they were probably worried about being ambushed on the way back carrying a load like that.'

'There was a Browning 9mm pistol,' she said.

'I know what you're thinking,' Caton replied. 'But it can't be the one that was used to kill Maureen Flinn. That was taken and tested by the RUC CID team, along with the AK-47 and the M-16. It must still be among the other crime scene evidence.'

'Worth checking though,' she said.

'I will,'

His phone rang.

'It's DCS Gates,' he told her. He took the call.

'Yes, ma'am?'

'Tom. You were supposed to be keeping me in the loop. I haven't heard from you since you got there.'

'Sorry, ma'am.' He grimaced for Joanne Stuart's benefit, forgetting how hypersensitive Helen Gates could be.

'Have you someone there with you?' she asked, proving the point yet again.

'Yes, ma'am. DI Stuart.'

'Acting DI Stuart,' she reminded him. 'How's she doing?'

He smiled.

'Exceptionally well, as it happens. Just this morning she really helped to move the investigation forward.'

Joanne Stuart gave him a mock bow in appreciation of his praise.

'Never mind that,' said Gates. 'Just tell me where you're up to.'

So he did.

'Curiouser and curiouser,' she said when he'd finished. 'So you were right about there being a connection. What do you propose to do next?'

'Check those names, and find out where they are now. It's odds on some of them will be dead by now, but the rest must be worth a visit.'

'To what end exactly?'

'We need to know if our victim was there at the farm when the rest of her family was massacred,' he said. 'If so, who knew that, and why was there no mention in the report of her or her sister? If she wasn't there, we need to know where she was, and how she ended up being put up for adoption.'

'Fair enough. How long do you need?'

'I won't know that till I've found out where they all are. 'I'm hoping no more than another couple of days.'

'You'd better get on with it then. You are keeping in touch with DI Holmes, I hope?'

'Yes, ma'am,'

It would have to be the next phone call he made before she had a chance to check for herself.

'And how are you getting on with our Belfast cousins?' she asked.

'Swimmingly,' he lied.

'Mmm,' she said, which left him none the wiser as to whether or not they'd already been on to her. 'Give my regards to Acting DI Stuart.'

'I will, ma'am.'

He waited for her to end the call, and then speed-dialled his Deputy.

'She sends you her regards,' he told Stuart as he waited for Gordon to answer.

'Yes, and I heard the Acting bit as well,' she told him. 'It's beginning to wear thin.'

Chapter 24

After he'd briefed Gordon Holmes they decided to stretch their legs before dinner, and explore the city centre like tourists. They were strolling along Donegal Place, on their way back from the impressive Belfast City Hall, when Jo saw something that took her fancy in the window of Next.

'Do you mind if I pop in here and have a look?' she said.

'No problem.' He pointed to the adjacent Easton stationery store. 'You'll find me browsing the books in here.'

Used to Kate's brief shopping trips lasting for hours, he was pleasantly surprised when she appeared at his shoulder ten minutes later.

'What's that you've got?' she said, pointing to the brown paper bag tucked under his arm. 'Something from the top shelf?'

He opened it wide enough for her to see the A4 hardback notebook.

'What's it for?' she asked.

'You'll be seeing later,' he said. 'How about you? What did you buy?'

She held up her bag.

'It's a nude strapless slip, with seam-free stitching.' She smiled impishly. 'Which you won't be seeing later.'

'This is a side of you I've never seen before,' he said.

'And?'

He chuckled.

'And it certainly makes a change from DI Holmes.'

'I bet. I don't see Gordon in a strapless slip.'

They laughed all the way to the door, where suddenly she stopped and bent to adjust one of her shoes.

'Don't look now,' she said, 'but there's a man on the other side of the road who I think is following us.'

She brushed her trouser leg, straightened up and turned to walk along the pavement.

'Mid-thirties, mid-brown hair waxed into a little peak on top, casual joggers and a light-brown windbreak,' she told him.

'Sounds about right for a perfect blend-in.' Caton, checked the shop windows as they passed, hoping to see the man reflected there. 'What makes you think he's been following us?'

'I saw him on Bridge Street, just after we'd left the hotel. It was his hairstyle that stuck in my mind. Then he was there again on Castle Street. And I swear he was standing under the trees close to the big wheel when we turned round at the City Hall. And now he's here.'

'It was the most direct route from the hotel to City Hall, down one of the main streets,' he said. 'It could easily be a coincidence.'

'Let's cross over,' she suggested. 'See how he reacts.'

They left it until the last minute then stopped suddenly at the kerb. Caton looked left, and right, and left again as though checking there wasn't a bus coming.

'Did you see?' she said as they started to cross.

'You're right,' he said. 'He was a fraction too slow pretending to look in the shop window. Poor choice too; I don't see him in Jane Norman outfits. I'm tempted to ask him if he knows the way to Loughside, but let's just see if he tries to stick with us.'

They turned left and continued up Donegal Place. As they turned right into Waring Street, the follower continued straight ahead into North Street.

'Exactly what we'd do,' said Caton. 'Except that he's wasting his time. We ought to complain to the Parliamentary Ombudsman about them squandering public money.'

'I've been wondering,' she said, stopping just short of their hotel. 'Why did that Wetherall guy give in so easily? It was obvious neither of them wanted us to see those names, so why did he suddenly hand them to us on a plate? And before you say it was down to my eloquent reasoning, we both know that isn't true.'

'You may be right,' he said, 'but you helped to make it easy for him. I can only think that there's actually nothing sinister for us to find, or that even if there is, he thinks that there's no chance of us finding it.'

'Then why all the fuss in the first place?'

'Because of all the current sensitivity about the Historical Enquiries Team. You remember what Jack Layer told us? Right now there's a debate going on as to whether or not they should replaced, or wound up. The last thing they need is us questioning the veracity of RUC investigations they're due to review, even if they are thirty-five years old.'

'I suppose so,' she said. And then there's the "on the run" debacle.'

'On the run?'

She tapped the side of her bag. 'I came across it last night when I was Googling stuff. Forgot to mention it.'

'Go on.'

'The Hallett Review?'

He shook his head.

'Following the collapse of that trial of the guy accused of the Hyde Park bombing?' she said.

Now he remembered.

'Wasn't it something to do with amnesty letters sent out to suspected terrorists who had left the UK, telling them they were no longer wanted by a UK police force.'

She nodded.

'Only this guy was arrested as soon as he set foot in England. The trial collapsed when the letter was brought up, and Lady Justice Haslett found that while the scheme was legal, it was never properly administered by the PSNI or the Northern Ireland Office, and he, along with the other 136 allegedly "on the run" Republican terrorists who received the letter were relying on an incorrect and misleading statement therein. They thought it was an amnesty for all time. Like a Monopoly get-out-of-jail card. Only it wasn't.'

'But it did help to convince the IRA and Sinn Fein to sign the Good Friday Agreement.'

'Exactly, only no one told the other side.'

'No wonder they were both edgy,' he said. 'Although putting us under surveillance seems a bit over the top. I have a funny feeling there's a lot more to it than that.'

He looked at his watch.

'We'd better go in. I need to ring Kate, then I suggest we have room service. We can do some work as soon as we've finished eating.'

'Fine by me, boss,' she said. 'And when we've finished that, we could swing by Kremlin.'

He laughed.

'I'll tell Kate. She'll be really impressed.'

He used his BlackBerry in the en suite bathroom, with the tap running. He doubted that it was really necessary, but when he had briefly worked undercover they had been taught that whenever you suspected that you were under surveillance, it was important to go through the motions. That way they became habitual, and ingrained. After Joanne's experience in the Cutacre Case, he had no doubt she would be doing the same right now, even though it was unlikely she'd be discussing the case with Abbie, her partner.

Kate was far from impressed when he told her he wouldn't be home for at least another two days.

'I don't know what it's like over there,' she said, 'but it's sweltering here and I'm ready to drop. In both senses of the word. I could really do with you being here, Tom.'

'I know,' he told her. 'And there's nothing I want more. But you know how it is. And if we get this right there'll be no need to come back again.'

'I'm worried about you,' she said. 'There was a report on the news about policemen in a Land Rover being shot at, and something about a letter bomb at a sorting office.'

'There's nothing to worry about,' he assured her. 'The shooting was in Derry, that's miles away. And the attempted bombing was a couple of weeks ago, a small affair, on an industrial estate. Two packages were intercepted. Nobody was hurt. There wasn't even an explosion.'

But she wasn't really listening.

'And there was all that trouble over the parades,' she continued. 'There were twenty-seven police officers injured with petrol bombs, and pipe bombs, and masonry being thrown.'

'That was over a week ago,' he said. 'Honestly

Kate, It's all quiet here now.' It wasn't like her be this anxious. He put it down to the pregnancy, but there was no way he was going to say so. 'Where have you got all this from?' he asked. 'Have you been trawling the Internet?'

He could hear her sucking her teeth.

'If I didn't care about you,' she said, 'I wouldn't be concerned.'

'I know,' he replied. 'But promise me, no more hunting for negative headlines. These are isolated incidents in a really peaceful city. The Peace process is not in doubt. It's just a few losers on either side. I'd be just as much at risk back home. The official threat level for the mainland right now is substantial. That means there's a strong possibility of an international terrorist attack.'

'And is that supposed to make me feel better?'

'Come on, Kate,' he pleaded. 'You know what I'm saying. The UK is a big place. The odds of either of us being caught up in a terrorist attack are the same as winning the Euro Millions Lottery.'

'Someone wins that every week.'

'Give me a break, Kate,' he said. 'I rang to hear your voice. To find out how you are. To tell you how much I loved and missed you. Not to end up with both of us feeling worse.'

'Okay,' she said, 'just so long as you promise me you'll stay safe.'

'Of course I will. For you, and for Junior.'

'Make sure you do. Give my best to Jo.'

'I will.'

'Love you, Tom.'

'Love you, Kate.'

Caton felt strangely unnerved by their conversation. It concerned him that Kate was so worried about him. It wasn't like her. And this was not a good time for her to be anxious about anything. He'd read somewhere, probably in one of her magazines, that anxiety during pregnancy could lead to premature childbirth. And it would be his fault. But it wasn't just that. For all his confidence in the situation in Belfast, he felt a creeping unease. Those 'losers' he had told her about had become increasingly active in recent months. And what he had neglected to tell Kate was that some of the witnesses he needed to speak to had been involved in acts of terrorism themselves. He wondered how they would feel about a pair of British detectives wanting to dig up the past.

He put the phone in his pocket, splashed his face with cold water and turned off the tap. There was only one way to find out.

'That was better than passable,' said Joanne Stuart, placing on the trolley the remains of her smoked salmon niçoise salad. 'How was your hand-battered fish and chips, boss?'

'It's not Harry Ramsden's, but it's pretty good.'

He smeared the last of the mushy peas between two slices of buttered brown bread and took a bite. A green slime slid out from between the layers and headed for his lap. He caught it deftly with the back of his hand and licked it up.

'If only the rest of the team could see you now,' she said. 'Do wonders for your street cred.'

'If I catch you taking any sneaky photos while we're out here, you're finished,' he said.

She laughed.

'Might be worth it though.'

She poured herself another glass of the Sauvignon Blanc and topped up his glass. When he'd finished, he put his plate and the empty bottle on the trolley, wheeled it into the corridor, came back in and closed the door.

'We should make it a habit of working like this when we get back home,' she said, waving her glass in the air. 'Do wonders for morale.'

'But not for our success rate,' he said. 'Not to mention what the accountants would have to say. And can you imagine Martin Hadfield's face when he sees twenty-four bottles of wine, and sundry fish and chips and salmon niçoise on the expenses sheet?'

'Might be worth it just to see that.'

'You're repeating yourself, DI Stuart. Could it be you've had too much wine?'

'Shush.' She looked at the phone, the television and the imaginary cameras in the walls. 'Are you trying to get me sacked?'

They both laughed at that.

'Come on,' said Caton. 'Down to work.'

He took his iPad from his bedside table, and from the drawer beneath it the hard-backed notebook he had bought. He put them on the bed between Joanne Stuart and himself.

'I've already put the names in here,' he said, opening the notebook.

He had listed them all on the first page, and then repeated them again on the pages that followed, one page per name.

'I also asked DI Holmes to get Duggie Benson to find out everything he could about them, and email the results over to me asap.' He powered up his iPad. 'Hopefully there should be something here by now.'

They waited for his emails to come up. There was one from Benson, which simply said: Here You Go.

Caton opened the attachment. It was only two pages long, but it was the quality of the content that mattered. He smiled.

'This will do nicely for starters,' he said.

Chapter 25

As you can see, wrote Duggie Benson, of the seven names you sent me, three are dead, the whereabouts of one is not known – don't worry, I'm on to that – and of the other three I think you'll find the last two particularly interesting.

> Patrick (Paddy) Kileen. RUC Constable. Retired as an Inspector October 2008. Died of a heart attack four years later, aged 64.
>
> Michael Antrim, RUC Sergeant. Killed in March 1991 whilst pursuing suspected Ulster Volunteer Force Terrorists. His killers were never caught.
>
> Stuart Gilchrist – Captain 14th Int. – East Det. Seconded from Ulster Defence Regiment. Killed in a bomb explosion 1989.
>
> George Ellis – Ulster Defence Regiment. Arrested in 1989 on suspicion of giving confidential information to the UDA. Convicted, and jailed for 11 years. Served six. Present whereabouts unknown.
>
> Michael Walsh – Royal Military Police – trained driver on attachment to 14th Int. South Det.

Fermanagh. Honourable discharge September 1987. Entered St Patrick's College Maynooth – an RC seminary near Dublin – Currently parish priest in Westmeath, Eire.

Francis (Frank) Finucane – 14th Int. East Det. Palace Barracks Belfast. Currently an Agent with the National Crime Agency.

Andrew Blair – Sergeant, RUC; Joined Merseyside Police 1985. Retired as Sergeant 2009. Currently working as a civilian with the Category C Team in Manchester.

'I can see what he means about interesting,' said Joanne Stuart. 'One's in the NCA and the other one's right on our own doorstep, in Dad's Army.'

Caton shook his head.

'I'm surprised at you,' he said. 'Okay, so they're all retired, but they get paid half what a DC gets paid in our team, and their clear-up rate is eighty-five per cent. They deserve our respect for that.'

She pulled a face.

'Should be a hundred per cent if you ask me. There's twenty-three of them, and they get all the easy ones where the perp' is already known and the evidence is staring them in the face.'

'Even so, think what our workload would be like if they didn't exist.'

'Instead of supplementing their pensions,' she persisted, 'there'd be thirteen more warranted detectives in our squad. It's creeping privatisation.'

'At least they've all been detectives,' he reminded her. He smiled. 'I didn't have you down as a Police Federation Rep. You've been spending too much time with DI Holmes.'

She shrugged.

'Whatever. Anyway, the good news is when we get home all we have to do to question Blair is pop over to Chadderton nick. That's all of two miles.'

Caton was busy considering the ramifications of having to investigate a member of the Cat C team. Jo's attitude was not uncommon among the rest of the detectives. He could already hear Helen Gates' voice telling him to tread carefully. The same with the other one, NCA agent Francis Finucane. The National Crime Agency had been up and running for less than a year. Sensitivities were still raw. But at least he had several contacts he could use.

'You'll have to fill me in on all these acronyms, boss,' she said. 'Most of them were before my time.'

Caton ran his eyes down the list.

'They're still relevant now though,' he said. 'In one way or another. The Royal Ulster Constabulary is now the Police Service of Northern Ireland. The change of name was supposed to lay some ghosts to rest, signal a shift in attitude, and boost recruitment from the Roman Catholic community.'

'Has it?'

'It's getting there. About thirty per cent among the serving officers are now Roman Catholic. Less among the support staff.'

'What about this UDR that Gilchrist and Ellis were members of?' she said. 'Where did that fit in?'

'It was the biggest regiment of the British Army,' he told her. 'Raised in 1970, mainly from volunteers to start with, its role was to support the police in defence of life and property, especially against terrorist attacks. It replaced the RUC's military role, and let them concentrate on policing.'

'And that was largely Protestant too?' she guessed.

'Even more so. It started off with about seventeen

per cent Catholics, but by the time they were recruiting full-timers it had fallen to less than five per cent.'

'Hardly non-partisan then.'

'Hardly. The IRA and Sinn Fein accused them not only of sectarianism, but also of collusion with loyalist paramilitary organisations like the UDF and the UDA. With some justification, as it turned out.'

'Which was what this George Ellis was convicted of.'

'Exactly. Incidentally, and this should impress you, they were the first British infantry regiment to fully incorporate women. '

She didn't look that impressed. She crossed her legs and leaned back on her elbows.

'So, what's the difference between the UDF and the UDA?'

It felt to Caton as though this was turning into a Q and A session from Sophie's World. She was even beginning to sound, and look, like a curious adolescent. Right down to the swell of her sweatshirt.

'Good question,' he replied, forcing himself to concentrate. 'Formed in 1971 the UDA was, in theory, a legal organisation, but it had a terrorist wing called the Ulster Freedom Fighters, so in reality it was the largest of all the Ulster loyalist paramilitary organisations. The UFF killed mainly Catholic civilian targets in what they claimed was retaliation for the IRA killings. From 1992 until it ended its armed campaign in 2007 the UDA was formally classified as a terrorist organisation.'

'And the UDF?'

'The Ulster Defence Force have never been anything but an active loyalist terror group. Smaller than their rivals, the UDA/UFF, who incidentally they called the Wombles – and don't ask me why because I don't know – were nevertheless well armed, highly trained and very resourceful. Like the UFF their targets were primarily civilians, and they were known for giving no advance warning when setting off a bomb.'

'Are you saying they're still active?'

'That's what the Chairman of the Police Federation claimed last November. Although it's difficult to tell if it's politically motivated or just organised crime. And they're not alone in that. The Real IRA are still active, although until those letter bombs in February, they seemed to be more concerned with fighting drug gangs south of the border.'

'I remember that,' she said. 'They sent them to seven Army recruitment offices down South.'

She pushed herself upright and straightened her sweatshirt, as though suddenly aware of how provocative it may have looked. She frowned.

'It's just struck me,' she said, 'these paramilitary groups are still out there, and for all we know one of them might have been responsible for the killings on that farm, and for the murder of our Maureen Flinn.'

She looked directly at him.

'We may need to question some of them.'

He grimaced.

'There's no may about it. We are going to have to, if only to eliminate them.'

She turned her attention back to the list of names.

'That just leaves this 14th Int.,' she said. 'That Gilchrist and Finucane were both in. What's that when it's at home?'

Caton hadn't heard that expression in years. It seemed strange coming from someone Joanne Stuart's age. Probably a favourite expression of one of her parents.

'It was the British Army 14th Field Security and Intelligence Company,' he told her. 'Also known as the

Det. Recruits came from all over the armed forces, but primarily from the SAS and the Special Boat Squadron of the Royal Marines. They were trained by 22 SAS and, in the main, led by SAS officers. They also had embedded links with Special Branch and MI5. Basically they carried out surveillance against people suspected of being members of paramilitary organisations.'

'On both sides?'

'On both sides. Although there have been a number of accusations of the unit passing on information to the loyalist paramilitaries, and even helping them directly to take out suspected Republican paramilitaries.'

'Are they still here?' she asked.

'Not officially. They've recently been absorbed into the Special Reconnaissance Regiment, which does the same things, but on a global scale. The odds are that anywhere in the world that we, or our allies, need surveillance, "eyes-on" intelligence or close target reconnaissance, you'll find a unit of the SRR. Only don't ask me anything else about them because I wouldn't know. It's the most secretive unit in the British Army. A lot more secret than the SAS, MI5, MI6 or GCHQ.'

She looked back down at the list. Caton could tell that she was running the implications through her head, just as he had already done. The PSNI, Graham Wetherall from the Northern Ireland Office, MI5 or who knew where, Special Branch, the NCA, all those terrorist organisations, and to top it all the man that had been following them. And now this.

She raised her head and stared into his eyes.

'What the hell have we got ourselves into?' she said.

It was the first of her questions for which he had no answer.

Chapter 26

Caton had spent a good part of the evening chasing numbers around Dublin trying to contact Detective Chief Superintendent McCarthy of the National Bureau of Criminal Investigation, who had been such a help to him and his cousin Niamh a couple of years before. When he finally got through and explained what he wanted, McCarthy had been cautiously optimistic.

'I'll do what I can, Tom,' he said. 'But if the one you're looking for is still active as a paramilitary, he definitely won't want to meet with you, and even if he isn't, it doesn't mean he'll be willing to meet a British police officer.'

'But what if you can convince him that I'm not interested in the Troubles?' Caton urged. 'That I've nothing to do with the Historical Enquiries Team, and that I'm only interested in clearing up a murder on my own patch?'

'But if he was involved, he's unlikely to want to admit it. He may even have had something to do with your murder back in Manchester.'

'Then if he isn't prepared to meet with me, it'll make me suspicious. You can tell him I'll be forced to dig deeper. Find another way to eliminate him from my investigation.'

He heard a sharp intake of breath.

'I hope you know what you're getting into, Tom,' said McCarthy. 'There's a fragile peace up there, and the extremists have still not given up. It's still a minefield this side of the water. Literally as well as metaphorically.'

'I don't have any option, Eamon.'

The Irishman sighed.

'Fair enough. I'll give it a go. But don't hold your breath.'

It was over breakfast the following morning that McCarthy rang back.

'You're on,' he said. 'I think I've found your man. He was understandably suspicious at first. He took a lot of convincing, but I think his curiosity got the better of him. What's more, and it's only a feeling I've got, I don't think he had anything to do with it. Not in a bad way at least. But I could tell straight away that he knew what I was talking about.'

'Eamon, that's brilliant,' said Caton. 'Who is he?'

There was a long pause.

'Not over the phone, Tom. I'll email it to you. There was something he wanted you to do as well. It'll all be in the email.'

'What happens now?'

'He didn't want your phone number or your email address, but he did ask which hotel you're staying at in Belfast. He said someone will contact you.'

'That's it?'

'That's it, Tom.'

'I owe you, Eamon.'

McCarthy laughed.

'That's the second time you've said that, Tom. You still haven't paid me back for the last time.'

'I will. Maybe if you could wangle a trip over to Manchester, Kate and I can take you out. Show you a good time?'

'That'd be good. How is Kate?'

'About to give birth anytime now.'

'That's wonderful. You'd better get this wrapped up and get back there then. If you miss that, she'll never forgive you.'

'Don't I know it.'

'Give her my love and best wishes.'

'I will.'

'Niamh, too. And the fragrant Helen Gates.'

'I will.'

'Bye, Tom.'

'Bye, Eamon. And thanks again.'

'Just make sure you stay safe, Tom.'

'I will.'

Caton ended the call and placed his mobile on the table.

'Fragrant?' he said, shaking his head.

'What is?' asked Joanne Stuart, putting her cup down.

'Who is,' he replied. 'But you don't want to know.'

'I do,' she said. 'I really do.'

So he told her.

When they'd both stopped laughing, he relayed the substance of the call.

'Contact you how?' she said.

'I've no idea. A knock on the door, an envelope under it, a tap on the shoulder as I'm leaving? Your guess is as good as mine.'

I doubt they'll do it in plain sight,' she said. 'Just in case we're being followed.'

When they got back to his room Caton switched on his iPad and opened his emails. The message from DCS McCarthy was waiting.

The man's name was Gerald Martin MacMahon, aka Gerry Mac. A former Commander of the Monaghan–Cavan Brigade of the IRA. The thing that

MacMahon wanted him to do McCarthy had reported verbatim. It was brief, and cryptic.

If You'se don't know about the Glenanne Gang You'se might want to look them up. Save us both a heap of time.

'Right,' said Caton, opening the browser. 'Let's have a look.'

There was a full page in Wikipedia about MacMahon, plus various newspaper items. He had been one of a number of successive commanders of the Monaghan–Cavan Brigade. One of the most successful ones, judging from the fact that he had never been convicted of anything, despite having been suspected of numerous attacks on army targets and several reprisal killings. As a young man in his twenties, he had been arrested during Operation Demetrius in 1971 and interned for four years without trial in Compound 19 of the notorious Long Kesh camp, along with three hundred and forty-one other suspected IRA militants. Released in 1975, he had risen steadily through the ranks of the brigade until his 'retirement' in 2008.

'What about the Glenanne Gang?' said Joanne Stuart.

'As it happens, I do remember reading about them,' said Caton. 'And there was an ITV programme about them too. If I remember rightly, they were a group of loyalist extremists working hand in glove with rogue elements of the Security Services. But let's check it out all the same.'

Joanne Stuart was already searching on her own iPad.

'You're right,' she said. 'It was mainly the UVF Mid-Ulster Brigade, together with UDR men and RUC reserve officers. They had a bomb-making site and an arms cache at Glenanne Farm in Armagh. Hence their name. Although they called themselves the Protestant Action Force, and sometimes claimed to be part of the Red Hand Commando.'

'We're drowning in names and acronyms, Jo,' said Caton. 'Why couldn't they have just chosen one and stuck with it?'

'They carried out sectarian attacks in the area,' she continued. 'And even in Dublin. Scores of attacks from the mid '70s right up to 1980. It lists forty-one names, with details of the convictions of the ones who weren't killed before they were arrested.'

'Which goes some way to explaining why the Historical Enquiries Team was set up,' Caton observed. 'And why there's so much controversy over it right now.'

'Boss,' she said, 'I've just found an interesting link.'

'What is it?'

'Hang on,' she replied. 'I'm just having a read.'

He checked the rest of his emails while he was waiting. Then he went through the texts on his phone. He had just replied to one from Kate when Jo looked up.

'Bloody hell!' she said.

'What?'

'Have a look for yourself.' She handed him the iPad.

'I'm going screen crazy,' he replied. 'Just tell me.'

'Okay,' she said. 'In a nutshell. South Armagh. Early 1979. Same year as the massacre at Malon Farm. The British Army sets up a paramilitary unit to carry out surveillance and covert operations along the border. Twenty-eight men recruited from the RUC, UDR and other British Army regiments. SAS-style training. And guess where they operated from?'

Caton shook his head.

'Surprise me.'

'Bessbrook Mill. They were supposedly based in Armagh Barracks but they were called the Bessbrook Support Unit. It's where they jumped off from.'

Caton could see where she was going with this. 'The same place where our seven names came from? The ones who just happened to be in the area, when the call came in to the RUC.'

'Exactly.' She was excited now. 'And guess what?'

'Come on, Jo,' he said. 'This is exhausting.'

'They were split into three units, each with seven or eight men!'

'Some coincidence,' he said.

The shrill sound of the in-room telephone caused them both to jump. Caton stood up, reached over and picked up. He listened for a moment.

'Thank you,' he said. 'I'll be down shortly.'

He replaced the handset.

'That was quick,' he said.

'What is it?' she asked.

'What we've been waiting for. I think this is our contact.'

'You mean he's waiting downstairs?'

'No, you were right. It had to be indirect. A package has been left for me at reception. By a taxi driver. He was paid to deliver it.'

'Clever,' she said.

The package lay on the bed between them. A padded envelope. She hefted it in her hand.

'Two hundred grams,' she said. 'Give or take. A mobile phone?'

He took it from her and ran his fingers carefully along the edges, checking for wires, contacts, anything unusual. Satisfied, he prised open the flap and tilted the package. An object slid out onto the bed. It was the same size as a mobile phone, but squatter. Caton flipped it over. There was a small screen on the reverse.

'Close,' he said, handing it to her. 'It's a GPS device.'

'Clever,' she said for the second time, examining it closely.

Caton felt inside the package and extracted a sheet of folded paper the size of a beer mat. He unfolded it.

'Is that the coordinates?' she asked.

'No. He wants me to leave the hotel at eleven a.m. precisely, and to come alone. Then to drive south out of Belfast on the M1. Take the A1 after Lisburn, and switch on the GPS when I reach Dromore, and not before.'

He handed it to her.

'Very clever,' she said. 'He's taking no chances. But you can't go alone, boss.'

'I don't have an option.'

'What if I followed you as far as Dromore, and waited there for you to come back?'

'What would be the point? And what if he has me followed from the moment I leave the hotel? Surely that's the reason he's been precise about what time I leave.'

'What am I supposed to do?' she said. 'Sit here twiddling my thumbs?'

'No way,' he told her. 'You can bring Gordon up to speed, and find out where he and the rest of the team are up to. Don't use the phone, do it by email on your iPad. Then you can follow up on the names of the seven men in that patrol. See what you can dig out from their service records.'

'Won't that start to ring alarm bells?'

'No more than those that Duggie rang when he did the initial search for us. Whoever it is that's started taking an interest in us, they won't be surprised to find us going down that route.'

'Okay, boss.'

She looked at her watch and stood up.

'Have you seen the time?' she said. 'I'm off back to my room. And you'd better get a move on. Eleven a.m. precisely he said.'

She opened the door.

'You take care, boss,' she said. 'I'd be lost without you.' She paused. Then grinned.

'I haven't brought my credit card.'

Chapter 27

On the outskirts of Dromore, Caton pulled off the dual carriageway of the A1 and cut the engine. If someone was following him, they were good. He had changed lanes with no good reason, accelerated suddenly, slowed down again, taken slip roads on the M1 several times and then immediately rejoined the motorway. Now he sat in this lay-by, outside the premises of a tyre factor and car wash, with just a builders' merchant's truck for company.

He took the GPS from his glove compartment and switched it on. He waited until it told him that the requisite satellites had been detected and then selected Saved Routes. There was only one. He tried the Show Map option, hoping to discover his destination; there was no response. He had no choice but to follow the sequential directions. He balanced the GPS in the cup holder behind the gear stick, had a drink of water from the plastic bottle in his cooler compartment, and set off.

The road climbed as he approached Bainbridge. He passed quarries and empty fields, then the town itself, before dropping down towards Newry. He wondered if they were taking him south-east towards Warrenpoint, Carlingford Lough and the Irish Channel coast. At the last moment he was directed straight on towards Dundalk. He found himself joining the M1 again and almost as quickly turning off onto the N53, heading west.

This was familiar territory. They had passed through here on their way to Monaghan to visit the former convent. His own satnav told him that this would eventually become Concession Road, which would intersect with Drumboy Road at a point less than half a mile from Malon Farm, the site of the murder of the Malone family. He wondered if this was where he was being taken. If so, it would save him a journey. It was a place he felt a need to see for himself. The place where it had all begun.

He was wrong. Half a mile short of that intersection he was sent left down a side road that led past farm fields, roadside hedges and trees whose branches met to create brief tunnels of shade. He passed a sign for Tattyboy. A mile further on, he left the road and followed a single track of tarmac up into the hills. The sky was blue and cloudless. The outside temperature was 26 Celsius and he was grateful for the cool breeze from the air conditioning across his face and arms.

A brief right turn, followed by an immediate left signposted Atiduff Lough, had him climbing higher through rough pasture. The road narrowed until it was barely wide enough for a tractor. In places, grass was growing through the tarmac. He passed three sets of farm buildings, and then as he rounded a corner he was forced to stop. A black Vauxhall Enigma was parked to one side beneath a tree, effectively blocking the road.

Caton left the engine running, applied his handbrake, and checked the GPS. There were no instructions. He waited what seemed an age. He checked in his rear-view mirror that the road was clear behind him, released the handbrake and slipped into reverse. His foot rode the clutch.

The driver's door of the Enigma opened. A man emerged. He wore a black windcheater over black jeans. He was big man. Well over six feet tall, muscular. He'd make a perfect bouncer. The man turned to face Caton's car, noted the tension in Caton's expression, and the fact that his engine was running, and raised both hands to show that they were empty. Then he began to walk towards the car.

As he came closer Caton realised that this was not Gerry MacMahon. This man had to be at least twenty years younger, closer to his own age. Late thirties, early forties perhaps. He looked intelligent, confident and hard. As the man reached the bonnet, Caton lowered his side window. The man placed a hand on the roof and bent to bring his face close to Caton's. His breath smelt of menthol. Like he'd been chewing gum.

'You see those gates on the right, opposite my car? Drive in there. Park up and get out.'

A softer accent than Belfast, with the quiet assured tone of someone used to being obeyed.

'Then you follow the hedge on your left into the trees. It becomes a path that takes you to the side of the Lough. When you get there, your man will be waiting.'

'Will I need the GPS?' said Caton.

'No.' He straightened up, and put out his hand. 'You can leave that with me. You'll not need it again.'

Caton reached down for the GPS and placed it in the man's palm. It was a strong hand. Smooth, not rough. He looked up into the man's face. His expression was unreadable. Hard and inscrutable. The look they taught you at training school, but hardly anyone managed to master until they were doing it for real. It reminded him of every Royal Protection Officer he had ever met. The man turned and walked back to his own car, where he stopped and watched as Caton drove forward and turned into the field.

Caton halted just beyond the gates. Although the ground was hard, it was also rough and uneven. He did not want to take any chances. As he climbed out of the car he found the metal five-barred gates being closed behind him.

'Don't worry,' the man told him. 'It'll be here when you get back.'

Caton alarmed the car and set off up hill beside the hedge. After a hundred and fifty yards the path turned sharply to the left to take him along the flank of a steeply wooded section. He paused, and looked back down the hill. The man was still there. He had a companion with him. They were leaning on the metal gate watching him. Caton turned and continued along the path. Another hundred yards, and it led him into the woods. The trees crowded in, their canopy dense. The only sound was the crunch of twigs beneath his feet. Now he was descending rapidly. In the half-light he struggled to find secure footing and feared that he might tumble. Suddenly, he found himself in the open. He stopped, drew breath and looked around.

He was in a large bowl, wooded on all sides. In the centre of the bowl was the Lough. Almost circular. Over a hundred yards in diameter. Inky black but for a fringe of green slimy bloom along the margins. The reflections of white clouds punctuated the surface. To the south the hills rose beyond the woods. One of the fields had recently been mown, the stripe of yellow stubble stark against the surrounding green. He could just make out a motionless figure standing at the top of the field staring in his direction. A lookout?

He waited for five minutes. It was chilly here, especially when the sun slipped behind a cloud. He turned up the collar of his jacket and pulled it tighter around him. When Caton had all but given up, a figure stepped out from the woods twenty yards to his right. It was a man, at least twenty years older than himself. He wore a green parka with a hood, over black jeans. Inappropriate for the season, but making perfect sense down here beside the Lough. Perfect camouflage too. When it was obvious that the man had no intention of coming to him, Caton set off towards him.

Chapter 28

Lived in, was an expression that Caton thought overused, but it certainly applied to the face of Gerry MacMahon. A full six inches shorter than Caton, his body looked strong and wiry, much younger than that face. Every wrinkle around the eyes and mouth, every furrow across the brow, told of tortuous decisions made. Of proud success and haunting failure. There were shadows behind the intelligent eyes that studied Caton.

'You're police,' he said. 'From over the water?'

His voice had the gravel-like quality of a heavy smoker. His accent was hard to place. Part West of Scotland, part South of the Border.

Caton held out his warrant card.

'Yes. From Manchester.'

MacMahon glanced at it and handed it back.

'Caton. Is that the English or the Irish Catons?'

'Both,' Caton told him. 'Originally from Caton-with-Litterdale, in the Trough of Bowland. Then into County Kerry.'

He nodded.

'The Irish Catons round here were part of the Protestant settlements,' he said, as though it was only yesterday, not five hundred years ago.

MacMahon cleared his throat and spat into the lake.

'From Manchester then?'

'Yes.'

'You're not with the HET then?'

Like there was a smell under his nose.

'No,' said Caton, giving nothing away.

'That's something I suppose. They're not worth the shit on my shoe. Did you know they've been protecting their own?'

'I've seen the allegations.'

He snorted.

'Allegations my arse. Did you know there'll be no inquiry into the massacre of innocent civilians by the British Army in Ballymurphy in '71?'

Belfast's very own Bloody Sunday.

'I had heard,' said Caton.

'So much for Historical Enquiries then. So much for impartial.'

'There'll be no inquiry into the burning to death of civilians at the La Mon Hotel by the IRA in '78 either,' said Caton.

It was an instinctive, pathetic, unnecessary response. Unhelpful. He regretted it as soon as he'd said it. Too late to take it back now. MacMahon's response surprised him. The IRA man smiled.

'That's just to justify not owning up to Ballymurphy,' he said. 'Brits' tricks.'

Caton thought he was probably right. He said as much.

MacMahon appraised him anew.

'So you're not part of that bollocks?'

'No.'

'Then what's your interest?'

'There's been a murder. On my patch. In Manchester. We think it may be connected.'

'So you want to know who slaughtered that family at Malon Farm?'

'Yes.'

MacMahon made sure he had eye contact. He paused for effect.

'Well, it wasn't us. They were our weapons Michael was hiding. Why would we be killing him? And I never believed it was the UVF neither. In fact, they swore to me it wasn't them or the UDA. If it had been them they'd have been crowing about it.'

He raised thick wiry eyebrows, streaked with grey.

'We all knew it was the security forces.'

'The security forces?'

He nodded.

'Or loyalists embedded within the security forces. We thought it was the Glenanne Gang, but we couldn't prove it. They've since denied it, and it's never been attributed to them.'

He paused.

'Did you look them up like I told you?'

'Yes.'

'You'll know what I'm talking about then.'

'So who do you think it was?' said Caton.

'At first we thought it was the security forces in revenge for Narrow Water.'

'Narrow Water?'

'Warrenpoint?'

Caton nodded. Eighteen members of the Parachute Regiment blown up and shot in an ambush by the IRA South Armagh Brigade. The worst loss of military life in the province in a single incident. On the same day that Lord Mountbatten, the Queen's cousin, was assassinated in Mullaghmore a hundred and fifty miles to the west.

'August 1979,' he said. 'Just a few months before the murders at Malon Farm.'

'27th of August,' said MacMahon. 'A little over a month. So you can see why we thought there was a connection. The security forces were edgy, trigger happy, out for revenge. But we never found out if we were right or not, which was odd, because we had plenty of people on the inside.'

'Of the security forces?'

'Yeah.'

'Which ones?'

MacMahon laughed.

'The lot of them,' he replied. 'The UDR, RUC, Special Branch, and especially the Det.'

'So who do you think it was?'

He shrugged.

'A rogue unit. Small enough not to be on anyone's radar, and tight enough to keep silent all this time.' His smile was rueful. 'Just like a PIRA cell. We were desperate to find out – with being blamed for it – but we never did.'

He shook his head as though chasing demons away.

'I helped to clear up the mess.'

'You were there?'

'Not at the farm. Not at first. But not far away. Over the border.'

'You know about the girls then?'

'The girls?'

'Caitlin and Finnoula.'

MacMahon's eyes narrowed. Surprise and suspicion suffused his face.

'How the hell do you know about them?'

'Because they are the reason I'm here. It was one of them that was murdered in Manchester a week ago.'

'Murdered, how?'

'Shot in the head, and in the heart.'

He nodded sadly.

'Executed,' he said.

He searched Caton's eyes.

'Which one?'

'Caitlin.'

He flinched.

'The youngest,' he said. He crossed himself and muttered an invocation.

'We think it's connected,' Caton told him. 'We believe that Finnoula may be at risk. We need to find her.'

MacMahon turned his head and stared out across the Lough. Caton waited patiently, letting him weigh up his options. Out of a clear sky appeared a flight of swallows, swooping in turn to skim the water. The former IRA man seemed not to notice. Somewhere in the woods a warbler trilled a high-pitched warning. And repeated it. And again. Finally, the man turned.

'We were close when it happened,' he said. 'We'd been going to get some weapons for an operation, but we learned that the Brits had had it under surveillance for two days. So we laid up to see what happened. We heard shooting, and I made the decision to get out of there. We were back over the border when word came that the family had been slaughtered, but there were two survivors.'

'Word came?' said Caton. 'From whom?'

He smiled thinly.

'Now that would be telling.'

'My guess is one of the neighbours, or more likely one of the constables,' said Caton.

A gleam in the man's eye told Caton he had hit the mark.

'It isn't relevant,' said MacMahon. 'We got those poor cailín beags out of there and into safe hands.'

'Sister Monica and Sister Agatha,' said Caton.

This time the man's expression was a mixture of surprise and respect.

'You've done your homework.'

'We know that the parish priest, and Henry Hoey the judge, helped to arrange the adoptions,' Caton told him. 'We've even met Caitlin's adoptive parents.'

He nodded sagely.

'And then you hit a brick wall?'

'Until now.'

MacMahon thrust his hands deep into his trouser pockets.

'I don't know where she is exactly,' he said. 'Finnoula. But I know through a cut-out that she's safe. Once a year I'm told. That was the arrangement.'

His eyes clouded over.

'The other cut-out, across the water, lost track of Caitlin some years back. Now the parents know, I suppose she'll be contacting me anytime now to tell me what you've just told me.'

'Can you arrange for us to meet her, Finnoula?'

Slowly and deliberately, MacMahon shook his head.

'She'll have forgotten all about it,' he said. 'Her adoptive parents were never told anything. Only that it was a tragedy best forgotten, best never spoken of. That it was the only way to keep her safe.'

'Caitlin's parents were told the same,' Caton replied. 'It wasn't enough to keep her safe.'

The former IRA man looked down at his feet, wrestling with the inescapable logic. If they had found one, then why not the other? When he raised his head Caton could see that he had won. MacMahon fixed him with hard, cold eyes that hinted of the pitiless anger that had driven him to eliminate those he saw as legitimate enemies.

'We do it my way,' he said. 'Through my cut-out. If Finnoula doesn't want to meet you or talk to you, that's it. Her choice. Do you understand?'

'Of course,' said Caton. 'But I think she will.'

'What makes you so sure? You don't even know her.'

'She was seven years old when it happened. Too old to simply forget. She knows that she has a sister who also survived. When she hears what happened to Caitlin she'll want to help us.'

'You can't know that.'

'Maybe not, but there's only one way to find out. Like you said, her choice.'

MacMahon half-turned to his left and then back to his right. He was less concerned about checking for watchers Caton decided, it was more about playing for time.

'Do they know you're here?' said MacMahon. 'That you're doing this?'

'They?' said Caton.

'The HET, the PSNI, the Security Services?'

'All three,' Caton told him.

He nodded.

'Tell one, you tell them all.'

He pulled something from his pocket and handed it to Caton. It was a mobile phone.

'I'll contact you on this,' he said. 'They'll be listening into yours, however secure you think it is.'

'How will I contact you?' asked Caton.

'You won't. Don't even try. If she wants to hear what you have to say, I'll let you know.'

'What if she doesn't?'

'I'll tell you that too. Then it's over.'

Caton could tell that it was pointless arguing with him. MacMahon turned to go.

'Please,' said Caton, 'just one more question?'

The former IRA man turned.

'What?'

'Who was the UDA commander you spoke to?'

He scowled.

'My word's not good enough then? I told you, they had nothing to do with it.'

'I believe you,' said Caton. 'It's just that if you're right about a rogue unit with links to the loyalists, he may know things he didn't share with you at the time.'

MacMahon looked sceptical.

'And you think he'll share them with you?'

Caton shrugged.

'It's worth a try.'

Once again the man surprised him.

'I can arrange a meet if you like?'

'You can do that?'

He grinned.

'He's retired now, like me. We've more in common than you think.'

'Just like Gusty Spence said at the funeral of your colleague, Jim Lynch?'

If he was surprised that Caton had taken the trouble to check him out that fully, he didn't show it.

'Exactly.'

He turned and walked towards the wood.

Caton could not resist it. He called after him.

'So you've both renounced the use of violence for political ends?'

'Now you're pushing your luck, Mr Caton,' he said without breaking stride. 'And there's precious little of that over here.'

Chapter 29

Caton waited for five minutes. The figure on the hill had disappeared. The sky had clouded over and was threatening rain. He retraced his steps.

The gate was open. The Enigma, complete with driver and passenger, had gone. Caton drove out onto the lane, got out, closed the gate and climbed back in again. He set his own satnav for Drumboy Road and switched on the engine.

Less than ten minutes later, he had arrived. He faced two problems. The first was that, try as they might, neither he nor DI Stuart had been able to find an address for Malon Farm. The second was that Drumboy Road consisted of one and a half miles, divided in the middle by a sharp right-hand bend, along which were close to twenty substantial properties. Many were relatively new, set back from the road behind low walls and metal gates, some of which were electrified. At least five looked like working farms, but it was clear that many of the newer properties had been built on land where farms previously stood. All of the buildings were cared for. The hedges neatly trimmed. They radiated a sense of pride, and better than modest incomes. After driving up and down the road several times he chose what he took to be one of the oldest farms, and pulled up outside.

The woman who answered the door eyed him with suspicion. She was in her forties he guessed and, judging by her manner, either the owner or the farmer's wife.

'Malon Farm?' she said. 'You're wasting your time. It no longer exists.'

She edged back a tad into the hall, one hand pressed against the wall to prevent him from entering.

'Are you another one of those journalists?' she said. 'Poking around like ghouls.'

He showed her his warrant card.

She glanced at it and shook her head.

'You're thirty odd years too late,' she said.

'I assumed the farm was no longer here,' he told her. 'I was hoping to find someone who lived in the vicinity of Malon Farm back then.'

'That would be my mother,' she said.

'Is it possible to speak with her?'

'I doubt it,' she said. 'She's been dead these past six years.'

'I'm sorry.'

'Why's that then? You never knew her. You don't know me.'

She was not reproaching him. Her tone was neutral. She was simply letting him know he couldn't charm her round. Undeterred, he pressed on.

'You were a child at the time,' he said. 'Were you not here, with your mother?'

A ghost of a smile flitted across her face.

'Detective, is it?' she said. 'Not that it would take a smart one to figure that out.'

'So you were here?'

'I was at my granny's in Crossmaglen when it happened,' she said. 'So you're wasting your time.'

She began to close the door.

Caton placed one foot over the sill.

'But you must have known Finnoula and Caitlin,' he said.

She froze. Her expression reflected shock, and then anxiety.

'What do you know of them?' she asked, her voice wavering.

'Then? Very little. But right now, far more than you think, Mrs…?'

'Connolly,' she said. 'Teresa Connolly.'

She opened the door wide.

'Show me that identification.'

She took her time reading it, handed it back and retreated into the hall.

'You'd best come in then,' she said.

'Would you like some more tea?' she asked, reaching for the pot.

Caton drained his cup and handed it to her.

'Thank you, Mrs Connolly.'

'And can I tempt you with another piece of fruit cake?'

'It was delicious,' he told her, 'but I don't think I could manage any more. That was a gradely slice.'

'Gradely?'

'It's a Northern expression. It means fine, good, decent, or in this case humungous.'

She handed him his cup back.

'Gradely. I like that. I'll be adding it to the Ulster lexicon.'

He blew on his tea to cool it.

'Speaking of definitions,' he said, 'why do you call it boiled fruit cake?'

She smiled.

'It's only the fruit, the butter and the sugar that get boiled before being added to the flour and eggs. Then it's baked the normal way.'

'There's was something else though,' he said. He

sipped his tea. 'A touch of this?'

'You're right,' she said. 'I steep a bag of Earl Grey in the boiled water. A trick my granny taught me.'

'Earl Grey,' he said. 'Didn't he vote against Home Rule?'

She nodded.

'But that's not all we remember him for. It was his scheme that helped four thousand adolescent girls flee an gorta Mór.'

She noted his expression.

'The Great Famine. The first of the ships to take them to Australia, in June 1948, was called the Earl Grey. All the girls on the first two crossings were from Ulster.'

A silence descended on the room. They were both thinking about two other girls who had fled from Ulster. And they both knew that the tea and cake and inconsequential conversation had been about avoidance. Teresa Connolly had guessed that he was not the bearer of good news. After all these years she was loath to hear of another unhappy ending.

She placed the cake on the tray together with her empty plate and cup and saucer. Caton handed her his. She stood, and took them away. He heard the rattle as she placed them on the kitchen table. He imagined her standing there looking out of the window. Putting off the inevitable. Finally, she came back into the room and sat down opposite him. He could tell that she had steeled herself.

'Tell me,' she said.

He told her enough, but not everything. She listened in silence, dabbing her eyes from time to time with a handkerchief that she took from the pocket of her apron. When he had finished she blew her nose, folded the handkerchief neatly and placed it back in her pocket.

'I was at my granny's,' she said. 'My mother came to stay with us that night. She was in bits. I heard her telling Granny what happened. I couldn't believe it. I'd played with the Malones all my life. I was in the same class as Patrick, the eldest of the boys. I was great friends with Finnoula. Like a big sister to Caitlin. I wept all night. And the following day.'

'Did you know that Finnoula and Caitlin had survived?'

She shook her head.

'Not at first. But a few days later, when my mother saw that I was inconsolable, she let me in on the secret. She said if I ever told a single person they would end up being killed, and I would burn in hell.'

'Did you?' he asked. 'Tell?'

'No,' she said. 'It was the hardest secret I ever kept. Until now.'

She looked down at her hands folded in her lap.

'And still Caitlin was killed.'

'Her death is not on your conscience,' he said.

She looked up. If it had been her own child she could not have looked more sorrowful.

'No,' she replied. She placed her hand over her heart. 'But it is in here.'

Caton waited until she had composed herself.

'We'll catch whoever killed her,' he said. 'And possibly whoever killed the rest of her family. And at least Finnoula is still alive.'

She stood up.

'I suppose you'll want to see where it happened?'

They stood on a small hillock, less than three hundred yards from the farmhouse.

'It was our neighbouring farm,' she said. 'After it happened, it slowly began to fall into disrepair.'

'What about relatives?'

'There were only a couple in America, and a second cousin in Australia. They didn't want to know. Hardly surprising after what happened. In the end my father was allowed to buy it for a pittance. He pulled it down before it fell down. He kept the barn for a while. But as you can see, even that has gone.'

Caton looked around him. The only signs that something might have stood there was the unevenness of the ground, and the faintest trace of the former farm track between here and a gate in the hedge bordering the road.

Try as he might, he had no sense of how it might have been on that night. In truth, he was glad of that.

'Will your husband be with you tonight?' he asked as they walked slowly back.

'He's away in Bundoran for the week, playing golf with his pals,' she said. 'It's the only break he gets all year. It wouldn't be fair to disturb him.'

They stopped beside his car.

'Will you be alright, Teresa?' he asked.

She smiled wanly.

'I'll be fine,' she said. 'On one condition.'

'Go on.'

'Promise me you'll keep Finnoula safe?'

He took her hands in his.

'You remember the oath you swore to your mother? The one you kept despite everything?'

She nodded.

'Well, I promise you I'll do everything I can to make sure that Finnoula comes safely out of this.'

'Thank you,' she said.

He watched her waving as he drove away, and fervently hoped that his everything would be enough.

Chapter 30

He was five miles from the A1 when the promised rain arrived with a vengeance. Menacing black clouds unleashed a torrent that hammered the roof of his car and cascaded down the windscreen. His wipers were overwhelmed. The ditches on either side filled with miraculous speed, spilling over into the fields and onto the road. He had no option but to pull into the nearest passing space and wait it out. He killed the engine, made sure that his parking lights were on in case some foolhardy motorist decided to chance it and failed to see the Skoda in time. He reclined his chair and closed his eyes.

When he awoke, the rain had lessened. He checked his watch. It was five p.m. He levered the seat upright, switched on the engine and was about to set off when his phone rang. He reached into his right-hand pocket, then realised that it wasn't his phone. This was a different ringtone. Harsh and insistent. It was the one that MacMahon had given him. He found it and took the call.

'That was quick,' he said.

'You're in luck,' said MacMahon. 'He'll see you. Not only that, he'll see you now.'

'Where?' said Caton.

'It's on your way back, only you'll have to make a little detour.'

'How much of a detour?'

'Just a couple o' hundred yards.' MacMahon's laugh was hollow. 'Wasn't that what they told the 36th Ulster Division at the Battle of the Somme?'

'I wouldn't know,' Caton replied.

'Four VCs they got given. Your man will tell you all about it if you ask him. And if you play your cards right, you may get a medal yourself.'

'Is there an address, or a postcode?' said Caton.

He laughed again.

'You're joking, aren't you? Just leave your phone switched on. I'll ring you when you're near.'

'Okay,' said Caton, wondering how they would know when he was near.

'And that medal,' said MacMahon.

'Yes?'

'Let's hope it's not posthumous.'

Caton called DI Stuart to bring her up to speed.

'It sounds really dodgy, boss,' she told him. 'Do you want me to come and join you?'

'Since I've no idea where this meeting is going to be,' he said, 'I can't see how you could. In any case, he's only expecting me. If you turn up too it may spook him completely. Then he won't talk to either of us.'

'Well, as soon as you know where you're meeting him make sure you call and tell me,' she said. 'Then at least if it goes belly-up I'll know where to send the PSNI.'

The image of him floating belly-up like a fish in some Irish Loch stayed with him for the rest of the journey. After all, as Helen Gates had been at great pains to remind him, the terrorist threat level in Northern Ireland was still severe and had been since 2010, despite the progress that had been made. This year alone there had been seven incidents – two fatal shootings, pipe bombs, the letter bombs and a mortar bomb discovered. But, he reasoned, they had all been the work of dissident republicans. He was going to meet the other side. They had been quiet recently. Surely they would not see him as a threat. In any case, the man he was going to meet had retired, hadn't he?

These thoughts, and others like them, plagued him all the way to the outskirts of Belfast. Which was when the mobile phone rang.

'Leave the motorway at the next exit,' he was told. 'At the roundabout, take the third exit. At the next roundabout at the Westicle sculpture, big balls to you and I, take the third exit onto Donegal Road. After half a mile there's a Texaco garage. Pull in and check your oil.'

'That's it?'

'Did you get all that?' MacMahon replied curtly.

'I did,' Caton told him.

'Good. Then just do it.'

The call was terminated.

Caton looked in his rear-view mirror, just as he had been doing throughout the journey. There were no obvious suspects. Certainly none that had been following him for any length of time. Perhaps they'd had someone waiting closer to the city. Watching for the make and registration. He thought that unlikely on a motorway. In any case, it was not relevant how they knew, only that they did. The exit sign loomed ahead. He signalled, took the slip road and followed the instructions.

At the second roundabout the name MacMahon had given it became clear. It was dominated by two huge geodesic spheres, white and silver globes, supported by slender steel stanchions. The exit he had been told to take was marked City Hospital, Shaftesbury Square [Donegal Road]. A loyalist flag flew high above the sign. There was another on the next lamppost. He was entering South Belfast.

A little further on, Caton pulled into the garage and stopped outside the attached Spar supermarket. He lifted his bonnet and removed the oil filler cap. He was pretending to inspect the oil level on the rod when a man emerged from the supermarket and sauntered over.

'How're you?' he asked. His accent was broad and solid, like the city.

'I'm fine,' said Caton.

The man spat onto the ground beside him.

'Stickin' out is what you say if you want to blend in,' he said. 'Now give me the phone.'

For a second Caton wondered if this was a mugging, unconnected to the reason he was here. Then he saw the knowing look in the man's eyes. He took the phone from his pocket and handed it over. The man put it in his own pocket and handed Caton a slip of paper.

'Your instructions are on there,' he said. 'You're to walk. Your car will still be here when you get back.'

'Walk? Is that really necessary?' said Caton.

The man's expression hardened.

'If you want to meet your man it is. And take it from me, it's more in your interest that the two of you are not seen together than it is in his.'

With that he turned, walked over to a black Golf that had followed Caton into the garage and was now parked up beside the boundary fence, and got into the passenger side.

Caton replaced the rod and filler cap, closed the bonnet and alarmed the car. He could feel the three men in the Golf watching him as he walked across the forecourt and out onto Donegal Road. He took consolation in the fact that they were watching his car too.

This was like any other gentrified street in the United Kingdom wending its way towards a city centre. A significant artery improved to present the best face of the city to a visitor fresh from the motorway. A street where the best of nineteenth-century architecture had been retained, the worst demolished to be replaced by modern maisonettes and high-profile facilities such as the City Hospital, which he was approaching on his right. A fifteen-storey-high square pod, clad in yellow wood, proudly declaring modernity and expertise. Immediately opposite the hospital was one of the waypoints mentioned in his instructions. A faux Gothic Edwardian building in brick and stone. A sign advertising office space informed him that this had been the Carnegie Library. In many ways this street reminded Caton of Princess Parkway back in Manchester.

One hundred yards further on was the second waypoint. A modern glass and redbrick building with large blue letters declaring it to be the Sandy Row Rangers Supporters Club. He checked the piece of paper, and turned left into Sandy Row. On the end gable wall were painted two impressive murals. The first was of a life-size George Best about to strike a football. Details of his greatest soccer triumphs surrounded him. The second mural was a memorial to Robert Dougan. His image had pride of place in the centre. To the left was the badge of the UDA, to the right that of the UFF. The inscription left Caton in no doubt as to whose territory he was in.

In Proud Memory of Our Fallen Comrade.
Murdered By The Enemies. 10th February 1998.
Gone But Not Forgotten.
South Belfast Brigade.

The last time he had felt this exposed was walking the streets in Moss Side immediately following the riots in 1981, and the siege of the police station at the heart of them. Common sense told him that he was far safer here now than he had been then, and he had come through that unscathed. Nevertheless, he decided to text Joanne Stuart to let her know where he was right now. It wasn't something he wanted to advertise. Using his phone could easily be interpreted as calling for support. As far as he could tell, no one had been following him, but as a precaution he stepped into the gap between the end wall and the next house, and sent the text. When he had finished he left his phone on silent, stepped out onto the pavement, and then proceeded as instructed.

Even this street, he reflected, had much in common with South Manchester. The Victorian and Edwardian terraces, the eclectic mix of corner shops, and bookies, tailors and fast-food outlets. He could easily be in Rusholme, or Moss Side. Except that he wasn't.

The last waypoint appeared. He turned right down a narrow street, his apprehension mounting.

On the right was the high wall of a factory. On the left was a wooden fence behind which he assumed building was taking place. Ten metres ahead of him a door opened in the fence, and a man stepped out into his path. He stood several inches taller than Caton, and was broader and more muscular. He wore a black windcheater over black jeans, and ankle-high black boots. Curly ginger hair, shoulder length, framed a sallow face and pale-blue eyes. He looked confident. This was his turf.

'You're Caton,' he said.

It wasn't a question. Caton merely nodded.

The man stabbed his hand towards the hole where the door had been.

'In here,' he said.

Chapter 31

A patch of land half the size of a football pitch. Houses had been demolished. The bricks had been bulldozed, crushed and compacted to form a temporary car park. On the far side of the perimeter fence Caton could see two wooden booths, each beside an identical pair of metal gates. Strange, then, that at this moment there were just three vehicles parked in the centre of the space in a loose triangle, nose to tail. A white Transit van, a smart black Audi saloon and a battered red Seat Leon. He turned to look at the doorkeeper who had fallen in behind him. The man urged him forward with a thrust of his chin.

As Caton approached, the passenger doors of the van and the Seat opened. A man emerged from each, and stood, arms folded, beside his vehicle. Identically dressed to their colleague stalking Caton from behind, they cleared intended to project a sense of menace. The comedic juxtaposition of their respective frames had the reverse effect on Caton, who had already christened them Fat Van Man and Little Leon.

The passenger door of the Audi opened. A man built like a bouncer, of the compact variety, materialised. He opened the rear door of the saloon and gestured for Caton to get in. As he ducked, a hand grasped the crown of his head and pushed down firmly. Less, he suspected, to help him avoid cracking his skull on the window moulding, than to demonstrate his isolation and powerlessness. The door slammed shut. He heard the click as locks engaged.

'Youse are Caton.'

With his pale complexion, watery blue eyes and ginger stubble peppered with grey on an otherwise bald pate, the man seated beside him could easily have been the father of the one that had opened the gate. Probably was. Or his grandfather.

'You've got balls, I'll say that fer yer.'

'I was told that I could trust you,' Caton replied.

'Were you now?'

'I was.'

A slight raise of the eyebrows.

'Well, isn't that nice? You know what they say?'

'No?'

The man in the driving seat laughed and glanced at Caton in the rear-view mirror.

'Never trust anyone,' he said with the voice of a life-long smoker.

'I thought everyone knew that,' said the man beside him.

'Sometimes you don't have a choice,' said Caton.

A shake of the head.

'You always have a choice.'

He stared out of the window at Fat Van Man and Little Leon leaning against the bonnet of the Seat, smoking hand-rolled cigarettes.

'I'll tell you what me father told me, the first time he took me down to the beach at Bushfoot Strand,' he said. '"If you're going to swim in these waters, Willie, you'd better keep your wits about you. There a currents hereabouts that'll pull you down and sweep you out where the sharks are waiting to pick you clean."'

'Willie?' said Caton.

The man turned to look at him, held his gaze, and then smiled.

'Willie-John Denny,' he said. 'You'd only look me up anyway. And you'll have no trouble getting hold of my life history, will he, Sam?'

'He will not, Willie,' came the reply. 'Wikipedia, Facebook, YouTube, sure you'll be on Twitter next.'

'So, if you have nothing to fear from me, nor I from you, why all the secrecy?' said Caton. 'Why all these precautions?'

Denny sighed.

'To protect the two of us, Mr Caton. To protect you and me.'

'From whom?'

'Now that's a very good question, isn't it, Sam?'

'It is that, Willie. It is that.'

'Let's start with me then, shall we?' said Denny. 'There are young bloods out there, hotheads like I used to be in my youth, who will be wondering why Willie-John Denny would be speaking with a British detective from over the water. Hotheads on both sides who still believe that the bullet and the bomb are the answer to our problems. And then there are my business partners. But we'll not be going into that, will we, Sam?'

In the mirror, a shake of the head.

'We will not, Willie-John. We most certainly will not.'

'What about me?' said Caton. 'From whom do I need protecting?'

'Now that's an even more interesting question,' Denny replied. 'If we knew that there wouldn't be a need for this meeting, now would there? In fact, I'm as interested as you to discover the answer to that question. As is my good friend, Gerry MacMahon.'

'You're very much alike,' said Caton.

'Why wouldn't we be?' said Denny. 'We're both Ulstermen. We both care with a passion about justice and freedom. Back in the day, we just saw it from different perspectives.'

He took a paper bag from his pocket and offered it to Caton.

'Would you like a Liquorice Twist?'

'No thanks,' said Caton.

'What about yourself, Sam?'

'No thanks, Willie,' he replied. 'I've given them up till Lent.'

The two of them had a laugh at that. The driver's became a fit of coughing. Denny popped a liquorice into his own mouth.

'Do youse know how we met?' he said. 'Gerry and me?'

'No,' Caton replied.

'In The Maze. RAF Long Kesh?'

Caton nodded.

'They were supposed to keep us apart in the H Blocks, but we got talking through the wire.' As he sucked his sweet, a melancholy expression crept over his face. 'Best thing about being locked away is that it gives you time to think. Sometimes, when you're too busy doing, you lose sight of the bigger picture.'

Caton was finding it hard not to let his impatience show. He was tempted to tell Denny to forget the history lesson and the self-absorbed trip down memory lane, but experience told him otherwise.

'Do you know the Famous Five?' said Denny.

Caton had no idea where this was going. 'Enid Blyton?' he said.

That set the two of them off laughing again.

'Enid Blyton! That's a good one,' said Denny. 'We'll have to remember that one, Sam. That's a cracker, that is. Enid Blyton!'

The smile vanished as quickly as it had come.

'I'm talking about the Famous Five techniques they used to try and make us talk,' he said. 'Do youse know about them?'

Caton thought he had a pretty good idea, but the question sounded rhetorical.

'Of course you don't,' said Denny, 'because you weren't there. And if you had been, you'd have been the one using them, and we wouldn't be sitting here having this nice cosy chat, now would we?'

'I suppose not,' said Caton.

'You suppose right,' replied the former UDA brigade commander.

His eyes never left Caton's, but they seemed to stare right through him to another place. His voice had changed too. Flatter, robotic, almost distant.

'Each time before they were going to interrogate us, they deprived us of food and drink. Not completely, just enough to make us hungry, thirsty, dehydrated. At the same time they deprived us of sleep by waking us up at regular intervals so we never really got any. Then they put us in a room filled with a loud continuous hissing sound. White noise, they call it now. Even if you put your hands over your ears you could still hear it. It made you feel like yer head was going to burst. Then when you couldn't take any more, they'd put a hood over your head and spread-eagle you against a wall. Your fingertips so high up that wall and your feet so far back, you had to stand on tippy-toe to stop you falling flat on your face. The pain in your wrists, your arms, your shoulders, your back, your calves, was indescribable. When you got the cramps, which was all the time, and fell to the floor curled up in a ball, screaming with pain, they'd straighten you out and shove you back up against that wall. Only when you'd been through all that would the bastards start the interrogation.'

His gaze seemed to retreat until it was focused clearly on Caton again.

'That's what Gerry and I both went through,' he said. 'Where do you think the Americans got the idea for Guantanamo Bay from, Mr Caton? And I tell yer something, when you've been through that together it forges bonds that'll cross any political divide.'

'I can understand that,' said Caton.

His voice hardened.

'No, you can't. Because you weren't there.'

Caton knew that he deserved that. 'You're right,' he said. 'I apologise.'

Denny shook his head.

'I wasn't looking for an apology. What I'm trying to tell you is that it's the same guys that were doing that to us that murdered that family at Malon Farm. That's who you need protection from.'

'You know that for a fact?'

The driver snorted. Denny took a deep breath and then exhaled slowly.

'I'll tell you what I know as facts,' he said.

He leaned closer to Caton, raised a clenched fist and extended one digit at a time as he counted them off.

'Number one, it wasn't us. Number two, it wasn't Gerry's boys. Number three, there was a Brit observation on the farm that night that was mysteriously called off shortly before the attack. Number four, there was a Det' patrol in the vicinity that night that conveniently turned up shortly after the local Guard, and took over the search of the farm. And, number five, nobody was ever fingered for it. No one.'

He raised his other fist, extended the little finger and wagged it to and fro.

'And, number six, now you have one of the wee girls rescued from that massacre murdered with a Service revolver…'

He stayed Caton's interruption with the palm of his left hand.

'…with a Service revolver, just as the Historical Enquiries Team is being investigated for a partisan approach to their review and investigation of cold cases.' He paused for three beats. 'Like the killings at Malon Farm.'

He lowered his hands and sat back in his seat.

'You're the detective, Mr Caton. You tell me who your money's on.'

'Everything you say leads back to the Security Services,' said Caton, 'I can see that. But I get the sense that it's more than surmise on your part. That there's something you're not telling me.'

'Surmise,' said Denny. 'That's a good word that one, isn't it, Sam?'

'It is that, Willie. Is that what you call an educated word?'

'It is indeed, Sam. An educated word.'

Denny stared thoughtfully at Caton. The fingers of both hands drummed lightly on his thighs like a pianist trying out a tune for the first time. The drumming stopped. Caton could tell that he had arrived at a decision.

'Just like they had informers in our ranks…'

'FRU grasses!' The driver spat it out again. 'Bastard grasses!'

'So we had our own intelligence officers in theirs.'

Caton noted the neat distinction he had made between the two.

'In the RUC?' Caton guessed.

Denny smiled.

'And the UDR, and Special Branch.'

'And?'

'And nothing,' said Denny. 'All they knew was that a blanket had been thrown over the whole thing. No one was saying anything for sure. Only that the official line was that it was either Gerry's lads or ours, and nobody seemed interested in finding out which of us it was. That was the giveaway. They knew there wasn't any point investigating, because they already knew it was neither of us. The RUC were told to turn over their case notes to Special Branch at Bessbrook Mill and leave the investigation to them and Army Intelligence. That was the last anyone heard of it. Apart from the press statements blaming it all on us.'

Caton could see movement outside. Fat Van Man had turned and was looking over his shoulder. Little Leon tossed his butt on the ground and began to open the Seat's passenger door. There was a rap on the roof of the Audi.

'Time to go, Mr Caton,' said Willie-John Denny. 'It's been nice talking with yer.'

Before Caton could reply, the door beside him opened wide. A hand reached in and grasped his shoulder.

'Thank you,' he said as he was pulled bodily from the car.

The door slammed. The engines of all three cars started up in unison. The rear passenger window retracted. Caton leaned down to look inside.

'Watch your backs, Mr Caton,' said Denny. 'You and your lady friend. And one more thing. Let us know when you find out who did it, and what the fuck's going on right now.' He smiled grimly. 'Unless of course we find out first.'

The window rose silently. Caton found himself spun round. A hand in his back propelled him towards the fence. He began to walk.

When he reached the door in the fence he turned. The car park was empty. Both of the booths were occupied. A young man, almost a boy, was sitting in the exit booth, an older man in the one at entrance. A car swung into the entrance and stopped. Money changed hands. The car drove forward and parked alongside the perimeter fence. Caton stepped out onto the pavement and retraced his steps.

His car was still there on the forecourt. The VW Golf was not. He was tempted to get down on his knees and look under the bumpers, the engine block and the wheel arches. He told himself he was being paranoid. He unlocked the car and got in. A cursory search reassured him that no one had been inside the car. He crossed his fingers and started the engine.

Chapter 32

DI Stuart had news of her own. She was unusually animated. He couldn't decide if it was driven by excitement or anxiety.

'You won't believe this,' she said. 'I got a phone call.' She held up her mobile phone. 'On this.'

'Who from?' said a puzzled Caton.

'Someone called MacMahon, Gerry MacMahon.'

'How did he get your number?'

'That's what I wanted to know.'

'What did he say?'

'He told me to shut up and listen.'

'That sounds like MacMahon.'

It was her turn to look puzzled.

'You know him?'

'It turns out that's who I was going to meet.'

'You gave him my phone number?'

'No, I didn't. And I've no idea how he could have got it. Although after the day I've had nothing would surprise me.'

She put her phone down on the bedside table.

'Well try this for size,' she said. 'Your Mr MacMahon has only gone and found Finnoula Malone!'

Caton nodded.

She sat down on the bed. Her enthusiasm evaporated.

'You already know, don't you?'

'He told me that he knew where she was, and that he'd find out if she was prepared to talk to us.'

'Well, she is. He's given her my number and he said to leave it switched on because she'll call. And not to try to trace her number, because if we do, he'll know. Can he do that?'

He shrugged.

'Probably. Like I said, after today nothing would surprise me any more.'

He sat down beside her.

'In that case,' she said, 'you'd better tell me all about it.'

They were laughing about him wondering if he should search under his car when her phone rang. Caller unknown. She offered him the phone.

'You take it,' he said.

She swiped to answer, cranked up the volume and held the phone to her ear.

'Hello?' she said.

'Hello?' Tentative. Female. North American, with a hint of Irish.

She looked at Caton and nodded. He nodded back.

'I'm DI Stuart,' she said. 'Are you Finnoula?'

They heard a gasp, as though someone had been punched in the solar plexus. They waited.

'Frances,' came the hesitant reply. 'Frances Fenton. That's who I am now.'

'Is that what you'd like me to call you?'

'Yes.'

There was an uneasy silence.

'You know why we would like to meet with you?' said Joanne Stuart.

'Yes.'

A beat.

'Because…'

Another beat.

'Because of … Caitlin.'

Her voice was heavy with emotion. Little wonder, Caton reflected. Bad enough to lose your parents and your brothers in that way, but then to be torn from your home, your country and your sister, only to learn that she too had been brutally murdered. He could not begin to imagine what that must feel like.

'I am so sorry, Frances,' said Joanne Stuart.

'Thank you.'

Stuart put her hand over the phone to mask the microphone.

'How are we going to do this?' she whispered.

'Ask her where it's best for her to meet us,' he said.

She removed her hand and spoke into the phone.

'We are in Belfast at the moment,' she said. 'But we'll be returning to Manchester shortly. Where would it be best for you to meet us?'

'I am in Montreal,' she replied. 'Visiting my parents. But I work in Belfast. I'm flying back at the weekend, but I'd rather meet you in Manchester.'

A beat of three.

'I want to see Caitlin.'

Another beat.

'Can I do that?'

'Of course you can, Frances. You can meet her adoptive parents too, if you'd like to?'

'Yes, I would. Very much.'

'Good. We'll arrange that then, Frances. You ring me when you know which flight you're on, and we'll come and meet you at the airport.'

'You'll come and meet me?'

'That's right. With my boss, Detective Chief Inspector Caton. He's with me now.'

Another uneasy silence. Stuart was wondering whether she should say something, but Caton shook his head and put his finger on his lips.

'Have you been to the farm?' Frances Fenton said at last. For the first time her voice was firm and steady, as though she had been steeling herself.

Stuart looked at Caton. He nodded.

'I haven't, but my boss has.'

'I've never been back,' she said. 'I've often wondered if I should. You know, living that close. If it might chase the ghosts away?'

They could tell that she was really talking to herself. That no reply was required.

'I can't tell you anything about her,' she continued. 'About Caitlin. About her life.'

'We don't need you to, Frances,' Stuart replied. 'That's not why we want to talk with you.'

A longer silence.

'I was only seven,' she said. 'I'm not sure I can help you.'

Caton gestured urgently for the phone. Stuart handed it to him.

'Frances, this is DCI Caton,' he said. 'DI Stuart's boss, I have no idea whether or not you'll able to help us to find your sister's murderer. We won't know that until we have this discussion, but I do know that we shouldn't be having it right now, over the phone.'

'You think I'm in danger?' she said.

'I'll be honest with you, Frances,' he said, 'we don't know. We just don't want to take any unnecessary risks.'

There was long pause before she responded.

'The man who sent the message. He gave Mrs Sweeney the impression that I was in danger. And that it might be safer if I agreed to talk to you. But that it was my decision.'

'Mrs Sweeney?'

'She does the flowers at our church. She's been there since forever.'

'Well, I'm afraid that she was right, Frances. Given what happened to your sister, and the fact that we think it may be connected to what happened to your parents, we have to consider that you may be at risk. That's the other reason that we need to meet with you.'

It was his turn to pause.

'But you'd worked that out for yourself, hadn't you?'

'How did you know?' she said.

'Because you mentioned the farm first.'

'I see.'

'Frances, we have no reason to believe that you are in any immediate danger. However–'

'You don't have any reason not to.'

'Which is why I'd rather we met up as soon as possible.'

'I'll fly direct to Manchester,' she said, 'instead of coming back to Belfast. You will be there by then?' She sounded anxious.

'Definitely,' he said. 'Wait until you are about to board, and then text DI Stuart the flight details. Can you do that?'

'Of course.'

'Until then–'

'You want me to be careful?'

'I wasn't going to say that, Frances,' he said.

'You didn't need to, Mr Caton.'

'I was going to say don't call or text unless you absolutely have to. But if you do need to, don't hesitate, day or night.'

'I will,' she said.

Two beats.

'If I need to.'

'Thank you for this, Frances,' he said. 'We look forward to seeing you.'

'Thank you,' she said. 'And please thank DI…'

'Stuart.'

'DI Stuart for me.'

'I will.'

'Goodbye.'

'Goodbye, Frances.'

Caton handed the phone back.

'God, that was hard,' he said.

'Harder for her,' observed Joanne Stuart, putting it back on the bedside table. 'She's a smart lady though. She had it all sussed out before she rang us.'

'It wasn't that difficult to work out, was it? She receives a mysterious message from Ireland, via the lady that does the flowers in church, telling her that her sister has been shot dead, the police are desperate to meet with her, and she's in danger. Given what happened all those years ago she'd have to be pretty dim not to realise what's going on.'

'When you put it like that, boss,' she said. 'You could tell it had hit her hard. Did you clock her reaction when I used her birth name?'

He stood up and helped himself to a glass of water from the complimentary bottle of Rocwell mineral water.

'Hardly surprising,' he said. 'When nobody's called you that for the past thirty-five years, and it's the one part of you that reminds you of who you were before your world fell apart.'

He held up the other glass.

'Do you want some?'

'Go on,' she said. 'Let's live dangerously.'

She saw his expression change, and laughed nervously. He poured the water and handed her the glass.

'She's not as smart as she thinks she is,' he said.

'What do you mean?'

'She shouldn't have given you her adopted name.'

'Come on, boss. That phone is as secure as it's going to get. Okay, so MacMahon was able to get my number, but that's all. There's no way he could listen in.'

'It's not him I'm worried about,' said Caton. 'When a teenager on the autistic spectrum can hack into the Pentagon, you tell me what's secure any more.'

'If not him, then who?' she asked. 'PSNI? The HET? Special Branch? GCHQ? MI5?'

'Who tasked the Special Patrol Group that turned up at Malon Farm immediately after the RUC arrived?' he asked.

She twirled her glass, studying the whirlpool of water as though an answer might magically reside there.

'The Det?'

He nodded.

'Correct. They were part of the Army Intelligence Corps. And where do you think they got their intelligence from?'

She shrugged, and took a gulp of water.

'All of the above?'

'Exactly. Except the HET did not exist at the time, and the PSNI replaced the RUC.'

She placed the glass on the bedside table.

'You still think that thirty-five years after the Malon Farm murders someone with access to national security intelligence surveillance resources is worried enough about what we might dig up to be listening in to all of our phone calls?'

He shrugged.

'I'm only saying it's a possibility. It would explain why we were being followed.'

'If we were,' she said. 'But not how MacMahon got hold of my mobile number. Not unless you're suggesting that he's working for one of the security forces?'

'I know it's unlikely,' he admitted, 'but it's not beyond the realms of possibility.'

'That he's some kind of double agent for the organisations he hated most in the world? Are you saying Willie-John Denny is in on it too?'

'I know,' he said, 'maybe I am paranoid. But you know what they say?'

She'd heard him say it that many times it was getting boring, but she decided to humour him.

'Just because you're paranoid, it doesn't mean they're not out to get you!'

Caton stood up.

'Either way, it's time we found out,' he said.

Chapter 33

'Nearly there.'

She looked at her watch.

'About time too,' she said. 'I thought it was only ninety miles or so.'

He pointed to the on-board computer display.

'Ninety-one point three to be exact. You didn't take account of the fact that most of it was on the N51. It was fine until we found ourselves behind a tanker, four artics and a couple of tractors.'

'I was surprised there wasn't a discernible border crossing,' she said. 'And the countryside still looked the same until we reached those peat moors. It's just like one big country.'

'You could be saying that when you travel up to Scotland in the future,' he said. 'It's ironic really; Northern Ireland fought to stay in, but there are Scots who can't wait to get away from us.'

'I know,' she said. 'I think it's sad, for so many reasons. And it's like trying to turn back the clock to a golden age of independence that never really existed. The last thing we need in this world is nationalism. You'd think people would have learned that from Hitler's experiment. Not to mention the Balkan wars, Ukraine and what's going on in the Middle East.'

'I didn't have you down as political,' said Caton. 'I'm seeing you anew.'

'That's how it is in this job though, isn't it, boss? When do we ever get any time to socialise? And when we do, it's either celebrating putting a scrote away for life, or drowning our sorrows because we couldn't.'

'Scrote?' He brought the car to a halt and cut the engine. He turned to look at her. 'There you go again, another surprise. When you joined us you'd have called anyone using that word sexist and insensitive.'

She grinned broadly.

'Like you said, that was before I spent time with DI Holmes. Besides, it's a technical term that refers specifically to males, which was how I was using it.'

He shook his head.

'I knew it was only a matter of time.'

He pointed to the view beyond the windscreen.

'This is it.'

A grey stone granite church, with a small matching porch, surrounded by a drystone wall. Three narrow windows on the front, below a small bell tower. Five gothic windows along the side. A graveyard with white marble headstones. Three windswept yews leaned like drunken sentinels among the graves.

'Are you sure?' she said. 'I don't see a house anywhere.'

'This is the postcode he gave me,' he said. 'It must be up ahead. We certainly haven't passed anything that looked like a presbytery.'

He started the engine again and set off.

'Strange place for a soldier to end up,' she said. 'Strange profession too, a man of the cloth.'

'Tell that to an army chaplain,' he replied. 'He'll tell you it makes perfect sense.'

'Or she will.'

'Touché,' he said. 'When we get there, do you mind taking notes on your iPad? We can arrange for him to make a formal statement at the local Garda station.

Assuming he's willing to.'

'No problem. So long as you don't mind me throwing the odd question in?'

'I doubt I could stop you if I wanted to.'

'I bet this it.' She pointed to a bungalow just ahead of them on the right-hand side of the road. 'Small, tidy, no sign of any ostentation. It's got priest written all over it.'

Caton drew up outside the gated hedge. Before they had time to unfasten their seat belts, the front door opened. A man stood there dressed in black trousers and a black pullover. Around his neck was the telltale clerical collar.

'Bingo!' she said. 'What his name again?'

'Michael Walsh. Father Walsh to you and me, unless he tells us otherwise.'

As they walked down the short path, Father Walsh retreated into his hallway.

'You made good time,' he said. 'Come on in and close the door behind you.'

'We didn't expect it to take as long as it did,' said Caton.

The priest led the way into his lounge.

'Ah well, you'd not have made any allowance for the state of that road. I don't think a pothole has been filled since the recession started. Then there are the tractors and the lorries and such.'

He pointed to the three-seater couch.

'Please take a seat. I'll put the kettle on.'

The room was dual aspect, open-plan, L-shaped. There was a hearth with a multi-fuel burner. Beside it was a stack of peat blocks. The burner was lit. The priest disappeared around the corner. They heard the tap running and the sound of a kettle being plugged in. The rattle of cups and saucers. A cutlery drawer being opened. He appeared suddenly.

'Tea is it? I've got coffee too, only I'm not too sure how old it is.'

'Tea's fine,' said Caton, answering for the two of them.

Father Walsh disappeared back into the kitchen.

'How did you know that I didn't want a coffee?' she whispered.

'Because you always accept the first thing that's offered to you when we make a house call.'

She frowned.

'I didn't know that.'

'Ah well, I'm a detective, I'm paid to observe things.'

'Things?'

'And people.'

'He hasn't asked to see our ID,' she said.

'That's because he's a priest. It's all about trust.'

'He should try our job,' she said. 'He'd soon wise up.'

Father Walsh appeared with a cake on a platter and three small plates. He put them down on the wooden coffee table.

'It's a Victoria Sponge. You have to try it; the women in the parish seem to be vying with each other to see who can fatten me up the fastest.' He chuckled. 'That Great British Bake Off has a lot to answer for.'

'I didn't realise you get BBC television over here,' said Caton.

'Sky Ireland,' he said. 'Isn't technology a wonderful thing?'

They waited until he had disappeared back into the kitchen.

'That means he could have seen the news items about Maureen Flinn,' she whispered. 'And the GMP appeal, with her photo.'

'It's possible,' he said. 'Although they had most

coverage on the North-West channels. In any case, he wouldn't have recognised the name, or her photo. She was only four at the time, remember. Plus as far as we know he never saw her.'

'But if you're right, one of them must have done. Or recently found out that she existed, and that she was there at the time. For all we know she might have started digging into her past. Maybe that's what brought her to her killer's attention?'

He was about to agree that it was the most likely scenario, when the priest returned carrying a tray with two cups and saucers, a mug and a bread knife. He placed the tray on the table beside the cake.

'Anyone for sugar?'

They told him no.

'Good,' he said. 'That saves me a trip. Help yourselves to cake.'

He picked up the mug, cradled it in his hands and sat down in the one remaining chair beside the multi-fuel stove.

'That was my church you passed,' he said. 'What did you think of it?'

'It looked perfect in that landscape,' said Caton. 'Like it had been there forever. How old is it?'

'Older than it looks, and nowhere near as old. It was built in 1841. After the Act of Toleration, as neat a legal condescension as you're likely to come across, thousands of Roman Catholic churches were built. The one you saw was constructed using stone from one that was destroyed by Cromwell's men. The original chapel was Celtic. Over a thousand years old.'

'Do you have many parishioners?' asked Joanne Stuart, following Caton's lead to keep the pleasantries going a little longer.

He drank from his mug and turned it in his hands.

'Just fifty here, but I have three churches to manage

in the Deanery. Roughly a thousand souls altogether, but only a couple of hundred come to Mass and the Sacraments. Mostly female, the old, the sick, the lame and the halt.'

He smiled to himself.

'But weren't those the ones that Jesus was most often drawn to?'

'So,' he said, 'this is all very mysterious. Why was it you wanted to see me?'

Caton put his cup down and took out his warrant card. Joanne Stuart did the same.

'DCI Caton, and DI Stuart,' he said. 'As I explained, Father, we are with the Greater Manchester Police Major Incidents Team.'

'So you did, but you didn't say what the incident was you were investigating. And it's Michael, by the way.'

As though to emphasise the point, he put his mug down, hooked two fingers around his clerical collar and took it off. He held it up for them to see, before placing it on the arm of his chair.

'I cut them out of Fairy Liquid bottles,' he said with a smile. 'It's not only cheaper, but I'm helping to save the planet.'

Caton told him the bare details. A young woman found murdered in Angel Meadow. That she was of Irish heritage, and a prostitute.

The priest seemed genuinely saddened, and surprised that they might think he could help them solve her murder.

'What was her name?' he asked.

'Maureen Flinn,' said Joanne Stuart.

He searched his memory banks, then shook his head.

'I don't know that name. Was she from round here? Did you think she might be a parishioner of mine? Is that it?'

'No, Michael,' said Caton. 'She was from North of the Border. From Armagh.'

'Armagh?'

He seemed genuinely surprised.

'I don't remember a Maureen Flinn in Armagh. Or Belfast for that matter. But then she would have been…' He looked up. 'How old?'

'Four,' said Joanne Stuart. 'She would have been just four years old.'

His forehead furrowed.

'Then I don't understand…'

'She lived on Drumboy Road, Michael,' said Caton. 'She lived at Malon Farm.'

Chapter 34

The priest's face drained of colour. There were so many emotions captured in his eyes that it was difficult to register them all. They saw shock, confusion and guilt. And something else. A long repressed memory forcing its way to the surface. When he spoke, his voice was faltering, and barely audible.

'She was at the farm?'

'That's right, Michael,' said Caton. 'She was there.'

They could tell that it had registered, but that he found it difficult to believe. He muttered something inaudible.

'Sorry, Michael,' said Caton, 'could you say that again?'

He raised his head.

'They didn't tell me,' he said.

'They didn't know. Nobody did.'

The man's wretchedness was so obviously genuine that Caton decided to take a risk.

'They didn't know about her sister either,' he said.

'Her sister?'

'There were two of them, Michael. Her sister was six years old. They were both there. Their neighbours found them and spirited them away before the RUC arrived.'

The priest searched their faces in turn.

'Did they see what happened?' he whispered. 'To their family?'

'We don't know yet,' said Caton. 'But we will, soon.'

'Oh dear God,' he said. 'What have we done? Dear God.'

He put his head in his hands and began to weep.

Joanne Stuart put everything back on the tray, including his mug, and took it into the kitchen. She returned with a glass of water for each of them and sat back down next to Caton. They waited patiently until he had no more tears to shed.

Five minutes had passed when he took a handkerchief from his pocket, wiped his eyes and blew his nose. He put it back in his pocket and raised his head. His eyes, almost lifeless, were bloodshot and red-rimmed.

'How much do you know?' he said.

'Most of it,' said Caton. 'We were hoping you could tell us the rest.'

'This sister,' he said, 'you think she may be in danger?'

Caton made sure he had eye contact before he replied.

'Maureen Flinn, formerly Caitlin Malone,' he said. 'was shot a week ago in Manchester, with a 9mm Army Issue pistol used by IRA terrorists during a chase in Castlederg in 1978. We suspect that it was part of the cache you discovered at Malon Farm. So, Michael, what do you think? Is her sister in danger?'

Walsh placed his head in his hands again. This time he did not cry. Caton sensed that he had already made his decision and was composing himself. When he raised his head and placed his hands on the arms of his chair, Caton knew that he was right.

'I was just twenty years of age,' the priest began. 'A

corporal in the Royal Military Police. When I heard I was being seconded as a driver to 14th Int…' He paused to see if he needed to explain, saw that he didn't and continued. 'I was over the moon. Our RSM told me that they only seconded the best. That I should remember I was lucky because I was a Catholic and they hadn't held that against me. And that whatever happened I mustn't balls it up. His words, not mine. We were trained by 22 SAS. That made us feel even more important. Like we were the elite?'

They both nodded their understanding.

'We were supposed to avoid direct action. Our main task was reconnaissance. Gathering information on the terrorists on both sides. We had specially modified saloons – "Q" cars – with covert radios, alarms, Kevlar armour plating, even stun grenades that you could trigger with your foot to put off pursuers.' For a moment he sounded almost wistful. 'Proper James Bond stuff.'

'But not that night?' said Caton.

He shook his head.

'No, not that night. That night I was given a Series 111 Land Rover, not marked or camouflaged, but with a long wheelbase, so a bit of a giveaway.'

'Why were you given that?'

'I don't know for sure. You have to remember, it was straight after Mountbatten's yacht was blown up, and all those men from the Paras and the Highlanders were killed at Warrenpoint. There was a lot of panic about. Incredible pressure to find those responsible. The rule book seemed to have gone out of the window.'

'You mean Shoot to Kill?' said Joanne Stuart.

Caton nudged her with his elbow, but Walsh took it in his stride. He turned his attention to her.

'No, I'm not saying that. There was nothing official,

or off the record even. Just a feeling.' He thought about it for a moment. 'A kind of wild, raw energy about the place.'

'That night, Michael,' said Caton. 'You were telling us about that night.'

He nodded. Took his time. His breathing was laboured. His face was now ashen. For a moment Caton was worried that he might be about to have a heart attack. Then he began to speak. Only now his head was bowed. It was as though he was talking to the table rather than to them.

'There were five of us. Finucane, Blair, Ellis, Gilchrist and me. We had been a regular team for about six months. Frank was the officer in command.'

'Frank?' said Caton.

'Frank Finucane,' he replied without raising his head. 'He was a Captain in 14th Int. He briefed us that night.'

He paused, reached for his glass of water, drank and placed it down again.

'Intelligence had been received that there was a large IRA arms cache near the borders with Monaghan and Louth. There was suspicion that it belonged to the South Armagh Brigade. There were rumours the guns and explosives used at Warrenpoint had come from there. A two-man SAS reconnaissance unit had been in place for forty-eight hours carrying out surveillance. Our task was to stay well clear, but to be ready to provide backup if called upon.'

'But that wasn't your usual role?' Caton, wanted to be clear.

He shook his head.

'No. But you have to understand that everyone was stretched to the limit. The Army, the RUC, us. There were rumours everywhere about impending attacks. The highest possible state of alert.'

He took another drink, and carried on.

'It was coming up to nine p.m., a couple of hours after sunset. We were laid up on a disused farm track just south of Crossmaglen. Finucane got a phone call. He got out of the Land Rover to take it. I watched him pace up and down. At one point he seemed to be arguing with whoever was on the other end of the line. He got back in the passenger seat. "Right, lads," he said. "Listen up. The cache has been confirmed, but they don't want to risk Tangos moving it before they can task a search and recovery team. The SAS observers have pulled out. We're going in."'

'What was the reaction of the rest of the team?' said Caton.

He thought about it. Closed his eyes. Then opened them.

'The atmosphere was suddenly electric. You could almost taste the adrenalin. You could certainly smell it in the close confines of the vehicle. Ellis and Blair were really up for it. You could tell they were excited. Gilchrist and Finucane were calm on the outside. Quiet, professional. What they were feeling on the inside I have no idea.'

'What about you?' said Caton.

He looked up.

'Me? I was bricking myself.'

He picked up his glass and had another drink. This time he held onto it. He seemed to have recovered a little of his composure. It was as though the telling of the story had stopped him from dwelling on the consequences of what had happened.

'It was two miles to the farm. We parked up in the lane behind a hedge. It was a full moon and cloudy, so visibility was poor, but we'd just been equipped with one individual weapon night scope. The lights were on in the farmhouse. The rest of the buildings were in darkness. Finucane briefed us again. He, Gilchrist and Ellis were going to the barn where the SAS said the arms were stashed. Once they'd confirmed that they were there, they'd come back to the Land Rover and plan the next step. Blair was to keep watch on the farmhouse with the night scope. If anyone came out he was to tell me, and I'd start the engine as a sign to them to take cover. If anyone came to see where the engine noise was coming from we were not to worry. Just switch the engine off. They would deal with it. Then the four of them took it in turn to use our camouflage sticks on each other's faces.'

He had another drink. Put the glass down, took his handkerchief from his pocket and wiped his forehead. It was only then that Caton realised Walsh had begun to sweat profusely. He kept the handkerchief in his hand and continued.

'They were gone ten minutes. When they came back they were excited. Ellis was really keyed up. They'd found what they were looking for. There was a stash of guns: rifles, shotguns and small arms. There were also timers, and a rocket-propelled grenade. Finucane said they were going in to detain the farmer and anyone else who looked like a terrorist. He, Gilchrist and Ellis were going in the front door. Blair was to circle around the back and cover the rear exits. I was to stay in the car with the night scope, and keep my eyes and ears peeled. If I heard or saw anything problematic I was to sound the horn three times, grab my gun and use my initiative.'

He mopped his forehead again and either side of his eyes. The colour was coming back into his cheeks, Caton noted, but if anything his eyes had sunk deeper into their sockets.

'I watched them head towards the house. Blair peeled off to the left and disappeared around the side of the farmhouse. The other three headed to the barn first. They were in there less than two minutes. When they came out they headed straight for the front porch. I saw the three of them go into the porch. Then there was a flash of light as the door was opened. I couldn't see anything because the sudden contrast caused a dramatic loss of resolution. The door closed. I heard shouting and screaming, and gunshots.'

He crushed the handkerchief in his fist and looked down at the table.

'In what order?' said Caton.

He shook his head slowly.

'There wasn't any order. It was as though they all came at once.'

'Automatic fire or single shots?'

'Automatic. Short bursts. Then a long one.'

'How many guns?'

'I don't know. How could I?'

Caton was not convinced. There was something about the speed with which he had replied. And he had answered with a question; one of eight potential signs of verbal deceit.

'You were an elite soldier,' Caton said. 'You must have had some idea. What did your gut tell you?'

This time he gave it the reflection it deserved. When he answered, Caton could tell that he was trying to be honest. The cues were in his tone, and in his eyes.

'One. Maybe two.'

'Carry on,' said Caton.

He closed his eyes for a moment, so it was impossible for them to tell if he was remembering, having an internal dialogue with himself or constructing a story. He opened them and continued his account from the point where he had been interrupted.

'Then there was this awful silence. Heavy. Full of foreboding. All sorts of things were going around in my head. What the hell had happened? What should I do? Get on the radio? Leave the Land Rover and go and investigate? What if they'd all been killed? Where was Blair? Then I saw Blair come running around the side of the farmhouse. I heard him call Frank's name, then he went inside. The door closed. Two minutes later, the four of them came out and headed back to the Land Rover.'

'How did they seem?' said Caton.

'Tense, tight-lipped. Like they had been arguing. They climbed in in silence. Finucane turned to me and said…' He closed his eyes as though forcing himself to remember the words verbatim. '"We were fired on. We had no choice but to return fire. It was self-defence." "But those screams, Frank," I said. "It sounded like there were women, and children."'

He looked up at Caton and Stuart, as though seeking their understanding at least, if not their forgiveness.

'He didn't have to say anything. I could see from his expression that whoever had been in there, they were all dead. He said because of how it might look we had to get out of there. I was numb. I couldn't believe it. I started the engine, backed down the lane and headed back towards Concession Road. Five miles away he told me to turn right and follow a track into some woods. Then he said to park up so we could listen to the Comms on the radio. In my wing mirror I saw Glichrist get out of the back of the Land Rover and head up the track. He was carrying a sack. When he came back, he no longer had it.'

'What did you think was in it?' said Caton.

He shrugged.

'I had no idea.'

'Now, on reflection? After all these years?' said Joanne Stuart.

'That he was hiding some kind of evidence.'

'What kind of evidence?'

He paused.

Three beats.

'Weapons.'

'What makes you say that?' said Caton.

He stared down at his glass and found it empty. Stuart poured some of her water into his. He drank it.

When the airwaves started buzzing,' he said, 'Finucane reported that we were in the vicinity. Did they want us to attend? The answer came back in the affirmative. When we got there it was chaos. There was an RUC Special Patrol Group on the scene, a local farmer and his wife from a neighbouring farm, and a local police car. It looked like the police had just got there. Frank jumped out and hurried over to them. He waved the other three over and they went into the house together, leaving the police outside. Then they went to the barn, came back out and waved the RUC officers over. They all went inside. Then Finucane and the others came back to the Land Rover. Forty minutes later, a Westland Wessex helicopter arrived from Aldergrove. There was someone from the Northern Ireland Office, a Colonel from 14th Int., and someone from the Army Investigation Branch. We were asked to account for our presence. Then they checked if our weapons had been fired. To my surprise none of them had been. They did the same with the RUC Special Patrol Group. We were told to return to base and write up our reports.'

'What happened to the arms dump?' said Caton.

'I heard it had been destroyed,' he said. 'Blown up. The next thing I knew, the official story was that an arms cache had been found. An IRA sympathiser and his family had been found shot. And it was likely that either the PIRA or UDF had been responsible.'

'What about your reports?' said Joanne Stuart. 'Surely they would have told a different story?'

He shook his head slowly.

'They didn't. There was really only one report. Frank Finucane wrote it. Ours were written to fit in with his. He said it was what the chain of command wanted. What he had been told to do. What he had been told to order us to do. He said because it had been self-defence this was only a white lie. The truth, if it ever came out, would undermine the work of the armed services, set back the fight against terrorism and put everyone – including ourselves – at even greater risk.'

He Joanne Stuart fighting to keep the contempt she felt from showing.

'Whatever you feel about me,' he told her, 'about what I did, I've felt a thousand times over and a hundred times worse. That night has haunted my waking and sleeping hours. It was why I left the army. Why I entered the seminary. Why I do what I do now.'

He paused. When he spoke, his words seemed to catch in his throat.

'It was intended as some kind of atonement.'

He wiped his forehead again, and then looked her in the eyes.

'And I can tell you, Detective Inspector, that it hasn't worked.'

Chapter 35

They took a short break while DI Stuart filled up their glasses with water. Michael Walsh followed her into the kitchen, splashed his face with cold water in the sink, wiped it with a hand towel and returned with several pieces of kitchen roll to replace his sodden handkerchief. When the three of them were settled, Caton pressed on.

'Did you then,' he said, 'or have you now, any sense of which of those three fired the fatal shots?'

'I'm sorry,' he said, 'but I didn't, and I still don't. It's something you're bound to want to know. And I did. But there was nothing about their demeanour that gave it away. It was clear that they were shaken by it. Frank … Finucane, that is … recovered first. He was still in charge, making the decisions. But that didn't mean he'd done it. He could have been covering for one of the others, or both of them.'

'Or all three?' said Caton.

He nodded.

'Or all three. But it was as though they had made a pact never to speak of it again except through him.'

'Couldn't you tell from the way they looked at each other when they thought no one else was watching?' asked Joanne Stuart.

'No. They didn't really look at each other, or me. It was like they were too ashamed.'

'Or too scared,' she said.

He thought about it, and nodded.

'Or too scared.'

'Of Finucane?' asked Caton.

He shrugged.

'Of the consequences.'

'What was it like when things had settled down?' Caton asked. 'It must have been difficult, the five of you working together with that hanging over you?'

'We didn't,' he said. 'Within a fortnight we were split up. Ellis and I were sent back to our respective regiments, Blair went back to the RUC.'

'What about the other two?'

'As far as I know, they both stayed on with 14th Int., but not as part of a mobile unit.'

'What did they do?'

He shrugged.

'I have no idea.'

Caton decided there was nothing to be gained from pursuing it. Walsh wasn't covering for any of them. He genuinely didn't know. Unless of course it had all been a lie, just as the report he had colluded with had been a lie. But if it was an act, he was convinced it was one of the best he had ever seen.

'I have to ask you this,' he said. He waited until the priest's eyes were locked onto his. 'Where were you on Friday the 13th and Saturday the 14th of June?'

He frowned.

'A week last Friday?'

'That's right.'

'That's easy,' he said. 'On Friday afternoon I played a round of golf with the other two priests in the diocese, then we had a fish and chip supper, and played cards until about ten o'clock. On Saturday morning I took Holy Communion to the sick of the parish. In the evening I said the six o'clock Mass, watched the TV, said my office and was in bed by eleven.'

'You don't need to check?' said Caton.

He smiled weakly.

'No need. It's what I've done every summer weekend for the past twenty-seven years.'

They were on the final leg, Caton decided, perhaps the most important part.

'Have you had contact with any of the other four over the years?' he asked. 'And do you know the whereabouts of any of them now?

DI Stuart glanced at Caton. It was shrewd of him, she realised, not to have revealed what they already knew about the members of his former unit. She turned her attention to the priest, watching for any blatant lies.

It was obvious that there was an internal struggle going on. To tell or not to tell? And what to tell, and just how much?

They waited. She with her index finger poised over the tablet, Caton leaning back against the sofa, his hands behind his head. The former military policeman finally decided.

'Blair, I'm sure you already know about,' he said. 'Given that he's working for you.'

He waited for Caton to acknowledge the fact with a slight nod, before continuing.

'Ellis was convicted of being an informer for the Ulster Defence Force. I know he went to jail, but I have no idea for how long.'

'Nine years,' Caton told him. 'He served five.'

It was the priest's turn to nod.

'Then I heard a rumour about eight years ago,' he said, 'that he had been killed in an RTA. Stepped off a kerb into a white van?'

It was the first they had heard of it, but they didn't comment.

'Frank Finucane,' he continued. 'Remained in 14 Company. Moved up the ranks, apparently. Then he crossed the water. London, I was led to believe.'

'And Stuart Gilchrist?' said Caton, knowing full well that he was dead.

'Gilchrist is dead,' he replied. 'A bomb on the Shankill Road. But then you'd know that too.'

He looked at each of them expectantly. Waited for Caton to nod, then carried on.

'I might have gone to the funeral, but I wasn't invited. It was a private funeral, apparently. Just the widow and immediate family. No three-gun salute over the grave.'

'It sounds as though you went out of your way to keep track of them,' said Caton. 'Why was that, Michael?'

'I didn't really,' he said. 'Ellis's conviction and the two deaths were in the papers, of course.'

His pause lasted so long that Joanne Stuart looked up from her iPad.

'And the others?' said Caton.

'James Bell told me about them,' he said, reaching for his glass.

'James Bell?' said Caton.

They waited impatiently as he emptied the glass, wiped his mouth with a piece of the polyroll and folded his arms. Caton was unable to tell if this was a piece of theatre or a kind of delaying tactic. When he began to answer the question, it was clear from his eyes that it had been the latter.

'James Bell was Stuart Gilchrist,' he said, taking them both by surprise. 'That is to say, he was, for a time. Now he is James Bell again.'

'You're saying that Stuart Gilchrist is still alive?' said Caton.

He smiled and shook his head, almost indulgently,

like a teacher with a slow learner.

'Stuart Gilchrist never actually existed,' he said. 'Except in name alone. When Captain James Bell was seconded from the UDR he did so under a false ID. After Malon Farm he remained in the Det operating under that same ID. My guess is that he became involved in undercover work for the security forces, as quite a few did in 14th Int. At some point he, and the operation he was engaged in, became compromised, and Stuart Gilchrist became the victim of a convenient bombing.'

'Someone else died in the bombing?' said Caton.

'When the body parts are fragmented and the security forces control the aftermath, who's to say what belongs to whom, and who was really there?'

'So what happened to James Bell?'

'As I understand it, he re-emerged on the other side of the water with an MOD back-story placing him in British Forces Germany 102nd Logistics Brigade. Then the Falklands, then MI5. Which is where he worked until he retired.'

'And you know all this because…?' said Caton.

'Because he told me so.'

He mopped his forehead, which had begun to sweat again. It made Caton conscious of how hot he had become himself. It's that damned peat fire, he reflected. In June.

'But why would he confide in you?' he said.

'I was on holiday, in Scotland. A sort of golf tour with a couple of friends I'd made at Westmeath … the seminary. We were in a pub, in Aberfeldy, and there he was. I knew he'd seen me because he tried to hide behind his newspaper. But it was too late. He couldn't leave without passing me. I was staggered. And curious. When it was time to move on I told the others I'd join them back at the hostel we were staying in.

Then I ordered two double whiskies and took them over.'

'And he told you all this, just like that?'

He smiled wistfully.

'Only after another five double malts.'

'Did you talk about Malon Farm?'

His face clouded over. He was slow to reply.

'It was always there between us, like a Pandora's Box that neither of us dared to open.'

'How long ago was this?'

'Four years,' he said.

'Are you still in contact?'

He nodded.

'A card at Christmas.'

'Do you have his address?'

He rose unsteadily, as though he had aged ten years in the course of that single afternoon.

'I'll go and get it,' he said.

They got up themselves, and waited in the hall. The priest returned and handed Caton a slip of paper.

'Thank you,' said Caton. 'I am going to arrange for the Garda to take a formal statement from you,' said Caton. 'Then they will send it on to us. Are you willing to do that?'

'Of course,' he said.

'They will also want to check your alibi, and take your fingerprints and a DNA swab, for the purposes of elimination.'

Walsh nodded his understanding. Caton opened the door, and he and DI Stuart stepped out onto the path.

'It could have been any one of us you know,' Walsh said. 'Even me. Nerves on edge, scared witless. Safety off. White knuckles gripping the rifle. Finger on the trigger. The farmer makes a sudden move. Is that a gun? Trigger pulled. The gun's on automatic. Bullets spraying everywhere.'

'That's what you told yourself, was it, Father?' said Caton. 'That's how you managed to live with a secret like that?'

'I suppose it was,' he said. 'I tried to put myself in their place. Then I realised that only they, and God, knew what really happened. That only He was in a position to judge.'

'Try telling that to Maureen Flinn's parents,' said Joanne Stuart as they turned their backs and walked down the path. 'And her sister.'

As they drove away Caton looked in the mirror. He was still there, in the doorway, his clerical collar hanging loose in his hand.

Chapter 36

They covered the first two miles in silence. DI Stuart was the first to speak.

'Do you think he will, boss?'

He glanced at her.

'What?'

'Provide a formal statement?'

'I don't see why not. It isn't as though you haven't got a record of everything he said. There's enough on your iPad to spark an urgent review of the case by the Historical Enquiries Team. What has he got to lose by continuing to cooperate with us?'

She stared at him in open amazement.

'Not a lot,' she said. 'Apart from his loss of reputation in his parish, and as a priest; a couple of years for conspiracy to pervert the course of justice; revenge from the IRA and UDF people they tried to pin it on in the first place; and the unwanted attention of whoever it is we think killed Caitlin.'

'When you put it like that,' he said.

His phone rang. He checked the display. It was Duggie Wallace.

'I'm driving,' he said. 'I'm on hands-free, but try to keep it succinct, okay?'

'No problem, boss. DI Holmes told me to let you know that we've tracked down George Ellis.'

Caton and Stuart exchanged a look.

'He's still alive?' said Caton.

'Very much so. He came out of prison with a dishonourable discharge from the services, and on licence for the remaining portion of his sentence. Within six months he'd changed his name by deed poll to Gordon Edwards. That's why we had so much trouble tracking him down.'

'I didn't think you could change your name by deed poll if you were on licence,' said Joanne Stuart. 'Otherwise all those convicted paedophiles would be onto it like a shot.'

'DI Holmes reckons someone in the Establishment must have pulled strings,' said Wallace. 'Probably because Ellis knew too much about how the Security Services had been operating. It's even possible Ellis was a double agent.'

'Where is he now?' said Caton.

'Probably where DI Holmes found him. Propping up the bar of a pub in Hull.'

'What did he have to say for himself, Duggie?'

'Not a lot. To say he was not forthcoming is a massive understatement, according to DI Holmes. His favourite phrases, and I quote, were: "I served my time. I have nothing to say."'

'Did DI Holmes ask him about Malon Farm?'

'Yes. He came out with the same phrases. When Gordon pressed him, he gave him the old name and number routine, and referred him to the Secretary of State for Northern Ireland.'

'The cheeky bugger,' said Joanne Stuart.

'So DI Holmes told him why we were interested in what happened back then.'

'What was his reaction?'

'Apparently, he was shocked and surprised to hear that there were two girls in the farm that night. And even more surprised to learn that one of them had just been murdered, and that we think there's a connection.'

'Where was he at the time that Maureen Flinn was murdered?' said Caton.

'Right there in the pub. He claimed he'd been at a quiz night, followed by some pretty heavy late-night drinking. The manager alibied him. Said he was as drunk as a skunk when he left at four a.m. Even came up with a CCTV tape that proved it.'

'Has he been in contact with any of the other three?'

'He claimed not. Said he had no idea where any of them were, and he had no desire to find out.'

'Is that it?' said Caton.

'Yes, boss. DI Holmes told him not to go anywhere without letting us know. And to contact us straight away if any of the old unit got in touch.'

'Did Gordon say what Ellis is doing for a living these days?' asked Joanne Stuart.

'Funny you should ask that,' said Wallace. 'Apparently, he's on the dole. But from what DI Holmes can gather he has a nice little apartment down on the Quayside, a three-year-old BMW, and not a care in the world.' He paused dramatically. 'Until now.'

'Why do you say that?' said Caton.

'Because according to DI Holmes, when he left him he was pale as a ghost, and giving a very good impression of someone who was scared witless.'

'Where is DI Holmes now?' said Caton.

'He's gone straight down to London to find out where Finucane was the night that Maureen Flinn was shot. He's taken DI Carter with him. He said to tell you he'd give you a ring as soon as he gets there.'

'Thanks,' said Caton.

'You're welcome, boss. When will you both be back?'

'Tomorrow. In fact, you can do us a favour there. Ask Ged to book DI Stuart and me on the seven a.m. Flybe flight from Belfast to Manchester, and to call a team briefing for nine thirty a.m.'

'Right you are, boss,' said a cheerful Wallace. 'We'll have breakfast waiting for you.'

Caton ended the call.

'It won't be a patch on the ones we've been having over here,' he said, with just a hint of disappointment.

'Suits me,' Stuart said. 'One more Ulster Fry and nothing's going to fit me.'

She opened the glove compartment and raided his bag of Imperial Mints.

'Do you want one?'

'No thanks.'

'Gordon's been busy.'

'And he's helped us to eliminate another suspect. That only leaves Finucane, Blair and Bell, formerly known as Gilchrist.'

'Assuming that it was one of them.'

'God, I hope so,' he said. 'They're all we've got.'

She sucked the mint and rolled it around her mouth, clicking it against her teeth as she did so. Caton found it inexplicably irritating.

'Please don't.'

'Sorry,' she said, 'I should have known. Abbie hates it when I do that.'

She inclined her seat a touch and settled back to enjoy the journey.

'So we're heading back in the morning,' she said. 'What are you going to tell the PSNI, boss? And specifically the Historical Enquiries Team?'

'The HET? Nothing. Not yet. Nor their bosses. They didn't seem keen to revisit that case, and they certainly didn't want us to.'

'But we have to tell them something, surely?'

'Eventually, but not just yet. If we did, I have a feeling they would create all sorts of problems for us. I tell you what is interesting though.'

'Go on.'

'That no one else appears to have given either Walsh or Gilchrist–'

'Bell,' she reminded him.

'Gilchrist as was, Bell as is, that no one has given them a heads-up. If someone was really trying to run interference I would have expected them to give all of them a warning, maybe even have briefed them on what to say.'

'I think we can safely assume that didn't happen.' She inclined her seat all the way back. 'Let me know if you want a turn with the driving,' she said. 'If not, wake me up when we get there.'

Then she closed her eyes.

They were walking into the hotel when he switched his BlackBerry back on. Seconds later, it pinged.

'Hell!' he said.

'What is it?' she asked.

'A missed call. From Kate.'

He had been so obsessed with the case that he had forgotten to ring her. Now he was concerned that with just weeks until her due date something had happened.

'You go on,' he said, stopping in the lobby. 'I'll have to deal with this.'

He sat on one of the leather sofas and rang home. It went to voicemail. With a rising sense of unease he called her mobile. She answered on the sixth ring.

'Hello?'

'Kate, it's Tom.'

'Do I know you?'

'Please don't mess around,' he said. 'I really was worried about you. How are you?'

'Not worried enough to ring me last night, or this morning.'

He sensed that beneath the veneer of frosty indignation she was close to tears.

'I am so sorry, Kate,' he said. 'I can't apologise enough.'

'No, you can't.'

'I'm not going to try to excuse it by telling you what's been going on–'

'Good, because I've heard it all before.'

'But if it helps, you should know that we're flying back first thing in the morning.'

She didn't answer, but he sensed her relief.

'I can't wait to see you,' he said. 'And I'll make it up to you, I promise.'

Three beats.

'Whatever you think you've got planned,' she said, 'it had better be pretty bloody spectacular.'

'It will be.'

'Don't think you're going to get away with row Z at the Arena to see Kings of Leon, followed by a fish and chip supper.'

'How about VIP seats for Bruno Mars, followed by a champagne dinner at a restaurant of your choice?'

'Now you're talking,' she said. 'But you'll have to wait until our daughter has deigned to arrive and I can really enjoy it.'

He heard the laugh in her voice and felt his own tension leach away.

'How are you, love?' he said. 'When I saw your missed call I panicked.'

'Good, because as it happens I could have done with your support. I had a false alarm.'

'Now I feel even worse.'

'It's not all about you Tom. How do you think I was feeling?'

'You know what I mean. And you still haven't answered my question. How are you, really?'

'I'm fine. My back hurts, my feet are swollen, I'm tired all the time, thirsty and running to the toilet every five minutes, but I'm fine. I just wish it was all over.'

'You're on the final straight.' He realised that it was trite, but didn't know what else to say.

'Do you know what, Tom?' she said. 'I'm so relieved that you're coming home. I don't know how I've managed without your words of wisdom. I really don't.'

Chapter 37

Gordon Holmes and Nick Carter were late for the briefing. Only ten minutes late, but Gordon was flustered. His face had developed a ruddy hue. He had loosened his tie and undone a button, and kept tugging at his collar as though it was still far too tight.

Caton had seen a gradual deterioration in his Deputy's appearance over the past few months, and a few days separation had brought it home. Gordon was overweight, his breathing laboured whenever he exerted himself and his colour troubling. Caton found himself checking that the defibrillator was still on the wall beside the fire extinguishers.

'Boss,' said DI Stuart.

He realised that they were all looking at him expectantly.

'It's your turn,' she said, 'to tell them what we've been up to.'

There were some murmured comments, and a chuckle or two.

'Alright,' he said. 'Settle down and concentrate. This will take a while.'

When it came to DI Holmes' turn, the reason for his demeanour was immediately apparent.

'Finucane,' he said. 'Complete tosser! I was given a number. Rang it. They said he was out on a job at the minute, but he was expected back in the office that afternoon. They'd make sure he knew we were coming. So Nick and I set off. All the way down to London. When we get there, he's not back yet. We wait. Two hours we sit twiddling our thumbs, drinking rank coffee, then someone comes and tells us they're really sorry, but this job's taken him up North.'

He looked around the room, working his audience as only he knew how.

'Where was he? Only bloody Manchester!'

Someone at the back sounded as though he was about to laugh, and then thought better of it.

Gordon tugged at his collar.

'He's going to be up here for a couple of days they say, so perhaps we could arrange to meet him in the morning? So, we come back. I ring National Crime Agency North-West Region. They're only too happy to set that up. That was before I knew about this briefing. So Nick and I get over there first thing. Guess what?'

'He's had to go back to London?' suggested DC Hulme.

'Give that man a prize,' said Gordon. 'What d'you want, Jimmy, a cuddly toy or a punch ball with Mr Frank Finucane's face on it?'

'Leave it with me, Gordon,' said Caton. 'I'll get onto the Deputy Director General straight after this briefing.'

They didn't need reminding that he and Barbara Bryce had a history in relation to her role at the Serious and Organised Crime Agency during two of his recent investigations.

Head bowed, his Deputy headed off towards his own desk.

'You tell her this is a murder investigation,' he said. 'And we're not some kind of toy town ceremonial outfit that can be messed around willy-nilly.'

Caton decided to let it go, for now. The rest of the team were staring at Gordon Holmes with a mixture of surprise and disappointment. It was clear to everyone that he was out of sorts in more ways than one. Best dealt with one to one.

'Next actions,' he said, regaining their attention.

He looked at the sheet Ged had handed him before the briefing, and the scribbled amendments he had made during the briefing.

'I will arrange that interview with Finucane. Then there's Andrew Blair.' He looked up. 'Where are we up to with Blair? Why has nobody seen him yet?'

DS Carter looked over nervously to where Gordon Holmes was sitting staring at his computer monitor.

'Err, that's in hand, boss,' he said. 'Mr Blair is on annual leave. He's due back the day after tomorrow. DI Holmes has spoken to the head of the Cat C Team and has arranged for him to be interviewed first thing.'

'Thank you, DS Carter,' he said. 'Then there's the remaining member of that unit, James Bell, who we had recorded as Stuart Gilchrist. According to Father Michael Walsh, his last known address was close to Aberfeldy in Perthshire.'

A hand shot up. It was Jimmy Hulme.

'I wouldn't mind that one, boss. J K Rowling lives in a haunted mansion near there. I could pop in afterwards for a chat.'

'Like she hasn't got enough ghouls around the place,' declared a female DC, prompting ripples of laughter.

'Thank you, DC Hulme,' said Caton, 'I'll bear it in mind.'

He checked his notes again.

'Ged, I want to see Father Walsh's statement as soon as it's faxed over, and I want his fingerprints and

DNA fast-tracked when they get here. DI Stuart, I want you and DS Carter to take Andrew Blair's interview, but I'd like to discuss your interview strategy after lunch. DS Carter and I will go and see James Bell. I'd like you to definitively check his whereabouts first. I don't want us traipsing up to Scotland to find that he's not there. But don't let him know we're coming. I don't want him giving us the run around like Mr Finucane.'

'What about Finucane, boss?' said Joanne Stuart.

'When I've pinned him down I'll decide who's going to interview him,' he replied. 'But if I'm still in Scotland it will be you and DS Carter, so we'll discuss his interview strategy too. And, finally, Frances Fenton – formerly Finnoula Malone – is intending to fly into Manchester on Saturday morning. DI Stuart and I will meet her. Ged, I'd like you to organise for her to see her sister's body at the mortuary. I know it's a Saturday, but don't take no for an answer. I'll contact the Fentons and let them know that she'd like to meet them. I'm sure they'll be fine with that.'

'What about protection, boss?' asked Nick Carter.

'We can't do anything until she gets here, but I'll work out something for when she does. Safe accommodation, a driver, and a shadow.'

He had no idea how he was going to get approval for the funding it would involve. If it came to it, he wouldn't ask. Just deploy two of his own team and fudge the overtime.

'Right,' he said, 'that's it. Thank you, everyone.'

He walked over to Gordon Holmes' desk.

'Gordon,' he said, 'we need to speak. Now. Not here, outside.'

He waited for his Deputy to place his hands on the desk, push back his chair and stand. Then he headed for the door.

'What the hell is going on, Gordon?' he asked, switching off his BlackBerry.

They were sitting on one of the concrete benches outside the Fujitsu Building opposite Central Park. It was the only place that Caton felt was completely private, and he sensed that his Deputy needed space.

Gordon was bent forwards, head bowed, his elbows on his thighs, hands hanging loose between his knees. He took a deep breath, straightened up and loosened his tie another notch.

'I'm sorry, boss,' he said. 'I shouldn't have kicked off. It's just that bastard Finucane–'

'No, it isn't,' Caton interrupted. 'It's you. Look at you. You've been letting yourself go for months. You're overweight, your drinking's getting out of control and you're tetchy with everyone. You keep this up, and you're heading for a heart attack.'

He saw the despair in his colleague's eyes and softened his tone.

'Look, Gordon, we are more than colleagues, we're friends. You need to tell someone what's going on, and if you can't tell me, who can you?'

Gordon bent forward again, as though trying to avoid Caton's gaze.

'It's Marilyn,' he said. 'I think she's going to leave me.'

'Come on, Gordon,' said Caton, 'that's never going to happen. You've known each other since you were at high school. You two are rock solid.'

He shook his head.

'Not any more we're not.'

'Why not?'

'It's complex. For a start, Marilyn's bitterly disappointed in me.'

'Disappointed?'

'I think she thought she was marrying a future

Chief Constable, instead of someone who had to be bullied into applying for every promotion.' He turned his head to look at Caton. 'Do you know when I was happiest?'

'No.'

'When I was a Sergeant in uniform, at Bootle Street. A bit of cut and thrust, still one of the lads, not too much paperwork.'

'I thought Marilyn hated you working shifts. I thought that was why you applied for CID?'

His laugh was hollow.

'Ironic, isn't it? What do they say, be careful what you wish for?'

'I thought you loved being part of FMIT?'

'It's not me, Tom,' he said, 'it's Marilyn. She reckons it's changed me. That I'm knackered, and more uptight. She wants me to retire, take the pension and find another job.'

'Looking at you right now, would that be so bad?' said Caton.

When Gordon replied, he looked and sounded like a wounded animal.

'Are you saying I'm no longer up to it?'

'Honestly? Of course you're still up to it. Providing you get a grip, stop feeling sorry for yourself and tell Marilyn how you feel. And what you want out of life.'

'Trouble is, it's not just the job.'

Caton had no idea where this was going. And he had no intention of trying to double-guess his friend. There were too many possibilities, all of them tricky.

'Go on,' he said.

Gordon took a grubby hankie from his pocket and blew his nose.

'Jimmy's waiting for his A-level results. If he's done as well as he thinks, he's off to university. Newcastle.'

'That's brilliant, Gordon,' said Caton. 'It's what you've both always wanted. The first in the family to go to uni.'

He shook his head.

'When he's gone there'll be no reason for us to stay together.'

Empty nest syndrome. Caton knew he should have seen that coming.

'How about the fact that you love each other?' he said, more in hope than expectation.

When Gordon failed to reply, he pressed on.

'Has Marilyn actually told you that she feels like that, or is it just what you fear might happen?'

'She hasn't actually said anything, but I can see she's worried about him going. And we just seem to bicker all the time.'

Caton wondered if this was how it would be for him and Kate in eighteen years time. If so, what would he do about it?

'Look, Gordon,' he said, 'you two need to talk. Of course Jimmy going off to uni will change things for both of you. And of course Marilyn's going to miss him. But think of the quality time the two of you are going to be able to have together. Reallocated rest days. It doesn't have to be all bad. It could be the best thing that's happened in years.'

Gordon smiled weakly.

'How would you like to come round to ours and tell her that?'

'That's your job. So, as of now, you're on leave till Monday.'

Gordon straightened up. Startled.

'But, boss…'

Caton put a firm hand on his shoulder.

'Gordon, you've been working flat-out for months. You've worked more rest days in the past year than ones you've actually taken. You were recalled from two days of your last annual leave when that court hearing was changed. I can swing this without affecting any of your leave entitlement.'

'But, boss–'

'The alternative is, I suspend you.'

'But you can't–'

'Yes, I can. I'll call it enforced sick leave on the grounds of Duty of Care.'

He adopted the formal tone he used when addressing Human Resources personnel.

'I have serious reasons for believing that the work patterns DI Holmes has been required to operate are impacting negatively on his health, to the extent that there is a distinct possibility that he could have a breakdown. Or, worse still, suffer a heart attack or a stroke.'

Caton slipped seamlessly back into empathy mode.

'You'd have to have a medical of course, but in the meantime you could take a nice long rest. Get your equilibrium back, sort things out with Marilyn.'

'But, boss–'

'On the other hand, I could make it a "query" alcohol addiction.'

Gordon's shoulders slumped. Caton couldn't tell if it was resignation or relief. He suspected a bit of both.

'I'll go on leave,' he said. 'Only till Monday, mind. But what am I going to tell Marilyn?'

'That I thought you'd been working too hard. That you had some TOIL leave coming and that I persuaded you to take it. Or better still, that you wanted to spend some quality time with her, so you took the leave you were entitled to.'

'That's not true though, is it?' he said. 'Inspectors and above are not entitled to time off in lieu.'

'Tell her you're a special case,' said Caton gently. 'That would be true.'

Chapter 38

He was barely through the door when Ged hurried across the room to meet him.

'You switched your phone off,' she said.

'Sorry.'

'And you didn't tell me where you were going.'

He reached into his pocket to turn it on again.

'Sorry, Ged.'

'You could have left it on vibrate.'

She handed him a note.

'I took this phone call ten minutes ago.'

It wasn't like Ged to reproach him like this. When he read the note he understood why. It was from the Head of the National Bureau of Criminal Investigation in Dublin, Detective Chief Superintendent Eamon McCarthy, who had been so helpful to him and to his cousin Niamh three years before. It was short, and to the point.

Tell him Father Michael Walsh is dead, and that I need to speak with him as soon as possible.

'Call him back, Ged,' he said. 'Please.'

It only took her a minute or two.

'When you gave me that courtesy call to tell me you were coming south of the border,' said McCarthy, without so much as a hello, 'you didn't mention anything about people dying as a result.'

'What happened, Eamon?'

'He had a woman from the parish who went in three times a week to do a bit of housekeeping for him. It was her that found him. She was lucky it was in the morning. If she'd had to switch a light on she'd have blown herself to kingdom come. He was in the kitchen, with his head in the gas oven. His blood alcohol level was through the roof. There was an empty whisky bottle on the kitchen table. Suicide is the obvious conclusion. There has been a lot of it among priests over the past decade. Most of them linked by rumour or allegation to the abuse scandals. That was the senior investigating officer's first thought.'

'I can't see Michel Walsh being involved in child abuse,' said Caton.

'He wasn't,' McCarthy replied. 'Not as far as we know.'

'Nor was he in the frame of mind to commit suicide,' Caton told him. 'Not when we left him. I'd stake my reputation on that.'

'Tell that to the SIO, Tom. I'm at the crime scene. Inspector O'Hannlon is right here beside me. He has some questions for you. Go ahead, Inspector.'

'Mr Caton,' said the SIO. 'Good morning to you. How about you tell me why you were here, what you talked about and how he was when you left him? Then I'll tell you where we're up to at the minute.'

'Fair enough,' said Caton. 'I have the feeling we are going to need each other's help.'

He told him about the murder of Maureen Flinn, the link to the 14th Intelligence unit and what Michael Walsh had told them about Malon Farm. He said nothing about his talks with the former IRA and UDF Commanders, or the names of the rest of the unit. He told him how Father Walsh had seemed when they left him, and that he had promised to provide a formal statement the following day.

'Our sense was that he was relieved to get it off his chest,' he said. 'That it was going to be his last attempt to atone for remaining silent all that time.'

He had to wait for a response.

'Unless he found he couldn't do it,' said the SIO at last. 'Or had second thoughts. Perhaps he decided that the shame that followed would be to hard to bear.'

'Superintendent McCarthy said that suicide would be the obvious conclusion,' said Caton. 'I sensed there was a but?'

Another long pause.

'There are a few things that don't add up,' O'Hannlon admitted.

'Such as?'

'The housekeeper called the local Garda. The officer responding, a bright young man, noted that the dishwasher was beeping. When he investigated he found that it was flagging up that it had finished. Rather than touch the end-cycle button he found the socket and switched it off. Then he told me as soon as I arrived that the dishwasher was less than half full. Two questions: why would you switch it on with so little in it? Why would you switch it on immediately before sticking your head in the oven? I'm thinking that's taking OCD a little too far.'

'What was in the dishwasher?' said Caton.

'Four mugs, a cereal bowl, a side plate, two dinner plates, a tall glass like you'd use for fruit juice, milk or water, and assorted cutlery.' There was a long pause. 'And a whisky tumbler.'

'He didn't drink himself close to oblivion, put the tumbler into the washer and then take his own life,' said Caton.

'No, he did not. Not in our estimation. Nor did he drink straight from the bottle. Sure, his prints were all over the bottle, but we found another identical tumbler on the floor beside the armchair in the lounge. It has his prints on it, and I've no doubt when the results come through we'll find his DNA on it.'

The implications were obvious.

'Not only that, but our forensics people reckon that the downstairs toilet, the kitchen and the lounge had been cleaned. And when we checked the hoover, the bag was empty. The contents were not outside in the dustbin.'

'You checked with the housekeeper?'

'Naturally. The last time she used it was four days ago, and she didn't empty the hoover because it wasn't even half full.'

'You dusted the handle of the hoover?'

'Someone had wiped it clean.'

'There was someone with him that night,' said Caton, 'someone forensically aware.'

'My thoughts entirely.'

'He might have got away with it but for that end-of-cycle alert on the dishwasher,' said Caton.

'Quite possibly. It was that which led me to request a comprehensive forensic examination. His housekeeper told us he'd seemed a bit down when she rang. She mentioned he'd had visitors. With a UK licence plate. It was you.'

'How did she know about that?' said Caton.

'This is a tight-knit community. Things like that get noticed. It's the kind of thing people can't wait to speculate about.'

Caton hadn't seen any curtains twitching, but he knew that it would have only taken someone driving or cycling past to spot the car.

'If those two things hadn't roused my suspicions,' said the SIO, 'it would have been easy to take it at face value.'

'Which was what the perpetrator was banking on.'

'Not that it couldn't still have been suicide, with the second party waking up to find him dead and cleaning up to hide the fact he'd been there, for whatever reason.'

'But you don't think so?'

'I do not,' said O'Hannlon.

'Nor me,' Caton replied.

'Hang on, would you?' said the SIO. 'Chief Superintendent McCarthy wants a word.'

'What I want to know, Tom,' said McCarthy, 'is do we need to involve our Special Detective Unit?'

The last thing Caton wanted was to have the Garda Síochána's security service on-board; the major Irish counter-terrorism and counter-espionage investigative unit in the country. Protocol meant that they would have to contact the MI5 centre at the Palace Barracks near Belfast. They in turn would contact the PSNI. That meant the Historical Enquiries Team finding out. His hopes of getting a clear run at the remaining suspects would be blown out of the water.

'My investigation is a criminal investigation, pure and simple,' he said. 'If there is a connection with Michael Walsh's death, as we both suspect, I can assure you it will be a criminal one. I don't believe there is any terrorist involvement, or a security issue for you or for the UK.'

Even as he said it, Caton was hoping that he was right.

'If anything happens to change that view I need to know immediately, Tom,' said McCarthy. 'Otherwise we could both be in a great deal of trouble.'

'Don't worry, I will,' said Caton.

'I'll make sure DI O'Hannlon has all the resources he needs, and that he keeps you up to speed. I'll pass on anything that may be of help to you. And I assume,

Tom, you'll let me know of any developments that have the slightest relevance to his investigation?'

'Of course, Eamon.'

'Like the names and whereabouts of the other men in Michael Walsh's unit?'

'Naturally.'

'Because if we don't have those soon, DI O'Hannlon will have to get on to the PSNI and see if they can dig them out for him.' He paused. 'But then you'll have tried that already.'

Caton knew that he was being backed into a corner. In McCarthy's place he would have done the same.

'I did,' he said. 'They were very cagey. Something to do with the Historical Enquiries Team and all the political issues surrounding that at the minute.' That at least was true. 'But I managed to get Michael Walsh's name, and I expect to have the rest within forty-eight hours.'

The length of time it took for McCarthy to respond told Caton that he was deciding whether or not to call his bluff. Caton crossed his fingers. He needed time to interview Blair, Finucane and Bell before anyone else got to them.

'Very well,' said the Irish detective. 'I can hold back the pack for forty-eight hours. It'll give us a chance to look at the forensic results. That might narrow the suspects down for us, and for you. After that they'll be snapping at your heels.' He chuckled. 'Metaphorically, of course.'

He paused again.

'And I won't be far behind them.'

Chapter 39

Caton called the team together and told them about Father Michael Walsh.

'The possibilities are limited,' he said. 'Either he did commit suicide, or he was murdered.'

'I don't buy suicide, boss,' said DI Stuart. 'Okay, he was down when we left him, but I'm certain he wanted to put things right. He wouldn't have gone and topped himself.'

'I agree,' Caton replied. 'Which leaves murder. He was a well-loved and respected priest with, according to the Garda, no known enemies. The manner in which his death appears to have been staged, and the relative absence of trace evidence, suggests a professional.'

'A contract killer?' muttered Jean Harper, one of the new Detective Constables.

'Not necessarily,' said DC Hulme. 'Someone trained to kill and to cover their tracks. Secret Service, SAS, Special Boat Squadron, and that's just the ones we know about.'

'Police officers, forensic scientists, pathologists, they'd all know how to cover their tracks,' Harper pointed out.

'Trained to kill?' said DC Hulme. 'That lot? Then we would be in trouble.'

Those around him laughed. Harper's neck flushed red.

'Harper's right,' said Caton. 'You don't have to be a trained killer to get a man drunk, stick his head in the oven and turn on the gas.'

The laughter died away.

'So that brings us to motive. Either someone wanted to stop him talking to us and was not aware that he'd already done so, or they did know, and wanted to make sure he didn't make a formal statement or get to testify if any of it came to court.'

'That wasn't likely to happen though, was it, boss?' said DS Carter. 'From what you said earlier nobody wants the Historical Enquiries Team to reopen the Malon Farm case.'

'And they don't want us dragging it into our investigation either,' Caton reminded him. 'If it turns out there is a link and we expose it in court, they'll have no option but to re-examine it.'

There was silence as he let his words sink in. He turned to face the whiteboard on which the face of Michael Walsh had now appeared alongside that of Maureen Flinn.

'Except,' he said, 'that it won't get to court if we can't make that link, or if someone gets to silence all of our witnesses.'

As he turned back he caught sight of DCS Gates standing in the doorway of the Incident Room. She beckoned him with one finger.

'You are not going to Scotland,' she said sitting down behind her desk.

'I can be there and back in less than a day,' he told her.

'It'll take you just shy of five hours each way, and that doesn't include interviewing this Bell character. Assuming he's actually there.'

'He is. Police Scotland have just confirmed it.'

She glared at him.

'That doesn't change anything. I need you here. Send DI Holmes.'

'DI Holmes has taken a bit of leave.'

'Gordon, taking his leave? That's not like him. Especially in the middle of a high-profile case.'

'That's why I've approved it,' he told her. 'Gordon's looking tired. He needs to take it or he'll burn out.'

She nodded thoughtfully. They all knew about that. And about relationships wrecked by the strain of the job and the long hours. Furthermore, she was no fool. She would have noticed that Holmes was below par, and probably suspected that his drinking was getting out of hand.

'All the more reason to send someone else. DI Stuart for example.'

'She's just come back from Belfast.'

'So have you. She's younger, and she hasn't got a wife who's on the verge of giving birth.'

Not only was Helen wearing him down, he could see her point. He had been away for close on a week. Without Gordon here it needed someone with experience to keep the investigation on track. He didn't have to do it all himself.

'I'll send DS Carter and DC Hulme,' he said.

She nodded.

'Good. Now, what's this about a dead priest?'

The rest of the day passed slowly. He spent an hour reviewing the Policy File and bringing it up to date with his account of the decisions he had taken whilst in Northern Ireland. He was relieved to see that his Deputy had done a good job while he was away, and had left no hostages to fortune, or to Counsel for the Defence. Then he worked through those emails he had not dealt with on his iPad, signed off a stack of overtime and expenses claim forms, and speed-read close to two dozen internal memoranda, each of which was testimony to the three floors full of policymakers and administrators that had survived the austerity cuts, and were determined to prove the need for their own existence.

Over a quick lunch in the canteen he and DI Stuart drew up their interview strategy for David Blair. By the time they had finished, they had less than twenty minutes to get over to Chadderton Police Station.

They were shown up to the second-floor office. It looked like any other Incident Room. Same blue carpet, white walls, white ceiling, standard beige workstations, whiteboards. Only there was one big difference. Every one of the twenty or so members of this murder squad, apart from their SIO, consisted of civilians. Most of them former police officers, now unwarranted and without powers of arrest. Not that they needed them. Their perpetrators were already known to the police. For each case there was a single prime suspect, many of whom had already admitted their guilt. The job of this team was to screw the supporting evidence down tighter than a drum and hand it on a plate to the Crown Prosecution Service.

Caton recognised some of the team. Several had worked with him in the past. Friendly nods were exchanged. The rest regarded the two of them with suspicion. Word had got round. One of their own was about to be questioned.

'Bit on the chunky side this lot,' whispered DI Stuart. Forestalling accusations of sizeism, she hastily added, 'Just an observation, boss.'

She had no need to worry.

'Hardly surprising,' Caton whispered back.

'Retired, and deskbound.'

DCI Tony Andrews, the head of the unit, waved them into his room.

'Tom, good to see you.'

'You too,' said Caton. 'It's been too long.'

Apart from brief episodes of senior officer training, they hadn't worked together for over twelve years. Having trained together at Bruche and joined GMP at the same time, they had developed a strong bond until their work had taken them in different directions. It was a job that made it difficult to sustain such relationships. Something Caton strongly regretted.

He introduced Joanne Stuart.

'Pleasure to meet you, DI Stuart,' said Andrews, offering his hand. 'I've heard all about you. Congratulations on your promotion.'

'Thank you,' she said. 'But I'm only Acting DI at the moment.'

'If it really was acting she'd be getting an Oscar,' Caton told him. Fearing that she'd find that patronising, he hurriedly added, 'So far.'

'You can have a chat with David in here, Tom,' said Andrews. 'I'll clear off and grab a coffee. I'll send drinks in to you. I know David will have coffee; what would you two like?'

'If it's all the same to you we'd prefer to use one of the interview rooms,' said Caton.

The SIO's face clouded over. He moved past them and closed the door.

'I assumed he was giving you some background. That this was an informal chat.'

'It's not a formal interview under caution,' said Caton. 'Not yet.'

Andrews slumped into his chair, and ran his hand through his hair.

'What's he been up to? No, don't tell me.' He

scanned their faces, hoping to discover how bad this might get. 'Will he need his Federation Representative? He's still entitled.'

'I don't know, Tony,' said Caton. 'That will be for him to decide. Although if we do get to that point I would expect him to ask for a lawyer instead.'

Chapter 40

Blair looked older than his fifty-eight years. But then some of that could have been down to the nervousness he was trying hard to disguise.

'This was the last thing I expected,' he said. 'Coming back from leave to an interview with the A team.'

'I'm surprised our paths have never crossed, David,' said Caton, easing his way in.

'That's probably because most of my time in GMP was spent in Wigan, and Bolton,' he replied. 'Five years in uniform, and then eleven in CID.'

'You were with Merseyside before that?' said Joanne Stuart.

He switched his attention to her, as though seeing her for the first time,

'They'd only become Merseyside six years before, and it was still a shambles. Took them another four years to really sort it out. Still, spent most of my time in Liverpool, which suited me.'

'When was the county of Merseyside formed?' said Caton.

'1974.' He grinned. 'What is this, Mastermind?'

'So that means you joined up in 1980,' said Caton. 'You'd have been, what?' He looked down at the notes in front of him.

'Twenty-four,' said Blair.

Caton nodded.

'Straight from the Army. How many years had you served?'

Blair looked genuinely confused.

'Eight,' he said, 'but I don't see–'

'How many years did you sign up for?'

'Nine.'

'You were lucky they let you go early. Right in the middle of the Troubles?'

'It was a reorganisation.' He shifted uneasily in his chair. 'Look, I got an honourable discharge if that's what you're wondering.'

They remained silent, as agreed beforehand. He looked at each of them in turn. It was clear that his anxiety levels had risen.

'Look, what has all this got to do with GMP? What exactly are you investigating?'

'Murder,' said Caton.

Blair's pupils dilated momentarily, and then narrowed again. He paused too long before asking the question. Classic signs that he was considering the possibilities, and his options.

'Go on then,' he said. 'Ask me where I was at the time of the incident.'

'Where were you at the time of the incident, David?'

He folded his arms and shrugged.

'I don't know. When was it exactly?'

'Where were you, David, between one thirty a.m. and five thirty a.m. the Saturday before last?'

'The Saturday before last?' He smiled, and appeared to relax. 'In bed. It's where you'll find me at that time regardless of what day it is.'

'Do you need to check your diary, David?' said Joanne Stuart.

'No need. I was definitely at home, in bed.'

'Can anyone vouch for that?' asked Caton.

He shook his head. His face contorted into a wry grimace.

'Chance'd be a fine thing.'

'No wife then?' said Joanne Stuart.

'Not since she walked out twenty years ago.'

'Any special reason for that?'

For the first time his body language and the tone of his voice betrayed hostility.

'None of your business, sweetheart. Not unless it has something to do with your murder.'

'What did you do that evening, David?' said Caton.

'The usual. Watched tele. Put an M&S curry in the microwave, cracked open a couple of cans. Went to bed. Probably about midnight.'

'Do you remember what you watched?'

He gave him a look, and shrugged. 'Saturday night, was it? A film. Graham Norton. Match of the Day.'

'Was it a live film, one you'd recorded, FreeView or a DVD?'

He looked wary suddenly. Aware that anything other than live they could probably check against the memory on the set top box.

'Live, probably,' he said. 'If I did watch one.'

'Fair enough,' said Caton.

He looked down at his notes again.

'You've been away on leave for the past week, David.' He looked up and stared at him. 'Away where exactly?'

Blair stared back.

'I don't get it,' he said. 'What's that got to do with this murder you're investigating?'

'It's a long story,' said Caton. 'Humour me, and answer the question please.'

He shrugged, at ease once again.

'It's not a problem. I was in Kyle, in the Highlands. Knocking off a few Corbetts.'

Joanne Stuart leaned forward.

'Corbetts?'

'Mountains over 2,500 feet and under 3,000 feet,' said Caton. 'Lower than a Munro, and higher than a Graham.'

Blair nodded enthusiastically and leaned forward himself.

'Spot on! How many have you done?'

'I've no idea,' said Caton. 'It's some years since I went climbing, and I wasn't keeping count. In any case, the Lake District was my regular haunt.'

Blair sat back and laughed.

'Climbing for softies,' he said. 'Give me Scotland anytime.'

'I'd have thought you were getting a bit old for mountain climbing,' said Joanne Stuart, still stinging from the sweetheart comment, but managing not to make it sound like an insult.

'Wainright was still climbing in his seventies,' he told her. 'I'm hoping to go one better.'

'Where did you stay in the Highlands, David?' said Caton.

'In a rented a cottage between Lienassie and Dorusdain, about twelve miles east of the Kyle of Lochalsh.'

'On your own?'

'On my own.'

'People will have seen you though? In the pub, the shops, out climbing?'

He shook his head.

'I'm not one for the pub. Not where I'm a stranger. Didn't use the local shops either. Mainly because there aren't any. I bought everything I needed on the way. I can show you my debit card receipts for that. As for fellow climbers, you know what it's like. Bob hat, anorak, climbing gear, it's difficult to remember one from another. Not unless you have a meaningful conversation.'

'Which you didn't?'

'Which I didn't. Morning. Afternoon. Lousy weather we're having. Any problems up there I should know about? That's as good as it got. But I suppose someone will remember me.'

Caton and Stuart exchanged glances, but said nothing.

Blair sat up straight.

'Hang on,' he said. 'The Saturday before last? Is this about that woman found shot in Angel Meadow? Maureen–'

'Flinn,' said Caton. 'Maureen Flinn.'

Blair smiled.

'That's it. Maureen Flinn. Well, in that case you are wasting your time and mine. I'd never heard of her till it was on the tele.'

'Okay, David,' said Caton. 'Let's move on.'

He pushed his notes aside and relaxed back in his seat.

'Tell us about Malon Farm.'

Surprise leached into anger. Blair lurched forward and slammed the table with the flat of his hand.

'Is that what this bollocks is all about?! Why the hell are you dredging it up now? That investigation was closed nigh on thirty years ago.'

Caton waited for him to sink back into his seat.

'What's the matter, David?' he said. 'Why so excited? According to the case notes it had nothing to do with you, other than securing the scene of the crime.'

Blair waited until he had recovered his composure before replying, but when he did, Caton noticed that there was still a vein pulsing at the side of his neck.

'That's right,' Blair replied. 'It was either the Provos or the Proddies. 'We were completely exonerated.'

Caton and Stuart exchanged glances again.

'Exonerated?' said Caton. 'I wasn't aware that your unit was ever under suspicion.'

Blair's reaction was almost imperceptible. No more than a little squirm, but evident to trained eyes.

'We weren't,' he said. 'It was just a figure of speech.'

'Why so upset then?' said DI Stuart.

'If you'd been there you'd be upset,' he told her. 'It never leaves you, something like that.'

'Tell us about it, David,' said Caton. 'Don't worry, this is off the record.'

His account was word perfect. Too perfect. A carbon copy of the one they had concocted together all those years ago. As though he had been rehearsing it for just such an occasion as this. They listened without interruption, until he reached the end.

'You can see why I was upset,' he said. 'A whole family butchered. It's not something you want to be reminded of.'

Caton exchanged a smiled with his DI and nodded his permission for her to respond.

'Not the whole family, David,' she said.

He stared back at her, uncomprehending.

'What do you mean?'

'You missed the girls.'

He looked at Caton, and then back at her. There was a hint of desperation in his eyes.

'Girls? What girls. There was only one girl.'

'The Malones had two more daughters,' she told him. 'They were there in the farm that night. Only you missed them. Maureen Flinn was one of them. Her name was Caitlin, in case you're interested. And while you claim you were away climbing Corbetts in Scotland, your former colleague Michael Walsh was also killed. Within twenty-four hours of telling his version of events.'

'That's two witnesses down and only four to go,' said Caton.

'And you are one of them,' said Joanne Stuart. 'Which makes you either the killer, or potentially the next victim. 'Which is it, David?'

His face was ashen, and his mouth had gaped open.

'Don't answer that,' said Caton. 'Not until I've reminded you of your rights.'

When Blair finally managed to speak, they had to strain to hear him.

'I want a solicitor,' he said.

Chapter 41

'What do you think, Jo?

They had left David Blair in the care of his boss, Tony Andrews, until the solicitor and his Federation Rep arrived. Now they were sitting drinking tea out of plastic beakers, in a cramped exhibits room barely big enough to swing a cat.

'He seemed genuinely surprised to learn about the girls, and about Father Walsh's death,' she said. 'If it is him, he's a bloody good actor.' She cracked a wry smile. 'Not as good as me though.'

'Sorry about that,' he said, with a sheepish grin. 'I meant it though. You've done well.'

She dug him in the side, almost causing him to spill his drink.

'So far.'

'Okay,' said Caton. 'Enough already.'

He put his mug on the floor in the only space available.

'This is how I propose we approach the interview.'

They had barely finished when there was a knock on the door. It opened, and DCI Andrews put his head round it. He looked upset.

'They're ready for you, Tom.' He paused, wondering whether to say anything else. Then he made a decision and went for it. 'Look, he's told me what this is about. Not all of it, but enough. It sounds like a bloody mess. For what it's worth, I've advised him to be straight with you. Hope it helps.'

They stood up.

'Thanks, Tony,' said Caton. 'I appreciate it. If it's any consolation, none of this will reflect on your team.'

They walked the gauntlet of hostile expressions from those who had the courage to look up from their computers. The door closed behind them and they started down the stairs.

'That felt like we were from Internal Affairs,' she said. 'It's a bit uncalled for, given they don't even know what we're doing here.'

'We are about to give one of their own a hard time,' he replied. 'That's all they need to know. It's called closing ranks.'

He stopped on the first landing.

'If Blair and his pals hadn't closed ranks thirty-five years ago,' he said, 'Maureen Flinn and Michael Walsh would be alive today.'

Introductions over, and the formal caution given, Caton pointed to the brand new digital recording device.

'This is our first time with this,' he said. 'Copies will be made available as per normal. This interview is also being video recorded. Should you require an audio cassette or MP3 version, we can provide those. To help us check the sound levels, it would be helpful if you could each introduce yourselves on my prompt. Everybody ready?'

They nodded. He switched on the device.

'Interview with David Blair, under caution, sixteen thirty hours, Thursday 22nd of June 2014. At North Manchester Divisional Headquarters. Present are…'

He nodded for each of them to speak in turn.

'David Blair.'

'Michael Mickleson, of Mickleson, Waters and Hope. Solicitor.'

'James Harnot, Police Federation Representative.'

'And,' said Caton, 'conducting the interview, Detective Chief Inspector Caton and…'

'Detective Inspector Joanne Stuart.'

'Mr Blair,' he began. 'How would you like us to address you?'

Blair was still pale, but had clearly steeled himself for the ordeal. His professionalism seemed to have kicked in. He was sitting upright and appeared composed.

'David will do,' he replied.

The first half of the interview, led by DI Stuart, was a repeat of the informal questions put to him about his whereabouts at the time of the murder of Maureen Flinn, and the suspected murder of Michael Walsh. His answers remained unchanged. He was able to provide no new corroborating evidence for his whereabouts.

'Moving on,' said Caton. 'I have to make it clear, for the tape, that this part of the interview relates to another case which is not currently part of GMP jurisdiction.'

He could see that both Mickleson and Harnot were about to interrupt and headed them off.

'However, we do have reason to believe that it is connected with the murder of Maureen Flinn.'

'Whose case does it relate to, Detective Chief Inspector?' asked the solicitor.

Caton hesitated.

'The Police Service of Northern Ireland, Mr Mickleson,' he said, deliberately avoiding mention of the Historical Enquiries Team.

'And will a tape or transcript of this interview be shared with them now, or at some time in the future?'

'Their case is currently awaiting review,' he said. 'If what your client tells us is likely to have relevance for that review then yes, we will be duty bound to inform them that this interview has taken place. If they then requested a copy we would be obliged to provide it. As with any other UK police force.'

Blair turned to his solicitor.

'I know where you're going with this,' he said. 'I told you, I'm prepared to make a statement, and I'm prepared to answer any questions put to me. I'm well aware of the potential consequences, and I have nothing to hide.'

He smiled ruefully.

'Not any more I don't.'

Mickleson sat back with a sigh that made it clear he was accepting no responsibility if it all went bottoms up. That suited Caton. It meant far less chance of further interruptions. Harnot the Federation Rep simply sat there looking bemused.

'Very well, David,' said Caton. 'I would like to keep this simple. Let's take it from the point at which you and the other members of your detachment arrived in the vicinity of Malon Farm.'

Blair nodded. He took a deep breath and began.

'Walsh was driving. Finucane was in the front. I was in the back with Gilchrist and Ellis. We parked up in a lane.'

'Did you know there had been an SAS observation on Malon Farm?' said Caton.

'Yes.'

'Were you told why they withdrew shortly before you went in?'

He looked surprised. Thought about it. Shook his head.

'No. I assumed it was standard practice.'

'It wasn't standard practice for a 14th Int. detachment to conduct a search and seize operation though?'

'No.'

'Weren't you at all suspicious?'

'Not really. You have to understand that the balloon had gone up after Mountbatten and Warrenpoint. Nobody knew where they were going to strike next. It was a bit like the US after 9/11. Panic stations. We were stretched. Everyone was running around like headless chickens. If you were told to do something you just did it.'

Caton let the words hang there for a moment. Then he nodded.

'Okay, David. Please carry on.'

'Finucane said we were going in to establish if there was an arms cache on the farm. If there was, that meant we'd likely be facing hostiles. He didn't want anyone taking any risks. Then he said, "If in doubt, remember the Yellow Card para' 15."'

'I think you'll have to tell all of us what that means, David,' said Caton.

'The Yellow Card was the Army Code 70771. Our rules of engagement. We had to learn it by heart and carry it with us at all times.'

'And paragraph 15?'

Blair looked down at the table, as though reading from an autocue. Then he raised his head and repeated it verbatim in the manner of a private responding to his sergeant major.

'Relating to those conditions under which it is permissible to fire without warning, Paragraph 15 states: If there is no other way to protect themselves or those whom it is their duty to protect from the danger of being killed or seriously injured.'

Had Blair been standing, Caton would not have been surprised if he had clicked his heels and bellowed Sir!

'You have a good memory, David,' he said. 'Is there any particular reason that you still remember that paragraph?'

'Detective Chief Inspector!' exclaimed the solicitor.

'We are not in court,' Caton replied, resisting the temptation to add yet. 'But I'm quite happy for your client not to answer the question.'

Blair's reaction had already told him as much as he needed to know, for now.

'Please carry on, David,' he said. 'What happened next?'

Blair picked up the plastic beaker full of water in front of him, had a few sips and put it down.

'Finucane said that he, Gilchrist and Ellis were going to reccy the barn where the SAS reckoned the arms were stashed. I was to keep watch with a night scope. If anyone came out of the farm Walsh was to start the engine as a warning to the others. We all applied camouflage to our faces and our hands, then the three of them got out.'

'DI Stuart and I know what happened next,' said Caton. 'Let's fast forward to the point where they came back from the barn. Did you notice what they were carrying?'

He tried to look perplexed, but Caton could see that he knew where this was leading.

'Their weapons.'

'Was there anything unusual about any of them, their weapons?'

He shook his head a little too fast.

'I don't think so. It was dark. I wouldn't have noticed if there had been.'

'Carry on.'

'They were really excited. Especially Ellis. It was a major find, they said. Guns, grenades, bomb-making equipment. Finucane said it meant there were definitely hostiles in the farmhouse. They would never leave a stash like that unprotected. We were going in to seize and detain suspected Tangos.'

'He used those exact words, seize and detain?'

'Yes.'

'Carry on.'

'He said he needed me to join them. I was to go round the back and cover the rear in case they tried to escape that way and off over the fields. We set off together, in a classic four-man fire team wedge. Ellis led out, Gilchrist was on the left flank, Finucane on the right and I was centre rear.'

His voice had become constricted, as though his throat was tightening up. He took another sip and cleared his throat. His arms were now wrapped around him as though hugging himself. His gaze was fixed on a point in the middle of Caton's chest.

'After about thirty metres the other three peeled off and headed for the barn on the right where the arms were stashed. When they were in a position to cover me, I skirted the farmhouse, found a low stone wall about fifteen metres from the back door and hunkered down behind it. Then I waited.'

'Could you see any lights on in the farmhouse?'

'From where I was crouching?'

'Yes.'

He thought about it.

'There was a light in what was clearly the kitchen, and another in a small room upstairs. I assumed it was a bedroom.'

'Then what?'

'I waited.'

He paused. When he started talking again his

voice sounded strangely detached, as though he was reliving it all over again.

'I was sweating, despite the cool night air. There must have been a slurry pit close by because the smell was almost overpowering. An owl hooted somewhere nearby, and I could hear cows moving around in a barn off to my right. The moon came out from behind a cloud, picking out the lime-washed walls of the farmhouse. I ducked down a bit more. It must have been only a couple of minutes, but it felt like forever. Then I heard all three of them shouting, "Hands up! Hands up!" A woman screamed. Then there was firing. One short burst. Then one long one.'

There was a long pause.

'I kept my weapon trained on the back door. Strained to hear something, anything. I tried them on my Clansman, but there was no response.'

'Clansman?' said Caton.

Blair looked up.

'Man-portable patrol radio. We'd only just been issued with them. I didn't know if it was faulty or if they were just not answering.'

His eyes dropped again.

'I gave it another minute, then I tried again. Finucane replied. "All clear. Get round here," he said. So I did. When I got to the door it was closed. I shouted Frank's name, just to be sure. He responded. I went in.'

He stopped for another drink from the beaker.

When he looked up, his composure had slipped. His face had a haunted look about it. His voice cracked several times during the telling.

'It was like something out of a horror movie. A total fucking disaster. The parlour opened up into a dining area. There was a man lying face down, his left arm pointing towards the door. There was a shotgun lying beside it. The side of his chest was ripped open. On the bench behind him was the body of a woman. She was slumped over a child, a young boy, who must have been sitting beside her. The back of her dress was soaked with blood. Her head was on the table. The boy…'

He tried again.

'The boy … half his head had been blown away.'

He reached for the beaker, saw it was empty and put it down. He clung to it with both hands as though to steady himself.

'Finucane was standing to the left of the man's body. Ellis was slumped against the door that led to the kitchen. Gilchrist was stood over to the right. He was looking down at something, intently. I moved forward a pace and followed his gaze. There were two more bodies. Another boy, older, and a girl, about ten or eleven. They'd both fallen backwards, taking the bench with them. The boy had his back to me and his arm was flung around his sister as though trying to protect her. There was blood all over the floor, and on the wall behind them.'

He paused for a long time. Nobody spoke. Caton remembered the overworked analogy about the tension in a room being almost electric. Joanne Stuart pushed her untouched beaker of water across the table. Blair seemed reluctant to relinquish his hold on his own beaker, but he did. He picked up the full one, had a sip, put it down and hugged it with both hands.

'I remember feeling sick. Of fighting back this burning wave of nausea. I swore, over and over again. I remember shouting, "What happened?! What the fuck did you do?!" Gilchrist said something like, "Pull yourself together, Davey." I turned to Finucane. He was calm. He said, "It was self-defence, Blair. It had to be done." I pointed to the woman and her kids. I shouted, "How the fuck is this self-defence?" Ellis said, "You weren't here, Davey. Their dad's a Tango. He had a gun. Point blank. He could've taken two of us out." I pointed to the wife and her kids again. "Where's her gun? Where the fuck are theirs?" Then Gilchrist said, "That one, he got up. He was holding something. He pointed it at me."

'I walked over and had a look. All I could see was those two wretched bodies in a pool of blood. Then I caught a flash of light in the corner of the room. I went and picked it up. It was a knife. A table knife. I held it up. "Is this your gun?" I asked. "Is this your fucking gun?" I put it on the table and walked towards the door. Finucane said, "You shouldn't have done that." He took out his camouflage handkerchief, picked up the knife, wiped it clean and put it back down on the table. "We were never here," he said. He looked at each of us in turn. "Repeat after me, we were never here." The other two said it in unison. He looked at me. They all did. Ellis and Gilchrist stood up straight. Their rifles were raised. I sensed fingers tightening. "I want to hear you say it, Davey," Finucane said.'

Blair locked eyes with Caton. As though willing him to see inside his soul. Just like Father Walsh when he had sought forgiveness. His voice faltered. The three of them craned forward to catch it.

'I said it. I said we were never there.'

Chapter 42

Caton suspended the interview for a short break. Blair's solicitor had requested it, but he would have done so anyway. It gave him and Joanne Stuart an opportunity to review their tactics. When they recommenced, DI Stuart took the lead.

'Did you leave the farm together, David?' she asked.

He thought about it, and shook his head.

'No. Finucane told me to go first and wait outside. Two minutes later, the others came out. Finucane said that Ellis and me should wait while he and Gilchrist checked the barn again.'

'Why did they need to check the barn?'

'He didn't say. They were less than a minute in there. When they came out Finucane told us over the Comms to get back to the vehicle. He and Gilchrist joined us as we were exiting onto the lane.'

'Did you notice anything different when they came out of the barn that second time?' she asked.

Blair looked surprised. Caton thought it was less the question than him wondering how she knew.

'How do you mean?' Blair asked.

She leaned forward.

'You said you were going to be straight with us, David. Are you going to tell us, or do I have to spell it out?'

His shoulders slumped.

'Gilchrist, he was carrying a large sack over his shoulder. It looked heavy.'

'Of course it did. But then you'd know that. I bet it clanked a bit too?'

Blair's expression replied for him.

'So, you got to the Land Rover,' she said. 'What then?'

'Finucane told me to get back in the front. The other three got in the back. Walsh wanted to know what the hell had happened. He'd heard the firing and the screams. He was well spooked. Finucane told him what he'd told me. That it was self-defence, but that it might look bad. Especially to the Provos. He said we had to get out of there A-SAP.'

'A-SAP?'

'As soon as possible.'

'Of course.'

His saying it that way, rather than spelling it out, had thrown her.

'Then what?' she asked.

'He gave Walsh a map reference and we set off. We drove for about four clicks. Then he told Walsh to stop and back up a track that led into a wooded area. Then he parked up. We sat there listening to the Comms, waiting to hear if anyone had reported the shooting.'

'Did you see Gilchrist get out of the back of the Land Rover?'

Again, he looked surprised.

'No. But I heard him get back in.'

'Did you know that he'd taken the sack with him?'

'No.'

'What did you think was in it?'

He shrugged.

'I had no idea.'

'Now, on reflection? After all these years?' said Joanne Stuart.

'That he was hiding some kind of evidence.'

'What kind of evidence?'

It was a long pause.

'Weapons.'

'What weapons?'

'The ones that had been fired in the farmhouse.'

The Federation Rep exhaled noisily, sat back, folded his arms and shook his head. His client's position had just taken a nosedive. Covering up self-defence in a wartime situation was one thing, but this?

'We know that they were not their own weapons,' Joanne Stuart said. 'Because those were checked by the RUC Forensics team and found not to have been fired. Which begs the question, where did they come from?'

He shrugged.

'I don't know.'

'Take an educated guess, David,' she said. 'We won't hold you to it.'

He looked at his solicitor and then at his Federation Rep. Neither of them had anything to say on the matter. It wasn't as though they hadn't already worked it out for themselves.

He turned back to face her, folded his arms and shrugged again.

'The barn?'

'Which suggests premeditation, don't you think?' she said.

'You don't have to answer that,' said Mickleson, his solicitor.

He did anyway.

'If it was, I knew nothing about it,' he replied.

'Said nothing about it either,' she replied. 'Not until now.'

'His solicitor was right,' said Joanne Stuart.

They were back in the Incident Room, sitting in

Caton's cubbyhole of a work space.

'He volunteered that information, and the original incident at Malon Farm is something we're not even supposed to be investigating.'

'Only after he knew we'd already spoken to Michael Walsh. Besides, Angel Meadow and Malon Farm are connected. And he hasn't got an alibi for either.'

'He did agree to our searching his house, and checking his phone records,' she pointed out.

'Only because he knows we'd have no problem getting a warrant, and it looks better if he volunteers it first. All that means is that he's confident we won't find anything. That if he is involved, he's covered his tracks. He stays here till we've conducted that search.'

'Then what?'

'Then we get the custody officer to give him unconditional police bail while we carry out our investigation.'

'Either Mickleson or Harnot are bound to claim we're running a "bail and see" operation. Keeping him on a rope while we take as long as we like over it.'

'Let them,' said Caton. 'Besides, we won't be hanging around. Not with Finnoula, Frances that is, flying in tomorrow.'

'Did you believe him when he said he hadn't been in touch with any of the others since he left the Army?' she asked.

'Difficult to tell. Although if I was him I would want to put as much distance between me and them as possible.'

'Based on his statement he could be charged with conspiracy to pervert the course of justice,' she said. 'But the CPS won't want to take it on unless we can tie him to Maureen Flinn's murder, or to Michael Walsh's. And the HET, the PSNI and God knows who else have already made it clear they don't want to reopen the Malon Farm case.'

'I know.'

'And,' she added, 'there's all this talk of an amnesty.'

'Not for the security forces.'

'That's hardly a level playing field.'

'It isn't,' he agreed. 'But once law keepers are told they can break the law with impunity, we all go to hell in a dustcart.'

'That would be a handcart, boss.'

Wallace had suddenly appeared, as though teleported, in the gap between the two partitions that served as a doorway.

'First appeared in the Trenton Times, New Jersey, 1895. Probably a reference to the plague burials of the seventeenth century.'

'What's this,' said Caton. 'Are you doing an impersonation of DC Hulme?'

'Sorry, boss,' he said, 'but DS Carter sent me a Skype message. He tried to ring you but your phone was on voicemail. Then he tried Ged, but she's out of the office. I told him you were back in now. He's waiting for you to call back.'

'Skype?' said Caton. I didn't know we had that on our system.'

Wallace looked apprehensive.

'I do, boss,' he said.

'Did you get authorisation?'

'The Bedfordshire force are using it to let people report crimes,' Wallace replied. 'It's saving them thousands. There's even talk of them closing down some part-time police stations.'

'That's not what I asked you.'

'I talked to a guy in IT. He said it would be okay if I trialled it.'

'And you didn't think to pass it by me?'

'Sorry, boss,' he repeated. 'Do you want me to Skype him back? DS Carter? Then you can talk to him face to face.'

Caton stood up.

'Come on, DI Stuart,' he said. 'As for you Wallace, I'll talk to you later. Face to face.'

Caton had to admit, the picture was remarkably clear. Not only that, but as communications went it was more secure than a landline. And free, as Wallace had been quick to point out. DS Carter was seated at a desk of some kind. DC Hulme lurked in the background, every so often peering over Carter's shoulder.

'We had a job tracking Bell down,' said Carter. 'He's got a part-time job as a deerstalker. The season starts up here on Sunday apparently, and he was out scoping some of the prize stags in readiness.'

'What did he have to say?'

'We met him in the Black Watch Inn in town. He wasn't forthcoming. Basically he said he'd served his time and he had nothing to say.'

'I hope you didn't let him get away with that?'

'No, boss. I told him why we wanted to talk with him. He wanted to know what it had to do with Malon Farm. I think he was genuinely surprised to learn that there had been two other girls at the farm that night. He was even more surprised to hear that one of them had just been murdered.'

'What was his reaction?'

'He looked thoughtful. Then he asked me when it had happened. When I told him, he said he'd been right here in the pub all night.'

DC Hulme, obviously feeling left out, interjected.

'There'd been a quiz night, then he played

dominoes. It checked out, boss. There's no way he could have done it.'

Carter looked annoyed at having his thunder stolen. Hulme must have spotted his face in the tiny video window at the bottom of the screen, because he quickly backed off.

'What about the day that Michael Walsh died, DS Carter?' said Caton.

'He didn't have an alibi for that one,' the Detective Sergeant replied. 'He was out on the moors, then home alone. I reckon he favours solitude and a glass of malt whisky beside an open fire.'

'Don't we all. Did you try asking him about Malon Farm again?'

Carter shook his head, and his face blurred.

'I asked him, but it was all, "No Comment." He said as far as he's concerned it was put to rest years ago.'

'Has he been in contact with any of the others? Blair, Finucane, or Walsh when he was still alive?'

'He swears not. And I use the word swears advisedly.'

'Did he seem to be aware that he might be in danger?'

'I pointed that out to him. Told him to take care.'

'What did he say?'

'"You don't want to worry about me, laddie. I've a cabinet full of guns. I know this area like the back of my hand. And any stranger looking for trouble is going to stand out like a fairground target."'

'I hope you warned him about taking matters into his own hands?'

Hulme cut in.

'Tried to, boss,' he said. 'But you could tell it was a waste of time.'

'Right,' said Caton. 'The two of you get back here

as fast as you can. I'm going to need you.'

Their faces fell.

'We were thinking of booking a room here for the night,' said a hopeful Carter. 'And setting off first thing in the morning.'

'After breakfast,' DC Hulme reminded him.

'Sorry, guys,' said Caton. 'No malt whisky beside an open fire for you tonight.'

Chapter 43

The search of Blair's property provided no new evidence. Caton let him go on unconditional police bail while they checked his phone records, together with the passenger lists for all of the ferry's plying between Northern Ireland and the Republic, and the rest of the UK. Not just for Blair, but for Bell and Finucane too. He didn't hold out too much hope; all three were experienced enough to know to use a false identity.

He had just returned to his desk when his internal phone rang. It was Ged.

'You're back,' she said in a hushed tone. 'Barbara Bryce from the National Crime Agency is waiting on a secure line for you in the Comms Room.'

'Thanks, Ged,' he said. 'Tell them I'm on my way.'

'Tom,' said Bryce, 'I thought this was urgent.'

It wasn't like her to be this brusque. He couldn't tell if she was annoyed or simply run ragged.

'I'm sorry,' he said. 'I was interviewing a murder suspect when you rang back. They decided not to interrupt.'

'I hope it had nothing to do with the reason you want to interview our man?'

Now she was sounding cautious.

'I'm afraid it has. I think there's a connection. I

need to interview him for the purposes of elimination.'

'Elimination from what exactly?'

He told her.

When he'd finished she placed a hand over the phone and swore mightily. Caton heard it anyway. He couldn't blame her. One way or another this looked like bringing trouble to her door.

'You're not serious?' she said.

'About what? Malon Farm, Angel Meadow or the Irish priest?'

'All of them. An NCA officer going out on a limb like that? He'd know he'd never get away with it. It's far more likely to be one of the Irish Terrorist organisations. They are still at it you know.'

'Come on, Barbara,' he said, wondering if given the circumstances he should start calling her Deputy Director. 'This is too much of a coincidence. We know that your man was involved in the Malon Farm shootings; whether or not it was self-defence is another matter. I can see why either side in the sectarian conflict might want to take revenge on members of that unit for Malon Farm, but not for Maureen Flinn. It doesn't make sense. On the other hand, eliminating both her and the others as witnesses does.'

There was silence while she had a think. When she spoke there was both firmness and urgency in her voice.

'He's been giving you the run around you say?'

'We think so.'

'Right,' she said. 'Leave it with me. I'll get you your interview, but I want one of ours there in the room with him.'

'It's a deal,' he said.

'You bet your life it is,' she replied. 'Because it's the only one you're going to get.'

Caton settled down to wade through the remainder of the mound of paperwork that had piled up in his in-tray while he was away. He was astonished when, less than an hour after his phone call with Barbara Bryce, Ged came to tell him that there were two NCA Officers waiting for him at reception.

'Shall I show them up?' she asked.

'No way,' he said. 'Have them both shown to whichever interview room happens to be available. Make sure they get a drink, and tell them I'll be with them shortly.'

This was when he missed Gordon Holmes. For all his rough, bluff exterior Gordon had a wisdom born of years of experience. DI Stuart was intelligent and quick on the uptake when a change of direction was required, and she brought a different dimension. One he could not quite put his finger on. But Finucane was going to be a tricky interviewee. With an army background, years in Special Branch and now a trained NCA Officer, he would know all there was to know about interview techniques, and even interrogation.

'With any luck,' he told her, 'it might just make him over-confident. That's something we can use.'

Unfortunately, it wasn't just Finucane they had to deal with. The person accompanying him, arms folded, scowled as he and DI Stuart entered.

'You just can't leave us alone, can you, Caton?' said Simon Levi, Deputy Director of the NCA Organised Crime Command, brushing an imaginary fly from the shoulder of his suit.

Beside him sat a man in a navy hoodie over blue jeans. Because he was seated it was difficult to be sure, but he looked to be just below average height. He was lean and sinewy. There was no sign of the middle age spread that his age might have warranted. His hair was black, with a few streaks of grey at the temples. His eyes were dark brown, and bright. He regarded the two detectives with genuine interest. There was not a hint of anxiety about him.

Aside from his obvious intelligence, here was a man who exuded physical and mental toughness. Caton was reminded of every member of special services that he had ever met. Little wonder that he had been selected to lead a 14th Int. Detachment, and had been recruited to Special Branch and now to the National Crime Agency.

Caton wondered what impression Finucane was making on DI Stuart, and if she, like him, was already questioning that hopeful comment about the NCA officer's probable overconfidence.

Caton did not respond to Levi's comment. Instead, he and Stuart introduced themselves. Levi introduced Finucane, who merely smiled and nodded.

'Frank's come here voluntarily,' said Levi. 'So I'm assuming this is an informal interview which we can get over with asap, so we can all get back to doing something important.'

'You're right in as much as Mr Finucane has not been arrested,' said Caton. 'As to whether or not he is here voluntarily is open to debate.'

'What the hell are you talking about?!'

Finucane placed a hand on Levi's arm and squeezed.

'It's alright, Simon,' he said. 'DCI Caton has a point. I haven't exactly made it easy for him.'

Levi pulled his arm away and rubbed it furiously.

'And why was that?' said Caton. 'I'm curious.'

Finucane smiled. It was an open smile, seemingly without artifice.

'It's a difficult time, Detective Chief Inspector,' he said. 'I am currently involved with an operation, the details of which I am not at liberty to share. However, I can tell you that it involves serious organised crime and at least one undercover operative. That person's safety has to be my prime consideration. I'm sure you understand.'

'Both DI Stuart and I have covert experience,' Caton told him.

If only you knew, he thought, just how close I came to losing Stuart because I hadn't got all the angles covered.

'There you go then,' said the Finucane. 'You'll know why I can't guarantee where I'll be from one minute to the next.'

Caton pulled out his chair and sat down. Joanne Stuart sat next to him, opposite Simon Levi.

'But you do keep records of where you've been?' said Caton.

'Of course.'

'Good, that should speed things up.'

'What precisely have you asked us here for?' said Levi in an attempt to reassert his authority.

'Barbara didn't tell you?'

Levi glowered.

'Mrs Bryce, the Deputy Director, asked us to come over here and assist you,' he said. 'She did not say why.'

Caton pictured the conversation. They hadn't been asked to attend this interview, they'd been told. But it was interesting that she had not mentioned the reason why he wanted to interview Finucane.

'I think you know, don't you, Frank?' he said.

'Actually, I don't,' Finucane replied.

'On the three occasions that my colleagues tried to arrange an interview with you did they not mention the reason?'

'I don't believe so.'

'And yet you agreed to come and see us?'

'I'm basically curious,' he said. 'And always happy to help police officers,' he smiled. 'After all, I still am one really.'

'But not curious enough to ask why?' said Joanne Stuart.

He slowly turned his head, and calmly appraised her. The manner in which he did so was neither insolent nor sexist. It was a question of professional analysis. If anything, it made her feel even more uncomfortable.

'No,' he said. 'Sometimes it's much more interesting to wait and see.'

'Can we get to it?' Levi interjected. 'We're both busy, even if you're not.'

Caton flipped open the file in front of him.

'Where were you, Mr Finucane, between one thirty a.m. and five thirty a.m. the Saturday before last?'

Finucane's face was expressionless.

'This is in connection with what exactly?' he said.

'Please could you just answer the question?'

Finucane smiled. He was doing a lot of that, Caton noticed. Too much.

'Certainly. Providing that you answer mine first.'

Caton considered making an issue of it, and decided against. If Finucane already knew, then there was nothing to be gained by not telling him. If he did not, then it didn't matter anyway. He suspected that there would be battles worth fighting with this man; this was not one of them.

'In connection with the murder of one Maureen Flinn,' he said.

'Christ!' said Simon Levi. 'You can't be serious?'

Finucane looked surprised.

'We heard about that, obviously,' he said. He turned to Simon Levi. 'On the routine NCA News

Feed? Body of a prostitute found in the Green Quarter of Manchester. Head wound, if I remember rightly.'

'Maureen Flinn,' said Joanne Stuart. 'Her name was Maureen Flinn.'

He ignored her and turned back to address Caton.

'Why on earth would you think I had something to do with that?'

'We believe there is a connection to an incident with which you were involved in Northern Ireland,' said Caton.

Finucane raised his eyebrows.

'You believe? That sounds decidedly speculative. What incident are we talking about?'

Caton sensed Joanne Stuart's unease. He didn't blame her. It must seem as though Finucane was controlling the interview. He trusted her not to become impatient and jump in. He paused long enough to make sure that he had Finucane's absolute attention and then chose his words with care.

'The murders at Malon Farm,' he said.

There was not a flicker on the NCA Officer's face. Not even a blink. It was as though he had known it was coming and had resolved not to betray the slightest emotion. It was the reaction Caton had been hoping for.

'What the hell is he talking about, Frank?' said Levi.

'1969,' Finucane replied, his eyes still locked with Caton's. 'A nasty business. So, you think it was the Provisional IRA that shot her? What, did they use the same gun?'

'We think that one of the people who was involved in the deaths of the Malone family also shot Maureen Flinn.'

Finucane's forehead furrowed.

'I don't understand. Why would the IRA want to

kill that woman? What possible connection could she have with Malon Farm?'

'Take it from me, she did,' said Caton.

Finucane placed his elbows on the table and leaned forward.

'Just to clarify,' he said, 'has the PSNI investigation into the Malon Farm incident been reopened?'

'No.'

Finucane smiled and sat back in his chair.

'In that case, I shall not be answering any questions in relation to Malon Farm. I said all I had to in my report at the time, and in subsequent interviews with the RUC and the RMP Investigations Branch. Like I said, it was a nasty business. Upsetting. I had flashbacks for years. I'm not going there again.'

'You still haven't answered my original question,' said Caton. 'The Saturday before last, between one thirty a.m. and five thirty a.m., where were you, Mr Finucane?'

The NCA Officer held Caton's gaze for a moment, then he leaned across and whispered in his colleague's ear. When he straightened up it was Simon Levi who spoke.

'I need a word with my colleague,' he said. 'Alone. Then he'll answer your question.'

Chapter 44

'Well?' said Caton.

They had taken less than two minutes to confer. He had no idea if that was a good thing or not.

Finucane was sitting up straight. His expression was totally different. More professional. And his manner more formal.

'I was with an undercover officer,' he said. 'It's what I do. Manage covert assets.'

Of all the things that Caton had been expecting to hear, this was not one of them.

Simon Levi leaned forward.

'Officer Finucane was recruited by the National Crime Agency precisely because of his extensive experience of managing covert assets whilst with the 14th Intelligence Regiment and subsequently with SO13.'

Caton ignored his intervention.

'Can you provide me with details of the location and duration of this meeting?' he asked.

'In broad terms, yes,' said Finucane.

He consulted the small tablet notebook that was now on the table in front of him.

'I was in a safe house in Liverpool preparing to make contact from eleven p.m. until two-thirty a.m. I left to travel to the rendezvous, arriving at three twenty-one a.m. The meeting lasted two and a half hours. The asset left at five fifty-five a.m. I left at six-ten a.m. and returned to the safe house.'

'In Liverpool?' said Caton.

'In Liverpool.'

'And your undercover officer will confirm this?'

'In writing, yes.'

'I meant in person,' said Caton. 'And I'll need a name.'

Finucane shook his head and sat back. Levi banged the flat of his hand on the table.

'For Christ's sake, Caton!' he said. 'What don't you get about undercover? If he's seen meeting you it'll blow the entire operation. Months of work up in flames. No, hold that, years of work. Not to mention it could get him killed.'

'I thought we were supposed to be working together?' said Caton. 'On the same side? If you can't trust us, who can you?'

'No one,' said Levi, leaning closer still. His breath smelled of rotting fish. 'Least of all you. You almost blew that undercover operation with the Russian, remember?'

Caton shuffled his chair back, out of range.

'I have another date for you,' he said to Finucane.

Levi sat back in his seat and threw his hands in the air.

'I don't believe it,' he said.

Finucane looked on impassively.

Caton gave him the date and times when they believed that the suicide of Father Michael Walsh had been staged. Finucane calmly consulted his diary. He looked up.

'I was on leave.'

Caton and Stuart looked at each other.

'What?' said Finucane.

'Let me guess,' said Caton. 'Scotland. The middle of nowhere.'

Finucane smiled.

'Half right,' he said. 'I was in Ireland. Fishing.'

Caton felt his pulse quicken.

'Where in Ireland?'

'Just outside Arigna, in Roscommon.'

'Alone?'

'God, no. I was with a pal from the old days. I'd spent a week at his place in Belfast, then we rented a stone cottage outside the town for the fishing.'

Caton's mind was racing. Belfast and the Republic, close to the Borderlands. All the time he and Stuart had been over there.

'This pal of yours, were you in the Army together by any chance?'

Finucane nodded.

'In the Marines.'

'The Special Boat Squadron?' said Caton

Finucane folded his arms and relaxed back into his chair.

'You really have been doing your homework, haven't you?' he said.

'No,' Caton told him. 'Just a guess. And was this former colleague in the Det' with you too?'

'The 14th Field and Intelligence Unit,' said Finucane in a tone that implied only members of the Det' were allowed to call it that. 'Except that he was at the Main Det' at Aldergrove.'

'And he can vouch for your whereabouts throughout your stay in Roscommon, and Belfast?'

Finucane's smile had an edge to it. A hint of smugness.

'We didn't go to the loo together.'

Simon Levi had become increasingly dislocated from this conversation. His confusion had mounted to the point where he could no longer contain it.

'Look, Caton, are you going to tell us what the hell

this has to do with that woman's death in Manchester a good week before Frank was on leave?'

'I was wondering when one of you was going to ask,' said Caton.

He searched Finucane's face for a response, and was met with a blank expression.

'On the date in question, Mr Finucane, a Father Walsh was found dead in his home in Offaly. Does that name mean anything to you?'

The NCA Officer gave it some thought, then shook his head.

'Father Walsh? No, never heard of him.'

'You would have known him as Corporal Michael Walsh, formerly of the Royal Military Police. A member of the Det' Unit you led that day at Malon Farm.'

From the corner of his eye Caton could see Simon Levi staring at his colleague, whose face had now registered surprise.

'Mickey?' said Finucane. 'A priest? I had no idea. Dead, you say?'

'Murdered,' Caton told him. 'Dressed up to look like suicide.'

'By someone trained to cover their tracks,' added Joanne Stuart.

He looked at each of them in disbelief.

'And you think I had something to do with that too? What possible motive would I have had for either of these deaths'

He turned to Levi.

'You told me Caton was a comedian. I should have listened.'

'Maureen Flinn and Father Michael Walsh were both witnesses to the Malon Farm murders,' said Caton. 'To be more precise, Walsh was a witness to the aftermath. But then you know that already. Maureen

Flinn, or Caitlin Malone as she then was, witnessed the shooting of her family. Is that motive enough?'

Finucane's head turned slowly. The smile had been wiped from his face.

'And you know this how?' he said. 'I thought she was dead when you found her.'

Caton turned the pages of his file.

'Because there were other witnesses. We've spoken to some of them.'

'I thought you said the Malon Farm investigation had not been reopened.'

'It hasn't. But surely, as an experienced investigator yourself, and an officer with the NCA, you can see how it looks? That these two deaths, less than two weeks apart, have to be other than coincidental? I'd have thought you'd want to help us.'

Finucane placed both hands on the table.

'I'm sure you'll agree that I have tried to help you, to the best of my ability. I've answered all of your questions. I have told you where I was at the time of both of these recent suspicious deaths, including the one which I assume is also outside your jurisdiction. As far as Malon Farm is concerned, as and when the Historical Enquiries Team decide to take another look at that case I will be happy to assist them.'

He pushed back his chair and stood. Levi jumped to his feet beside him.

'I haven't finished,' said Caton. 'We have just two further questions.'

Both NCA Officers remained standing.

'Get on with it,' said Finucane.

'Do you possess any hand guns?'

He shrugged.

'I'm licensed and trained to use, and to carry when required, a Glock 26 pistol.'

'Nine millimetre.'

Simon Levi clapped his hands together sarcastically.

'Very good,' he said.

Caton ignored him.

'Any others?'

'No.'

'Did you bring any guns back from Northern Ireland with you?'

For the first time Finucane scowled.

'No,' he said. 'And that's four questions. Come on, Simon, we're done here.'

He walked over to the door.

'Before you go,' said Caton, 'I need the names and addresses of the two people you claim to be able to confirm your whereabouts at the times that I put to you.'

Finucane came back to the table. Joanne Stuart turned the page of her pad to a fresh one and handed him her biro. He took it, and wrote a name, address and telephone number. He handed her back the biro and stood up.

'Don't forget the Belfast dialling code,' he said. 'It's the 0295 one.'

Stuart held up the biro and the pad.

'You forgot the name and number for your undercover officer,' she said.

He smiled thinly.

'No, I didn't.'

He opened the door for Simon Levi.

'You'll have to get permission from the NCA Director to talk with him,' he said. 'Good luck with that.'

Chapter 45

'What do you reckon, boss?' said DI Stuart.

Caton tipped his chair back on two legs and sighed.

'He was exactly what we expected him to be. Intelligent, cunning, cautious, confident, prepared, trained by the best, and he knows his way around the law at least as well as we do.'

'And he's a bloody good actor,' she said.

'And he's a bloody good actor.'

'He did a good job of looking surprised when you told him about Maureen Flinn having been a witness to the Malon Farm killings,' she said. 'Although he was right. We couldn't have known that she saw what happened. It was clever of you imply to it though, boss. It did rattle him.'

'Odd that he didn't ask why I wanted to know where he was at the time that Michael Walsh was killed,' said Caton.

'Not if that was because he already knew.'

'True. He's right though, we have absolutely nothing to link him directly with the two recent murders. It's all hypothesis, and vaguely circumstantial.'

'I know we have to follow up his alibis,' she said, 'but they're both going to back him up, aren't they? Always assuming we're allowed to interview this mysterious undercover officer. '

'What makes you say that?'

'You know what it's like between undercover assets and their handlers,' she said. 'The bond between them? When your life depends on your handler, you're going to say whatever he tells you to say.'

There was an uneasy silence as the two of them reflected on those words: Your life depends on your handler. It was less than three years since Joanne Stuart, acting undercover, had almost died at the hands of a predator. Caton had been her handler. He had almost lost her. She reddened. Caton felt his cheeks burn.

'I'm sorry, boss,' she said. 'I didn't mean to...'

'It's alright, Jo,' he replied. 'You're right. And nobody is better placed than you to point it out.'

He paused for a drink of water. Glad of the excuse, she did the same.

'And I've no doubt you'll also be proved right about his mate in Belfast,' he continued. 'For all we know he was part of the cover-up. He may even have been among the people on that Wessex helicopter that Blair told us flew in from RAF Aldergrove to take over the investigation.'

'We could be looking at a joint enterprise,' she said. 'Two or three perpetrators, not one. Bell has an alibi for the Angel Meadow shooting, but not for Michael Walsh's. Blair doesn't have an alibi for either of them. And we've just established that both of Finucane's are sounding decidedly dodgy.'

'And Finucane was in Ireland,' added Caton, 'at the time that we were being followed and Father Walsh was killed. And Blair was close enough to get a ferry across and back at the same time.'

He grounded the legs of his chair and sat up.

'How near to Offaly is this...' He consulted the

notes she had made. 'Arigna in Roscommon?'

She opened her iPad. They had to wait while the Apps loaded. It took less than a minute. She showed him the screen.

'Thirty-three miles, give or take.'

He shook his head.

'That's too good to be true. But I bet there's not a CCTV camera along the route. Not that we'd know what vehicle we were looking for.'

'There was something else that struck me,' she said.

'Go on.'

'When we told him about Michael Walsh having been murdered, and it being made to look like suicide, he must have wondered if there was someone out to get the rest the of the unit, him included. But he didn't show any sign of being concerned for his own safety.'

'Maybe he thinks as an NCA Officer he's bullet-proof.'

'Even so, he should have been a bit bothered.'

'You're right. The question is, what are we going to do about it?'

'We could get a warrant to search his house like we did Blair's.'

'Blair volunteered that. Finucane isn't going to. And I'm not sure we have enough yet for a magistrate to sign a search warrant. Besides, with his experience and training he would never leave a murder weapon where we can find it. Would you?'

'No, boss.'

They sat in silence, pondering the possibilities.

'We could set up observation on both Blair and Finucane for starters,' she said.

'Tailing an NCA Officer who just happens to be running undercover assets? I don't think we're going to get approval for that. Not without a hell of a lot more than supposition.'

He pushed back his chair and stood up.

'Let's go and see how the rest of the team have been getting on. Then we'd better decide how we prepare for Frances Fenton's arrival tomorrow.'

Caton sent Stuart off to ring the Belfast number in the faint hope that she might get there before Finucane had time to ring it himself. Then he checked in with the rest of the team.

Given that all of the evidence pointed towards the Malon Farm connection, Caton was not surprised to discover that little progress had been made beyond what was already known about the circumstances of Maureen Flinn's death. He had pinned most of his hopes on the CCTV.

'Thanks to the new CCTV retrieval system,' Wallace told him, 'the delay in retrieval from private cameras has come down from seven days to less than two. Unfortunately, there's not a lot to go on.'

'Surely,' said Caton, 'at that time in the morning there can't have been too many people about?'

'You're right,' Wallace replied. 'Unfortunately, given the time and place, the few images that could be relevant are not that brilliant. There's a guy that appears out of Sandbanks onto Rochdale Road, about half a mile north of the crime scene, only his hoodie is up, hands in his pockets, head down, straight into the estate and away. Then there's another one, comes out from the tunnel under the railway line onto Bromley Street, straight across Danzig Street into the industrial estate, and that's the last sighting we have for him.'

'Also with a hoodie?' Caton guessed.

'Yes, boss.'

'But you must have a good idea of their height and build?'

'Of course. Couldn't swear to their gender. Although I'm sure when we've done an analysis of their gait it'll confirm that they are both male.'

Caton pointed to the progress board.

'See if you can get a general match to any of our suspects. I know it won't be definitive, but it could help down the line.'

He returned to his desk and rang the Garda SIO, O'Hannlon, in Roscommon.

'Tom, how are you?' said the Irish Inspector.

'I'm fine,' Caton replied. 'And yourself?'

'I'm fine too. Have you anything for me?'

'Nothing that'll have you reaching for a European Arrest Warrant. But I do have an interesting development.'

He told him about Finucane's proximity to the murder scene, and both Blair's and Bell's lack of alibis for the murder of Michael Walsh.

'That is interesting,' said O'Hannlon. 'Mind, we've already been checking for sightings in and out of Roscommon, and requested the same for the cameras on roads into all of our ports and airports. Plus I've got people checking the passenger lists, with an eye out for the names you gave me, including theirs. And I've asked the PSNI to do the same. Nothing so far.'

'Not that that means anything,' Caton reflected ruefully. 'These men would have no problem getting hold of false names and photographic ID. In any case, only one of the carriers actually insists on their passengers carrying a passport.'

'From what you've told me about the connection to the shooting of the Malone family, Tom, this could just as easily have been an IRA reprisal. Have you thought about that?'

'I have,' said Caton. 'Or one of the Loyalist terrorist groups, come to that, given they'd tried to point the blame in both directions. I haven't ruled it out altogether, but I'm dubious about it being either of them.'

'Well, if it is,' said O'Hannlon, 'I doubt we'll ever find out in our lifetimes. Not unless another super grass pops up.'

'Those days are long gone,' said Caton. 'And all this talk of an amnesty makes it less likely that anyone would bother putting their lives on the line.'

'Here's the thing, Tom,' said the Irish detective. 'That amnesty only seems to cover the terrorists themselves. It seems to me that them that worked for the police, the army, and security services are as vulnerable as ever. Have you thought about that?'

'I have,' said Caton. 'That's the only reason I can see why someone would want to kill Caitlin Malone. Sorry, Maureen Flinn that is.'

'What I don't get,' said O'Hannlon, 'is if they didn't know those two little girls were there in the first place, how would they know to kill her? How would they know she was a threat?'

'That's been worrying me all along,' Caton replied. 'But I have a feeling it was nothing more than a voice half-remembered in a pub bar, a stare held too long and a family photograph on a bedside table.'

'Wrong place, wrong time?'

'Sometimes that's all it takes.'

'Tell me about it.'

They agreed to request access to the CCTV footage from the ports, the airports and the carriers in their respective jurisdictions, and to speak again as soon as anything new came up. Caton had no sooner replaced the phone in its charger than it rang again. It was Ged.

'I'm sorry to bother you, sir,' she said, 'but ACC Hadfield has called an urgent review of Operation Stardust.'

Caton groaned.

'When is it, Ged?'

'In forty-five minutes. In the Meeting Room on the

Fifth Floor of the Headquarters building.'

He took a deep breath.

'Okay, Ged. You know what we'll need. Find out how many copies he wants and we'll take them with us.'

Caton replaced the phone. Less than an hour to pull it all together, and no Gordon Holmes. He stood up and went in search of DI Stuart. The Fifth Floor was a lonely place at the best of times.

Chapter 46

This was no ordinary Case Review. The faces around the table confirmed it. It was packed with members of the Command Team.

Chief Superintendent Helen Gates he had expected, together with Assistant Chief Constable Martin Hadfield, Head of the Serious Crime Division. There was also the inevitable stenographer and a Holmes 2 operator, complete with computer access. It was a surprise to find the ACC Professional Standards and ACC Corporate Communications there too. There was also a woman Caton recognised from an Association of Chief Police Officers course back in 2013, although he couldn't put a name to her.

'All we need is the Chief Constable and the Police and Crime Commissioner, and it's a full set,' whispered Joanne Stuart as they took their seats.

'Be careful what you wish for,' he whispered back.

'Incidentally,' she said, 'I've told DS Carter to keep ringing that number in Belfast. All I got was an answerphone.'

Hadfield tapped his glass with a biro and called the meeting to order.

'Everybody knows everybody else,' he began. 'With the possible exception of Detective Chief Superintendent Alison Grey, ACPO-appointed Senior Investigative Consultant to this review.'

He stretched his right arm out towards Caton and Stuart, who were seated at the opposite end of the table.

'Alison, this is DCI Caton, the Senior Investigating Officer for Stardust, and Acting DI Stuart, a member of the Stardust Investigative team.'

While the three of them acknowledged each other with polite nods, he checked the notes on the table in front of him.

'I realise,' he said, 'that this review has been called at short notice, but there are compelling reasons why we should take stock at this point.'

Compelling for whom? Caton wondered. The NCA, MI5, the Home Office even?

'I intend,' Hadfield continued, 'for this meeting to be an opportunity for the SIO to brief me as the reviewing officer, and DCS Grey as the Investigative Consultant. DCS Grey is with us until next Wednesday. This will give her time to immerse herself in the investigation. I have scheduled a second meeting at the same time next Tuesday to conclude the review, and to arrive at conclusions and recommendations to drive this investigation forward.'

He looked up.

'Is everybody clear?'

There were nods all round. Caton had a number of questions, but he doubted that any of them would receive a satisfactory reply.

'Good,' said Hadfield. 'Quick reminder, then. The purpose of this review is to ensure that the Stardust investigation currently conforms to the nationally approved standards, is thorough, is being conducted with integrity and objectivity, and that no investigative opportunities have been overlooked. Furthermore, that should any good practice be identified, it is recorded for sharing across UK police forces.'

His tone and expression left no doubt that he would be surprised if any such good practice were actually identified. Alongside him, DCS Gates looked in Caton's direction, smiled and raised her eyebrows.

'Right, DCI Caton,' said Hadfield. He consulted his notes again. 'I assume you have brought copies of the Policy File and your log of events, including their sequence, statements from witnesses, schedules of exhibits and a current situation report?'

'Yes, sir,' said Caton. 'Would you like me to pass them round?'

The ACC sneered.

'Well, they're not going to be much use to us sat down there, are they?'

That earned him a surprised look from DCS Grey. Everyone else took it in their stride. It was after all typical of Hadfield to posture in front of strangers.

It took over an hour for Caton to take them through everything. Each time he asked Joanne Stuart to lead on a section she had acquitted herself well. Now it was the part he dreaded. Question time. Not because he didn't have the answers, but because sometimes it was hard to contain his frustration. Experience had taught him that the review process had a useful part to play, but there were always those who had little to contribute but an irrepressible need to have their voices heard.

'Thank you, Caton,' said Hadfield, ignoring the contribution Joanne Stuart had made. 'Given that we will be reconvening next week I suggest that we begin with questions of clarification, and then move swiftly on to issues relating to the pace and direction of this investigation. In particular, I am interested in identifying potential fast-track actions.'

The issues of clarification were mercifully few. Caton hoped that was down to the job that he and

Stuart had done, not to mention Ged and the Analyst Manager. Unfortunately, when it came to the most important part, Hadfield took it upon himself to lead.

'So,' he said, 'the shooting of Maureen Flinn. Initially you had four suspects, one of whom is now dead himself. Of your remaining suspects, one…' He had to consult his notes. 'Bell, has an alibi that has been corroborated. A second, Blair, has no alibi. And the third, Finucane, has an alibi which has yet to be confirmed.'

'In relation to the killing of Maureen Flinn, that is correct,' said Caton. 'But there is also the murder of Father Mi–'

'This is a review of Operation Stardust,' said the ACC Crime. 'Not Operation Emerald Isle.'

'But–' Caton began.

Hadfield cut him off again, this time with an imperious wave of his hand.

'Let's be clear,' he said. 'There is no physical or trace evidence of any kind to link these two deaths. Furthermore, your rationale for suspecting these men, two of whom are serving police officers…'

That was not strictly true, but Caton, with more important skirmishes looming, remained silent.

'…is wholly hypothetical. According to you, the men you currently have down as suspects were unaware that those two girls were even in the house–'

'Farm,' said Helen Gates.

'Farm. What's more, the girls didn't see what happened. There is no way that Maureen Flinn could have identified any of them.'

'The killer doesn't know that, Martin,' said Helen Gates.

He ploughed on regardless.

'As for the alleged involvement of the rogue security forces in the killings in Northern Ireland, that is none of our business. That's one for the Historical Enquiries Team.'

'The HET has been accused of illegal activities in covering up just such incidents,' said Caton. 'Their future is under debate as we speak.'

'Nevertheless,' said Hadfield, 'it's their remit. Have you spoken to them?'

There were raised eyebrows around the room. It was all there in the case notes.

'I went to see them,' Caton told him.

'And?'

'They don't want to know.'

'Why not?'

'They have it down as unsolved, but attributed it to an unidentified terrorist group.'

'And all you've come up with is that it was actually self-defence?'

'I've no doubt that's what they'll claim. But the fact that they took weapons other than theirs from the barn, used them to kill that family, then dumped them and fabricated their reports, suggests otherwise.'

Hadfield's face reddened. The pitch of his voice rose as it always did when he felt his authority undermined.

'Suggests is not enough. As I understand it, you have two men – one of whom is now dead – claiming that it wasn't them. That they were told it was self-defence involving Finucane, Bell and a fifth man since dead. Finucane and Bell are refusing to comment until the case is reopened by the Historical Enquiries Team. And, if and when they finally do give their account, there is no one and nothing to contradict them.'

'You can see HET's point,' said the ACC Professional Standards. 'They've got enough on their plate.'

'But what about the fact that the gun that was used to kill Maureen Flinn originated in Northern

Ireland?' said Helen Gates.

'Coincidence,' said Hadfield. 'Hundreds of ex-servicemen must have smuggled guns back as trophies and whatnot.'

He looked down at his notes, and then spoke directly to Caton.

'In my view, this operation is in danger of developing tunnel vision. Stick to the girl's murder, and consider other possibilities.'

'Such as, sir?' said Caton.

'Drugs, a war between pimps, robbery, a random shooting.'

'I think you'll find the initial phase of the investigation did all that, Martin,' said Helen Gates.

'Then they need to do it some more,' he said. 'And Caton…'

'Yes, sir?'

'No more jollies across the water. Is that understood? And stay away from the NCA undercover operation. You're in danger of getting another man killed. And by the way, the Chief Constable has not supported your request to suspend Mr Blair. He has been returned to duty while your enquiries continue.'

'But–' Caton began.

'His service record is exemplary. You have no evidence to connect him to the murder of Maureen Flinn.'

'He has admitted to being part of a conspiracy to lie about the Malon Farm shooting,' Caton pointed out.

The ACC Professional Standards raised her hand.

'On active service, thirty-five years ago,' she said. 'Under conditions of which none of us have any comprehension.'

'But surely–' Caton began.

'You're not listening Caton,' said Hadfield. 'Mr Blair was not employed by GMP at the time to which this unsubstantiated allegation refers. He was seconded from the Ulster Defence Regiment to the 14th Field and Intelligence Company. It's a matter for the Northern Ireland Office and the Ministry of Defence.'

'Both of whom have a vested interest in not–'

'Are you trying to become another Stalker?'

The ACC Crime had almost shouted it. Enough to startle DCS Grey sitting beside him.

'I don't understand, sir,' said Caton, even though he did.

Hadfield thumped the tabletop.

'John Stalker, man! The Stalker Report.'

Caton was tempted to reply that that was exactly what he was prepared to become; an honourable man besmirched by the Establishment, rather than one who would bow to political pressure and turn a blind eye to murders, just because they had been committed by members of the security forces.

'He's been got at, boss,' said DI Stuart as she closed the door behind them. 'The Chief Constable too by the sound of it.'

'It looks that way,' he agreed. 'Look, you go on ahead, I'm going to try and catch DCS Gates when she comes out. Let the mortuary know you'll be bringing Frances Fenton by in the morning. And see if you can find out where the NCA are up to with our request to interview Finucane's covert alibi.'

'Right you are,' she said. 'Nil carborundum, eh, boss?'

He watched her walk purposefully down the corridor. It was time she was boss in her own right, he reflected. Behind him, voices were being raised. He moved closer to the door and listened, even though he knew he would regret it.

'He's a bloody good detective.'

He smiled. That was Helen Gates. A different voice carried above the others. Predictably, it was Martin Hadfield.

'But now you know why he's never gone any further. Overweening pride. No understanding that justice isn't always black and white.'

'You can't say black and white, Martin, not any more.'

'What the hell am I supposed to say?'

'A million shades of grey?' suggested the ACC Corporate Communications.

'More like fifty,' he replied.

Their laughter followed him down the corridor.

Chapter 47

Carter intercepted Caton between the lifts and the Incident Room.

'The NCA have set up that interview you wanted, boss,' he said. 'Only we have to go over to the Media Suite.'

Caton wasn't sure he'd heard correctly.

'The Media Suite?'

'Yes, boss.'

'He's in the Media Suite?'

'No, boss. They're not prepared to let us meet him in the field. They say it's too dangerous for him. And likely too dangerous for whoever it is that goes to meet him. The best they'll do is a three-way video hook-up. They've set strict conditions. And they don't want anyone else in the room but you. Their Director has cleared it with the Chief Constable apparently.'

Caton shook his head.

'And I suppose ACC Hadfield was only too happy to oblige.'

'I beg your pardon, boss?' said Carter.

'Forget it, Nick,' he said. 'Just let DI Stuart know where I am. I'll be back as soon as this charade is over.'

Charade was an understatement. The Media Suite technician had set up the three-way conference, and then left with the two other members of staff. Caton stared at the screen. His own image appeared in the bottom right-hand corner. Simon Levi's was in the bottom left. The bulk of the screen was taken up by someone wearing a black sweater and a matching balaclava, sitting in a small room. In the corner was an unmade bed. The wall above it showed signs of damp. The wallpaper was peeling.

'You have got to be joking,' said Caton. 'This could be anyone. It could even be Finucane himself.'

'Wake up, Caton,' said Levi. 'Our guy has put himself at considerable risk doing this. If someone bursts in on this he's toast, and the whole operation is blown.'

'I am here you know,' said the balaclava.

Dark eyes, in shadow. Impossible to read. At least the voice was not distorted in any way. It was Manc. Extenuated vowels. Occasional glottal stops on consonants. If he had to narrow it down, more North Manchester or Salford than Wythenshawe. Like a character from Shameless. Of course, he might just be a bloody good mimic.

'Can I at least see your face?' said Caton. We are on the same side, and I promise you that there is no one else in the room.'

'Show me.'

'No way,' said Levi.

'The camera is integrated into the screen,' said Caton.

'So turn the monitor.'

'I said no way!' shouted Levi.

Caton stood, moved to the side so that his half of the room appeared in the little window, and then proceeded to rotate the screen in both directions and back to the centre. Then he sat down.

'Fair enough,' said the undercover officer, lowering his head and raising his right hand to remove the balaclava.

Levi bellowed in vain. 'Don't!'

The balaclava came off and was dropped to the floor. The head came up. Caton found himself staring at a face that would have looked at home as a police EvoFIT. An oval face, short dark hair cut to a widow's peak. Thick, dark eyebrows over equally dark hooded eyes. A broad nose with flaring nostrils. A thin mouth turned down at the corners, and ears flaring back like aerodynamic fins. He was immediately put in mind of the photos the CIA had released of Matt Damon in the Bourne Inheritance.

'It's your life,' muttered Simon Levi.

'Thank you,' said Caton. 'Do you have a name?'

'Not one that you can write down.'

'I have to have something.'

'Call me Harry.'

'Okay, Harry,' said Caton. 'But if this goes to court you'll have to give me more than that.'

There was a brief, wry smile.

'If it goes to court we'll let the judge decide. My guess is anonymity, with all my testimony given from behind a screen. That's less than you're getting now.'

Caton knew he was right. Levi cut in.

'I'm here on behalf of the Agency to vouch for him being who he says he is. Now, for God's sake can we speed this up?'

'Can you confirm,' said Caton, 'that you had a meeting with your handler, Frank Finucane, the weekend before last? That's Friday the 13th and Saturday the 14th of June?'

The man called Harry ran his hand through his hair where the balaclava had presumably caused him to sweat. He wiped his hand on his thigh.

'Yeah. I can.'

'What time was the meeting?'

'It was supposed to be three a.m. Saturday morning.

He was late.'

'How late?'

'Long enough. I was just about to get out of there.'

'How late, Harry?'

'It was almost half past.'

'Did he say why he was late?'

'Yeah, he did.'

'And?'

'He said there was a drug deal going on outside the gates. He waited till they'd gone.'

'He didn't ring you, or text to let you know he'd been delayed?'

'Too risky, Caton,' said Levi. 'You should know that.'

'I'd prefer that you let Harry speak for himself,' said Caton.

'Then stop asking dumb questions.'

'The only one slowing things down here is you, Levi,' said Harry. 'So why don't you button it?'

One advantage of this video hook-up, Caton realised, was that he was able to see Simon Levi squirm.

'How long did your meeting last?' he asked before Levi had time to respond.

'About two and a half hours.'

'That's a long time. Especially if you're undercover.'

'We had a lot to talk about.'

What time did your meeting finish?'

'Just before six.'

'Is that when your handler left?'

'No, I left first. He was going to wait till I was well clear. Standard procedure.'

'So you can't be sure when he left?'

'Nope. I have no idea. But after six, obviously.'

'Where was the meeting?'

Another thin smile.

'An industrial estate. Nice and remote, but with loads of different ways in and out.'

Caton nodded. That was also standard procedure.

'Do you have a record of the meeting?'

Levi snorted.

'I'll assume that was a joke,' said the undercover officer. 'Frank will have written them up though.'

Frank. Neither Finucane, nor my handler. Evidence of the bond between them, which DI Stuart had so perceptively surmised.

'Any CCTV around that location?'

Another wry smile.

'Frank said you were a comedian. We choose these places specifically for their lack of surveillance of any kind – including police and public safety cameras. You never know who's working for whom. Know what I mean?'

It had been a complete waste of time, Caton reflected. It was impossible to know if he had been telling the truth. The man was a consummate actor. He had to be to do what he did, and stay alive. Caton was still trying to work out where that left them as he pushed open the door to the Incident Room. This time it was DI Stuart who couldn't get to him quickly enough.

'Boss,' she said, 'we have a problem.'

'I doubt things could get much worse.'

'Sorry to disappoint you, boss. Frances Fenton. She's already here.'

'What?'

'She's already here.'

'When?'

'Yesterday, apparently. She flew into Belfast and out again the same day.'

'How did you find out?'

'When I rang the mortuary like you told me to, they said she'd already been there. This morning. They assumed we knew because we'd told them to expect her.'

'Christ!' he said. 'Not today we didn't. Was she on her own?'

'We're not sure.'

'Did anyone meet her at the airport?'

'I've no idea, boss. But as soon as I put the phone down I got on to Border Control at Manchester Airport. She came in on the eight thirty a.m. FlyBe flight. Arrived at nine fifty-five. Which means that she went straight to the mortuary. Stayed about twenty minutes.'

'Where is she now?'

'I've no idea. I rang her sister's parents, but they said they hadn't heard from her since the day before yesterday. They were expecting her to arrive tomorrow. I could tell my call had made them anxious. I said not to worry, it was my mistake. That I'd got my wires crossed. I'm not sure they believed me.'

'We have to find her, Jo,' he said.

'Boss!' Nick Carter pushed his chair back and stood up. 'That phone call to Belfast? I got through at last. He confirmed what Finucane told you. Reckons he was with him for the entire–'

'Not now, Nick,' said Caton. 'Not now.'

Chapter 48

'Listen up.'

Caton scanned the room to make sure everyone was present.

'Other than DS Carter, I want all of you on this . Ged is going to give each of you a block of hotels or bed and breakfasts to ring. You want to know if Frances Fenton has checked in, or has made a booking. If you get a positive result, find out what room she's in and if she's there now. Tell them not to let on that you've rung. I don't want her spooked.'

'What if she's using a different name, boss?' said DC Hulme.

'Good point. If you get a no to Fenton, ask if they've got a Malone. A Finnoula Malone. Failing that, if a woman in her forties with an Irish or Canadian accent has checked in.'

'That's going to generate quite a few names,' muttered someone near the back.

'I don't care,' he said. 'This is about more than catching the killer, it's about preventing another murder.'

A mile and a half south west of the Central Park complex Frances Fenton stared through the passenger window of the stationary car. The house was at the end of a row of decrepit factory buildings, each displaying a For Sale notice. The front door had a metal grill across it, secured with a padlock. The two ground-floor windows on either side of the door had panels of wood where glass should have been. Likewise, the three first-floor windows. White paint peeled from stone lintels. Judging by the long vertical crack in the bricks on the front elevation, in which purple blossomed buddleia had found a home, the gable end was in imminent danger of collapse. To the side, a corridor had been hacked through undergrowth between the gable end and the wall of a neighbouring builder's yard. She sighed, opened the car door and got out.

DS Carter had been dispatched to see if the CCTV at the mortuary gave them any clues as to the identity of the mysterious uncle, or the direction in which Frances Fenton had travelled when she left. When it came, his call was a disappointment.

'Sorry, boss,' he reported. 'A taxi dropped her off and stayed till she came out again. I got the registration from the CCTV, and tracked down the firm and the driver. He said there was a guy with her. He stayed in the taxi all the time she was in the mortuary. He dropped them at the temporary car park at the back of Red Bank.'

'Let me guess, no CCTV?'

'You guessed right, boss.'

'They had a car parked up waiting for them,' Caton surmised. 'Did you get a description of her companion from the taxi driver?'

'Average height, average build. Black baseball cap pulled low over his eyes. Worse than useless except for one thing, and that wasn't all that brilliant.' He paused. 'He said he had a funny accent.'

'Funny in what way?'

'Just funny,' he said. 'Which was priceless given the taxi driver was Turkish.'

After that conversation Caton had a sinking feeling that the rest of the team were also wasting their time. Frances Fenton did not want to be found. Not yet anyway. He asked DI Stuart for an update. She confirmed his suspicions.

'It's not looking good,' she said. 'There are three women in the right age range with Irish accents for whom further details are being sought, but two were accompanied by children and partners, and the other one sounds too heavily built to be Fenton. More problematic is the number of women with North American accents. Just our luck there's a global medical symposium at the university and most of the hotel receptionists are Eastern European. They can't tell an American accent from a South African one, let alone a Canadian one.'

Caton turned to look at the photos on the whiteboard.

'Keep going,' he said. 'She must be somewhere.'

'Speaking of medical matters, boss,' she said. 'Shouldn't you be at home? I thought you said the baby was due any time now?'

Caton's attention shifted to the large clock on the Incident Room wall. It was eight fifteen p.m. He had promised to be home two hours ago. Even worse, he hadn't been in touch all day. DI Stuart read his expression.

'Just go,' she said. 'There's nothing you can do here that I can't do. I'll ring you as soon as we've got something. And let's face it, if we can't find her, neither can anyone else.'

Kate's mother opened the door. He didn't blame her for the frosty reception.

'The prodigal returns!' she announced as much for Kate's benefit as his. 'You'd better come in, Tom.'

'Lovely to see you too, Marge,' he said, bending to

kiss the proffered cheek.

She stepped aside to allow him to pass, closed the door, and followed him down the hallway and into the lounge.

'You're not a father yet, in case you're interested.'

'Leave him alone, Mum,' said Kate. 'I'm going to need him when you've gone.'

The coffee table had been pulled to one side. She was on all fours on the rug.

'Bloody hell!' he said. 'It's coming!'

Kate laughed; her mother rolled her eyes.

'I'm doing the cat stretch, you silly beggar,' said Kate. 'You'll know when it's for real. There'll be bodily fluids all over the place.'

He breathed deeply and relaxed.

'I'm sorry I'm late,' he began.

'Forget it,' she said. 'Lucky for you, Mum's been keeping me company since lunchtime. Now you are here you can do something useful.' She sat back on her haunches. 'You can help me up.'

Tom hooked his arm beneath one armpit while her mother took the other one. Slowly they raised her to her feet. She placed her hands beneath her bump and arched her back.

'God, I'll be glad when this is over,' she said.

Amen to that, thought Caton.

'I'll just go and change out of these clothes, and freshen up,' he said, heading for the bedroom.

'I hope you're not thinking of going out again,' said Kate's mother.

'No, Marge,' he said. 'I'm not.'

'Bloody good job, or you'd have me to deal with.'

'Leave him alone, Mum,' said Kate, sitting down on the dining chair, with the lumbar roll hooked over the back. 'There'll be plenty of time for that when Junior's arrived.'

Chapter 49

Caton had a fitful night on the sofa. Kate would have been tossing and turning all night trying to get comfortable. Her mother had slept in the spare room. He was already half awake when his phone rang. It was DI Stuart. The display told him it was five fifty-eight a.m.

'Boss, we've just had an urgent call from Crimestoppers,' she said. 'They had an anonymous message about a body in East Manchester. The caller specifically mentioned your name. Said you'd be interested. I'm on my way there.'

Caton's heart pounded as he wrestled with the zip on his sleeping bag.

'Give me the address,' he said. He wrote it down.

'Don't go alone,' he told her. But she had already rung off.

He didn't need to look at the map on the satnav display to know what to expect. It was less than half a mile from his apartment in New Islington. The small triangle of land bordered by Cambria Street, Upper Helena Street and the Rochdale Canal was one of the few patches of land untouched by the regeneration of East Manchester. A stone's throw from the Etihad stadium, it was a jumble of car breakers, scrap metal yards and dodgy car repairers.

Joanne Stuart's car was parked outside a dilapidated

end-terrace house. Behind it was a uniformed response car, its lights still flashing. At the far end of the street was what looked like a black BMW. The rest of the street was deserted. Caton had a sense of foreboding. In the pre-dawn gloom, dwarfed by the Bradford gasholder, red and blue flashes of light strobing the ramshackle buildings, it had a post-apocalyptic feel about it.

He parked in front of her car and got out. He tried the metal gate over the front door. The bolt was secured by a chunky brass padlock. The sound of muted conversation drew him to a narrow gap between the end of the house and a high brick wall. The beam of a torch swung up in his direction, blinding him.

'It's alright,' said DI Stuart's voice. 'It's my boss.'

The beam swung back to the ground where it had been before. Caton regretted having left his own Maglite in the car. He waited for his eyes to readjust, and then, one hand on the gable end and the other out in front of him, he carefully felt his way forward. Bushes slapped against his legs. Something honey-scented brushed his face.

DI Stuart and a uniformed constable were standing over a body slumped in an open doorway. It appeared to have fallen forwards onto its left side, with the upper body inside the house and both legs poking out across the step. As the beam of the constable's torch travelled up the body towards the head, Caton felt a guilty wave of relief. It was a man. It was only when it came to rest on the face that he recognised it, and only then with difficulty.

It was Frank Finucane. That he was dead was self-evident. As was the cause. The otherwise perfectly circular hole in the side of his temple showed classic signs of a gunshot entry wound. Three deep blood-filled crevices, and two smaller ones, radiated outwards where the gases had expanded between the skull and the skin, dissecting it. Blood had pooled on the kitchen floor from the hidden exit wound.

'It's here, boss,' said Joanne Stuart, shining her torch on the floor beside her feet.

He didn't need a manual to recognise the matt black handgun, even with the silencer attached. This was the unmistakeable Browning Hi-Power Mark 1, locked-breech, semi-automatic, single-action, recoil-operated pistol. The same make of weapon that had been used to murder Maureen Flinn.

'Is the house clear?' he asked.

'I don't know, boss,' she replied. 'We've only just got here ourselves.'

'I'm going to check,' he told her. He turned to the Constable. 'I'll need to borrow your torch.'

'Shouldn't you wait for Armed Response?' she said. 'I've called it in.'

'If he did this himself,' he said, 'then there's no longer a threat. If he didn't, whoever did it is long gone. I need to see if there's anyone else in there.'

She did not need it spelling out.

'Be careful,' she said as he stepped over the body and disappeared.

As he moved forward he swept the beam from right to left, and floor to ceiling. The kitchen fittings had been ripped out. Even some of the floor tiles had been lifted. Praying that gas pipes had not been ruptured, and that if they had the supply had been cut off long ago, he held his breath and flipped the light switch. There was no response. In the empty lounge, cold grey half-burned logs lay in the grate. Here, and in the narrow hallway, the radiators had been pulled from the wall and taken away. The carpets had also gone. He placed a tentative foot on the first wooden tread of the stairs. In the empty house the sound reverberated like a pistol shot.

'Police!' he shouted. 'Is there anyone there?'

'Only me,' came the reply.

He took the stairs two at a time, stumbled near the top and had to put his hands out in front of him to stop his head from crashing onto the landing. He scrambled to his feet and hurried from room to room.

He found her in a rear bedroom, sitting on the bed in the dark. Her face was lit by the stark white beam of his torch. Her shadow filled the wall behind her. She smiled wearily.

'I didn't see anything,' she said.

Chapter 50

'What do you think?' said Caton.

An hour had passed. Frances Fenton, wrapped in a foil blanket, was sitting in the back of Caton's car with a female PC. The crime scene had been secured. The area around the door, hidden from prying eyes by a tarpaulin suspended between the wall and the gable end, was now floodlit. Caton was reminded of a horror film set he had once stumbled upon in the Northern Quarter.

Professor Flatman was uncharacteristically cheerful. Caton wondered if that had anything to do with Gordon Holmes' absence from the scene.

'Apart from the fact that he's dead?' the pathologist replied, sitting back on his heels. 'Well, for once I can give you a pretty good indication of the time of death.'

He lowered and raised the body's right eyelid, then lifted the right arm a few centimetres and let it drop.

'Primary flaccidity. Given the ambient and body temperature, this strongly suggests that he died no more than four hours ago, and not less than three.'

Caton eased back the sleeve of his Tyvek suit and checked his watch. The phone call had come three and a half hours ago. DI Stuart had arrived twenty minutes later. He had only been a minute or two behind her. The body had still been warm. The blood that had pooled on the floor barely congealed. Even allowing for the silencer, Frances Fenton must have heard something. Must be able to pin it down. In any case, he suspected that the phone call had been made within minutes of the fatal gunshot.

'Thank you,' he said. 'That was more or less what I'd expected.'

The pathologist raised a gloved left hand.

'Give me a hand up, would you? My joints aren't what they used to be.'

Caton held Flatman's wrist with one hand and his elbow with the other as he helped him to his feet.

'As to cause of death, you won't be surprised to learn that you'll have to wait for the autopsy. But there are no signs of any other head wounds, strangulation or asphyxia. And given the degree of exsanguination, he was definitely still alive when the bullet penetrated his skull.'

He rubbed at an itch on the side of his face with the knuckle of his right hand.

'Funny thing though,' he said. 'Suicide by gunshot is pretty damn rare, but I've never before come across one that involved the use of a silencer.'

He looked down at the body and shook his head.

'I'd have thought that worrying about making a noise would have been the least of his concerns.'

He bent down and picked up his case.

'Still, that's your field of expertise, isn't it, Detective Chief Inspector? Happily, mine begins here and ends on the slab.'

He nodded at the corpse. 'I'll squeeze him in as soon as I can. Have a nice day.'

He started to pick his way carefully along the walkway Jack Benson's team had erected over the common approach path. Part way along he stopped and half turned.

'By the by, Caton. This is the third weekend in as

many months that you've got me out of bed early, and cocked up a morning's golf. Do me a favour, have a word with your perpetrators, or call someone else for a change.'

As he walked away his laughter developed into a hacking cough that made Caton smile.

'He's right though,' said Jack Benson. 'Why a silencer? And why did he take his glove off the hand he used to hold the gun?'

It had been one of the first things that had struck Caton. Finucane's left hand still wore a glove, the other glove had been found beneath the body when Flatman had asked for it to be raised so that he could examine the exit wound. Everything else pointed to suicide, including the gun residue and blood back spatter, both of which were evident on his right hand and his clothes, and the powder burns on his head. No doubt his fingerprints would be found on the butt and trigger guard of the pistol. That must surely be the only reason why the glove had been removed from his right hand. But by whom?

'And why would he do it here?' Joanne Stuart was asking. 'Was it for her benefit? In which case why didn't he do it upstairs, where she could see him do it? But he didn't strike me as the remorseful type last time we saw him, did he, boss? Let alone suicidal.'

'No, Jo,' he said, 'he didn't. And there's another thing. Why would he shoot himself in the side of his head? Having that silencer on would have made it really difficult, and nowhere near as certain as placing it under his chin or against the roof of his mouth. His training and his experience would have taught him that.'

'He was on his knees at the time,' said Benson. He pointed to the partially open door. 'Have you seen the blood splatter?'

Caton hadn't noticed it. He had been too preoccupied by the body itself and checking if Frances Fenton was still alive. And then setting things in motion. Now, in the intense glare of the LED floodlights, it was obvious. The projected blood and tissue from the exit wound had formed a classic high-velocity impact spatter just below the mid point in the centre of the door. The angle and direction of this random mist-like pattern told him that the door had been open, just as they had found it, and that either the barrel of the silencer had been angled slightly up or the bullet's angle of exit had been deflected as it travelled into and through the brain cavity.

'You're right,' he said. 'He must have been kneeling, and then pitched forward with the impact of the blast. That would explain why we found him half in and half outside the room.'

'The recoil causing the gun to fall from his hand as he fell,' said Benson.

'Or it was placed where we found it to make it look like that,' said Stuart.

'Suicide, or execution?' said Caton. 'That is the question.'

He heard steps and voices on the walkway, and glanced over his shoulder. An impatient queue of crime scene technicians had formed.

'Come on, Jo,' he said. 'Let's leave them to it.'

They squeezed past the SOCOs and stopped on the pavement outside the house while he climbed out of his barrier suit. Along the street, uniformed officers with clipboards in their hands were knocking on the doors or standing talking on the steps of the few houses that were still occupied. He did not hold out much hope of the door-to-door yielding anything worthwhile. So far there had been no reports of strangers in the area, or of anyone fleeing the scene.

Nobody had stirred at all until an area car had arrived with sirens wailing. Furthermore, the only CCTV in the area appeared to be inside the yards of some of the business premises.

'There's someone I bet could tell us, boss,' she said, nodding towards the car in which Frances Fenton's head could just be seen above the rear seat rest. 'She was bait if I ever saw one.'

'But she didn't need to actually be there,' he said. 'It was only necessary that he should believe that she was there.'

'Maybe she wanted to be there. Maybe she wanted to be sure. If he'd killed my sister, I'd want to.'

'I didn't know you had a sister.'

She grinned.

'I don't. But if I had.'

'Assuming you're right,' he said, 'someone must have brought her here; she would never have found it on her own. And the same person would have needed to give Finucane the address.'

'Unless he followed her here.'

'But how would he know she was even in the country?'

'The same way he found out about us looking into the Malon Farm incident. The same way he found out about us visiting Father Michael Walsh. Surely he, or people he knew in the Intelligence Services, would have access to passenger lists.'

One of the crime scene technicians approached with a brown paper bag and a plastic biohazard bag. Caton placed his booties in the paper bag for testing for trace evidence, and his gloves and mask in the plastic bag for eventual disposal. He signed and dated the attached labels. Then he folded his Tyvek body suit ready to place it in the box provided.

'Make sure they get everything they can from that

scene,' he said. 'I know there wasn't any sign that he'd been restrained, but I want every inch of his clothes tested for DNA. There must be fibres on those bushes. The same in that bedroom. If there was anyone with her, odds on they accompanied her to that room. And don't let them forget shoeprints in the soil.'

'I don't know about that, boss,' she said. 'It hasn't rained for days. The ground is rock hard, and two of us tramped over it before the scene was made secure.'

'I don't care,' he said. 'They'll be able to eliminate your footprints if they have to. As well as his, and hers.'

He could tell that she thought he was clutching at straws. But he hated people thinking they could pull the wool over his eyes. Besides, it was a simple matter of justice.

Chapter 51

'How is she?' he asked.

'She's fine,' said DS Carter. 'She had some breakfast in the canteen, like you said. And a woman from Family Liaison has been sitting with her in the atrium. I'm surprised you didn't see her when you came in.'

'I had other things on my mind,' said Caton. 'Find out if there's an interview room free, let Ged know, then escort them both there. Then find out who the duty solicitor is and ask them to stand by. I'll be with you shortly.'

She looked up as he entered.

The colour had returned to her face. It was a face full of character. But that was not what stopped him in his tracks. It was the resemblance to her sister. Jet-black hair, piercing blue eyes, high cheekbones, a long, slim nose and small, yet firm lips.

She saw the flicker of recognition in his eyes.

'I know what you're thinking,' she said. 'We were peas in a pod, Caitlin and me.'

He pulled the chair out and sat down next to Carter.

'How are you?' he asked.

She smiled.

'I'm fine, thank you. A bit tired, that's all.'

'Only you've had quite a shock.'

She smiled again.

She didn't look as though she was in shock. He thought he probably looked a damn sight worse.

'No,' she said, 'I'm fine. Really.'

'In which case I need to ask you some questions.'

'Of course.'

'I am going to need to record this interview,' he told her. 'Under caution.'

Caton noted a brief dilation of her pupils.

'Does that mean I am a suspect?'

'Not necessarily. But this is a suspicious death. At the very least it is currently unexplained.'

She nodded her head.

'I can see that.'

'In such a case,' he said, quoting almost verbatim from the PACE guidelines, 'we have to be diligent in recording statements by key witnesses when we believe that they may provide important information revealing further lines of enquiry.'

'If nothing else,' added DS Carter, 'it saves us having to ask you to go through it all over again.'

'That doesn't answer my question though,' she said. 'Am I a suspect?'

'Not at this stage,' Caton replied. 'Not unless something you tell us, or some other evidence, were to suggest that you ought to be. Which is why I also have to offer you the opportunity to have a solicitor to advise you.'

He looked at Carter.

'Do we have a duty solicitor available?'

'Yes, sir, we do.'

'No,' she said firmly. 'It's alright, I don't need one.'

'If you're sure?'

She smiled.

'I'm sure.'

'Very well then.'

He took her through the caution, stated the time and date, and the names of those present, and began.

'I would like to begin by getting a sense of how you ended up in the bedroom of the house where the body was found,' he said. 'Is that alright with you?'

'Of course.'

'Good. Can you start by telling us why you flew to Belfast? I thought you were going to fly direct to Manchester.'

She looked surprised. It was not where she had expected the questioning to begin. She placed her hands on the table; the palm of one hand slid over the back of the other.

'There were a few things I needed to do. Work mainly.'

'You called in at work?'

She hesitated a microsecond too long.

'Briefly.'

'What is it you do exactly?'

'Exactly? I am a solicitor. I specialise in cases involving the abuse of Human Rights.'

Little wonder that she didn't feel the need to be represented.

'Challenging discrimination? Defending the rights and freedoms of ordinary people?' he said.

'And of organisations.'

'Was that the only reason you went to Belfast? To call in at work?'

The same hesitation. He guessed that she was trying hard to stay as close to the truth as possible, whilst hiding something. Her answer confirmed it.

'It was the main reason.'

He waited, letting the tension build. He noted how the topmost hand closed over the bottom one and gripped it.

'You went back to Drumboy Road, didn't you, Frances?' he said.

She nodded. He had a feeling that admitting it was almost a relief.

'Those ghosts you talked about,' he said. 'Did going there chase them away?'

Her eyes met his. He was reminded of the Bruce Springsteen lyric. Sad eyes never lie.

'No,' she said. 'I've discovered that nothing in this world will achieve that.'

'Not even the death of the man who took your family from you?'

Her gaze was steady, unblinking.

'Not even that,' she said.

It felt as though there were only the two of them in the room and a silent secret had passed between them. Caton was the first to tear his eyes away. He looked down at the sheet on which his interview strategy had been typed.

'Did you go there alone?'

'No.'

'With whom did you go?'

'With a friend.'

'Does this friend have a name?'

She nodded.

'Of course. But I would rather not involve my friend.'

'Why not?'

'Because it isn't relevant.'

'Let us be the judge of that.'

'I'm sorry,' she said, 'but you have my answer.'

Carter looked as though he was about to speak. Caton shook his head. They couldn't make her answer, and there were more important questions that he felt sure she would also refuse to answer.

'Very well,' he said. 'Moving on. Why did you

decide to come to Manchester a day early, and without informing us?'

She folded her arms and sat back in her chair.

'I was worried that sticking to our agreement might make me even more vulnerable,' she said.

He had no difficulty sounding incredulous.

'You thought there might be a leak within my team? Within the Greater Manchester Police Service?'

'I am surprised you haven't considered that yourself,' she said. 'Given what happened to Father Michael Walsh the day after you visited him.'

Caton found himself exchanging glances with DS Carter.

'How do you know about that?' he asked, even though he suspected he knew what the answer would be.

She smiled.

'A friend told me.'

'The same friend who accompanied you to Drumboy Road?'

'No comment,' she said.

He leaned forward.

'The same friend who was in the taxi with you when you left the mortuary?'

Her expression had become fixed.

'No comment.'

'The same friend who took you to the house where we found you?'

'No comment.'

He sat back and made a conscious effort to relax.

'Why were you there, Finnoula?' he asked. 'Why would you let someone take you to that rat-infested house?'

There was a flicker of a smile at his use of her birth name. She did not bother to correct it.

'I was told that it would be safe,' she said. 'Safer than

Angel Meadow was for Caitlin. Or the presbytery for Father Walsh. Or any place that you might take me to.'

'Told by whom?'

'No comment.'

'By your friend?'

Before she had a chance to reply, the door burst open.

'Detective Superintendent Gates has entered the room,' said Caton for the tape.

'Suspend the interview,' said Gates. 'DCI Caton, a word please. Outside.'

She waited until the door had closed behind him.

'It's Kate,' she said. 'She's on her way to Manchester Royal.'

He felt a flutter in his chest.

'Is she alright?'

She placed a comforting arm on his shoulder.

'Tom, according to your mother-in-law there's nothing to worry about, except that your baby is likely to arrive before you do.'

'What about her in there?' he asked.

'Don't worry,' she said, 'I'm on top of it. Just go.'

His footsteps echoed as he ran down the corridor beside the custody suite and out onto the central circulation area. As he exited the building and sprinted towards the car park, it dawned on him that the woman who had held the door open as he rushed past had been Barbara Bryce, Deputy Director of the NCA. It was a fleeting image. There were other, more graphic images, vying for his attention.

Chapter 52

Blue lights flashing, and being careful not to jump any red lights, Caton sped down Hathersage Road. After all, it was an emergency, of a kind. His hands-free told him that he had four missed calls from a number he did not recognise. Attempts to return the calls proved fruitless. With a mounting sense of panic, he ignored the multi-storey car park on the corner and turned onto the Boulevard, hoping there would an empty space or two in the Disabled and Emergency Services bay outside the entrance. For once, there was not. Cursing his luck he turned back onto the Boulevard and drove back to the car park. Five minutes later, he arrived, panting, at the entrance to St Mary's Hospital.

He hurried into the vast glass and steel atrium that eerily reminded him of the GMP Headquarters building, ignored the queue at reception and stopped a young man wearing an identity badge suspended on a blue lanyard around his neck.

'My wife's in labour,' he said. 'She's been brought in here.'

The man glanced at the busy reception desk.

'You can try the Delivery Suite,' he said. 'Come on, I'll show you.'

A midwife in a crisp blue uniform stepped out into the corridor where Caton anxiously paced.

'It's Tom, isn't it?' she said. 'Kate is doing really

well. Come on in.'

'But Kate's always said she didn't want me to be there ... at the birth,' he said. 'You see, I wasn't able to get to all of the prenatal classes. She said I'd only be a distraction.'

She smiled to reassure him.

'Well, she's changed her mind. She definitely wants you in there with her.'

He looked down at his clothes.

'I'm not sure,' he said. 'I've just come from a particularly bloody crime scene. I don't want to risk any infection.'

'That's no problem,' she told him. 'I'll get someone to bring you a gown, a cap and a pair of booties, and in the meantime...' She pointed to the wall-mounted sanitizer beside the door. '...rub some of that all over your hands.'

The young woman who brought the items watched with amusement as he struggled to put them on.

'There's nothing to worry about,' she said. 'The midwife will tell you what to do. It's just about being there for your partner. It's about reassuring her. Helping her to focus. To remain calm. That means you have to be all those things too. There's nothing worse for switching off the oxytocin release that she needs to deliver your baby than to have waves of male adrenalin flooding the room.'

She reached for the door handle.

'Your mother-in-law's in there too. So you're not on your own.'

'That's all I need,' he muttered.

Kate lay on the bed, propped up against two massive pillows, with her legs drawn up. The midwife in blue stood with her back to him, leaning over Kate. Another midwife in a white uniform stood beside her. Marge stood to the right of Kate at the head of the bed.

'Here he comes,' she said. 'Better late than never. I've been ringing you all morning.'

'Mum, don't,' said Kate, before tailing off in a sustained burst of swearing that took Caton completely by surprise.

'Don't worry, Tom,' said the midwife, turning to smile at him. 'It's perfectly normal. We call this the transition stage. It's an opportunity for the mum-to-be to rant and swear about the female condition. Usually it's directed at us, God, and the father in particular. It won't be long now. Why don't you go and stand by Kate and give her some encouragement?'

'I don't need bloody encouragement!' shouted Kate. 'I need gas and air!'

She pushed into the bed with her arms. Droplets of sweat trickled down her forehead. Caton took a tissue from the large box on the bedside unit and made to wipe them away.

'Don't!' she yelled. 'Don't you dare touch me!'

Marge reached across, took the tissues from his hand and proceeded to mop her daughter's brow.

'Ignore her,' she said. 'She always hated being sick.'

'I'm not fucking sick!' Kate screamed. 'I'm giving bi……rth!'

'Breathe, Kate,' said the midwife.

Kate's face was bright red with the strain of pushing. It looked to Tom as though her lungs might explode.

'Breathe, Kate,' he urged. 'Breathe.'

She exhaled, and immediately filled her lungs again with a huge gulp.

'I am breathing,' she growled on the next exhalation.

'Pant, Kate,' said the midwife.

'Pant,' said Marge.

'Pant, Kate, pant!' said Caton.

'What is this?!' she yelled between pants. 'The sodding Hallelujah chorus?!'

'Nearly there,' said the midwife, placing her hand on Kate's perineum. 'Just one more push.'

'It's coming,' said Caton. 'I can see its head.'

'Her head,' said Kate.

'Give me your hand, Kate,' said the midwife.

Caton supported his wife as she reached forward with her left hand. The midwife placed it on the top of the perfect mound of slick red hair that was the baby's head.

'It's a girl,' announced the midwife. 'You have a baby girl.'

As their daughter slipped gently into this world Caton experienced an overwhelming wave of wonder tinged with relief.

'Told you,' said Kate, collapsing back onto the pillow.

Half an hour later, the initial checks had been carried out. Kate, Marge and Caton had taken it in turns to have a hold and a cuddle. Now their daughter, washed, weighed and measured, lay in the crook of Kate's arm, her face against her breast.

'It looks as though she may be ready to take her first feed anytime now,' observed the midwife. 'We're going to move you to the ward. You can feed her there. We're exceptionally busy at the moment, but I expect Dr Wakefield to be free to carry out the full newborn examination in about two hours' time. Then, if everything's fine, you'll be able to take her home.'

'Mum's got a list for you, Tom,' said Kate. 'Things I'm going to need that I didn't have time to get. You can pop into Boots and pick them up. Then you may as well go straight home. There's a stack of ready meals in the fridge. You can lay the table. Mum will microwave or oven cook them when we get home. And you can get a bottle of red out for the two of you.'

She grinned.

'We'll save the champagne till I've stopped breastfeeding Emily and she's started bottle-feeding. Then you'd better watch out.'

'Emily?' he said. 'That wasn't on the list.'

She beamed at him.

'It was on my list.'

Chapter 53

Other than having to park in the city centre the nearest Boots store, Caton discovered, was on Cheetham Hill Road, less than a mile and a half from Central Park. That meant he could check on the investigation, do the shopping and be back at the apartment with an hour and a half to spare. He could even pick up some flowers along the way. He started the engine and set off.

The Incident Room was strangely quiet. Apart from Ged, DC Hulme was alone in the room. He was busy taking the case photos down from the whiteboard and placing them in a box.

'What are you doing?' said Caton. 'And where is everybody?'

Hulme dropped the photo. He turned, seemed uncharacteristically flustered and struggled to reply. Ged hurried over protectively.

'I think you'd better ask Detective Superintendent Gates,' she said. 'I was told to send you straight up if you came in.'

Caton turned and headed for the door.

'I assume congratulations are in order?' she called as he disappeared into the corridor.

Helen Gates was waiting for him.

'Tom,' she said. 'Congratulations. How is Kate? And the baby? It's a girl I gather.' She smiled. 'You're in trouble now, mother and daughter, they'll run rings around you.'

'Helen,' he said. 'About the case.'

The smile vanished. It was replaced by her serious face. She pointed to the chair closest to him.

'Sit down, Tom.'

She waited until he was seated.

'You're off the case, Tom. You're on paternity leave.'

'But–'

'Come to that, we're all off the case.'

'I don't understand,' he said.

'Finucane. The NCA have taken it over. After all, he was their man. Something to do with national security. Apparently, he was working across Serious Crime Division and Terrorism Command.'

'That's bollocks, Helen!' he said. 'And you know it. There are too many unanswered questions.'

'Be careful, Tom,' she said. 'There's a limit to how much I'm prepared to take.'

She paused, hoping that he had got the message.

'Face it,' she said at last, 'as far as the NCA are concerned it was suicide.'

He felt his anger growing.

'What was she doing sitting in that godforsaken hole? Who told him she was there? Her mysterious friend? And who was that? Why didn't Finucane kill her, like he killed her sister? He could have walked away, and covered his tracks just like he did with the others. Why didn't he? And why did he remove one glove?'

She waited patiently until he ran out of steam.

'It doesn't really matter how he found out,' she said, 'because in the end he took his own life. It was suicide.'

She raised her hand to stop him interrupting.

'His role with the NCA was particularly stressful. They have people lining up to attest to his state of mind. Throw in long-term untreated post traumatic stress from his time in Northern Ireland, and it's hardly surprising that he flipped when he thought Maureen Flinn had dredged him up from an even more traumatic, long-repressed memory. He pitched up at that house full of remorse. Unable to go through with it he topped himself. End of story.'

She shrugged, and gave him an apologetic smile.

'Their story, that is.'

'It won't wash,' said Caton. 'When the forensics come through there'll be fibres on the bushes, footprints, DNA. They must have touched him, held him.'

She let her expression reply for her.

'What?' he said.

'They cancelled your request for all those tests, Tom. And before you start shouting, think about it. If you're right, and it's a bloody big if, it's unlikely they'll have anything or anyone to match forensics to. This early in their existence the NCA can do without the publicity. The suicide of one of their officers is bad enough, but a revenge killing for a massacre he was responsible for thirty-five years ago? You know what the media would do with that. Face it, they have to minimise the fallout.'

She sighed wearily, as though the world was on her shoulders. He couldn't decide if it was genuine, or if she was simply letting him know that she was as unhappy with all of this as he was.

'Look, Tom,' she said, counting them off on her fingers, 'the Northern Ireland Office are happy. The PSNI are happy. I've already spoken to Chief Inspector Burke, by the way, and the Garda are happy. As soon as Finucane's fishing expedition alibi was told he was dead, he had another think. There were a couple of times when Finucane might have gone off on his own. Sorry, it completely slipped his mind. So, their prime suspect is dead. Case closed. The Chief Constable is happy, because it closes your investigation, Operation Stardust. No doubt by now Finucane's undercover officer will have had a similar memory recovery. Either that, or he'll claim his handler told him to lie for some mythical state security reason.'

She closed her fist and placed it on the table.

'The man who killed Maureen Flinn is dead. You tracked him down, and you solved the Malon Farm killings along the way. It's a result.'

'If Finucane was such an embarrassment to everybody,' he said, 'how do we know it wasn't a blue-on-blue?'

She made sure that he was looking directly at her. There was a bleak, almost haunted look in her eyes.

'We don't, Tom. And I doubt that we ever will.'

Slowly but surely Caton's anger had leached away. Now all he felt was bitter resignation.

'Christ, Helen,' he said, 'this is like something out of one of those John le Carré novels, A Delicate Truth, or A Wanted Man.' In this case, both at once.

She sensed his change in mood and smiled.

'He was a spook, wasn't he, le Carré?'

'He worked for MI5 and MI6 before he started writing.'

'There you go then,' she said. 'He knows a thing or two.'

Caton suddenly felt exhausted. In less than six hours he had been through the full range of human emotions. He shook his head, put his hands on the desk and stood up.

'One other thing,' said Helen Gates. 'How is DI Stuart doing?'

'Well, very well. Why?'

'The Director of the National Crime Agency has just contacted Human Resources branch. They would like to borrow her. A secondment.'

'For how long?'

'A year.' She paused. 'Initially.'

'Why her, why now?'

'Apparently, the Deputy Director has been impressed by what she's heard about her. I gather they're also a bit man heavy at the moment. Especially on the operational side. So, what do you think?'

'We'd miss her,' he said. 'I'd miss her. And we're a bit man heavy ourselves. Except for you, of course.'

'Don't worry,' she said, 'I'm working on that. Frankly this could be good for her prospects, and earn us brownie points with the Agency.'

She registered his scowl and held up her hands.

'You don't have to say it,' she said. 'They owe us, not the other way round.'

She sighed and stood up.

'If you see her, Tom, please don't mention it; I haven't discussed it with her yet.'

'I won't.'

'And, Tom,' she said, 'your paternity leave? Take it. All of it.'

He was walking across the atrium as DI Stuart entered.

'Congratulations, boss,' she said. 'A girl. That's wonderful.'

'Thanks, Jo,' he said. 'Yes, it is. She's adorable.'

It wasn't difficult for her to pick up on his mood. He was too tired to try to hide it.

'Let's go outside,' she said. 'We need to talk.'

They walked slowly side by side towards the car park.

'I'm sorry about the way it's going,' she said. 'You

know, with the NCA muscling in.'

'Don't be,' he said. 'Whether or not it was suicide, the man who killed the Malone family, Father Walsh and Maureen Flinn is dead. That's good enough.'

Surprised and disappointed, she stopped in her tracks and stared up at him.

'You don't mean that. Remember when you told me the end can never justify the means? That way leads either to anarchy or fascism, you said.'

'It does,' he replied. 'I still believe that. You still have to believe that. It's just that sometimes what we believe doesn't count, except to us. You can only control what you can control.'

He carried on walking, and she fell into step alongside him.

'Gerald MacMahon is in Manchester,' she said.

He stopped.

'How do you know?'

'Frances Fenton asked to speak to you after DCS Gates had left the room. Nick told her that wasn't going to happen, that you were on paternity leave. She said to give me a message for you.'

'She knew your name?'

'Only because MacMahon does. "Tell her," she said, "that Gerry Mac is waiting for him at the Irish Centre."'

'The Irish Heritage Centre? On Cheetham Hill?'

'Presumably. There are others though.'

'He must be confident that we can't tie him into Finucane's death,' he said.

'I was just going to tell DCS Gates, and find out what she wanted me to do about it.'

'You do that, Jo,' he said. 'But don't hold your breath. And don't tell her, but I'm going to go and see what he has to say. I just happen to be going in that direction.'

He started to walk away towards the car park, then stopped and turned.

'By the way, DI Stuart,' he said, 'I meant it when I said you'd done a great job. And not just on this investigation. I owe you an apology. I should have given you more responsibility sooner. More investigations of your own as the Senior Investigating Officer. You're bloody good. You're bright, brave and morally courageous. You've got great instinct, and brilliant man management skills. You're going to go a long way.'

She was too stunned to reply. Besides, he was already walking away. She stood there wondering what that was all about as he disappeared into the car park.

Chapter 54

Caton turned off Queen's Road onto Irish Town Way, and then turned right up the asphalt drive. A sign on the stone wall beside the gates read Fáilte – Irish Town. He had no idea what kind of welcome was really waiting for him. He parked at the top of the slope outside the brand new complex and got out.

He had not been here since the building of the new Irish Heritage Centre had begun. With only the first phase completed – the two-storey bar and function room – it still impressed. It had the appearance of a modern sports and social club, which, in a sense, he supposed it was. He alarmed the car and went inside.

As he entered the atrium Caton was reminded, for the second time that day, of Central Park. The same bright white walls, grey slate floor and blue tinted glass. The bar was another matter entirely. Everywhere in this circular room wood was burnished gold beneath the lights. Globes of perforated wooden slats suspended from the ceiling, planet-like, lit a 5,000-year-old black and silver bogwood sculpture rising like an avenging angel from the centre of a circular table. The only people in the room were two middle-aged women chatting to the barmaid. They looked across at him as he stepped into the room, raised their glasses, smiled and returned to their conversation.

Outside on a veranda, a man stood by the wooden railings staring out across the walled garden and football fields beyond. It was the former IRA commander, Gerry MacMahon. Caton went to join him.

'I knew you'd come,' said MacMahon, still looking out across the bare fields. 'Only I didn't think it'd be this soon.'

He turned to face Caton.

'I'd have thought you'd want to be with your wife and baby, Mr Caton. Congratulations by the way.'

Caton fought to hide his anger and surprise. Only his colleagues knew. There had not been time to tell anyone else. Perhaps someone had let it slip in front of Frances Fenton? It was, he realised, pointless in speculating.

'Come on,' MacMahon was saying, 'it's coming up to lunchtime. We'll go upstairs; they tell me it's the only place we can be sure not to be disturbed.'

The Irishman led the way, stopping at the bar to order a double shot of Jameson whisky.

'What'll you have yourself, Mr Caton?' he asked.

Caton was about to decline completely when he realised how thirsty he actually was. He hadn't had a drink since he'd left home, and it felt like he'd lost a pint or two in the delivery room.

'I'll have a pint of tap water,' he said.

'Dear God,' said MacMahon. 'Have a Guinness at least, why don't cha?'

'Water's fine,' said Caton to the barmaid.

They took their drinks up to the function room. MacMahon was right. It was empty. They sat opposite each other at one of the tables by the floor-to-ceiling windows. MacMahon raised his glass in salute and took a sip.

'Save you the trouble of asking,' he said. 'I was here last night till late, with friends. Then I went back to theirs in Middleton, cos' it's where I've been staying the night. I woke up around six. Dessie's mother brought me a cup of tea around seven thirty. I had breakfast with the household at eight o'clock,' he smiled. 'Will that do you?'

'You could have slipped out in between going to bed and your friend's mother bringing you breakfast,' said Caton.

'Not a chance. They've got a Jack Russell that's better than a burglar alarm. I wouldn't have got past the landing.'

Caton took a long, slow draught of water and put the glass back down.

'How is it you know what timescale I'm interested in?' he said.

'She rang me.'

'Frances Fenton?'

'Finnoula Malone.'

Caton nodded thoughtfully.

'And I'll find a record of that call on her phone?'

'And on mine.'

'She stopped off in Belfast to meet you,' said Caton.

MacMahon leaned forward.

'Why wouldn't she? I was the one they brought them to when they were rescued from that farm. The one who got them put up for adoption. The one who made sure no one would ever find her. Who's kept tabs on her ever since.'

'Like a guardian angel?'

'You could say that.'

'What happened with Caitlin then?'

MacMahon frowned and sat back.

'She slipped through the net. Went AWOL. Her choice.'

Caton let it go. There was no point in rubbing salt in the wound.

'You came to Manchester with her.'

'Same day, different plane.'

'To choose the place to which to lure Finucane?'

The Irishman was unmoved.

'To see my friends. And to be there if she needed me.'

'It was you that gave Finucane the address.'

'Me? Do you really think he would have gone there if he thought that I was the source?'

'An anonymous tip then.'

'Would you have pitched up there all alone on the strength of an anonymous source? If I were him I'd assume it was your lot trying to get him to show his hand.'

'Who then?

He spread his hands.

'I thought you were the detective?' He lifted his glass and had a sip of whisky. 'Besides, how was I to know it was him that massacred the Malones and shot Finnoula's sister in cold blood?'

'You've known the names of everyone in that unit for years,' Caton said.

MacMahon smiled.

'Of course. What we didn't know for sure was if it was actually them, and if so, who was really responsible. If I had, we wouldn't be sitting here now discussing it. There'd be no need.'

'So how did you find out it was Finucane?'

He raised his eyebrows.

'That's easy; he admitted it when he shot himself, didn't he?'

'I meant how did you know that he was the one you needed to give the address of the house where Frances was waiting?'

The former IRA man tutted and shook his head slowly.

'Nice try, Mr Caton. But like I said, it wasn't me.'

He took a mobile phone from his pocket and slid it across the table.

'Here. Check the texts and the calls. You can swab me and take my prints if you like. Be my guest.'

Caton recalled the men in the black Vauxhall Enigma by the lane to Loch Atiduff Lough; the black Golf on Donegal Road; Fat Van Man, and Little Leon in the car park in South Belfast. Not to mention the contacts that must still exist in the police, the army and even the secret services.

MacMahon watched him. Then he reached out, picked up the phone and replaced it in his pocket.

'You're right,' he said. 'No point. Finucane finally saw the error of his ways. Took the coward's way out. End of story.'

It was the second time someone had used the phrase that morning, Caton realised.

'So that's it,' he said. 'As far as you're concerned justice has been done?'

MacMahon looked at his watch, drained the last of the whisky and pushed back his chair.

'Justice? Do you know what they say about justice, Mr Caton?'

'That justice is blind?'

MacMahon glanced towards the doors and stood up.

'That's not it. The one I was thinking of was, You only get justice after you're dead. Until then all you have is the law. Well, Mr Caton, let's face it, the law did bugger all about him while he was alive. Now he's dead, God will decide.' He waved a hand across the room.

Caton turned to find Frances Fenton standing in the doorway.

'Now, if you'll excuse me,' said MacMahon, 'I'm

taking Finnoula to meet Caitlin's adopted parents.' He held out his hand. 'You look after yourself, Mr Caton, and that little girl of yours.'

Caton ignored the proffered hand, thrust his own in his pockets and watched as the two of them embraced, linked arms and left the room.

Chapter 55

He heard the sound of a key turning in the lock and hurried into the hallway. Marge entered first, carrying her daughter's hospital bag. Tom took it from her and backed up towards the lounge. Kate followed on, carrying their baby high up against her chest in a soft pink wrap that appeared to have been crossed over and tied to create a perfectly snug cocoon.

It was a long five minutes before Kate was finally settled and ready to hand over her precious cargo for him to hold.

'Be careful,' she said.

Caton cradled his daughter as he had been taught; one hand and arm beneath her bottom, the other cupping her tiny head. Her eyes were closed. He was amazed by the curly strands of auburn hair, so much richer than her mother's, and the tiny, perfectly formed fingers complete with long, soft fingernails.

Suddenly, her eyes opened. Tiny dark-blue pools stared up at him, trying to focus.

'You're too close, Tom,' said Kate. 'Move your head back a bit. That's it.'

Now those eyes were scanning his face with a hint of fascination. He smiled at her. Her lips twitched. Not so much a smile as an attempt to copy. She radiated unconditional love, innocence and a life full of endless possibility. Caton held her tight and made a solemn, silent promise to protect her from the worst that life could throw at her, and from the evil that men do. At that moment, nothing else mattered in the entire world.

The Author

Bill Rogers has written ten crime thriller novels to date, all of them based in and around the City of Manchester. His first novel, The Cleansing, received the ePublishing Consortium Writers Award 2011, was shortlisted for the Long Barn Books Debut Novel Award and was in the Amazon Kindle 100 Bestsellers for over one hundred days. His fourth novel, A Trace of Blood, reached the semi-final of the Amazon Breakthrough Novel Award in 2009.

Bill has also written Breakfast at Katsouris, an anthology of short crime stories, The Cave, a novel for teens, young adults and adults, and Caton's Manchester, a book of walks in and around Manchester based on the crime series. He lives in Greater Manchester, where he has spent his entire adult life.

www.billrogers.co.uk
www.catonbooks.com

If you have enjoyed
Angel Meadow,
why not try the other novels in the series?

In order:

The Cleansing
The Head Case
The Tiger's Cave
A Fatal Intervention
A Trace of Blood
Bluebell Hollow
The Frozen Contract
Backwash

All of these books are available as paperbacks from bookshops or on Amazon, and as eBooks on Amazon Kindle, Smashwords, Nook, Kobu, Apple and most other platforms.

The Cleansing is also available as an Amazon Audible AudioBook, narrated by Michael Troughton.

The End